JESSIE FORD

Her millions of fans have waited over four years
—since the publication of her great bestseller
LOVE REMEMBER ME—for Jessie Ford's
new novel.

From the opening pages of
THE BURNING WOMAN,
they will know it was worth the wait.

Jessie Ford has written a rich and compelling
love story that goes to the heart of the passion
between a woman and a priest. The glorious
love between Cathryn Godwin and Father
Vittorio is an affirmation of their Creator. But
the powerful forces of organized religion—from
Rome to England to the New World—see any
passion between a man and a woman as the
work of the Devil.

Please turn the page to meet Cathryn, Vittorio, and
the other marvelous people in

THE BURNING WOMAN

CATHRYN GODWIN

"Father, forgive me, for I have sinned. I have loved a man who is a priest and with that love have been granted breathtaking ecstasy—and torment that far surpasses all my fantasies of Hell. I accept my exile in England, banished like a leper from his presence, as fitting penance."

FATHER VITTORIO

"Though I swore to love God only, I find I love you more.... You alone bring out the unwritten music of my soul."

VANYA RUSSO

"The very acts the fathers of the Church despise are ones which bring us very close to God ... and draw down power from the cosmos."

COMTESSE DANSETTE

"Perhaps, if the flesh of her priests were satisfied, the clergy would be free to be more imaginative, and, perhaps, then the Church would refrain from depicting God as little more than a heavenly voyeur."

GERALD SEYMOUR

"You have gifts, don't you, dark and lovely, Cathryn? Your look sears a man's soul, leaving his flesh to crave and think of naught else but purging himself of lust—but it is folly for a man to believe that even then he can be done with you."

WEYLIN RODMAN

"You've seduced me to your needs, Cathryn, but your power is not so great that I cannot inflict great harm to you.... You, my wife, are a witch!"

Also by Jessie Ford
Published by Ballantine Books:

LOVE, REMEMBER ME

THE
BURNING
WOMAN

Jessie Ford

BALLANTINE BOOKS • NEW YORK

Library of Congress Catalog Card Number: 85-90713

ISBN 0-345-31046-2

Manufactured in the United States of America

First Edition: September 1985

With love to Ted, Greg, and Christopher, and to Zephyrus, who came out of the mists as a bright omen.

With gratitude to my editor, Cheryl Woodruff.

Acknowledgments

I wish to thank Erica Jong and Harry N. Abrams, Inc., for granting permission to use poetry from the volume WITCHES, and Mitchell Hooks for the wonderful cover art.

For All Those Who Died

For all those who died—
stripped naked, shaved, shorn.

For all those who screamed
in vain to the great Goddess
only to have their tongues
ripped out by the root.

For all those who were pricked, racked, broken on the wheel
for the sins of their Inquisitors.

For all those whose beauty
stirred their torturers to fury;
& for all those whose ugliness did the same.

For all those who were neither ugly nor beautiful,
but only women who would not submit.

For all those quick fingers
broken in the vise.

For all those soft arms
pulled from their sockets.

For all those budding breasts
ripped with hot pincers.

For all those midwives killed merely for the sin
of delivering man
to an imperfect world.

For all those witch-women, my sisters,
who breathed freer
as the flames took them,

knowing as they shed
their female bodies,
the seared flesh falling like fruit
in the flames,

that death alone would cleanse them
of the sin for which they died

the sin of being born a woman,
who is more than the sum
of her parts.

—Erica Jong

PART ONE

Republic of Venice
1687

The
Harrowing

Witch-woman,
burning goddess,
every woman bears
within her soul
the figure of the witch,
the face of the witch,
beautiful and hideous,
hidden as the lips
of her cunt,
open as her open eyes,
which see the fire
without screaming

from "Figure of the Witch"
by Erica Jong

Prologue

Signorina Perdita Fabiani looked up from the terse missive she had received earlier in the day and sighed, admitting she had expected nothing more expansive. But after fourteen years of giving loving attention to Cathryn Godwyne, Perdita wanted more than a simple announcement of Cathryn's departure from Venice. The generous settlement of Cathryn's expenses as promised gladdened Signorina Fabiani, but it did not suffice as an expression of gratitude for the care Perdita and Bianca Fabiani had bestowed on Lord Ashley Godwyne's only child.

Perdita shivered. This final letter was no exception to the unyieldingly cold correspondence she had received from England over the years. Such a society would be unbearably alien to a warm and generous soul like Cathryn Godwyne.

From the age of three, Cathryn had made her home with Perdita and her sister Bianca Fabiani at La Casa degli Innocenti, an orphans' school for girls, and with no false modesty Perdita believed she had mothered the child exceptionally well. She further deemed that the warmth and vitality of Venice, coupled with the gypsy blood the girl inherited from her mother, had usurped any icy English temperament Cathryn might have inherited from her father. But now, as Signorina Fabiani pondered the final message from Cathryn's guardian, Master Gerald Seymour, Perdita harbored the fear that the potency of English blood might tell after all.

No! No! Perdita denied the possibility to herself.

The girl was more than her English blood. She was a Venetian! She would forbear her new homeland and life. Perdita's precious child would never lose heart!

Perdita looked up from the letter embossed with the Godwyne seal and sighed, then pulled an elaborate lace handkerchief from a pocket hidden in the folds of her robe. She dabbed her lashes to quell a shower of tears, then rested her eyes on a page of music that Cathryn had left behind only minutes before.

A smile curled Signorina Fabiani's mouth. She had known the composer's name even before Cathryn had divulged it. Father Vittorio's impatient scrawl was unmistakable, his hasty notation making it clear that his first love was music—its creation and not its preservation.

For the first time this evening, Perdita, a proficient musician herself, picked up Father Vittorio's latest score and eyed it critically, reading the notes of his latest inspiration. It was another brilliant composition with a lilting flow of melody, and closing her eyes, Perdita could recall perfectly the crystal-sweet voice of Cathryn's violin.

The girl had dropped her usual mask of serenity to perform Father Vittorio's newest composition, and, as the music escaped from her instrument, Cathryn's joyfulness touched Perdita and left its mark once more.

Earlier Cathryn had stolen from her bedchamber already dressed for bed, her nightgown covered with a white dressing gown of heavy satin brocade. However, the promise of Cathryn's full womanhood was hardly concealed; her lithe young body was much like a blossom ripe for plucking. Unnerved, Perdita sorrowed and realized that soon the young woman would be far from the cloistered security of degli Innocenti.

At seventeen, Cathryn was hardly a child, and Perdita worried that the girl's almost perfect beauty would endanger her in the world outside. In viewing Cathryn's delicately etched features, one was certain God had granted the full breath of life to this particular young woman, her physical beauty enhanced and illuminated by an enchanting vitality.

Perdita now remembered that tonight the girl's raven hair had held an especially healthy shine, and if Perdita was not mistaken, that tumbling mass of unruly curls exuded a warm, inviting fragrance.

Perdita had looked into Cathryn's clear, startlingly deep brown eyes and observed only their innocence, and insisted her imagination was playing tricks on her. Cathryn was incapable of the seductive ruse of perfuming her hair. Engaged by Cathryn's feverish excitement, Perdita Fabiani also chose to overlook the disturbing Eastern slant of the girl's beautiful eyes, a feature that served to aggravate Cathryn's foster mother whenever the young woman sparked her ire.

Now, even in her absence, Perdita could feel Cathryn's presence in the room. "Isn't it marvelous?" the young woman had bubbled even before she put her violin down. "Can you think of anything more glorious than to have Father Vittorio's gift for music?"

"He's most dedicated."

"Oh, no, Dita! Surely it is more than that! His music comes from his heart. His very soul! You can hear it clearly," Cathryn insisted, picking up her violin to play the lilting melody again. "Please, *listen* this time. Truly it is the best he's ever written." She played Father Vittorio's song again for Perdita, who, for the heaviness of her heart, did not hear it better the second time.

"Yes, yes, Cathryn, it is very good" was all the enthusiasm she could muster.

"It's my fault," Cathryn muttered, defeated by her inability to infect Perdita with her enthusiasm. "I've failed to capture what he's written."

"No, Cathryn. Your teacher would be proud of you, just as I am," Perdita had answered, and now, to her grief, she realized there soon would be no more impulsive visits from Cathryn to her private rooms within the walls of La Casa degli Innocenti.

The matronly Signorina Fabiani leaned back into her chair and reflected for a moment on the thirty years since the founding of the orphans' school by her father, Antonio Fabiani. Many girls had come and gone, and nowadays very few true orphan girls resided at degli Innocenti. In fact, Cathryn Godwyne was not an orphan, or, at least, had not been at the time of placement fourteen years ago. When Cathryn entered the school, she was left behind in Venice by parents who were very much alive.

Signorina Fabiani blanched at the thought of Cathryn's parents—her father, Lord Ashley Godwyne, a notable former member of the English mission to the Venetian court, and her mother, Vanya Russo, whom all of Venice knew by reputation, at least.

Rumored to be of Chinese and Russian blood, the bastard issue of a Russian prince by his Chinese mistress, Vanya Russo one day had descended out of nowhere on the Venetian lagoon to be relentlessly pursued by one besotted man after another. Men of all stripes clustered to her, drawn by her luminous beauty;

enchanted by her exotic and passionate nature. She traveled from one man to another, a *cortigiana*, until, one day, she came under Lord Godwyne's spell.

Nothing less than an evil spell explained Vanya Russo's behavior to Perdita's satisfaction, because in addition to her attachment to the acerbic Lord Godwyne, the woman abandoned her only child to strangers when she followed her lover to England.

Perdita reminded herself that although Cathryn had been left in Perdita's capable hands, she had never comprehended how anyone could leave such a winsome child behind for the sake of a man.

The fact remained the mother had, and, after secluding herself for weeks, regaled in brilliant silk and ermine, Vanya Russo had been seen to go aboard an English sailing vessel with Lord Godwyne, never to be heard from again.

For seven years following, Lord Godwyne corresponded with the Fabianis, handling all matters concerning Cathryn with brief instructions in elegant script drawn on paper embossed with the golden Godwyne seal. He referred only to Perdita's favorite charge as "the child, Cathryn," neither acknowledging nor denying her legitimacy.

Perdita Fabiani judged it most unlikely that a gentleman of Lord Godwyne's stature would marry an Eastern seductress the likes of Vanya Russo, but she gave Cathryn the surname Godwyne. If she was not Lord Godwyne's legitimate heir, His Lordship at least had assumed the role of her patron.

After Lord Godwyne's death, Cathryn's affairs were overseen by her guardian, Gerald Seymour, who never divulged a word about the circumstances of Lord Godwyne's death, nor the fate of Vanya Russo. Master Seymour referred to Cathryn using the Godwyne surname, but never as Lady Godwyne, as might be expected if her birth were acknowledged as legitimate.

To Perdita's mind, Cathryn Godwyne was as much an orphan as any child discovered on a convent doorstep, and Perdita openly confessed her almost immediate and unalterable attachment to the child.

Cathryn was special, and on many a night Perdita had comforted the child while she waited for "Mama" to arrive and take her home. Night after night, the elfin Cathryn sat at the foot of the stairs dressed in a long silk nightgown befitting a princess with her long black hair cascading down her slim back like a heavy satin cape. ''*Mamma* will come for me tonight,'' she would declare, and then fall asleep in Perdita's arms.

Cathryn's memory of her parents had faded after a reasonable time, though Perdita felt the child had cried for her mother longer than was due the woman.

Eventually Cathryn seemed to forget she had ever belonged to anyone and La Casa degli Innocenti became her home; the other girls, her sisters; the Fabianis, her parents. She began to speak of herself as an orphan and appeared to have no memory of the parents who had deserted her.

Perdita deemed it a cruelty to suggest differently.

It was obvious Lord Godwyne and his foreign paramour would never return for their child, and Perdita began to refer to Lord Godwyne as Cathryn's benefactor rather easily. When Perdita became the school's directress, there was no one to dispute her word, or even to remember.

With her striking intelligence and enchanting desire to please, Cathryn soon became a favorite of her tutors. She kindled the young Perdita's maternal desires, and for years Cathryn was allowed to share Perdita's rooms, until eventually the demands on Perdita's time as directress of degli Innocenti required that she have greater privacy.

By then Cathryn was ten years old and quite ready to move from under Perdita's wing. She had already come to the attention of Father Vittorio, degli Innocenti's finest music teacher.

Almost from the moment Cathryn first touched a violin, she had exhibited an affinity for the instrument, immediately holding it as if it were a natural appendage of her body. More rapidly than any pupil Perdita could remember, Cathryn produced sounds with the instrument that could be described as music.

Signorina Fabiani could not suppress a smile to think of the first time Cathryn had played for the school's gifted new teacher, handsome Father Vittorio. The priest had already suffered through two score less talented students. He was weary and, though he would never have admitted it, fearful that he would never find a student worthy of his talent among the eager children residing at the school.

''Father, this is Cathryn Godwyne, and you will happily discover she has a gift that quite exceeds the . . . talent I fear you have already come to expect from my children.''

Young Father Vittorio had smiled at Perdita, but she'd noted little hope reflected in his eyes. He gazed at Cathryn with tenderness and requested, just as he had of the other students, that she play a few of her most difficult exercises and a favorite song. Then he settled back as though resigned to hear another uninspired performance.

Perdita smiled at her recollection of the priest as he listened to the child who not only looked like an angel but played her violin like one as well. As Father Vittorio listened, his weariness seemed to fade and, suddenly alert, a light of appreciation, even jubilance, filled his eyes.

Signorina Fabiani cherished the priest, who was himself a virtuoso violinist, for the sake of degli Innocenti's reputation. Under his brilliant guidance she imagined the school soon would be the finest academy of music in Venice, if not all of Europe. Quietly, Signorina Fabiani delighted in the fact that Cathryn's ability did not escape her genius priest.

"You must play something more for me . . . ah . . . Cathryn." He had smiled. "This time, choose the most demanding in your repertoire instead of your favorite."

"But it's not yet perfect," Cathryn protested.

The priest nodded. "I understand. I won't expect perfection—yet."

He listened attentively, and soon both teacher and pupil forgot Perdita's presence in the room. Father Vittorio would have forgotten the other students waiting for an audience with him as well had Perdita not finally interrupted them.

It was with obvious annoyance on that day that Father Vittorio had dismissed Cathryn Godwyne, and it had been the same ever since. He became devoted to this particular shining musician, and likewise, the priest became the child's idol. Many times her teacher expressed his gratitude for Cathryn's extraordinary talent to Perdita and even confessed having despaired of ever discovering a student who would begin to approach her talent within the orphans' school.

The priest nurtured Cathryn's gift for music with great care, demanding that she not neglect any aspect of her enormous talent, and now when they made music together it was as if their songs soared from one instrument; indeed, one soul.

Signorina Fabiani sighed and tears clouded her eyes. To think that soon she would never again be touched by their inspired music made her heart break—surely Father Vittorio would miss his prize pupil as much as she would miss her dearest child.

How would either she or Father Vittorio survive? Perdita wondered. How could it be that already the time had come for Cathryn to go from their midst?

In fact, all but the exact date of Cathryn's departure had been announced years ago. Soon after Lord Godwyne's death, the guardian of the Godwyne estate informed Perdita that Cathryn would remain at degli Innocenti only until she was seventeen years old and would then take up residence in England.

As a rule Perdita ignored the reality of Cathryn's eventual departure from Venice. The only concession she made was to see that Cathryn learned to speak fluent English. A wise decision; Perdita sighed, then smiled. Father Alberto boasted that Cathryn spoke English without a hint of an accent, but *that* would be a miracle, since Father Alberto spoke Italian with a French accent.

Perdita's smile vanished. "I have been remiss in my duty," she murmured, chastising herself for her behavior toward Cathryn over the years; for growing excessively fond of the child; for being a coward.

And to compound matters, tonight she had acted cowardly again. She had failed to tell Cathryn she soon would be leaving degli Innocenti.

Ah, well, would not tomorrow be time enough?

Tonight Signorina Fabiani gave herself yet another reprieve. A stay of execution. The sailing was still a few months away. Another few moments to prepare herself and her child for their lifetime of separation.

Chapter 1

Cathryn lifted her head from her pillows and in frustration swept the thick mass of her satiny black hair to one side. Tonight her trick of monotonously repeating her prayers until she numbed herself to sleep had failed. Cathryn feared that God disapproved of the method she employed to avoid her troubling thoughts, for true devotion required that she be more serious about her prayers.

Because she held her faith in high regard one part of Cathryn obediently feared God and tried to be a good Catholic. She avoided sin; confessed her errors; and observed and respected the rites of the Church, but she was, she acknowledged, not the angel some would have her be. The other part of Cathryn loved and trusted God, and allowed Him to love and forgive her, imperfect as she was. She often imagined Him as her very own father, and far more tender and understanding than the doctrines of the Roman Catholic Church allowed.

Cathryn squirmed and tried to settle herself more comfortably in bed. She stared into the room's darkness, gazing from one shaded object to another. Finally she breathed an exasperated sigh. She wished she shared her room with another girl, so that at least on sleepless nights like this, she would have a companion.

Cathryn felt dwarfed in her bed. The twenty-foot ceiling of her room loomed above her. She thought of her bedchamber and its relation to the scores of other rooms in the Fabiani palace, and of the grand house's position in the crowded Venetian lagoon. Surrounding the tiny islands that made up the lagoon was the Adriatic Sea, and tonight, its waters seemed to lap at Cathryn's very door.

She tried to imagine nothing had changed, but soon, Cathryn knew, she would step from La Casa degli Innocenti and glide away from all she loved. She would board a ship and sail for England and never again see Venice—or Perdita, or Simone, or Teresa, or her beloved teacher, Father Vittorio.

Cathryn shook her head violently on her pillow and forbade her tears.

Though no one knew of it, from the day she'd turned seventeen, Cathryn had dreaded the order that would send her from La Casa degli Innocenti, the home of innocents, to England.

"No wonder I do not sleep!" Cathryn muttered, and sat up, her long hair falling in soft waves against her back. Cathryn smiled, comforted a little by the pleasure of inhaling the lingering fragrance of her curls, and for the moment she turned her thoughts away from her troubles and thought of her friend Simone Barbera instead.

At her friend's persistent urging, Cathryn had added a generous splash of perfume to a pitcher of rinse water, and the result was warm and spicy-smelling curls, just as Simone promised.

However, Cathryn still doubted her friend's claim that fragrant curls would make her beautiful.

"You're beautiful, even though you don't seem to know it," Simone had insisted to Cathryn. "A little fragrance will only make you more so."

"Dear Simone, not a soul cares whether I've a hooked nose or straight, or if my eyes cross. And certainly no one cares whether my hair is scented," Cathryn had protested. "I shall only waste your rare perfume. I could shave my head and get more notice."

Simone had laughed. "Indeed, *that* would attract everyone's attention!"

Simone was a dear and loyal friend, but she never seemed to fathom that she, the daughter of a wealthy nobleman, was destined for a life that Cathryn, an orphan, was not.

"Your paternity will mean little in the end. As my mother insists, men are men," Simone always declared impatiently whenever Cathryn brought up her orphan's status.

In Cathryn's view, scenting her hair was a simple and frivolous squandering of costly perfume. "It is both pointless and sinful to be concerned with the condition of the flesh. Beauty is too often only a curse and a temptation."

Simone groaned. "You have lived at degli Innocenti far too long, Cathryn. The Fabiani women may all be saints, but there hasn't been a pretty face in the history of the family. Why, the gallery of portraits is enough to give you a fright! Frankly, I'd be ashamed to adorn my *palazzo* with such no doubt perfect likenesses."

Cathryn gave Simone a jab. "The condition of the heart is more important than the face."

"Only in heaven," Simone conceded, knowing quite well that most other people were not as oblivious to Cathryn's beauty as Cathryn was. Her vibrant, clear brown eyes and elegantly sculptured narrow face, delicate nose and slightly full mouth were noticed, if not envied, by almost everyone. It was to her advantage, Simone reflected, for Cathryn to be as innocent as she seemed; to have a soothing aura of purity and gentleness. But Simone also suspected that any vital man in Cathryn's presence couldn't help but speculate on the lithe young body hidden beneath her gowns.

Cathryn, however, knew her place far too well to spend much time in lengthy self-regard. Marriages were never arranged for the sake of acquiring a beautiful bride, and she had no need to worry whether, in addition to the dowry, her face and form would attract a handsome suitor. There was no dowry, and doubtless there would be no bridegroom in her future.

If Cathryn had her way, she would never marry; in fact, she would change little in her life. She would remain in Venice at degli Innocenti forever. She would emulate the Fabiani women and dedicate herself to the school's children. But in truth her life would be far richer than that of Perdita or Bianca Fabiani, for she had her music and the admiration and direction of an unsurpassed teacher.

If Cathryn stayed in Venice, she could teach music at degli Innocenti and free Father Vittorio to devote more of his time to writing music, which she would then play. Cathryn imagined, she would have everything she could ever hope for.

Cathryn sighed and lay back against her pillows. It was useless to dream, she then knew, and unwittingly her thoughts returned to her earlier visit to Perdita Fabiani.

Cathryn frowned at her foster mother's almost total lack of interest in Father Vittorio's latest inspiration. As usual, she felt the priest's most recent work merited total concentration, and certainly Perdita's undivided attention. After all, were it not for Father Vittorio's wonderful music, degli Innocenti would not have its excellent reputation. The school would be nothing more than an elegant and richly endowed retreat for the daughters of aristocrats and wealthy merchants.

As such, degli Innocenti would be an agreeable place to wile away one's life until one's marriage was arranged, but for Cathryn, since marriage was not in question, the education she received would have been quite vapid had it not been for Father Vittorio.

Cathryn was nine years old when Father Vittorio arrived at degli Innocenti, and when he came her life had changed forever. She worshiped him. Through his gift of music and his ability to impart what he knew, Cathryn had begun to live an enchanted life. Sounds that others heard indistinctly translated into rapturous music for Cathryn. Scenes that others barely saw Cathryn experienced as music. It was magic. Father Vittorio was magic.

Of course, it was unseemly, if not dangerous, to suggest that Father Vittorio was a magician. Magic was in the domain of witchcraft and, after all, her teacher was a priest; a man of God, inspired by the Holy Spirit. No one but a man under God's direction could create and perform the way he did.

"Father Vittorio. Father Vittorio. You have been my salvation in this place." Cathryn sighed, realizing that leaving her teacher behind was the most painful sacrifice of all. From the time of their introduction, they had been devoted to each other. Cathryn clearly remembered their first meeting, still able to recall the awe she had felt when ushered into his presence.

To the child she had been then, he had seemed distracted and remote; dark and forbidding in his priest's cassock. Cathryn recalled how desperate she had been to please him—this teacher who made her beloved Dita fairly dance for joy.

Father Vittorio conveyed his total dedication to his music and to God, and, revering the priest, each one of his students strove to match his faithfulness and his standard of perfection.

Though she was eager to please him, Cathryn did not always find it easy to meet Father Vittorio's demands. At times she dissolved into tears when she failed to attain his full approval. But, Cathryn had to admit, she never left his presence feeling she had not gained something by her efforts to please him. Perhaps that was why she relentlessly sought his approbation even when frustration with intricate fingering or failed interpretation made her want to pitch her violin into the Grand Canal!

Not that Father Vittorio's elevated position in Cathryn's mind always made it easy to obey him. He was an enlightened man, but he could also be tyrannical, and when she defied him, Cathryn could almost feel the fire of his temper, though the priest strove mightily to keep his composure.

Cathryn supposed it wicked to test the priest's patience; after all, he was no ordinary man. There probably was not a girl in the school who, when she reached a certain age, had not stared at Father Vittorio with more than respectful admiration at least once. He was the only handsome male in their midst, and indeed when Cathryn thought of Father Vittorio, she first saw his deep dark eyes surrounded by a bounty of black curling lashes. She was certain she saw mischief in those eyes, but perhaps there was more mystery than mischief—the hidden essence that fueled the priest's boundless creativity.

Father Vittorio's passion for music dominated his worldly existence, and his musical gifts seemed unlimited. In addition to the violin, he played a variety of other stringed instruments, both the flute, and the oboe. He wrote and conducted for all these instruments and the voice as well.

Cathryn closed her eyes and dreamed of Father Vittorio's smooth-shaven, still young face accentuated by high-planed cheekbones burnished by the bright Venetian sun. His warm smile touched her. Would his closely cropped black hair be as thick and as soft to her fingers as she imagined?

Cathryn sat up once more, suddenly aware of every nerve and fiber of her being; distressed by an urgent and inexplicable desire to be held and comforted; startled by the tingling sensation of her skin as it seemed to pull taut over her body. Her breasts seemed to swell beneath her gown, but most disturbing of all was the pleasurable warmth between her legs.

Unable to bear the sensations of her body, Cathryn bounded out of bed and into the corridor outside her room. Not pausing to collect her thoughts, she rushed down the stairs, only stopping when she came to Perdita's door. Light spilled from beneath the entryway, but just as Cathryn raised her hand to knock, she halted.

It was natural for Cathryn to run to Dita when she felt distressed, but she could not confess what troubled her now to anyone, most of all Dita! Still extremely upset over her earlier encounter with the woman, Cathryn stepped away from the door, again refusing to dwell on Perdita's disturbing attitude. For the moment, she focused her thoughts instead on the cold marble floor beneath her bare feet. Shivering, she silently hurried back down the long hallway.

Cathryn entered one of degli Innocenti's many music salons, closed the door behind her and waited for her eyes to adjust to the salon's dim light; then she sought her violin. Inching toward it, Cathryn took up the instrument with care, the familiar feel of the wood giving her odd comfort.

Music was the love of Cathryn's life, the most constant love she had ever known. The love of God, the love of Dita, the love of her teacher did not sustain her as her music did. It was all she truly cared for, except . . .

Cathryn moved to the window seat and pulled the draperies aside. She stood and looked out onto the dark waters of the Grand Canal, then sat down and, cradling her Amati, stared for a long while into the night. She tried to erase all thought from her mind.

Several minutes later, Cathryn sighed in frustration.

She'd run from her room to escape her thoughts of Father Vittorio, but his haunting presence followed her everywhere—especially in this room where they spent many hours of each day together.

Cathryn lifted her violin and began to play the score she had played earlier for Perdita, and just as Cathryn remembered, the fault was neither with the composer nor the violinist, but with her foster mother.

Her vision blurred with tears now, but in Perdita's presence, Cathryn's response to Perdita's indifference had been to play Father Vittorio's lilting song more passionately than she might have otherwise, faulting her own performance rather than face the truth. Earlier, simple cowardice had forced Cathryn to deny the letter Perdita had hastily concealed within the voluminous folds of her brocade robe. She could not escape the events that were about to unfold. In fact, she knew the precise reason for Dita's long face. Indeed, at seventeen she had been sheltered within the treasure-filled walls of the Fabiani's renaissance palace longer than she had a right to expect.

"Before returning to his homeland, your patron generously endowed the school with funds to support at least one orphan girl. The only stipulations he made were that this child be half English and take a good English name, and, finally, when she turned seventeen, the girl should go to live in England." Lord Godwyne had insisted also that his orphan *not* be raised a Catholic, but the Fabianis had flatly ignored this part of his request. "For the sake of your immortal soul," Cathryn had been told.

Signorina Fabiani had been discreet and never divulged more than a few details about Cathryn's munificent patron. She knew his name and that he was English, as was her own father. When Cathryn was younger, she had persistently inquired about her mother, but Perdita was always strangely silent on the subject.

Over the years, Cathryn had racked her brains but could not

remember anything before her arrival at degli Innocenti. Signorina Fabiani told her she was too young when she arrived to recall anything of her past and prompted her, instead, to feel blessed to have such a charitable benefactor, a man who had fallen in love with glorious Venice while serving the English mission to the Venetian court.

Lord Godwyne had been a man of the world, Perdita reminded her. He understood the charms of Venice and how the beautiful, richly sensuous city in the North Adriatic Sea might lead a man astray, if not for a lifetime, at least for a brief while. He understood well how a child might result from a man's waywardness.

Fortunately for Cathryn, her patron's generous concern had never ceased. Regular contributions and instructions about her care arrived at respectable intervals, though, as was witnessed this evening, the correspondence did not always inspire Perdita's happiness.

As Cathryn sat in the darkened music salon contemplating her departure, she could summon little gratitude for her patron's generosity. She felt apprehensive and desperately cold, and, shivering, she concluded that her life would soon be over.

Cathryn had heard often enough that life in the Republic of Venice was unparalleled, which meant, in her still unworldly view, that there was nothing to be seen beyond the Venetian coast. To Cathryn the tiny islands of the lagoon were heaven.

Built in the middle of the Adriatic Sea on the watery soil of ancient salt marshes by those fleeing the endless waves of barbarians who invaded from the East, Venice had from the start been an unlikely refuge. She was a nation built against the odds, emerging gradually over the centuries from hovels to grand edifices. She gained her separate identity as the spirit of her inhabitants and their installations proved to be, more or less, invulnerable.

Perhaps, as some said, Venice had already reached her zenith as a nation and was less a power in the world than she once had been; but for Cathryn Godwyne, Venice would always seem a haven. She longed never to leave.

England was a Protestant country, Cathryn knew, and she had heard many tales of the persecution of Catholics by those deluded rebels. She had been cautioned that she would have to keep her Catholic faith a secret once she set foot in England, for

Catholics were deemed enemies of the Crown. Father Vittorio said Catholics were sometimes burned at the stake for refusing to renounce their faith—as if those of the Roman faith were no better than witches!

Cathryn trembled with fear as well as cold and gathered her delicate, lace-edged nightgown tightly about her slim young body, desperate for warmth.

What would she do, she wondered, in cold, cold England? How would she survive without the comforting rituals of the Catholic church—without the sacraments that were one's only hope of salvation? How could she survive without her music? Without Perdita to look out for her?

Until this very moment, God had seemed a benevolent deity, answering nearly every one of Cathryn's prayers offered with her promise of faithfulness.

Sitting in the dark, Cathryn felt utterly hopeless and, at length, decided she would be better off returning to her bed.

But as she crept back to her room, through the cold, dark corridor, Cathryn began to feel more miserable than she imagined possible. By the time she reached the stairway, the dark had closed in on her. She shivered almost convulsively and, without a thought to tripping over the hem of her long gown, ran headlong up the stairs.

At the top she stumbled into someone's arms.

"Ohhh!" she shrieked; but then, with some relief and without knowing how, she recognized Father Vittorio. Above the stairs, Cathryn swayed precariously until he righted her. "Your pardon, Father!" she gasped. "I didn't see you!"

"Obviously," he said, sounding almost amused.

Self-conscious, Cathryn was surprised yet comforted by the sureness and strength of the priest's powerful grip on her. In contrast, she felt as light as air.

"Why are you out of bed?" he asked, concerned. "You're cold as death."

A weakness that Cathryn refused to acknowledge surged through her body, and she trembled as if to justify his words, savoring the warmth that seemed to blaze from him. His lips close to hers, she felt him tremble, also, and for a breathless instant Cathryn imagined that the priest was about to kiss her.

Then he released her.

"You're not dressed for wandering outside your chamber," he scolded.

Cathryn felt her nakedness beneath her thin nightdress, and her body flamed with heat. If they had been standing in the light, the priest would have seen her blush.

"I suppose your feet are bare," he said.

Cathryn could only nod in reply.

"Why are you out of bed? Did something frighten you? You're shaking even now."

She nodded once again.

"What was it, Cathryn? What troubles you?"

"I can't explain."

"Something in the dark?"

"Not exactly," she answered slowly.

"Well, did you pray?"

"Of course."

"Perhaps you should try again."

"Yes, Father, I shall," she promised as he escorted her to her door. "But I wonder if God shall ever again listen to my prayers."

Father Vittorio took Cathryn's arm. "What a foolish worry, *angelica.*"

"But soon I shall go to England, where I cannot admit my faith, and perhaps God does not wish to hear the prayers of one who will soon appear to be no longer faithful."

The priest hugged Cathryn gently to him to give her comfort. "If you do not abandon Him in your heart, God will not desert you, Cathryn," he promised.

Cathryn sighed against the priest. "How can you imagine He would stop loving you?" he murmured.

"I am not very important."

"Of course you are important!"

"I should be easy to forget, I imagine."

"You imagine wrongly!" the priest answered with force. "None of us who have known you will forget you, God least of all."

Father Vittorio felt Cathryn's ease and in a moment let her go.

"Thank you, Father."

He touched her cheek. "Good night, Cathryn. God's peace."

But in her bed again, Cathryn did not fall asleep immediately. More awake than ever, she lay tossing and turning in her featherbed. Her heart was heavy with sorrow, and to her other miseries and her sense of dread, Cathryn added the knowledge that soon she would not have Father Vittorio to turn to in distress. He was the only one who truly understood her. He sensed her moods, knowing how and when to draw her out and when to calm her down. He always knew just the right words to say and, better than anyone, how to exact her best.

Cathryn stared into the darkness. "If only," she whispered as she fell asleep, "if only he were a man and not a priest."

Chapter 2

"Holy Mother of God, protect me!" Cathryn beseeched under her breath as she scurried up the marble staircase later than usual. Again, she would have to attempt to slip unnoticed into Mass. Sometimes she succeeded. Sometimes she did not. "Please, save me this *last* time!" she prayed.

Perdita always reprimanded tardiness, and Cathryn tried to be penitent, but these days the early morning of Venice called more deeply than the Mass.

Lately, despite her sleepless nights, Cathryn woke early. She would bathe and dress hurriedly, then steal downstairs and out the entry to dart down myriad passageways into the Piazza San Marco. Before it was fully light, before the canals became crowded with gondolas and shopkeepers opened their stalls and narrow lanes became crowded with passersby, Cathryn would walk briskly with a purpose: to feel her blood pound in her ears and race through her veins; to soothe her desperate restlessness.

She would open her concealing cape and cast back its hood to let the freshness of the morning assault her freely. But all too frequently she would forget herself, stretching her allotted time beyond the limit, and returning very late for chapel.

This morning she had exceeded even her own liberal rationale for tardiness and felt almost deserving of the inevitable chastisement that would be meted out for her obvious disrespect. "I need the air to inspire me,'' she once insisted, less than contrite. The desire to banish her agitation seemed excuse enough to Cathryn for rushing about the city unescorted.

"I wouldn't consider waking anyone at this hour," Cathryn argued. "Besides, who would I find to accompany me at such an hour?" she demanded, thinking she made a very good point.

"Perhaps Father Vittorio? He's another restless sort these days," Perdita suggested dourly, knowing her offer to be out of the question, regretting her proposal the instant she uttered it.

Though she answered her foster mother flippantly, Cathryn nevertheless suffered over Perdita's disapproval. Whenever the directress expressed displeasure over Cathryn's behavior, it seemed to her the woman frowned more deeply than she did at any other offending girl. Cathryn tried to convince herself that Perdita's special fondness for her made the directress exceptionally cross whenever she was guilty of misconduct, but this knowledge rarely softened the burden of Perdita's disgust.

This morning, as she rushed into the always cool Fabiani chapel, Cathryn knew instinctively she would receive a larger than usual portion of Perdita's ire.

Cathryn pushed open the heavily carved chapel door then made an entrance that could not have been more poorly timed. Father Umberto turned toward the worshipers and let his gaze fall squarely upon Cathryn. He paused, seemingly confused by her entry, and all eyes turned to Cathryn.

She froze breathless and guilty.

To the offender the moment seemed endless, but shortly thereafter the priest resumed the ritual. Heads turned in his direction once more and Cathryn sank gratefully onto an empty bench, then kneeled and bowed her head. Only much later did she dare to raise her eyes in the direction of the altar. At last, Cathryn began to focus on the majestic and beloved ritual of the Mass.

She listened more attentively than most while tiny Father Umberto intoned his prayers, weighted down by elaborate, almost cumbersome priest's vestments. She was grateful for the familiar ceremony in musical Latin; though she knew the order of the Mass, she appreciated its beauty and mysterious, almost magical quality. With other worshipers, Cathryn sat in the Fabiani chapel, dwarfed by the marble altar and other fixtures, her breath stilled by the beauty of the early morning's light as it filtered through the jewellike panes of stained glass, and sensed that God was present. The Sacrament of the Holy Eucharist, the actual partaking of Christ's body and blood, conferred grace upon Cathryn and for a moment brought her a much needed sense of peace.

The sensation did not last long, for soon Cathryn felt the pull of eyes from the altar alcove, and when she turned her head, she stared into Father Vittorio's eyes.

At his look, Cathryn blushed crimson, certain his face portrayed the displeasure of everyone in chapel, though she felt his censure most.

How different he had seemed last night when he had prevented her from falling down the stairs! Then he had seemed genuinely concerned for her welfare. He had even expressed his worry that she might be cold. He had been tender and comforted her with reassuring words, but perhaps, Cathryn now considered, his words might only have been mechanical responses, words uttered for the thousandth time by a priest used to soothing troubled souls.

Father Vittorio's gaze riveted Cathryn's. How she ever managed to bow her head again, Cathryn did not begin to know, and as the minutes passed, she continued to feel the heat of his regard.

She knew he should be lost in the liturgy even more dutifully than she, and she forced herself to reason that the priest would scarcely concern himself with her. Please, let it be that though he stares, he does not truly see me, she prayed, and hoped he was in some sort of spiritual trance.

Cathryn worried that her tardiness convinced him she had not been sincere with him the night before. How could a girl who could not trouble herself to get to chapel on time worry whether God listened to her prayers?

Father Umberto continued to pray, and once more Cathryn tried her best to concentrate, pretending to be unaware of Father Vittorio's continued scrutiny. Yet she could not ignore him, helplessly drawn to lift her eyes to his by a pull she could not explain. He glowered and made it obvious to Cathryn that he was furious.

When, with the others, she filed past the altar for the final blessing, Cathryn was stunned to find Father Vittorio gone. In surprise, Cathryn stopped still, halting the procession until she felt a friend's impatient nudge.

"Cathryn!" Simone whispered, urging Cathryn on with a poke in the ribs. "What's wrong?" she demanded when they finally passed through the chapel doors.

"Nothing."

"Well, there *will* be when Signorina Fabiani is done with you, I warrant!" Simone insisted. "She was red-faced and late to chapel herself. Looking for you, I imagine. I thought you gave her your word not to go out again?"

Cathryn only had time to nod an answer before Signorina Fabiani rested a hand on Cathryn's shoulder and with a stern glance dismissed Simone, leaving Cathryn to face her sorely disappointed foster mother in the wide, cold marble corridor.

"Child, you test my patience unmercifully!" Perdita began the instant Simone's figure disappeared down the stairs. "Come with me," she motioned, and prodded Cathryn with a firm hand at the small of the young woman's back. She ushered Cathryn into a salon, pointing to an ornately upholstered chair, then motioned for her to sit.

For several minutes the older woman sat across from Cathryn in silence, uncharacteristically at a loss for words. She stared at her unruly charge while the morning sun streamed into the room and cast its brilliance on Cathryn. In response, Cathryn pulled the hood of her cape from her head.

Perdita was struck by the fragile but enduring beauty of the girl, and suddenly she was reminded of Cathryn's mother, which caused her to summon her sternest voice. "This willfulness of yours must cease instantly! You endanger my reputation, as well as yours, when you are so thoughtless and disobedient."

Cathryn lowered her eyes a moment, expecting Perdita to continue scolding her. When the silence lasted longer than she expected, Cathryn looked up and had to face Perdita's disturbing stare. "What possesses you, *angelica*? You say you toss and turn in your bed nights, yet you rise with the sun. I've asked you before, are you unwell?"

Cathryn replied with a shake of her head.

"Of course not. All one has to do is look at you for a moment to know you are fit." Perdita sighed. "I cannot fathom what possesses you. Soon, however, I'll no longer bear the burden of worry over your conduct—and suddenly, I'm not sorry to be free of that increasingly heavy cross," Perdita added harshly.

Cathryn winced invisibly, both too proud, too stunned by

Perdita's oblique confirmation of her fears to allow the sting of Perdita's last remark to show. She waited for the woman to continue.

"As you've known for a long time, Cathryn, your stay with us will one day come to an end, and it seems that day is almost here. Just yesterday I learned arrangements for your passage to England have already been made.

"Until this very moment I have been dreading your departure almost as long as I can remember. But if you continue to be ungrateful and disobedient, the day will not come soon enough for me."

Perdita's disgust was more than Cathryn could bear. Large tears welled in Cathryn's eyes and spilled down her cheeks.

Perdita steeled herself against the young woman's emotion. "From this moment until we part, let me see from your conduct that you are not ungrateful, *angelica*. Let us spend this time we have left enjoying each other," she said, then reached out for Cathryn, who readily kneeled and savored her foster mother's comforting embrace.

"I promise I'll be good. I want so for you to remember me gladly! Oh, Dita, I can't bear to think of leaving!" Cathryn cried. "I've known that the day for me to go was near—perhaps that's why I've been so wicked?"

Perdita sighed. "Perhaps, *angelica*, perhaps," she answered, believing Cathryn to be genuinely contrite. She tried her best to give comfort without completely erasing the effect of her carefully considered words. She hoped this scene would be their last unpleasant one, finding it a terrible effort to conceal her true emotions.

But Perdita Fabiani struggled and won, knowing without a shred of doubt that on that final day, she alone would shed enough tears to last them both a lifetime.

Chapter 3

Cathryn still felt desolate but at last realized she was hungry.
After her confrontation with Perdita, aware only of her tumultuous feelings, she had not ventured downstairs for breakfast and had missed the morning's usual light repast—as well as the morning's whispered gossip.

Blushing, Cathryn suspected she had been the subject of this morning's conversation.

Her stomach rumbled, and she covered the offending part of her body with her hands in an effort to smother the sound. Then her stomach growled at her again to remind her that the midday meal, the heaviest of the day, was still hours away.

Cathryn's usual tutoring duties had all been performed and her own lessons prepared, but her normal enthusiasm had been overshadowed by a very heavy heart. The knowledge of Perdita's displeasure, and, more heavily, the very real dread she felt about leaving Venice, had destroyed her concentration.

To make matters worse, Father Vittorio was due in the salon at any moment to coach her over any troubling passages before their afternoon lesson. Soon he would be standing over her—with a scowl, no doubt, she imagined.

"There is no need for you to inconvenience yourself today, Father," Cathryn muttered to herself.

Father Vittorio's morning visits interrupting her solitary practice had begun only recently. At first Cathryn welcomed his intrusion. During these interludes, he seemed unusually approachable. It seemed almost as if they were friends. But today, remembering his heated stare at chapel, Cathryn did not feel the least hospitable.

Nevertheless, the priest arrived.

He entered the room quietly, finding Cathryn deep in thought; when she turned around for no reason in particular, there he stood in silent appraisal. She was startled at the sight of him, but

24

more so by the slow approving smile that spread over his face when he looked into her eyes. He seemed at ease, as if he intended to overlook her misdeeds of early morning, and if his smile meant anything, he was happy to see her.

They stood close, staring at each other for a long moment. "What can I help you with this morning?" he said at last.

"With nothing—and everything," she stammered, feeling stupid.

"Perhaps I should have waited until this afternoon's lesson. . . ."

He chuckled at her response. "What troubles you the most?"

His gentle smile unsettled Cathryn's brain as she fixed her eyes first on the curve of his mouth, then on the firm line of his jaw, and at last on his magnificent dark brown eyes.

"The *presto*?" he suggested when she had no answer.

"No!"

"What then?"

"The dampness, I think," she offered, struggling to think of something concrete to complain about.

"The dampness?" he repeated. "I've not noticed it's especially damp." His eyes seemed to caress her face. "Have the cold nights also affected your violin?"

"Perhaps it's simply that my Amati needs a rest," she replied, choosing to ignore his mention of their encounter on the stairs.

"Then by all means, give it one."

I need a rest, too! Cathryn almost said aloud. A rest from your eyes, Father Vittorio!

"You have another violin at your disposal. Use it if the Amati is tired."

"Its voice has turned sour."

"No," he answered, disbelieving, but was concerned enough to pick up the instrument in question and sound it out. He made a slight adjustment, then tried again, his deft fingers and the bow sliding magically over the strings. He wrenched Cathryn's heart with his brilliance, forcing her into even deeper turbulence. The violin's voice was haunting and perfect, and Cathryn trembled at its beauty.

"There is nothing wrong with the violin, Cathryn," he said, and laid the instrument down gently. He looked at her bemusedly. "Are you sure your technique isn't the problem? Those passages you stumbled on yesterday will probably elude you for a while."

"I've perfected them already," she insisted perversely.

"You're bluffing and I know it, Cathryn," he answered, then challenged her by offering her the violin. "Match your boast with performance."

Cathryn refused, shaking her head.

"Sometimes, Cathryn, I fear you suffer from excess pride. You are on the verge, perhaps, of sacrificing your talent to become a dilettante."

Cathryn's face turned red and she whirled away from him, bursting into tears. "How can you accuse me! You know how hard I work—how I strive to please you! At the violin, I am your slave!"

Her outburst of tears baffled the priest. Instinctively he moved to her. "Cathryn. Cathryn," he whispered soothingly at her back. "You should be used to my scolding by now. I do not mean to wound you mortally, only to make you attend more carefully to your music." He put his hands on her shoulders and turned her to face him, gathering her into his arms. "I'm afraid this time you have taken me too seriously."

Cathryn was not in the least comforted by the priest's gentler words, and her tears fell harder.

He stroked her hair as she pressed her cheek against his chest. "I have never truly pleased you. You always find some fault with me."

Father Vittorio sighed. "You are quite wrong. You almost always please me. You lifted my heart from the very first time I saw and heard you play." He pushed her slightly away to look down into her face. "But it is my task to criticize, to help you strive for perfection. It would be wrong of me to declare you an angel when we both know you are not quite that." He smiled.

Cathryn nodded. "But you must admit you reserve your harshest judgment for me."

He brushed a wayward strand of her hair from her cheek. "If, like everyone else, I were enchanted by you, you'd learn nothing from me."

Her tears subsided and Cathryn gave the priest a slow smile. "I suppose I yet have a few things to learn from you," she admitted.

"I promise you, you do," he answered, releasing her. "Still, you and I are very alike in some ways, Cathryn. We both have been granted a gift from God, but we also have more than our share of pride and suffer from impatience.''

Cathryn looked at the priest. ''Are you trying to say you are not as perfect as you seem?''

His laugh was quick and light. Then he grew quite serious. ''I assure you, as a priest I fall a long way from perfection. . . .'' He paused to stare at Cathryn. ''But as a musician and a teacher I come much closer, and I promise I will continue to make demands on you as long as you are mine to influence.''

''You haven't much more time to impart your wisdom.'' Cathryn sighed.

He turned and reached for the Amati again. ''Then you had better continue your practicing,'' he said, handing her the violin.

Cathryn took her beautiful instrument and gently cradled it in her arms. She lifted her chin a little defiantly. ''I am not a dilettante, Father, but at times I see little use in practicing another note.

''I'm already well prepared for the children I will teach in my capacity as governess. I see no need to practice further. Only you care whether my lessons continue or not. And you will forget me the moment I leave, and, if not quite so soon as that, then the moment another student comes to take my place.''

Father Vittorio could only stare at the girl before him who was one moment a trying child and the next a disturbing young woman, but his eyes showed only shock at Cathryn's impudent tone. Then they darkened with an emotion Cathryn could not read.

''Perhaps if I refuse to practice,'' Cathryn rushed on in his silence, ''if I refuse to perform the music you write—music that none of your other students can perform—then you shall realize what you stand to lose when I leave. And perhaps you will come to miss me a little, even before I'm gone.''

Cathryn was startled by her boldness and a little frightened by the dark look the priest now gave her. ''You are more vain than I was aware,'' he chastised her. ''I've not spent my efforts on you, encouraging you to perfect your ability—your gift from God—for the selfish satisfaction of hearing you play my songs. Dear Cathryn, I hope you have been developing your skill for the glory of God and not with the notion that it pleases me.''

Her cheeks burning with color, Cathryn had to look away from Father Vittorio's blazing eyes.

"And I hope," he continued more gently, "that when I leave this room, you will lift your violin and once again praise God with your music."

Cathryn could not force herself to look up until the priest had left the salon and only barely managed to keep her tears at bay. When he was gone, her emotions still in turmoil, Cathryn lifted her Amati under her chin. She swore to practice until she dropped from exhaustion. Even if Father Vittorio continued to find fault with her, she hoped that God would not.

Chapter 4

The midday meal restored and elevated Cathryn's spirits and in the afternoon, while she waited for Father Vittorio, Cathryn practiced dutifully until she could play perfectly the passages on which he had challenged her. Satisfied at last, she held her violin and bow in her lap, feeling a little less in turmoil, less inclined to cry than she had been in the morning.

Her earlier display of emotion and her impudence toward the priest bewildered Cathryn—that she had actually suggested he should miss her when she left Venice was cause for furious blushing.

Cathryn tried to excuse her behavior by remembering her morning confrontation with Perdita and the woman's announcement of her now certain departure from Venice. As Cathryn continued to reflect, she confessed to not being quite as prepared to see her teacher as she wanted to be.

Even overlooking her latest outrageous behavior toward the priest, Cathryn admitted discomfort. Of late, Father Vittorio seemed mercurial in his responses to her, and his altering moods confused her, to say the least. One moment he might be gentle and consoling, as he had been on the stairs last night, or almost tender with her tears, as he had been this morning. A moment later he might thrash her verbally and glower as if he intended worse.

Cathryn mimicked the priest's dark furrowed brow, doubting she could scowl as impressively as the dark priest when he was in one of his exasperated moods. Perhaps he was sometimes plagued by demons, Cathryn thought, hoping it was more than her behavior that made Vittorio cast her such brooding looks.

Unable to suppress a shiver, Cathryn groaned aloud as she suddenly recalled that Father Vittorio would receive confession tonight. He had been quite right about her pride; she sighed.

"Father forgive me, for I have sinned," she whispered. "I am vain and prideful and disobedient. *Mea culpa. Mea culpa.*"

Cathryn stared at the music on the stand before her and prayed for the ability to overpower her confusing emotions; then, with a gesture of supreme frustration, she threw her bow onto the carpet, spilling the pages of music from the stand in front of her onto the floor. Then she all but dropped her magnificent violin onto the chair beside her. She wished that she had left Venice a fortnight ago!

Prior to the announcement of her departure everything in Cathryn's life seemed perfectly arranged. Every hour of her day was spoken for. She never had to worry about what came next. Now suddenly everything was uncertain. Soon everything would be foreign, the landscape, the people, the whole order of her life.

Cathryn felt close to tears again.

She supposed she could do as Father Vittorio suggested and practice, practice, practice! Then she would be too exhausted to deliberate and worry over her future.

Yes, he was right. He was *always* right! "God's most supreme gift to music since He created sounds for man to hear," Perdita proclaimed him.

Was it any wonder Father Vittorio also suffered from the sin of pride!

Cathryn smiled and conjured one of her more pleasant memories of Father Vittorio. This morning he claimed not to be a perfect priest—boasting instead that he *was* a nearly perfect musician. Cathryn grudgingly admitted her teacher did deserve her total devotion until the moment of her departure.

Yet she wondered now if she had dedicated herself to her music all these years to show gratitude to God, or if she had strived only to please the priest?

Before she could give the question thoughtful consideration, Father Vittorio entered the salon and interrupted her. His gaze immediately fell on her discarded bow and on the sheets of music scattered on the floor. Without a word, he bolted the door and went to stand by the gallery of high windows on the far side of the room; for several minutes he stared down onto the waters of the Grand Canal. When she had collected her things, he turned to face her.

Cathryn hoped to avoid the power of his thickly lashed brown eyes and was forced to look behind him out the windows. For a few moments she allowed herself to be distracted by a passing storm that threatened in the distance. Then, as her mind returned from wandering, Cathryn braced herself for an outburst from the priest who now stood before her brimming with displeasure.

There was no warm, approving smile upon his face to reassure her, and defiantly, Cathryn pouted in response to Father Vittorio's brooding silence. Finally, Cathryn looked him in the eye and locked her gaze with his.

At first she felt the fool staring at him, but gradually she forgot that feeling and was overcome by a disturbing warmth that made her feel quite faint.

"I've watched you these several years," the priest spoke to her at last, "and I've marveled at you every day." His voice was soft and though he stood very close to her, Cathryn had to strain to hear him. She waited for him to qualify his gentle remarks with the sting of criticism.

A strong current of emotion seemed to pass between them. He paused, and she was mesmerized. He seemed to hold her in a spell, and when he spoke again, Cathryn did not trust it safe to believe her ears.

"You accused me of indifference to your leaving me—I promise you nothing could be further from the truth. Dearest Cathryn, how can you imagine that I would not miss you?" he demanded.

Cathryn lowered her gaze, but as she did, he reached for her chin and raised her face. "Don't look away," he commanded softly. "We have so little time and I have so much to say." He seemed to struggle, as if his words were painful.

"How will I survive without you, *angelica*? Who will I turn to?" he asked as if Cathryn could help him. "Who else, here within these walls, begins to approach you?"

Cathryn sighed with audible relief. He was only concerned about losing his best student. "Surely you'll find someone you can develop among the younger girls. Or someone new will come to take my place," Cathryn offered, granting him a smile that did not reach her eyes.

Father Vittorio shook his head. "Never. Never." He sighed. "How can I let you go? You are the breath of life," he whispered, then handed her several sheets of music. "I wrote this for you—it speaks more clearly than my words."

Trembling, Cathryn was fully aware that her body responded to his affectionate words much differently than her mind would allow.

Feeling light-headed, Cathryn sat down to read Father Vittorio's new score and, as he began to play the music, closed her eyes to fully appreciate the composition dedicated to her; listening, she told herself she misinterpreted and assumed too much.

Occasionally, Cathryn forced herself to open her eyes and saw a gifted musician performing—a man of God, her teacher, instructing her on the mastery of the violin. Yet when her eyes were closed again, and her senses immune to all but the emotion of the music, Cathryn was tantalized by forbidden images.

She heard his music and dreamed of Vittorio: his perfect mouth; his intriguing deep eyes; his graceful but masculine hands; his lithe body strangely enhanced by the fine wool cassock that covered his well-muscled frame. She dreamed of his broad shoulders and the strength of his arms, and vaguely acknowledged visions of a man making love to a woman.

Cathryn drifted with the music, soon lost in a daydream that fast became clearer than the reality of her physical presence in the salon. She imagined the priest and how it would feel to be in his arms; to feel his cheek next to hers and, this late in the afternoon, the rough stubble of his usually close-shaven beard. She remembered his warm scent and the fact that this pleasant essence had often disturbed her senses.

Before this moment, Cathryn had been uncertain about the stirrings she had sometimes felt in his presence, but now the recognition was instinctual. It was desire—a woman's longing for a man to touch her—perceived by a girl who was in the instant no longer a child.

The music stopped too soon, and with reluctance, Cathryn pulled herself from her reverie. When she opened her eyes, Vittorio quickly closed the distance between them and lifted her into his arms. He kissed her passionately, his mouth devouring her with urgency.

She responded naturally, ardently, in a way unknown to her before. Vittorio the man caressed Cathryn the woman, holding her tightly against the fullness of his manhood, and they both completely forgot, as if they had never known, the restrictions that should have kept them separate forever.

"I love you," he whispered. "I have loved you always." He seemed almost fierce and for a while captured her entirely with his kisses.

"I remind myself I am your priest, and until now, I've kept myself from you. But dear God, you tempt me with your smiles, your grace, your gentle beauty. I lie to myself and to God when I say I do not love you."

He pulled her more tightly against him, and irrationally, Cathryn felt he did not hold her close enough, suddenly aware of a strange desire to melt into his body—to be one with him. Cathryn pressed herself to him, seeking that end, resenting the cloth that kept his hands separate from her bare skin. She felt no urge to stop him as he began to unfasten the pearl buttons at the throat of her shining gray silk dress.

Her usual modesty obliterated by the quickening of her desire, Cathryn was aware of nothing but his caresses and her own delicious responses. She wanted him to soothe the sudden tingling of her flesh; to ease the growing fever that threatened to consume her. Perhaps free of her clothes, she reasoned, she would feel cool again.

But no. The more exposed her skin, the more intense the heat became. Why was it so warm in the salon? she wondered as he undid her bodice. Why had he waited so long to free her of its restrictions?

When Vittorio exposed and finally touched her bare breast, Cathryn gasped softly, her eyes wide with awe and pleasure. "You are lovelier than I dreamed," he said.

Cathryn felt a shimmer of delight with each caress as he tantalized her nipples until they strained erect. When his mouth replaced his fingers, Cathryn trembled with the magnitude of her desire.

"I may burn for loving you—God knows I have tried *not* to—but still I love you," Vittorio confided when he raised his mouth to hers again. "I've prayed without ceasing for relief of my feelings for you. I've pondered my vows and begged to be sent from degli Innocenti—to be driven from your presence."

Cathryn's eyes widened with astonishment.

"I imagined I'd forget you if you were absent from me. Yet when I close my eyes, I dream, and you are with me. Surely I've fallen from God's grace, for there is no forgetting you."

Cathryn's eyes filled with tears.

"No, my love, don't cry," he begged. "When I think of you, my heart is filled with overwhelming joy."

Cathryn looked into Vittorio's eyes and saw his adoration and the depth of his contagious desire. When he bent to kiss her lips, she could imagine no greater pleasure.

Yet naked to the waist, her silk gown and soft underthings draped about her hips, Cathryn wished to be even more undressed. As he continued to caress her, the voice of her conscience warned that to be the downfall of one of God's own would have its price, but the voice was drowned out by her own soft cries.

Drawn to him by a force more powerful than any she had ever experienced, Cathryn completely ignored that spending her virginity on Vittorio, a man who could never marry her, would diminish her only value in the world outside his embrace. In the tight circle of Vittorio's arms, Cathryn could not consider anything but surrender, unable to discourage him though she risked her immortal soul.

His eager kiss traveled slowly over her face and to every inch of exposed skin.

"I love you, Vittorio," Cathryn whispered as her gown rustled in its descent from her body.

Naked, Cathryn was more gloriously beautiful than Vittorio had imagined. He sighed inwardly, adoring her, drawn to her by a mysterious tide against which resistance was useless. She was so trusting, so heartbreakingly innocent. But he was also aware that her young body was now a woman's and that his own flesh ached for hers. When she reached to caress his face, to place her hand against his chest, and called his name in a sweetly seductive whisper, he shuddered at the depth of his need.

For a long moment Vittorio gazed at Cathryn, his heart caught in midbeat by the radiance and sweet expression of her face. Her eyes were filled with trust and uncertain longing. When he could not resist her or himself a moment more, he caressed her lovingly, sensitive to her tender inexperience.

Vittorio respected the precious gift Cathryn was about to give him. She was an orphan, with nothing in the world but her virtue to offer, but he also knew no one would ever love Cathryn Godwyne more.

It seemed a lifetime since Vittorio had last made love to a woman, and never before, he realized, had he been with a woman whom he loved. He was as nervous and expectant as Cathryn, for this was no simple act of passion. It was a sacred commitment for which he was breaking sacred vows. Loving Cathryn—touching her was a step that might mean his eternal damnation, it was true, but deep in his soul Vittorio believed that Cathryn might also be the source of his redemption. "I pledge my love to you for all eternity," Vittorio vowed with kisses that made Cathryn weak.

Vittorio disrobed before Cathryn, displaying a body more powerful and masculine than she had ever envisioned. "You are magnificent," she breathed, touching the naturally bronzed skin of his chest as he bared it, lightly fingering the curling black triangle of hair that spread above his nipples to almost disappear just below his navel.

She felt it natural for her to look upon and touch him, and wanted him to hold and caress her—in fact, she could think of nothing else—but she was completely innocent of a man's body fully prepared to make love. What she had seen carved between the legs of nude male statues in the squares of Venice did not prepare Cathryn for Vittorio at this moment.

She could only stare. He seemed enormous and Cathryn was certain he would have to use terrible force against her. Fully erect, his body suddenly seemed a weapon. "I'm afraid," she whispered finally.

"I love you more than I've ever loved anyone," he tried to reassure her, pulling her tightly against his warm flesh, knowing nothing else to say, afraid promising not to hurt her might be a lie.

Heart pounding, Cathryn lay down with Vittorio, at first hesitantly welcoming his tight embrace, her dress and petticoats and his cassock pillowed beneath them. When she closed her eyes, he pressed her eyelids with gentle kisses, the pressure of his kiss kindling a small flame deep inside her. He made love to her slowly. He kissed her temples; the curve and hollow of each cheek; and settled his mouth gently for a moment beneath one ear. "I have never desired anything in life as I desire you," he whispered.

She yielded her mouth to him fully, letting him know by her responsiveness that she was willing in spite of her uncertainties. His tongue probed her warm, sweet mouth, which she opened to his insistence for his eager exploration. Cathryn likewise tested him, an imitation that gave him exceeding joy.

His mouth and fingers drifted lower, multiplying Cathryn's tension a thousandfold. Wherever he touched her, he created need. Her breasts, on which he lavished much attention, ached for more, and Cathryn pulled his mouth back to her pouting nipples repeatedly, protesting his seeming determination to desert them. By now she too, was driven, and the flame he had inspired at her center expanded and engulfed her completely.

She made soft sounds of pleasure, little by little, beginning to appreciate the wonderful hardness of him, to relish the idea of taking him into her, of surrounding his firm instrument with her supremely tender flesh. She forgot her fear, answering his patience with a soaring need to be fulfilled.

With each taste of her, he wanted more.

He caressed her thighs, admiring her graceful limbs, his touch still patient, yet sweetly demanding. She parted her legs, aching for him to explore more deeply, wet with the juices of her own desire. He used his tongue to prepare her further, while she emitted soft, excited cries and arched her back in eagerness.

Cathryn knew not what to anticipate, only that the sensations he was building made her desperate and feverish for some conclusion. When he slipped his fingers into her, she accepted him gladly, tight with newness at first, but as he fondled her, she suited him with ease.

His pace of exploration quickened then and she showed him with her touch, with fingers that had engagingly lost their innocence, that she wanted his body joined with hers. She caressed Vittorio's hard, silken shaft, at once aware that her body had been made for him to plunder, and begged with motions and with words for him to enter her. "Vittorio, Vittorio," she cried, gladly forgetting that she had never known a man before.

Almost forgetting she was new, Vittorio thrust into her, and she cried out and wrapped her legs around him in a fierce embrace. He groaned with pleasure and the effort to force his movements to be tentative. His body begged for swift release, but Vittorio sensed Cathryn was not quite ready and he lingered with her.

He smiled down at her and leaned to kiss her hungry mouth, then nibble at her still eager breasts. When her body eased and he felt her soar, he began to move within her for a purpose that would no longer wait. As he drove himself deep inside her, Cathryn consented and with her waves of joy brought him explosive and rapturous release. "We will burn, Cathryn, but you are worth it!" he cried, her sighs of ecstasy still echoing in his ears.

It seemed a long while before the glorious throbbing of their bodies ceased, and when Vittorio settled against her, Cathryn could only weep. In response, he gathered her more tightly in his arms. "Have I hurt you?"

"No. Never," she said, pushing herself away from him slightly to better see his face. Relieved, he smiled at her and Cathryn felt as if she would drown with her feelings of love. "But you speak of burning, and I fear that someday you will want me not to love you."

With a gentle hand, Vittorio brushed away Cathryn's tears and kissed her trembling lips. "I dread the day of judgment, Cathryn, but I love you and I gladly risk everything to have you in my arms. You are dearer to me than life—dearer even than my soul," he swore, and believed his words with all his heart. "That you love me, too," he whispered, "is more than I had dreamed."

Chapter 5

Father Vittorio was weary of waiting. Tonight he had heard the confession of every girl except Cathryn, and he assumed now that she would not appear.

He tried not to worry over Cathryn's absence, preferring to view her neglect as a form of childish defiance rather than a sign that something was wrong. Yet he harbored the fear that she might now be remorseful or ashamed or, perhaps, feel shy. In their lovemaking this afternoon, Cathryn had exposed herself in ways most respectable women never did. Perhaps, he feared, she was now regretful. Vittorio, the man, prayed not.

Cathryn was an angel—sweet, trusting, divine—and the love he felt for her was sacred. Surely loving her could not be a sin.

The chapel was dim and quiet, and, at this late hour especially, he enjoyed the silence, for unlike those of most priests, Father Vittorio's days were filled with sound. And some of the sounds to which he was subjected could only be described as pure noise.

Vittorio grimaced at the thought of his worst students. On occasion, it was almost more than he could bear to sit through a music lesson, though he invariably did. He was noted for his forbearance with the inept but eager, and at times he felt he more than deserved nomination for sainthood.

Vittorio smiled to himself. There had never been any possibility of his canonization, and now that he had declared his love for Cathryn, there was not even a remote chance for veneration.

In addition to their physical union, there were other counts against the priest with regard to Cathryn. As her teacher, lately he seemed to be always losing patience. He justified his flares of temper by saying that to tolerate careless study or performance from her was unthinkable, if for no other reason than because her ability was so great. There was no excuse to accept less than excellence from Cathryn. And yet, in light of the afternoon they'd spent together, Father Vittorio admitted his intolerance had had more to do with his physical desires than with his wish for Cathryn to properly honor her God-given musical ability.

Father Vittorio was aroused again by his memory of the time spent with Cathryn earlier in the day. For months and years he had successfully resisted his feelings for her, but now there could be no further denial of her effect on him or his love for her.

The priest recalled the moment when he first saw Cathryn and how he had been drawn to her by a selfish interest in her extraordinary musical ability. But her innocence, her eagerness to please him, soon touched him, and though young himself, he began to love Cathryn in a way he did not love the other children in his charge. Cathryn Godwyne became his very special child.

One day many years later, Father Vittorio looked at Cathryn and realized she was no longer a little girl. Before his eyes she had grown from a beautiful child into the most extraordinary and vital young woman he had ever known. She dazzled him, but for a blessed time his attachment remained paternal.

Father Vittorio did not know exactly when Cathryn began to affect him as a beautiful woman affects a man of ordinary desires, but there came a day when he could not ignore her presence in his dreams.

An innocent laugh, a look, a smile from her, and his man's body betrayed the priest. Without her knowing, he was sure, she haunted him. He knew she loved him: he was her teacher; her confessor; her priest. She trusted him. He prayed, begging for relief from sin. He said penitential psalms. Still he was seduced body and soul.

Until succumbing to his passion, Father Vittorio continued to tell himself Cathryn was a child, but now it was an unconvincing argument. If he had any doubt, he only needed to dwell briefly on the hour she had lain with him this afternoon. Cathryn was no longer a schoolgirl.

Vittorio inhaled deeply, conscious of the heat of his fresh desire. Did he only imagine that he could still breathe her scent? he wondered, not knowing how he would last the night without holding her in his arms. How would he survive the lifetime of emptiness that lay before them?

Until Cathryn began to obsess him, Father Vittorio had accepted his obligation of chastity, though becoming a priest had never truly been his calling. He had wanted to do much as his two older brothers had done, but as his father's third son, he'd never had the option of going to sea.

His musical brilliance only made his course more clear, at least to his parents. Their third born was foreordained to bring special honor to the family by the order of his birth and by his talent. There was nothing else to do but dedicate this son and his musical gift to God.

Vittorio had accepted this fate and, from the age of sixteen, had quelled his male urges. His vows were supported by the constant presence of his young charges as music master at La Casa degli Innocenti.

Fortunately, most of the schoolgirls who blossomed into young women aware of their wiles were bound also by their religion's rigid edicts, and to those who dared consider breaking those rules, Father Vittorio made himself convincingly unapproachable. From time to time there had been severe temptations to his basic human weaknesses, but until Cathryn, he had remained chaste. When he was twenty, a young noblewoman, Natalia Lamberto, new to degli Innocenti, made it her main amusement to seduce him. Though she was delightful to behold and charming, she did not stir him, nor did she capture his imagination. She did not call upon his soul as Cathryn Godwyne did.

But Signorina Lamberto was dedicated to her pursuit and tested the priest's determination at every turn. He rejected her advances, but to his astonishment, she seemed to be immune even to his warnings that God most despised a woman who dared seduce a priest.

Finally, she stole into his room one night and, while he was still sleeping, patiently touched and aroused him. On waking, he was inclined for a moment to submit to her seduction, but both the risk of discovery and the threat of eternal damnation served to dampen the fire in his blood.

Perdita's face was quite red when he marched the half-naked and guilty young woman to her chambers in the middle of the night, but Father Vittorio had no qualms about having Natalia discreetly but swiftly expelled.

But Vittorio's longing for Cathryn Godwyne was greater than his fear of discovery, greater even than his fear of eternal damnation. Vittorio made the sign of the cross. "God have mercy on us both," he muttered, and considered Cathryn's fate.

Would she be despised by God now that she had been party to the downfall of a priest?

Vittorio had loved Cathryn since she was nine years old. She had been a winsome child, her sweet face framed by pitch-black hair trailing behind her like a long braid of satin rope, and a suggestion of the Orient in the slant of her eyes. A rumor persisted that Cathryn's mother was part Chinese, but Signorina Fabiani remained steadfastly silent about Cathryn's background.

Whatever the truth of her heritage, as a mysteriously beautiful woman, Cathryn had proved irresistible.

Father Vittorio sighed at his most recent memory of Cathryn and opened the curtain of the confession box. Perhaps Cathryn only wanted to confess her sins to him in private, he defended to himself, determined to see her before going to his room to spend the long empty night alone.

The priest removed the fringed silk stole. With Cathryn's

departure drawing near, the nights seemed longer than he ever remembered.

Perdita had informed him of Cathryn's imminent departure even before the formal letter of announcement arrived, in the hope that he would help Cathryn face her future with optimism.

"Father, I am beside myself for thinking of Cathryn leaving us!" Perdita had sniffed. "How can she be called away from us to tend some household of wretched English children? And *please* don't say not to question God's grand design—for I've too often used that very argument with a tearful Cathryn, and am not convinced," she huffed, then rushed on, giving the priest no opportunity to reply.

"She is of better mettle than any girl within these walls, yet she will never have a marriage or a husband worthy of her. And if she marries at all, he will be, God forbid, an Englishman." Perdita sank into a chair, disconsolate.

The priest had chafed to consider her the bride of any man and, in private, shook his head at Perdita's choice of counselors for Cathryn. Truly, he was the worst choice she could have made. He could not begin to console Cathryn, for the priest could not bear to think of her departure and even considered begging her to remain in Venice.

Perdita's opinion of Cathryn aside, there was no chance that she would marry well, but it was quite likely she could find a tutoring position with an aristocratic family, and when he was in an expansive mood, the nature of Cathryn's musical ability did not make it impossible for Vittorio to imagine that someday she might return to degli Innocenti to teach beside him.

Father Vittorio winced. He knew he was dreaming.

Disturbed by the hopelessness of Cathryn's situation and his, the priest deserted the Fabiani chapel and walked briskly past the many salons where in daylight hours children studied ordinary subjects or practiced voice and other music. The teacher thought of his favorite instrument and of his favorite student. What remarkable fate it was that Cathryn's forté should be the violin, the instrument on which he was an undisputed virtuoso. Perhaps if Cathryn had preferred another instrument, she would not have come so keenly to his attention.

How fervently Father Vittorio wished it were that simple! For music was only one part of his attraction to Cathryn Godwyne. He was intensely aware of being drawn to her by a force even greater than their mutual gift and love for music. If anything, Vittorio believed their shared passion for music could have overwhelmed the love that lay beneath.

Nor was his attraction to Cathryn simply carnal desire. He knew from experience and from Church teaching that most men's affinity for a woman was lust alone. In cleaving to Cathryn, Vittorio felt a current so strong that he was helpless to resist, and although its origin was still a mystery, he knew the force that bound them was not mere lust.

Father Vittorio reached the landing and for several minutes stood before the marble staircase approaching the third floor. He took a deep breath and, realizing there was no retreat from the course he had set, took the wide steps of the staircase two at a time, rushing in the direction of Cathryn's room.

He paused before Cathryn's door, imagining her already nestled in the bed one floor beneath his own, and as he stood in reflection, the door was opened by Signorina Bianca Fabiani, who startled him with her sudden appearance.

Perdita's short but ample younger sister was equally surprised to see the priest and gave a small shout. "Oh, dear Father Vittorio!" cried Bianca, a little amused by the surprise that registered on his face. "Your forgiveness for my startling you— and for my shrieks. But you are an answer to my prayers!"

Then she gasped a second time. "But I fear you've been waiting all this time and you must be very tired. I should have sent word that Cathryn would not come to confession—she claims to be unwell and refuses to get out of bed, though truthfully, Father," the plump matron confided, drawing nearer to the priest, "I think, in spite of her contrary claim, there's not a thing wrong with her—for all the world she looks delicate, but in full bloom."

Bianca Fabiani lowered her voice further. "Would you be so kind as to sit with Cathryn a little while this evening? She is upset—about leaving degli Innocenti—and your words might console her in a way her sorrowing sisters and little mothers cannot."

Vittorio nodded at the kindly Bianca Fabiani, a little ashamed that he failed to blush. "It's natural for Cathryn to be unhappy. Surely a suitable place within the Republic where her great talent would be appreciated can be found," he suggested. "No one will value her the way we Venetians do."

Bianca nodded. "Believe me, Father, my sister and I agree with you completely. But, at last, Perdita and I are honor bound to obey the demands of her English guardian. She is not our possession, you know, Father, only a child to whom we have grown immutably attached." The woman let a long sigh free of her ample lungs.

"It has been a privilege to oversee this orphans' school. It was my dear mother's dream and we are proud of the many good girls who have made their home with us and then gone on to blessed lives in families needing their skills with music and children. And, also, we value those girls who have made their own families richer for what they have learned here. I've no regrets. Truly.

"But Cathryn is no ordinary girl, and her future troubles me as the future of no other child who has dwelled here has. Like you, I worry. I fear that in a foreign land she will not be appreciated. She does belong with us, does she not, Father?" Bianca shook her head sadly.

"It is sometimes difficult to accept God's will, is it not?" she asked. "Please, go to her, Father Vittorio, and though we are not to be consoled, give her what comfort you can."

The priest nodded. "I will do what I can," he promised as he brushed past Bianca and entered Cathryn's room.

For a short while, Bianca continued to stand in the doorway, wondering if the most demanding of Cathryn's teachers would succeed in cheering her. It seemed unlikely, somehow, yet she knew Cathryn was fond of this exacting priest. In fact, his name had been included in the few comprehensible words Cathryn had uttered this evening during a fit of dramatic tears. Bianca hadn't made much sense of what Cathryn tried to communicate, but it was obvious that she was deeply affected and deeply troubled.

In her distress she had even threatened to run away, to throw herself into the sea, then insisted in the next breath that someone would have to carry her aboard the ship that was destined to take her to England, promising she would make no cooperative move toward her new home. Bianca sighed. This was a side to Cathryn no one had ever seen before.

Usually Cathryn was a most pliant and agreeable child, but, Bianca realized, before this, no one had ever actually crossed

Cathryn's will. Or perhaps it was simply that Cathryn was no longer a child and, as a woman, would have at least a few independent notions of her own. And perhaps it was a very good thing, Bianca asserted firmly, closing Cathryn's door.

Chapter 6

Vittorio waited to hear the door close behind him.

The bedcovers were pulled over Cathryn's head and she did not stir, but he stood patiently, knowing she had seen and heard him whispering with Bianca. He had seen her peek at them from beneath the covers, though she thought she was unobserved.

"Do you want me to go?" he asked finally.

There was silence.

"Then good night, Cathryn," Vittorio said, and turned his back.

"No! Please," Cathryn called, rising from the bed to stop him.

When he paused and turned again to face her, Cathryn halted her movement toward him, conscious of his heated gaze. She retreated to the edge of her bed, reaching behind her for the comforter, pulling it before her to cover herself, and smiled shyly at Vittorio as he moved to close the distance between them.

"You failed to come to confession," he accused in a stern voice.

Cathryn lowered her eyes, then looked at him boldly. "What need is there to confess, Father? You and God both know my sin very well—if loving you is a sin." She raised her face to the priest temptingly. "Would it not be blasphemous to confess," she wondered, "when I know in my heart that I will sin again? Do you have the power to absolve me of that, Father?"

She paused for his reply, but he was silent.

"Perhaps, Father, like me, you suddenly question why love

between a man and a woman is evil and cannot reason why God would punish us with fire for loving one another.''

Vittorio could not summon an articulate reply.

"Why are you here?" she demanded, slowly smiling.

"I did not come to be interrogated, _angelica_. I came only because I am weak to the power you have over me. I cannot stay away," he said, and reached for her, pulling her into his arms. "I do not come out of any logic," he whispered, and kissed her hungrily.

"You corrupt me, Father, for in your arms I will sin again and again," she whispered breathlessly against his cheek when she could pull her lips away from his.

He tightened himself against her pliant body. "You mock me."

"No, Father, I love you," she replied, and reached to push the biretta from his head. "But this question you must answer— are you a man or a priest?"

"With you, first a man," Vittorio confessed, unlacing the bodice of Cathryn's nightdress, touching the smooth skin of her breasts with reverence, seeking her nipples to caress.

In response, Cathryn sought his mouth with hers, feeling he tantalized her unmercifully as he nibbled with his fingers at the tips of her sensitive breasts, wondering how this priest knew her secrets, secrets she hardly knew herself.

Vittorio's kiss was passionate as, with some reluctance, he moved his fingers from her breasts and pushed her nightdress lower to her hips, where it fell to her feet of its own accord. Eagerly he drew her hard against him, her firm round buttocks a pleasure in his hands, her flat belly yielding only slightly to the pressure of his erection.

Arms encircling him, she caressed and held him fast. She let him know with her sighs and by her motion against him that she was eager in their undulating embrace.

Cathryn tugged at Vittorio's cassock and freed her lips from his. "You hide from me, priest," she teased, but then was overcome with shyness, unable to watch him as he hurriedly disrobed. Instead, she turned away to pull the covers off the bed.

Naked, greedy to thrust himself into contact with her, Vittorio pulled her back against him, groaning with the pleasure of having her pressed tightly against him.

Once again his fingers sought her delightfully full breasts, their dusky pink tips seeming to beg for his attention. He gave that attention willingly, but an urgency in his loins forced him to linger there only momentarily. "I fear the more I have you, the more I want you."

Cathryn leaned against Vittorio and pressed him hard against her. "Please come into me now," she whispered, feeling herself warm and open to him, moaning softly with anticipation as he slipped his hand down her belly and tangled his fingers in her hair. He coaxed her gently and she opened her legs to his insistent, delicious caresses.

When Cathryn could not endure his touch another moment, Vittorio released her and lay down with her and, staggered by his own desire, covered her body with his own. He entered her swiftly, but even in his great excitement, Vittorio studied Cathryn. She closed her eyes and arched her body, splendidly eager for him, at every opportunity allowing him to drive himself more deeply into her, this time knowing she was at the very edge of ecstasy.

The intensity of her pleasure only magnified Vittorio's passion and when he crested, she followed, crying out, holding him fiercely to her, hoping the fast-breaking waves of pleasure that burst inside her would last forever.

Afterward they lay entwined, each cherishing the other, filled with the wonder of their experience, but soon kisses that at first were soothing and gentle, offered to ease the slow but advancing fact of separation, turned passionate.

Vittorio's languor vanished, and pursuing Cathryn again, he entreated her with caresses and words. "Your body is an opiate to me," he whispered, trailing kisses from her mouth along her jaw and slowly down to love-tender breasts and her sensitive waist. And though only minutes before Cathryn had felt vibrations that seemed to exhaust her, she yearned desperately for her lover again.

"Touch me, touch me," she implored.

Quite willingly he obeyed, continuing to explore her sweet body with his mouth, kindling flames that Cathryn imagined would take several lifetimes to quench.

Vittorio was also passionately vulnerable to her caresses and, wisely, Cathryn teased him cautiously. She filled his senses to the brim and then withheld herself, sweetly begging for his attention to her own erotic needs. For a time they were playful and abandoned, with Vittorio confirming that if he teased her nipples, Cathryn could very quickly be reduced to incoherent cries of ecstasy.

When she could endure no more and her body ached with need for him to fill her, Cathryn called to him invitingly. "I need you," she begged.

Vittorio gasped with both joy and worry as she caressed him with purpose and obliged her gladly, nestling himself between her legs. He pushed into her slowly and, mindful of her feverish need, struggled to delay his own release. Cathryn could not conceal her pleasure and moaned with every delicious thrust. He was almost too patient and soon his rhythm made her frantic for his sweet torture to end.

"Please, now!" she begged, and Vittorio needed no further supplication. He rode her fiercely then, until her jubilant cries seemed to madden him and he took his pleasure, feeling as though, in her embrace, he escaped from the bonds of flesh and blood and soared outside himself.

"The moment was all too fleeting, *cara*," he complained softly afterward. "You have brought me to the brink. In your arms I transcend into another domain."

Drifting to sleep, her legs and body wrapped possessively around him, Cathryn smiled at Vittorio. In his wonderfully strong arms she was, she knew, hopelessly charmed and bound to him through all eternity.

Chapter 7

They slept together until very early light, stirring occasionally to begin but not to finish making love, until, with the freshness of the new day, they greeted each other in passion. It was startling to Cathryn to wake in someone's arms, and it filled her with joy to see Vittorio's face against her pillows; to lie against him. Though it seemed the end of everything when morning finally came, Vittorio promised, "It is only our beginning."

Vittorio was accustomed to rising early, his usual course to attend Mass, then, before assuming his teaching duties, to seclude himself in his room and commit to paper the music that had disturbed his sleep during the night. But the night just spent with Cathryn made him restless in an entirely different way.

Though he had not completely forgotten the pleasures of making love to a woman, his experiences as a youth with mature women, friends of his older brothers, were not really comparable. His night with Cathryn had been a revelation.

In the nine years that he had been a priest, Vittorio had learned to tolerate the rules of his existence, to abide by the vows he had been persuaded to take. His religion taught purity as the ideal condition and virginity the natural state of man before his fall from grace. Man only experienced the curse of lust as the result of sin.

As a priest Father Vittorio had the opportunity to purify himself. It was God's will that he not live his life as an ordinary man. Vittorio accepted this fate but sometimes lamented what seemed to be God's obvious plan.

Yet what was the use of regretting? the priest had often asked himself. There was nothing to be gained by regret.

He never found a better answer.

Fortunately, he had much work to do and little time to bemoan his fate. His life was full and rich. Besides, life in the world outside the Church did not often run the course of one's choosing. Vittorio knew many a man who would gladly change places with him. The priesthood had much to offer.

That was his attitude the day before yesterday, Vittorio acknowledged as he lay beside Cathryn, deliciously warm and physically gratified.

His priesthood had been an unchallengeable notion only before Cathryn became fully real to him. Now that he had made love to Cathryn, her responses to him and his to her would color his life, his world, his music, forevermore. Their physical union had filled a final void in their communion.

Vittorio admitted loving Cathryn almost from the beginning, but until very recently, he had never allowed himself to think about loving her, except in the most esoteric way. He had convinced himself that love for God could be expanded to include love for others: for his students, including Cathryn. But the love Vittorio felt for Cathryn, that now had been unlocked from his heart and physically expressed, was unlike any other.

"Cathryn, you bewitch me," he gasped accusingly at dawn, settling himself against her after making love to her again.

Cathryn laughed joyously. "And what have you done to me, priest?" she demanded playfully, accepting the kisses he rained on the top of her head, and nestled into his arms more tightly.

"I was a virgin, pure and unblemished, until you seduced me. You are wicked—an evil angel," she teased, but Vittorio tensed against her. Cathryn only laughed more and began to kiss the uneasy priest to arouse him once again.

Vittorio could not resist her and lay back in resignation to accept her ministrations, and though she surprised him greatly, he had not the least desire to forbid her mouth on him.

She tantalized him until he believed he would die of pleasure. She tortured him delightfully, discovering his body to be a fertile plain of glorious sensation. Everywhere her lips and fingers lovingly trailed she left him burning with increased desire, and what had made her tremble with fear the day before now thoroughly enticed her.

At first she teased him lightly with her tongue; then gave quick nibbling kisses; then took him fully into her mouth, discovering a kind of pleasure that only yesterday she would have sworn impossible.

Vittorio nearly lost control; he was not even vaguely aware of how much enjoyment Cathryn's explorations brought her, nor did he have any wish to stop her.

When she finally sought his lips again, his blood was searing in his veins. He grasped her fiercely and drew her down on him, single-mindedly determined to satisfy the feverish need she had created.

He demanded that she ride him vigorously, and Cathryn moved at his bidding, greatly excited by his passion, until, abruptly, he stilled her movements and held her fiercely to him, groaning deep sighs of satisfaction.

Vittorio's heart raced. Smiling gently, he closed his eyes and waited to regain his breath. *"Cara,* you have talent no one within these walls imagines," he teased, unable to resist a playful jibe.

"And you, my able teacher," Cathryn replied quite seriously, "you have yet to test me fully."

Almost warily, Vittorio opened his eyes and took a long look at the young woman he lovingly called "*angelica*." She lay beside him, her eyes bright with love. He stared at Cathryn, drinking in her beauty, her skin reminding him of the satiny petals of a fragile flower, her bright brown eyes its deep contrasting center, her mouth a delicate blossom, opening to its full perfection.

Earlier he would have described her lips as gentle. But now, parted slightly and moistened by a pensive dab of her tongue, they were hungry and wanton. Cathryn was slim and small-boned, her narrow shoulders surrounded by a heavy cape of rich black hair that tumbled obediently to her waist. She seemed fragile, delicate, gentle, yet there was something exuberantly vigorous and wonderfully strong about Cathryn Godwyne.

Vittorio smiled. There was little danger that she would collapse in the midst of strenuous lovemaking.

Cathryn smiled back at Vittorio, a little impatient with his lengthy scrutiny. "You keep me waiting and in suspense," she cajoled. "Or is it, now that you have had your pleasure, you are tired of me?"

"It's certainly possible to be exhausted rather than rested in your bed, but I doubt I'll ever tire of you," he countered leisurely, and gestured to the window where the morning light was growing strong. "It's already late, and I am weary still. And you are to blame."

"Father, forgive me!" she pleaded unconvincingly, a devilish smile playing at her lips. "I promise the next time you come to my bed, Father, I will leave you to slumber in peace."

"And *leave* me is what you would have to do, for I'll never have any peace with you in my bed," he said, his smile matching hers at first. "But peace, *cara*, is something I've permanently disavowed now that I've made love to you."

"You're regretful, Father?" she asked, matching the pensive sadness of his voice.

Vittorio looked at Cathryn in cold appraisal. He touched the nipple of a breast that beckoned his fingertips even as his mind dwelled on deeper issues. "Regret? I regret only that I am not free," he said, and before she could consider his reply, he drew her against him and, at last, satisfied her longing.

Chapter 8

Reluctantly, Cathryn immersed herself in the warm sudsy bath and washed away the last traces of the night with Vittorio. "I won't be late to Mass this morning, Dita," she promised aloud, smiling saucily. This morning she had no desire to desert the *palazzo*. Her own bed was far more enticing than the fresh air of dawn that had lately beckoned her, and even in the chill that enveloped her as she rose from the tub, Cathryn felt a rush of warmth at the thought of her pleasure with Vittorio.

She raised her silvered mirror and gazed into it thoughtfully. She believed the actual risk of their being discovered while making love was small, for no one dared to interrupt Father Vittorio's lessons. As a rule, one could expect privacy in one's room, but while Cathryn did not expect to be discovered in her lover's arms, she wondered whether evidence of their passion could be seen in her face, her eyes.

Would Dita or anyone else suspect how she had spent last night? How could there not be a noticeable difference in her? she wondered as she turned her mirror to various angles.

Why had Bianca not been able to see that the hour of love she had spent with Father Vittorio that first afternoon had changed her forever?

It became a constant struggle for Cathryn to keep her mind off her beloved. And Father Vittorio likewise had difficulty thinking of much other than the young woman who, from midnight until dawn of the new day, had filled his arms with the pleasure of her love. He ached for her steadily and felt the lonely isolation of his priestly calling.

As the days passed, every stolen moment they shared heightened their need for each other, and Cathryn began to appreciate Father Vittorio's unspoken remorse: he was not free and neither was she. The priest was weighted with duty, not the least of which was his obligation to provide an example of strict obedi-

ence to the Church's teachings—to the commandments of God—
and in spite of her daring private challenge of Church doctrine,
Cathryn bore the burden of her upbringing: the call to be devout,
pure of spirit, and, above all, chaste.

At first, their feelings of guilt hardly touched them. Their need
for each other was more compelling, their passion only heightened by its forbidden nature. Cathryn's love for Vittorio lent her
a naive immunity from self-reproach and made it impossible for
her to concede that God truly would damn them. The perfect
love she felt for him surpassed all other emotions, and the
consequences in this life and the next were overshadowed by the
ecstasy of Vittorio's love.

The priest avoided complete self-condemnation with a dim
awareness that in time his passion might abate, rationalizing that
his obsession with Cathryn would diminish and the intensity of
his feelings, especially those physically expressed, might cool much
as his craving for oranges as a child was cooled after eating a
basketful.

But as Father Vittorio went about his daily routine, his craving
for Cathryn Godwyne did not cease. His taste for her was not
satisfied by consumption, for his appetite was more than physical. Cathryn Godwyne had captured more than his man's body—
she had claimed his heart and soul.

She filled his dreams at night, his thoughts by day. Her image
intruded on his lessons, his music, and his prayers. He continued
to petition God for release from his obsession with Cathryn
Godwyne, but he received no relief and worried he would not
survive without her.

Under her influence he was a different man, and a week
before Carnival, the most festive day of the year in Venice,
Father Vittorio stood before the celebrated degli Innocenti chorus
quite distracted. He listened to fifty eager-to-please voices and
should have found much to criticize, but the rehearsal was
clearly of very peripheral concern.

Normally, he would have demanded more unity and precise
harmony from his chorus. Even the youngest students noticed his
indifference. The girls eyed one another as obvious mistakes
failed to provoke his criticism.

The recital, to culminate the Feast of the Ascension and the
celebration of Venice's marriage to the sea, was the most
prestigious performance that the chorus gave all year. Its individ-

ual members fretted about their sound even if their conductor did not.

The girls expected Father Vittorio to stamp his foot impatiently and shout, "No! No! No, my misbegotten cherubs!" as he sometimes did when particularly vexed. At the very least, they assumed he would threaten them with excommunication for failing to meet his exacting standards. "Expressively! Not as if you needed to be carried one by one to your beds!"

But the errors of his willing servants passed over him as though his commitment to glorifying God through the creation and performance of music were no longer his sole reason for being. Many of the girls sensed that the priest had lost heart, that his energy was no longer dedicated to transforming the collection of their voices into one glorious choir.

Several of the older children complained of his obvious neglect, collecting around him in a circle after practice one morning.

"Ofelia sang off key all day and you didn't say one word to her," Susetta complained, near tears, offended because in the past her teacher had often spoken to her for the same offense.

"Please, Father, tell Marcellina not to sing so loud!" Paola begged. "I've nearly lost my hearing." She grimaced, dramatically holding a hand to one ear.

"What is it, Father? Why do you not scold us more?" Magda sighed. "Unless you do, we shall disgrace degli Innocenti."

Aware that they were justified in their concern for the reputation of his chorus, Father Vittorio doubled his efforts. He still cared that they be perfect but not as passionately as he once had.

A week before the Feast of Ascension, Cathryn stood before the priest and, as transfixed as any other of his worshiping students, watched him conduct. Chosen to sing the first solo for her matchless soprano, Cathryn sang the priest's music for all to hear, though in fact she lifted her voice to him alone.

To almost everyone who heard her clear, crystal voice, she declared devout and abiding love for God. In truth, she sang of her own human passion.

As Father Vittorio conducted the chorus, his eyes came to rest on her. He cued her then and listened to her luscious voice, moved by her perfection, touched by the true meaning of her voluptuous song. His gaze lingered and softened. He longed for her; she saw it in his eyes and in the tension of his body.

The solo she sang was written before he came under her spell, but just now, Father Vittorio could not remember ever being free from her influence. Her perfection and beauty overwhelmed his senses and his heart cried out to hers: I need you; I love you. He felt his essence pull from his body and flow into hers.

At the end of the aria, when he was silent and, to most who watched, morose, neglecting to recommend her performance to the others as an example of the kind of effort he expected, his students knew Father Vittorio was not well.

When he dismissed them at song's end, they regarded one another in disbelief, but not one of the girls demurred. Obediently, each girl climbed down from the choir loft and filed past the priest in silence.

He seemed not to notice.

"What do you suppose ails Father Vittorio?" Simone questioned as soon as she and Cathryn escaped the chapel doors.

"Perhaps he's ill." Cathryn blushed, but Simone didn't see her color as they scurried to the evening meal.

"He simply can't be! Carnival is only a few days away."

"What has that to do with his being well or unwell?" Cathryn demanded.

"Signorina Perdita would not permit it, that's all," Simone insisted.

Cathryn chuckled softly. "There are some things which even *la signorina* cannot forbid."

Simone looked at Cathryn thoughtfully. "I wouldn't put it to a test, Cathryn, whatever it is you have in mind."

For a fleeting second Cathryn feared Simone had sensed the current of passion that had passed between herself and the errant priest.

"Lately, you've been behaving almost as strangely as Father Vittorio and I wonder if, now that your days here are numbered, you might be planning some sort of mischief. Coming late to Mass in the mornings is but one sign." Simone eyed Cathryn with a cool, appraising gaze.

"Surely you've noticed I've repented," Cathryn protested. "Besides, you forget, my name is *angelica*."

"No. It is *you* who forget your name," Simone said flatly.

Cathryn was silent. She felt rebuked. "Have I done something wrong?" she asked, and slowed their pace so that they trailed some distance behind the others on their way to dinner.

"You would know better than I," Simone parried.

Cathryn touched her friend's arm. "Are you warning me of my misdeeds?"

Simone laughed gaily. "If you're feeling guilty, you must go at once and confess to your favorite priest—but only after we eat," she whispered, her eyes dancing.

Chapter 9

In all respects, time became the most precious element of Cathryn's life: time with Vittorio; time to think; time to plan; time to dream. Even now, as she dressed, Cathryn hurried, lacing the silk underbodice of her gown tightly over her full round breasts, her nipples pressing conspicuously against the soft chemise. Filled with desire, anxious to lie with him again, Cathryn longed for Vittorio's stimulating mouth at her breast.

Pouting, she tied the ribbons at her small waist and contemplated her seeming constant state of arousal. Whether in Father Vittorio's presence or not, Cathryn was preoccupied with him. In their rising passion, caution was often forgotten. She dreaded the shame of being discovered in his bed, or of someone reading an intimate look, or overhearing a whispered word of love, but fear did not overcome the need for his loving embrace. In her lover's arms she found justification and perfect peace.

Cathryn often caught herself staring at her friends or into Perdita's or Bianca's eyes, quite unable to believe they did not accuse her of her multitude of sins. Simone's recent teasing remarks plagued Cathryn, and she wondered whether her friend was innocent or merely being coy. Oftentimes she imagined that her friend spied on her. Yet when nothing came of Simone's remarks, Cathryn damned her own imagination, for she had ample reason to suffer from her conscience!

Cathryn smoothed a fitted chemise over narrow hips and tied a silk petticoat around her waist. I must hurry, she thought. At any moment, Perdita would knock on the door and be ready to dress her hair.

Cathryn raised her hand mirror and gazed into it, surveying her mass of hair, and knew exactly how she would have liked to have her wanton curls arranged this night—and just what Vittorio, who loved to see her hair down, would prefer. When she undressed for him, he loved to watch her unfasten the coils and unbraid the strands of the deepest black hair he had ever seen. "I sometimes dream of you taking down your hair. I watch and grow weak, knowing I'll soon touch you." He said he remembered the exciting fragrance of her hair and its satin texture against his cheek and palms. She shivered and recalled how well Vittorio could convey his appreciation with his hands!

If it was her decision, Cathryn would frame her face with a soft fringe of wispy curls and brush the remainder to a glossy shine and allow those vibrant strands to fall as they would, to cascade triumphantly down her back; but such a display was unthinkable.

Cathryn stared into the mirror, quite unable to believe that her love for Vittorio did not show, then blinked to interrupt her idle thoughts. She would have to hurry if she wanted to be ready on time.

This afternoon, Perdita Fabiani would spend a great deal of time persuading Cathryn's hair to lie in strict, obedient curls. In the end, Cathryn would look sweetly innocent, like the pet name Perdita had given her when she was very young, *angelica*.

"Angelica, angelica," Father Vittorio echoed in rapturous disbelief, but noted, still breathless from spending himself in her embrace, there was something inappropriate about the name applied to the woman to whom he was so helplessly drawn. "Strega," he said, was more precise.

At the name "witch," Cathryn visibly bristled in his arms. Vittorio laughed at her reaction, "You can't deny you enchant me," he said, continuing to tease. "Perhaps you are the Devil's woman sent to tempt this innocent servant of God?" he wondered, mounting her again. "Ah, but the Prince of Darkness has chosen his bride well—I cannot resist you.

"But why me, *angelica?* Why am I singled out? I'm of little account."

Cathryn cringed inwardly, though she believed he was only jesting. "To the Master of the Underworld," she parried, provoked by his taunts, "no soul is insignificant. Surely you know that, priest."

"May my case never come to trial," he half prayed aloud, but added a question. "Should I ever be tried for perfidy, Cathryn, whose side would you take?"

"Why, Father, whose do you think?" Cathryn smiled wickedly. When he shrugged his uncertainty, she answered, bubbling with laughter. "My lover's side, of course," she said, pleased that he was now the one who bristled. The conversation ended there, Cathryn remembered now, but that night Vittorio had made love to her at so intense a pitch it was as if he'd wanted to be certain that she would have cause to remember just who her lover was.

Trembling from her memories, Cathryn finished dressing, lifting the heavy trimmed velvet skirt of her gown over her head, weighted not only with that garment, but with a strange foreboding. She arranged the pearl-and-gold-embroidered fabric of the skirt and tried to push her uneasy feelings aside.

She reminded herself to be grateful that she was still in Venice, where rich and ornamental dressing was very much in vogue despite the sumptuary edicts condemning extravagant dress. Cathryn winced at the prospect of living in England, where she understood everyone dressed somberly.

She loved the fashion of lace and ribbons, of outer skirts hiked high upon the hip to show outrageous or even plain underskirts, and tight, padded low bodices that showed ample delicate flesh. She loved color and fine fabrics and jewels.

In secret, Vittorio brought her ribbons and lace; a lilac chemise; a gay lemon-yellow petticoat; a nightdress of sheerest red silk. Since the girls sometimes traded clothes amongst themselves, no one was the wiser.

One night he gifted her with a short knotted strand of pearls. "The knot is called a love knot and comes with a charm: firm be the knot; firm may our love endure."

"I did not imagine you would succumb to using charms."

"It is your influence that makes me do so."

"Does your agent not wonder what a priest does with these woman's things?" she asked curiously.

"He does not know that I'm a priest."

Cathryn stared. "Must I give these away when I go? They wear nothing but coarse wool in England, and no jewels."

"That is not quite true."

"My guardian, a Puritan, does not."

"Perhaps you'll find England more to your liking than you think."

Cathryn eyed her lover as if he were mad. "I shall send you in my place, Father."

He pulled her into his arms. "I would gladly go with you."

Cathryn began to cry. "I won't go! I shall run away! I shall drown myself in the lagoon!" she sobbed.

"Do you care nothing for me? You'll do nothing of the kind!"

"But even you've told me the English burn Catholics at the stake!" Cathryn shuddered. "I'd rather die in Venice!"

He took her by the arms and shook her. His eyes were wild, his voice low and fierce. "I forbid you to speak of taking your life—I forbid you to mention your leaving me ever again!"

His angry command made Cathryn cry harder, which he regretted. With a sigh of remorse, he pulled her into his embrace and tried to comfort her, in desperate need of comfort himself. "Oh, God, there must be a way to keep you here," he whispered.

But nothing more on the subject was said. Their time together was scarce, the moments fleeting, and if there was no plan, Cathryn insisted privately, there surely was no time, no reason to speak of her departure.

Cathryn's thoughts were interrupted when Perdita finally arrived to dress her hair, but as the doting woman adroitly used her combs and pins, Cathryn schemed. She warmed her voice with simple vocal exercises, and she dreamed of running away this very night.

Tonight Venice celebrated the annual Feast of the Ascension, and Cathryn imagined herself and Vittorio becoming lost in the gala masquerade. After the ceremony celebrating Venice's supremacy over the sea, in which the doge of Venice sailed upon the Lido in a magnificent galley followed by a legion of gondolas, there would be a public procession to Piazza San Marco and a Mass; then feasting and fireworks; music and dancing; and contagious revelry. In such an atmosphere Cathryn imagined it would be quite easy to slip away unseen, to hide herself forever.

But where would she flee? What would she do with herself?

Cathryn knew precious few people in Venice intimately, and no one outside degli Innocenti. She could not even approach anyone for a position as a tutor or governess, as she expected to be employed when she left degli Innocenti, without Signorina Fabiani's first interceding in her behalf. And clearly, in spite of her feelings for Cathryn, Perdita saw Cathryn's journey to England as a foregone conclusion. In Perdita's mind there was no question but that she should respond obediently to her guardian's summons.

Could Vittorio send her to his family for shelter and succor? she wondered. Under what pretense? It would be impossible. Clergy who had mistresses housed them in secret, not beneath the family's nose.

Cathryn halted her mindless song. She had never before considered the possibility of being someone's mistress. The mistresses of the wealthy noblemen that the musicians of degli Innocenti entertained were as foreign to her as were their wives. The mere idea of being someone's mistress was, until now, as impossible for Cathryn to imagine as marriage.

But Cathryn was now more than willing to consider herself as Vittorio's possession; willing to be his slave—if that was his wish. There was nothing, she imagined, she wouldn't be willing to do at his bidding.

Cathryn had never dreamed of being so completely at the mercy of another human being, but she now lived only for the look and the touch of one man.

Vittorio chided Cathryn for having possessed him. Yet from Cathryn's point of view, Father Vittorio was the one guilty of sorcery. At times he seemed a man obsessed.

"Stunning. Perfectly stunning!" Perdita exclaimed when she finished dressing Cathryn's hair. She paused to consider her handiwork. "I think you must wear your plainest cloak to cover yourself when you perform. Otherwise no one will hear a word you sing," she said, helping Cathryn into a padded bodice and sleeves.

Cathryn smiled coquettishly. She had only just begun to see herself through Vittorio's eyes, accepting his judgment that she was beautiful. Perdita's seconding of his appraisal delighted her. "Even if you have done your best, Dita, no one will notice me," she answered with false modesty.

Perdita grumbled. You are pitifully like your mother, Cathryn, she thought. Not a man in Piazza San Marco will be immune to you.

"I fear it is good that you will be leaving Venice soon," Perdita said, hoping to sober the girl a bit. She succeeded until they were interrupted by Father Vittorio's impatient knocking at the chamber door.

When Perdita admitted the priest, Cathryn forgot Perdita's admonitions directly.

"I've come to remind you to warm up your voice," he said by way of greeting. "It will be very cold tonight."

"When am I not ready?" Cathryn answered saucily.

Father Vittorio forced back a smile.

"Cathryn!" Perdita cautioned, surprised and embarrassed by Cathryn's sassy tone. "Excuse her, Father. I believe she's nervous," she said, eyeing her charge with more than a hint of annoyance. "One would never know it, however, unless one knew her as well as I do!"

Perdita gave Cathryn a vexed tap on her forearm with the hairbrush. Lately, she feared, Cathryn had begun to display the same haughty seductiveness for which her mother was famous. Perdita shuddered, remembering how the men had bowed down to Vanya Russo! "Thank God you are no ordinary man, Father, to be overwhelmed by such a vixen!" She sighed, assuming he of all people could contain Cathryn's impudence. "I leave you to take this unruly student of yours in hand," she said, making a respectful curtsy to the priest.

And take Cathryn in hand is exactly what Father Vittorio did. As soon as the door closed behind them, Vittorio swept Cathryn forcibly into his arms and smothered her with kisses, which she returned with a hungry ferocity.

"After the recital, when everyone begins to dance, follow me into the crowd," he ordered. "We'll make our way to an inn, a good way from the square. While the others are dancing and drinking themselves into oblivion, we'll spend the night together making love," he promised. "No one will know we're missing. Everyone without exception will be too occupied with their own revelry to notice."

This was the one night of the year when license was given for all manner of behavior. When the younger children were safely in their beds, even Perdita and Bianca Fabiani, normally the essence of restraint, would allow themselves to be carried away by the ebullient mood of Carnival. Both would drink more wine than was prudent, as did everyone else, and indulge themselves by dancing in the streets with any nearly sober partner.

It was the perfect night for almost anyone to disappear—
including a priest and his beautiful paramour.

Chapter 10

As the night descended, flamed torches glittered along the water-
ways, bridges, and passageways leading to Piazza San Marco.
The annual Feast of the Ascension was underway. Nearly every
citizen and resident of Venice and the surrounding lagoons
would participate, or so it would seem at the height of the
evening.

At the conclusion of the ceremony of the sea, the plaza
began to fill with masqueraders, and whether elegantly or
simply attired, the crowd seemed resplendent. Almost all wore
masks, adding to the effect that on this night, Venice was
magical.

Music from various instruments played by ardent if not accomplished musicians filled the air, as did succulent aromas
from a vast assortment of food spread out by vendors. Piazza
San Marco, the largest and grandest plaza in Venice, overflowed
with celebrators, man and beast; food and drink and wares,
though hardly any drink that by morning would leave one sober
could be found.

After the archbishop of Venice said a Mass to celebrate Christ's
ascent into heaven, the doge, His Excellency Marcantonio
Guistinian, unmistakable in the gold raiment and headdress of
his office, addressed the crowd. He toasted the throng with a
jewel-encrusted goblet filled with wine. ''The Son of God has
ascended into heaven. Alleluia! Alleluia!'' He drank the wine.
''We come to rejoice! Feast and enjoy the plenty of our fair
Republic,'' he cried to the crowd, and a cheer went up, signify-
ing their every intention to follow his advice.

When the doge took his seat in the royal box above the crowd,
it was a signal for the festivities to begin. On cue royal trumpet-
ers, dressed in red velvet doublets and trunk hose, sounded

brilliantly. Then all eyes turned to a second raised platform, where seven acrobatic jugglers began to prance and leap dramatically. They contorted themselves impossibly and dove bravely through hoops of fire with no apparent concern for their welfare. In unison the crowd gasped with awe at their feats of daring, then were stunned into silence as the performers began to dance with wild enthusiasm, seemingly oblivious to the swinging of vicious-looking swords their partners waved in their direction as if the weapons were merely paper replicas.

Next came a troupe of actors dancing in the latest style to be seen at court, and among them a gaggle of clowns jesting and mimicking their betters. The crowd roared their approval as the bizarrely costumed clowns imitated the formal dancing of fake noble personages, teasing the righteous matrons and poking the bloated belly of the aged suitor of a winsome maiden. They shamelessly raised skirts and patted derrieres and bosoms. The more ribald observers begged for more.

But soon their frivolity was over, replaced on stage by a chorus of fifty girls from La Casa degli Innocenti, and though the audience was still in the mood for immodest feigning, the renown and talent of the young musicians soon silenced the few loudly raised objections to the change of scene. Venetians loved splendid music above most other pleasures, and even an ordinary man knew well that he was about to be feted with the finest sounds to be heard this night.

None of the girls was visibly nervous before the audience of thousands. Almost all were veteran performers standing proudly with Cathryn centered in the arch of the chorus tier. She had performed during the Feast of the Ascension since she was seven years of age, but this occasion above all others would live in her memory.

Father Vittorio stood beneath the chorus almost at the level of the audience. He looked calm but purposeful, the eyes of every girl obediently on him. When the moment was right, when the crowd was attentive and hushed, Vittorio cued the voices to begin.

A cappella, the voices raised in unison and spilled sweetly over the listeners, clear and unobscured. They began quietly, a chant that signified the holiness of the occasion, then gradually filled with passionate gratitude, dividing into vocal parts to sing continuing rounds of exhilarating praise to God; rising finally to a thunderous crescendo, halting abruptly.

Before a breath of silence could settle in the air, Cathryn's crystal soprano soared into the night, almost stilling the heart-beats of her audience. But she was barely conscious of the rapt crowd as she watched the conductor. The lyrics spoke of sacred love, but she sang to her lover of a very human passion. To the ear of the innocent she was perfect in her rendition, and to the knowing priest who heard her meaning, she sang her song of love for him alone.

Lovingly Cathryn drew Vittorio into her spell, the thread of her beautiful melody enveloping him in a cocoon of isolation, and throughout the remainder of the cantata, he conducted as if in a dream.

Cathryn succeeded in captivating all other listeners as well, dominating the chorus when she should have, yet never completely fading into the background when she might. When the music ended and the general celebration began, Cathryn was sought as a companion for the night by a drove of masked and richly costumed revelers, and helpless, her priest watched as she was pulled light-heartedly away from him.

"Don't worry, Father; no harm will come to her," shouted one who sought Cathryn's favor. "She has a large following to see to her safety!" the man cried as, jubilantly, he danced away with her.

Father Vittorio followed her with his eyes, vexed in the extreme, unable, in the tangle of his students, to follow; prevented also by fear of attracting attention to his purpose.

"It is inevitable, Father." Perdita sighed with sad resignation. "She is her mother's daughter."

Vittorio turned to Perdita as much in surprise at her presence as by her words.

"We cannot prevent it. She's as much a gypsy as her mother was—she will always have a following. Men were hopelessly bewitched in droves in her mother's time, and I'm afraid Cathryn is cursed with the same wanton blood."

Perdita had no intention of elaborating and dismissed the subject in the next breath. "Father, kindly quide my younger charges home for the night so that I may begin to celebrate," she implored, wishing to have a glimpse of Cathryn before she completely disappeared. "Otherwise the festivities will begin without me."

Realizing he had completely lost sight of Cathryn in the crush of humanity thronging the plaza, Vittorio reluctantly accepted the task of leading the youngest students home. He hurried them along their way, which was no easy task with a dozen wide-eyed charges in tow. He knew every moment wasted would make it more difficult to find her. Cathryn was too beautiful and alluring for her own good, he feared, and terribly vulnerable to the dangers of the night.

Chapter 11

At first Cathryn was frightened by her pursuers, but their gaiety soon convinced her they intended her no harm. She was swept easily into the throng and launched into the spirit of the night's revelry. For a little while she watched for Vittorio, hoping against hope that he would rescue her. But she knew, just as he had, it would be unseemly for a priest to pursue her. This night she and the other older girls from La Casa degli Innocenti were expected to celebrate like all Venetians.

Shortly, Cathryn relaxed with the other merrymakers, dancing, eating, drinking, and changing partners as often as the fiddlers changed their tunes. She grew giddy and light-hearted from an ever-present brimming cup of wine offered by her admirers, and to the eyes of the men who wished for her attention, she grew more beautiful with every passing moment.

Cathryn recognized no one. Almost everyone was costumed and virtually everyone wore a mask. She was captivated by the strident gaiety of the crowd and soon was infected with the same enthusiasm. Flung into the primitive heart of the crowd, she felt only wild abandon. She became lost, strangely untroubled by the change in her plans for the night.

The myriad colorful costumes intrigued Cathryn. There were gargoyles, monks, kings, and lesser nobility by the score; barnyard animals and demons; butterflies and birds. In the dark, some of the masqueraders were so frightening that, had it been any other night of the year, meeting these creatures in a lane would have caused Cathryn's hair to stand on end. Tonight she only admired the ingenuity of the costumes.

When suddenly the Devil himself stood before her, Cathryn only laughed and smiled into his mysteriously vacant eyes. When he seized her with a determined forcefulness and danced, refusing to yield her to anyone, Cathryn's gaiety ceased.

No words could be exchanged for the din of the crowd, but still she protested. "Stop! Unhand me!" she screamed, and struggled against the demon, swiftly realizing that she was at his mercy with no one to save her. In the midst of the roaring whirling crowd, Cathryn appeared to be alone with the Devil.

He was dressed in black, his head covered with a fitted hood; his face covered by a hammered gold mask which was so cleverly designed that only darkness showed beneath the slits that were made for his eyes.

Small wings of gold fanned out from the place the creature's ears and nostrils should have been. Below, his mouth was exposed, and beneath his lower lip, the black hood appeared again to conceal the rest of the demon's face and neck.

The golden mask was florentined, burnished in such a way as to reflect light in all directions, and the demon's face shimmered in even scant illumination. When the fire of a torch shined directly on him, he appeared even more demonic, and as he moved with obvious purpose, with Cathryn held tightly in his embrace, her heart filled with terror.

Pulled hard against him, she moved as he willed, helpless to do differently, with a growing sense that he had seized his prey. She felt the demon's passion, but in her rising panic, she found herself unable to scream. She felt ravaged in the demon's hungry grip, vividly aware that his dark clothes disguised an all too human form. Beneath the costume was a man aroused by lust, and with deepening dread, Cathryn increased her useless efforts to escape. She struggled while he dragged her through the mob that only a short time before had seemed to have eyes only for her. Now it was blind, as he pulled her effortlessly from the plaza and into a darkened passageway. She had raised her voice in protest, certain she had objected, though even she did not hear the sound of her screams.

He dragged her with him, his long strides demanding that she run or stumble, finally pulling her into the shadows of a narrow lane, far away from the crowd. Cathryn was completely out of breath, gasping for air, terrified, pulled familiarly against his hard male form. Her heart beat wildly and her senses rebelled so that it was several moments before she heard Vittorio's familiar voice against her ear.

Cathryn's eyes widened with confusion and, as he took the mask away, she stared in disbelief. He raised her face and kissed her mouth, and she, at first, responded, then swooned into his arms.

Vittorio lifted her with ease then and carried her a short distance to the dark canal, down water-engulfed steps where, completely hidden in shadows, there waited a gondola and an impatient gondolier.

Chapter 12

The gondola wove a soundless meandering course through the sinuous canals as the dark night sky filled with bursts of ornamental fireworks and the air with cheers from the patrons of the feast. Resting her head on Vittorio's shoulder, Cathryn slipped an arm around him for comfort and nestled in his arms. "I was terrified by your demon pose," she whispered.

Vittorio bent his head and drew her lips to his, kissing her lightly only at first, easing her fear, reducing her trembling to desire.

The lovers floated to an inn that Vittorio had known years before, and because the dock where the gondolier should have landed was submerged far below the water, he drew up alongside the inn's steep stone stairway. Vittorio lifted Cathryn in his arms and carried her to the entrance of the inn, then set her down to enter an unremarkable building.

As usual, to accommodate flooding times, the first floor of the inn was devoted to storage. One stout candle at the foot of an inner staircase lighted the way to the upper floors. Cathryn climbed the stairs with Vittorio to find the inn itself almost deserted.

The inn was more mean than respectable, crowded with small tables and short benches, and oppressively dark. It was hardly a haven for the average citizen, Cathryn sensed, but a place for secret encounters and nefarious plans. Cathryn tried her best to hide in her cloak, inspecting her surroundings from the recesses of its voluminous hood.

Ill at ease, she would have been frightened, except that Vittorio seemed quite confident in the strange atmosphere. He murmured questions to a weary-looking servant, who glanced at Cathryn inquisitively as he spoke. The servant answered Vittorio's questions in a rough but equally quiet tone. Finally the woman gave Vittorio a key and a small lamp.

As Cathryn followed Vittorio down a narrow hallway, she could feel the servant's eyes on her back, imagining the woman knew just who Vittorio was and the nature of Cathryn's relationship with him.

Cathryn tried to dismiss her guilty feelings and told herself that the dismal surroundings of the inn could not help but make her feel uneasy. Once the door to the small room to which Vittorio led them was closed and locked behind them, Cathryn began to relax. She was surprised by the elegance of the room's furnishings and the walls covered in a lustrous silk brocade. The room held a large lace-canopied bed draped with the same fabric, an ornately carved wardrobe of shining walnut, a night table, and two chairs. "What an unusual room," Cathryn remarked with an obvious question in her voice. "I hardly expected it."

Vittorio smiled at her innocence. "A beautiful room for a beautiful woman," he said, pulling her gently into his arms. "I've made plans for us, *angelica,* and we will wait in this room tonight for men who will come to make my dreams become reality." He pushed the hood of Cathryn's cloak from her head. "I cannot conceive of parting with you, my love, unless it is your wish." He tilted her chin so that the lamp illuminated her face. "You will haunt my dreams for as long as I live," he whispered, kissing her inviting lips, forgetting for the moment that he had more to say.

Cathryn melted in his arms, her remaining uneasiness evaporating, her desire rekindled. "And I will never dream of another man, Vittorio. *You* are my life," she promised.

With reluctance, Vittorio forced himself to pull away from their embrace. "We must talk, Cathryn. I regret that I haven't time to approach you less abruptly, but I am forced to speak plainly—cold-bloodedly.

"Cathryn, I want you to be my mistress . . . perhaps forever. For now, I can offer you nothing better. But before you answer with your heart, you must understand what being the mistress of a priest will mean.

"First, Cathryn, imagine yourself as another man's paramour. You could expect to be flattered and admired; pampered and adored. Your lover would have great wealth, perhaps, and you would dress in the finest gowns and be decorated with jewels. Probably you would have everything you could want from life except what you most deserve: enduring love, honor, and respect. Surely you'd have the best of your lover's affections, for it would not be possible for a man to come into your heart and not love you, also. But you'd never have your lover's name, and the truth is, of course, you would be regarded as nothing better than a whore."

Cathryn gasped softly at the prospect.

"I'm sorry, *angelica*, what I say is only the sad truth. Most likely, those you'd come to regard as friends would not be, and you'd be shunned by many. Your beloved Perdita would despise you."

Vittorio paused and Cathryn looked away from his intense gaze and from the pain conveyed in his last statement.

He touched her face and she raised her eyes to him. "But as my mistress, *cara*, it is likely that your lot would not even be so fair. You'd be mine in secret; *never*, as long as I remain a priest, openly. You would live much like a captive bird in a confining cage. You'd have no public admirers; no festive entertainments to hostess; no recognition of any kind. If you say yes to me, you'll live well, but not handsomely. You'll be isolated; lonely much of the time. You will come to know all of the unpleasantries and few of the benefits."

"But I shall have you?" Cathryn asked.

Vittorio nodded. "My very soul."

"It shall be enough," she said, taking his hands and raising them to her lips. "I will be whatever you want me to be," she promised, tears welling in her eyes. "I love you."

Vittorio gathered Cathryn's supple body into his arms, holding her close to his heart, stirred by her tender pledge; by the knowledge that he would realize at least this part of his dream. He began to make love to her, first freeing her curls from their pins, and when they tumbled down her back, framing her face more to his liking, he began to kiss her.

Vittorio invited her to enjoy, and for a while Cathryn's hands roamed freely over the fabric of his costume that fitted him like a second skin. His eager body responded to her touch, and he pulled her tightly to him to confirm his pleasure. She stroked his back, then slipped her hands beneath the waistband of his costume to caress his skin.

Cathryn kneaded the firm muscles of his buttocks, managing to inflame him further. When he spread his legs, she searched between them to discover a tender place that with the gentle pressure of her fingers made Vittorio groan with deep appreciation.

On this occasion, it was Cathryn who took the lead. She undressed him, caressing his body with her lips, transmitting incredible joy with her tongue. When she took him into her mouth, he struggled for control. "You *must* cease," he pleaded and, reluctantly, she stopped.

Vittorio recovered slowly while he watched Cathryn disrobe, the task taking far longer than an unruly part of him preferred. He resisted the urge to rudely raise her skirts and quickly satisfy himself. "You fast turn me into a panting beast," he exclaimed when she finally lay beneath him in the bed.

"Perhaps the true disguise is the cleric's habit, Father, and the demon's mask, no mask at all."

Vittorio looked hard at Cathryn for a moment, then put his hungry mouth to an impatient breast and suckled her with vigor. Soon he made her sigh in rapture.

"The Devil crushed me against him, Father, and I felt his passion, but I swear—I've known the Beast before."

Chapter 13

They spent the night as they had planned, exhilarating and exhausting themselves with hours of lovemaking. Long after midnight, finally sated, they fell asleep with Vittorio captured beneath one of Cathryn's legs.

Cathryn dreamed vague dreams, comforted by Vittorio's presence, secure in the belief that she would never leave Venice, nor his embrace. When a loud knocking disturbed their bliss, she stirred but did not wake.

Vittorio, however, woke instantly, fleeing his love nest, closing the curtain around the canopied bed and covering his nakedness with a cloak. He was alert and eager to greet his expected visitors.

When he answered the knocking, two richly dressed men several years older than the priest stood in the doorway. One was a head taller than his companion, and the other nearly as short as he was broad.

Quickly smiles covered the three men's faces and they reached to embrace one another. "Brother," Vittorio said with emotion, hugging each man tightly in turn. The visitors were equally joyous, and somewhat louder in their greeting of the priest.

Piero and Luciano did not see their younger brother as often as they would have liked, and they also held him somewhat in awe. He was their beloved mother's youngest son, the one who had been denied nothing. While meeting Vittorio tonight was greatly inconvenient, it was their pleasure, and they said as much. They were used to going out of their way to please Vittorio.

"We're sorry to be late," Piero, the oldest, said after Vittorio motioned them into the room. They settled into the two available chairs. "And we are curious about our meeting place. This is not a place where a priest normally spends the night."

"I was last here in your company, you may recall."

"But you have good reason to remember the place, eh, Father?" Luciano chuckled. "You would not recognize Giovanna now, little brother." He used his hands to describe a woman of considerable dimension. "She is fantastic now in size as well." He laughed.

Piero frowned. "Father Vittorio is not here to reminisce about the women he has had," he scolded Luciano.

"Of course not! Your pardon, Father." Luciano's eyes sparkled once more before he cast them down, contrite.

Vittorio acknowledged him with a wave of his hand. "Indeed, I didn't ask you here to talk about the past, but to plan for the future," he began. At the same moment, Cathryn, still sleeping in the bed, stirred, making the curtains of the enclosed bed sway.

Startled, Father Vittorio's brothers looked at each other.

"We are not alone?" Piero inquired.

"No." Vittorio confessed in a hushed voice. "It is the reason for our meeting."

The older brothers looked at one another again. "Even *I* am shocked," Luciano said.

"Perhaps," Vittorio admitted. "I confess I never dreamed of coming to this place in time. I, too, thought I would never break my vows. But beneath the priest's habit beats the heart of a man I did not know existed. I never dreamed of passion so extreme as I have known because of one woman."

The priest's brothers lowered their eyes.

"You embarrass us, Father."

"I doubt it, Luciano, but I'm afraid it can't be helped. I've no one else to turn to. I come tonight to ask you to take Cathryn away with you, to provide for her, and to protect her from all harm until I can make other arrangements. I have a claim on my inheritance from our father that I've yet to designate, and I do so now. It will keep her for a very long while—at least until I can conclude some of the other details that must be arranged."

Luciano and Piero were silent.

"You are struck dumb, I see."

"Quite. Her name is?" Piero verified.

"Cathryn Godwyne."

"She is foreign."

"Part English."

"And the other part whore?" Piero demanded, his voice

registering his disgust. "What kind of woman would risk her soul by seducing a priest?"

Vittorio's face reddened in anger, but he strove to control his fury, knowing how crucial it was to enlist his brothers' cooperation.

"It is the Devil's doing, Father, surely. It is the only explanation," Piero suggested, trying to seem sympathetic.

Luciano had the answer. "A Witch, no doubt!"

"She is nothing of the kind! Have you never heard of a man being unsuited for the priesthood?!"

"Not you, little brother," Piero declared.

"How can you be sure she's not a sorceress? Have you investigated her? Have you seen her without her clothes?"

"She is pure and without contamination. If anything, I have corrupted her."

"This cannot be!" Piero insisted.

"You speak of having other plans. What are they?"

"I will leave the Church."

"Never! I will not hear of it!" Piero slammed his fist down on the night table.

"It is not *your* decision!"

"Nor is it yours alone! You will bring disgrace to our family. You will bring a curse on our enterprises. You will *ruin* us! A sailor needs the protection of God. He does not willfully invite His ire. He does not consort with the Devil!"

"You exaggerate, Piero," Vittorio said calmly. "I sense there is something else that troubles you besides my request, as unusual as it may be."

"There is nothing else," Piero insisted stubbornly, his voice only a little calmer than it had been.

Vittorio looked into Luciano's face for confirmation.

Luciano looked away.

"I am right. I know I am. What is it?"

"You're wrong," Piero denied again. "Let us view this Witch," Piero said, standing to draw back the draperies surrounding the bed, yanking the covers away from Cathryn's sleeping form.

The sudden commotion startled Cathryn and she roused with fright. "Vittorio?" she cried, seeking his face in the dimly lighted room, able only to focus on the furious countenance of the man who stood over the bed. "Vittorio?"

"I'm here," he said, moving to push his larger brother aside, but forcefully Piero shoved him back in Luciano's direction, causing Vittorio to lose his balance. He was caught and restrained in Luciano's muscular arms.

Piero was struck both by Cathryn's youth and by her great beauty. "The Devil sends his most perfect handmaiden, I see," he said, wrenching away the blanket that Cathryn had retrieved to cover her nakedness.

"Vittorio, who are these men?" Cathryn pleaded, grasping unsuccessfully for the covers again.

"Don't you mean *Father*?" Piero demanded.

Cathryn looked to Vittorio in confusion and fell silent.

"You don't deny knowing he is a priest of the Holy Church?"

Struck dumb under the man's thorough scrutiny. Cathryn drew her knees up and turned her back.

Piero surveyed Cathryn's straight back as she stiffened her spine under his harsh gaze. She tried to cover her breasts with arms crossed over them.

Piero reached behind him for the lamp. "Let us look for the Devil's Mark. Have you not noticed one, Father? If not, surely you've noticed she is too exotic to be English? Have you not noticed the slant of her eyes?" Piero grasped Cathryn's arm and with force dragged her to his side of the bed.

"You're hurting me!" she cried, struggling to resist him.

"Unhand her!" Vittorio demanded, straining against Luciano's grip. "You have no right!"

"I've every right to protect your immortal soul and my house from the Devil's control."

"You've taken leave of your senses, Piero!" Vittorio raged, and tried vainly to free himself from Luciano's iron grip.

Piero scanned Cathryn's body slowly with the light from the lamp. Even in faint light, Piero understood well how his little brother could be attracted to the woman. It wasn't necessary to be bewitched to desire this one. Her beauty was incredible. In spite of her obvious youth, her body was a woman's: her breasts ripe, her hips slender but full. She would be unmatched by the time she was twenty, he thought, admiring the supple lift of her breasts, imagining the soft touch of her skin and how responsive her nipples would be under his fingers, how yielding her woman's flesh would be to his thrusts.

But how did Vittorio come by her? he wondered, forcing

himself to concentrate on the issue at hand. He looked harder, then released his hold on her arm to cross himself, his eyes settling on a mark on the underside of Cathryn's left breast.

"Don't touch me!" Cathryn hissed, but he ignored her.

"Here!" he exclaimed, pulling Cathryn to a sitting position, then shoving her onto her side, roughly handling her breast, jabbing at a small, faintly dark spot on her skin. "There! Just as I feared. The Devil's Mark! You need say nothing more to defend her, brother. It is all the proof needed of her allegiance to Satan. She could be burned at the stake with less evidence."

Luciano let go of Father Vittorio to confirm what Piero described for himself, crossing himself when he gazed upon the spot Piero had discovered. He was convinced of her guilt the instant he saw the faint brown butterfly shape. "Holy Mother of God, preserve us!" he whispered.

Vittorio tried again to reach Cathryn's side but was prevented by Piero, who forced him back into one of the chairs. "Were you too busy shoving yourself into her to notice the Devil's Mark, little brother? Or has the Devil's Woman made you blind?

"You were spoiled from birth," he continued venomously, a light of pure hatred shining in his eyes. "As a boy you thought you could have whatever you wanted and usually did. But not this time, little brother. Go back to your cell and pray for deliverance. Get rid of her, Father, before she brings you along with herself to the stake! I will send someone to soothe your restless cock, if you desire, but for the sake of your soul do not traffic with the Devil, For the sake of us all, damn you!" he said, fearing he knew not what if he were to look back on Cathryn.

"Come, Luciano." He motioned toward the door. "Before she seduces us, also. We will pray for you, Father," he promised, and, with Luciano, abruptly left the room, shutting the door hastily behind them.

Immediately Vittorio rose to comfort Cathryn, taking her into his arms, comforting her as one would a distraught child. In a state of shock himself, Cathryn's tears battered his soul. He covered her nakedness with the blankets she had tried vainly several times to capture.

He held her and tried to soothe her and, unnerved, tried to soothe himself as well. He stroked her soft skin and with wonder touched the red marks left by Piero's jabs on the underside of her breast.

"All the while I thought this blemish only a birthmark—the trace of a kiss given by the angels when they sent you to live among us," he said tenderly, heartbroken by his brothers' cruelty.

Cathryn's tears of anguish had almost dried, and she began to weep again, this time with gratitude for Vittorio's abiding love.

"Some men are fools," he said in an effort to understand if not excuse his brothers.

And from the beginning—reminded a voice at the back of Father Vittorio's brain—some men are damned.

Chapter 14

*Vittorio and Cathryn returned to La Casa degli Innocenti with*out drawing any special attention to themselves, by agreement parting long before they reached the Fabiani palace, wending their separate ways along Venice's many narrow bridges and passageways.

When they next saw each other, Cathryn discovered Vittorio gazing down upon her during a silence in the morning Mass. She thought he gazed on her with love, then realized he did not even see her. Majestic and beautiful, dressed in splendid, pure white vestments that conferred divinity upon his motions, he was absorbed in the mystical liturgy of the Mass. As he spoke the Latin of the rite, his deep melodic voice held the congregation spellbound. Cathryn shivered. Vittorio the man, her adoring lover, was nowhere to be seen.

Cathryn turned her face away from the priest and bowed her head to pray. When she closed her eyes, in her mind's eye she saw Piero and Luciano staring at her in horror—at the woman who had defiled a priest.

Cathryn's mouth felt dry and her eyes burned with unshed

tears. The innocence of her love for Vittorio was swept away forever. She felt unclean.

"Lord, have mercy. Cleanse and forgive me," she begged in silence as the Mass continued.

She begged for pardon and for peace but knew her prayers would go unanswered: her love for Father Vittorio would not cease.

In the sermon of the first Mass after Carnival, Father Vittorio preached of rededicating oneself to God, of resisting the temptations of Satan, of avoiding the sin of fornication. "A virgin is holy in God's eyes, as holy as all mankind would be had only Adam and Eve chosen to obey God.

"Lust is the curse of mankind, God's punishment for man's disobedience in the garden of Eden. God loves the pure of heart and body above all others.

"In his first letter to the Corinthians, the Apostle Paul admonishes us against the sin of fornication, for the body as well as the soul belongs to Christ.

"The body of the believer is a temple of the Holy Spirit, to be kept pure and sacred. A person whom God has received as a Christian is God's property, bought with the sacrifice of His Son's blood and body. A Christian, whose body belongs to Christ and is eternally joined to Christ, who defiles himself with the sin of fornication, defiles Christ and offends God the Father."

As the Mass continued, silent tears spilled from Cathryn's eyes. After the confrontation with his brothers, Vittorio had returned to degli Innocenti a priest. His sermon this morning was his renunciation of her and a reaffirmation of his vows.

Cathryn fought her tears and tried to follow the remaining portion of the Mass. Father Vittorio prepared the Eucharist with prayers and called upon the believers to receive communion. *"Ecce Agnus Dei, ecce qui tollit peccata mundi,"* he whispered to Cathryn and to the others as they consumed Christ's body and blood. Behold the Lamb of God, who takes away the sins of the world.

Devastated, Cathryn was completely ignorant of Perdita's stare. In alarm, concerned with the paleness of Cathryn's face, Signorina Fabiani's heart lurched at the abject sorrow she read there. At once Perdita began to berate herself for indulging in the festivities of Carnival; for loosening her grip on the affairs of the children for whom she was responsible.

When Mass ended, Perdita lost no time in reaching Cathryn's side. "What has befallen you, *angelica*?" Perdita demanded in a voice showing her suspicion that something dreadful had occurred.

"Nothing at all," Cathryn objected, disoriented by weariness, afraid for an instant that Perdita knew more than she did.

"You look dreadful."

"I'm sorry. I tried to freshen myself before coming to Mass."

"It was a rather long night," Perdita said, convinced she had overreacted to the look on Cathryn's face. "I'm weary myself. Which is very light recompense for a hedonist, I suppose," she added cheerfully. "It was enjoyable," she reflected with a sigh. "Don't you agree?"

Cathryn nodded.

"And, you *angelica*, surely earned your name. You have the voice of an angel!" Perdita praised. Then she frowned. "But we mustn't fool ourselves on that score, child. You were much too easily carried away by your admirers last night. You intoxicated those hapless men, and you have no right. Your voice should be used for what it is, God's gift, not as an instrument of seduction."

Cathryn's face reddened, her vision suddenly clouded by a vision of the object of her wickedness: Vittorio's short lace-edged surplice and ornately embroidered chasuble covering his black cassock.

"Ah, you see, I am right. You know you are guilty of just such evil behavior. Oh, Cathryn, you make men drunk, just like your mother. What is to become of you?" Perdita fretted.

Overwhelmed by the Mass and exhausted, it was all Cathryn could do to hold back her tears, grateful that Perdita did not know the extent of her sins. It was infinitely better for Perdita to think her nature flawed by an innate penchant for the seduction of men, Cathryn sighed inwardly, than for Perdita to know the truth.

"You must meditate on this matter, Cathryn, for the sake of your soul. God's displeasure surely surpasses mine."

"Yes, Dita," she pledged, then hurried on to the first meal of the day, hoping not to attract any more attention to herself.

She was the last to be seated, and as she glanced around at the faces of her friends, she saw that like herself, except for the youngest girls who had spent their usual night in bed, everyone was worse for the previous evening. Today would be a long day,

Cathryn mused over buttered bread and strong, aromatic coffee laced heavily with cream and sugar.

Cathryn usually enjoyed the early part of the day's routine, in which she helped the youngest girls with their lessons, but this morning her great weariness and heavy heart distracted her. Cathryn was both a good student and a natural teacher. Past the need herself for formal academic studies, she both remembered and understood the restlessness of the youngsters who sat for long periods diligently poring over their slates and chapbooks.

Her approach was positive, as had been the normal approach used when she was very young. "Like this," she said when demonstrating a bowing technique or a stroke of the pen. Never condemning. Always offering hope for improvement.

Cathryn reflected on Perdita, her own first teacher. Just when had Perdita changed her attitude toward her? Cathryn wondered. When had Perdita become an angry scold?

Only recently—when she began to have cause, came the stern answer from out of nowhere.

Cathryn turned around, expecting to find Perdita behind her, and was relieved to find no one but five studious schoolgirls sitting in a row at a table before her, working diligently on their lessons.

Cathryn loved the five little girls for whom she was responsible, her duty to them to see they understood their lessons, giving them help if need be. They were, in many ways, her sisters, and in others, her children. Only one of the five, Constanza, was an orphan, and none was to be pitied in the least.

The only sadness Cathryn felt for Constanza, a fair maiden in a sea of dark-haired urchins, concerned the child's lack of an ear for music. She could not sing on key to save her soul, nor did she seem to have an aptitude for any of the instruments yet introduced to her. But she had a nature as sunny as her golden hair. She would find a good place in the world, Cathryn felt certain. A tutor raised at degli Innocenti was much in demand by the region's finest families.

Marietta's fate was already known. To seal a friendship and a bargain, the girl's father had promised her in marriage to the son of one of his comrades. Marietta spoke proudly of her father's choice for her. She would be a fine lady of prominence and staggering wealth. Now eleven, she would be a bride at thirteen.

Talented and devout, Delia would marry well, live quietly, and raise a family. Her father, one of Venice's most respected statesmen, would see to it.

And surely Editta and Olivia, both daughters of wealthy merchants, would also live out their lives as the other women of their families did, in comfort surrounded by husbands, children, and servants.

Cathryn bent to correct a bar of music Delia copied into her notebook. She smiled at Cathryn. "You were beautiful last night. My father said so." The other children nodded in agreement.

"Thank you." Cathryn smiled back. But to be beautiful was not enough, she thought, doubting that beauty alone could ever change one's destiny.

Certainly beauty would not alter her fate. In a few weeks hence she would leave Venice for good. In England she would wither and die, forced to live among foreigners far from her friends and far from the lover who now despised her. Soon she would be imprisoned with Protestants on yet another island, ostracized from the saving grace of Roman Catholic sacraments.

But I have been fortunate, Cathryn forced herself to acknowledge. For as long as she could remember, she had lived in an enormous, loving family. She could not imagine any other sort of existence, except . . .

Except to have a family of her own. With one mother and one father, and brothers and sisters. Had she ever had such an experience? she sometimes wondered. What did she remember and what were the idle daydreams of a curious child? Cathryn shook her weary head.

Occasionally, when she was very tired, it seemed she could remember something of another life. In Venice, but unlike the Fabiani *palazzo*. Her memory, if that's what it was, recalled a place with air heavy with spicy fragrances; walls covered with brilliant tapestries; open windows with billows of sheer vibrant-colored silk screening them.

Cathryn raised her hands to feel the contour of her eyes. "If only she didn't have that distinctly Eastern look," she'd once overheard someone say. And when she'd queried and insisted on an answer, Perdita had admitted Cathryn's eyes were slanted—

but only very slightly, she'd hastened to add. "One of your parents might have had some small degree of Oriental blood."

But there was never anything more. Ever. The subject of her life before coming to degli Innocenti was closed.

The remark Perdita made after Mass this morning now rattled in Cathryn's head—"Oh, Cathryn, you make men drunk, *just like your mother.*"

Cathryn frowned, shadowy memory filtering through her brain. Her mother. Seductive? Foreign? Evil? Cathryn shuddered as the vague image slipped away.

Perhaps her past was not *unknown*. Perhaps her past was *inadmissible*.

Cathryn felt certain now that there was something more than the simple stain of foreign blood that Perdita kept hidden. But unless Perdita had a sudden change of heart, Cathryn had no hope of learning anything more than she already knew from Perdita. More than likely, Cathryn's past would remain as dark as her future.

Chapter 15

The night following Carnival, exhausted in body and spirit, Cathryn slept without dreams, alone in her bed, waking before dawn of the next day to stare into darkness.

She woke from a vision of Vittorio's brother Piero, his angry face and words, to knowledge that her lover, regardless of his passion, was first a priest.

From the silence of her room, Perdita's words rose to accuse Cathryn. "You *are* your mother's daughter, a seducer of men."

"My mother's daughter," Cathryn whispered as she tried to conjure some memory of her mother. Only a shadow appeared.

Cathryn fled the discomfort of her bed, pulling a heavy cloak over her fine lawn nightgown and high-heeled clogs upon her feet. She stole from the dark *palazzo* into a foggy morning, hurrying as if pursued. Over narrow bridges and alleyways she ran from her miseries until she was out of breath.

She slowed her pace then but continued on until she came to the lagoon's outer shore, where she sat for a long while and stared out toward the mainland. For the first time in her life, Cathryn wanted to flee the tiny islands of Venice, reasoning, perhaps, the destiny that awaited her in England would be better than she feared. Perhaps far away from Venice and degli Innocenti, she would be purified of her wicked obsession. Cathryn held her tears at bay and acknowledged such reasoning sounded more like Perdita's than her own. Was there ever absolution for seducing a priest? she wondered.

Staring into dark waters, Cathryn remembered the threats she had recently made. She swore to run away rather than be forced to go to England. She had even threatened to throw herself into the lagoon, she recalled as she considered the deserted gondolas and empty skiffs tied bobbing only inches from her feet. She could easily steal one of the boats now and row to the far shore or end her life as she had threatened, she realized.

Cathryn shivered at the reality of cold water splashing gently at her feet—at the thought of her nose and mouth and eyes filling with salty water as she choked and drowned. Would ending her life truly be more unforgivable than the sins she had already committed?

Cathryn walked to the stone stairway leading down into the water. A high tide had left most of the steps submerged. She descended the stairway slowly and hesitated at the last dry step, then stepped down into the water, the hem of her nightgown and cloak quickly soaked by water that was not as cold as she had imagined. Vaguely comforted, the sea seemed to pull at her, the water's temperature now feeling almost warm. She took one more step, then another, oblivious to all but the suddenly hypnotic influence of the fog-shrouded sea.

Cathryn was aware of nothing else until, waist deep, she was seized and yanked backward and up.

"What insanity is this?" demanded an angry and familiar voice.

In confusion, Cathryn turned and stared into Vittorio's frightened eyes. It took a few more moments for her to realize he was not dressed as a priest, but wore tight breeches, an elaborate embroidered white satin doublet, and a long brown cloak—the disguise of a nobleman returning home in the early hours of morning after a long night's entertainment. As she tried to pry his hands from her, Cathryn considered that she might be dreaming.

He seized her more firmly. "There is no need to struggle," he said, and after a moment more she stopped. With relief, she put her head down on his chest.

"I saw you leaving the *palazzo*."

She pulled her head up and her body slightly away.

"I followed you for an hour."

"And only now approached me?"

Vittorio ignored her anger. "What were you doing in the water, Cathryn?"

"Bathing," she snapped. "Why are you dressed this way?"

"Sometimes the cassock does not seem to fit."

"It fit you well enough in yesterday's Mass!" she answered, and pulled herself from his arms. "Just as your sermon fit your mood," she said, her anger weakened by tears. "You renounced me with your sermon! You renounced *us*!"

"I am torn!" he defended with obvious pain.

"But you said you loved me!"

Vittorio pulled her back against him and held her to him fiercely. She struggled, and he fought with her until her tears subsided and she lay meekly in his arms. "Surely, dearest Cathryn, you can appreciate my agony!"

She nodded slowly, her own troubles seeming to fade before her knowledge of the priest's.

"Then you must try to understand my moods, for, God help me, though I've sworn to love God only, I find I love you more."

Cathryn leaned against Vittorio and wept. Soon he bent to kiss her, but amid their freshly stirred longings Cathryn became reluctantly aware of an angry chant of voices thrumming in her head.

"A woman is no better than a harlot!" cursed a priest.

"You are your mother's daughter," Perdita scolded.

"She's a witch and a whore!" Piero screamed.

Cathryn shivered, not with desire or from the chill of standing wet on steps that led into the sea, but from a chill of doubt and a growing sense of shame. "Please, Father," she begged, interrupting his feverish kisses, "take me back to degli Innocenti."

Chapter 16

For a short while, Father Vittorio continued to dream of a life
with Cathryn. He wanted Cathryn to be more than his mistress.
She deserved better: respect; acceptance by his family; a home;
his name. Yet, for a time, it seemed their only choice. But
eventually, he would leave the Church; they would live quietly;
he would seek the patronage of some nobleman or wealthy
merchant and he would write music. He and Cathryn would continue to make music together as they did now.

Father Vittorio's fondness for Cathryn and his apparent feelings of loss at the prospect of her departure were quite obvious to
the Fabiana sisters. They were touched by how often he sought
her company at dinner or even brought her something from the
open market stalls: a tart; a multicolored scarf; a nosegay.
Sometimes he took her with him on walks or simply took time to
work in the palace garden with her.

Perdita and Bianca smiled over his attentiveness and felt sorrow over his loss of his best student. He earned, they said, their
everlasting gratitude for his solicitous and tender consideration of
their favorite child. He smiled and thanked them.

Then the letter from Piero arrived.

Father Vittorio,
  I am in despair over our meeting the night of Carnival. I
am overcome with grief by your actions and by the course
I must take in response.
  I urge you to consider with care your fate and the fate of
your family in the course you choose to pursue. I am used
to acceding to your wishes on all counts, but you endanger
all of my enterprises by your liaison with the woman you
brought before us. You claim you love her. I remind you
that love for a woman is a sin, and for a priest, a
sacrilege.

Do not force me to act, brother. The woman means nothing to me, but I swear to you I would see you both dead rather than allow you to disgrace our family and besmirch its name by leaving the Church for the sake of an open alliance with a woman who is both a Witch and a whore.

Signed with my pledge to carry out my oath.

Piero R.

With the receipt of his brother's letter, Father Vittorio felt his heart constrict. Piero was not a man to make idle threats. All hope of a future with Cathryn vanished.

Father Vittorio contemplated life without Cathryn and felt himself driven almost to the brink of madness. Piero offered to procure a woman for him, as if the satisfaction of his loins would satisfy the priest's aching need for his beloved!

Vittorio despaired of his life without Cathryn, but still music continued to flow from his creative soul. Sometimes the melodies he wrote were filled with pathos, but always the notes sang of love and passion, for he could write honestly of nothing else.

Daily, he recorded notes he did not want to forget, yet he knew he could never perform the finished scores. No one, save his inspiration, would hear this passionate music; especially not his usual audience of schoolgirls and their cassock-clothed schoolmasters.

Not even the wealthy, self-indulgent noblemen, whom he often entertained in their splendid private salons, would ever enjoy these highly polished reveries. The bent of his mind and heart could never be broadcast in such a chamber for fear of raising a scandal or inspiring self-recognition and guilt in his amiable hosts.

A priest was expected to overcome his carnal nature and far too many of the measures Father Vittorio now composed vividly described the woman who possessed him, revealing how completely the priest had failed to overcome his baser instincts. Any astute listener would discern his love for the woman his music described, realizing her vagaries, her capacity for stillness, and her liveliness. One could easily imagine her lithe body and graceful limbs, or the smile that touched her tempting mouth and filled her eyes with a dusky glow. The softness of the silk that covered her supple body could almost be felt, the scent of her natural woman's perfume seemed intoxicatingly real. With lilting clarity, Vittorio contrasted her childish innocence with her woman's responsiveness. The relentless rhythms described a breathless drive. He spoke of his deepest and most elemental desires. The listener heard their sighs. Undeniably, his theme was love—the profane and not the sacred.

One after another, songs "For Cathryn" in every key accumulated on the table in his chamber, but only Cathryn heard the finished scores.

"Learn the music you've etched on my soul," he urged his inspiration.

Cathryn found the music incredibly complex, layered with intricate fingerings and breathless rondos. At a song's end, she herself was often breathless or in tears. "It is much like making love," she whispered.

"I make love to you with every note," he answered.

Sometimes Father Vittorio would accompany her, adding contrasting harmony, his tenor violin adding greater pathos to the song. "Your music makes me want you," she whispered, "as though your lips have already traveled over me."

"You hear exactly why no one else shall ever enjoy this music." Vittorio took Cathryn into his arms. "The Church demands a priest know nothing of passion, or love, for both are sins."

How can either be sin? she wondered in silence filled with doubt but unable to challenge her tormented priest.

Father Vittorio ached for Cathryn constantly and as usual found his attempts to repress his feelings futile. As often as he could, he held Cathryn crying out in ecstasy beneath him, at her every sigh of rapture and with each caress growing more despondent. The sensations he experienced loving her left him reeling, the responses of his body extravagant. He was certain in this realm of existence, at least, nothing could surpass them, and he was always reluctant to let her slip away.

"I must go, Vittorio, or else we shall be discovered," she pleaded.

Sometimes after midnight, she would steal into his quarters to lie with him, but she was always careful not to overstay. She enjoyed these nights in his bed one floor above her own. Both the austere elegance of his room (which contrasted with the decidedly feminine appointments of hers) and the forbidden nature of her visits appealed to Cathryn. If caught, it might be possible to invent a story to explain his leaving her room in the wee hours of the morning, but there could never be any legitimate excuse for her presence on his floor.

Now it was already growing light, and though she wished for nothing more than to stay nearly crushed beneath his hungry, demanding body, she knew Issaco, Vittorio's servant, soon would appear to dress him. "You don't really wish to be discovered, do you?"

Instead of releasing her as she expected, he held her fast. "I can imagine worse."

Cathryn tried to wriggle free. "Vittorio!" she exclaimed in exasperation, then lay back against his pillow. "What possesses you this morning, Father?" she demanded, worried and annoyed, and quite aware her motions to escape had only aroused her lover again. "Dallying will only lead us into trouble."

"No more trouble, surely, than we have already," he insisted, and began to kiss her, succeeding in distracting her, his tongue parting her lips to explore her succulent mouth.

She moaned softly and encircled him with eager arms, caressing the length of his muscular back slowly, forcing his hard shaft against her. "You hope to bring me to a swift end, imagining, in my weakness, that I'll release you," he accused.

"Perhaps you've forgotten Issaco's faithfulness."

"I remember nothing but my need for you."

Cathryn smiled at him indulgently. "How I love you, my heart! But surely, I must go."

"You don't merely love me, you possess me, Cathryn. You corrupt my very soul."

Cathryn had no reply. She lay immobile under him and stared silently into the dark pools that were his eyes, wondering if he really knew just how much she loved him. She noticed that his handsome face, which sometimes caused her to suck in her breath at its manly beauty, seemed haggard, the shading of his beard at dawn enhancing that impression.

She saw the blue shadows beneath his lower lids, revealing the sleep he'd lost of late and, ignoring his accusation, suddenly felt his vulnerability. "And if we're discovered, what will you say, Father?" she asked, almost afraid to hear his answer.

He rolled off of her and began to stroke her belly, filling his eyes with the luxurious promise of her round, shapely breasts. "I'll say you've bewitched me," he replied, and unable to resist her breasts, leaned to suckle and caress her.

Cathryn gasped with pleasure at the insistent pull of his tongue and fingers. He took his time with her, then raised himself to look at her. "Please stay a moment longer," he urged, knowing full well she became hopelessly excited whenever he tugged and twisted at her nipples the way he had just now. "Let us finish," he implored her, pleased by her clouded gaze, which told him that she was more than willing.

A stab of emptiness knifed through her center that could only be erased by the penetration of his body; she burned with desire to have him thrusting deep within her.

Cathryn persuaded him to open a small space between them, allowing her to touch him, and he moved his mouth to hers.

She stroked him slowly, savoring the satin skin beneath her fingers, and soon he slipped his fingers into her hair to tease and make her anxious for more. She lifted her hips slightly and thrust herself against his hand, begging him to seek her woman's softness, until, with pleasure, his fingers played deep between her legs. She was wet and eager but in her ecstasy did not forget him. He groaned both in torment and in pleasure, almost unable to restrain himself.

But Vittorio's ministrations to Cathryn soon forced her to still the rhythmic motion of her hand on him. Fully taken with the sensations he inspired, she reached to grasp his upper arms, clinging desperately. "Ah, Vittorio," she cried, undulating slowly, wishing and not wishing for glorious release.

He entered her with his fingers to find her tender with intense desire, and plundered her velvet warmth as though he knew her every secret. Excited by her incoherent whispers, he lowered his mouth to spread his kisses down her belly, then moved to coax Cathryn's pleasure with his tongue.

Cathryn began to tremble, closing her body tightly and convulsively around his fingers. She cried out almost shrilly as she felt herself shatter into pieces and saw the white light of a hundred swaying candles begin to flicker inside her head.

She panted with exhaustion and entwined her fingers in his thick black hair, letting him feast on her until she had the strength to move. When it seemed he should have had his fill, she pulled his face to hers and resisted his demanding motions that she wrap her legs around him.

She kissed his mouth and reached for him again, expressing sheer delight at his size. "You are made like a mighty stallion," she praised, "but I sometimes wonder whether you were made for your pleasure or mine." She laughed, gently freeing herself from his embrace, trailing quick, wet kisses down his torso to well below his waist. "I've wanted to have you this way for a long while," she confided, her voice beguiling and soft. "This morning, you must grant my wish," she insisted, but raised her head a moment to consider his response.

She saw in his countenance no desire to protest; indeed, his eyes were distant with bliss as she covered his throbbing shaft, first with splendid fingers, then with her mouth.

Her sucking ignited his emotions and he moaned, waging a strenuous battle to keep from reaching too hasty an end. The sounds he made came from deep within his chest and it was not easy to decipher whether pain or pleasure gave his voice its edge. When her mouth yielded to him further, Vittorio could not control himself a moment longer.

"*Cara! Cara!*" he exclaimed as he spewed himself, electrified with joy. When she again lay next to him, he hugged her to him tightly and breathed a contented sigh. "Why did you wait so long to share your wish?"

"I was afraid my desire might shock you," she whispered.

He cradled her as if she were a priceless treasure. "Perhaps," he answered with a sigh. "Perhaps."

But on reflection, her pleasure in this loving gesture did not surprise him greatly, and deep within his heart, he feared he knew the source.

Chapter 17

The undisguised fury of Piero's letter repeating his accusations against Cathryn haunted the priest. Often Father Vittorio imagined he heard his brother's voice: "Love is but lust; and the lust of a priest, an abomination and a sacrilege."

Tormented, but helpless with his love for her, Vittorio was driven to pursue Cathryn, and at every opportunity he implored her, "Pleasure me again."

His heart leapt for joy at her willingness to satisfy his longings for the satisfaction of her mouth. By deliberately prolonging the length of her seduction, she intensified his pleasure. "You deliver unbelievably sweet torture," he suggested, sweating; breathless; fascinated by her apparent craving of the act as enjoyment for herself. The blush of color upon her skin, the tautness of her nipples, the clear excitement in her eyes made it obvious to him. If he had not demanded her mouth, he was sure she would have taken him that way, for she was at least his equal in lust.

Father Vittorio had learned his lessons well and knew only a whore, or worse, could enjoy the debasing act in which Cathryn took such obvious pleasure. Piero's stinging judgment of Cathryn all at once began to hold up to light. A decent woman permitted only her husband the use of her body, and only for procreation as commanded by God. Replenishing the earth with souls for the Church to save in the everlasting battle with Satan was the only legitimate purpose of sex. The fact that Father Vittorio could not seem to keep himself from Cathryn only magnified her sin. Cathryn Godwyne might just be the Devil's woman.

Father Vittorio grew desperate with guilt and fearful of Cathryn's influence, and he began again to pray in earnest for deliverance from sin. In supplication, abject and contrite, Father Vittorio prostrated himself on the ice-speckled tiles of the Fabiani chapel. "Grant my heart ease. Destroy my love and the vile lust of my body. Deliver me from this evil obsession. Strike her from my soul." Yet God was not disposed to grant him freedom from his obsession with Cathryn, and through his guilt and by her loving nature, Cathryn was damned.

From the alcove of the Fabiani chapel, Father Vittorio regarded Cathryn in prayer. She looked like an angel, he admitted, captured by her innocence. Had he known the truth, he wondered even now, could he have kept away from her? She was beautiful beyond all others in his sight, so tender and so perfectly made, and he longed for her even as he damned her.

However, that she was wicked he had no doubt and marveled at the Devil's gift to make so incomparable a creature. Yet he should have known her origin by this attribute alone: such notable perfection was the Devil's way to trap a soul.

God's creations were all in some way flawed.

But Cathryn's beauty was not flawed, Vittorio admitted as he adored her, the bent of his heart slipping from hostility to more comfortable and familiar love.

She sat in profile, dark hair swept and knotted at the back of her perfectly shaped head. Even under the small chapel veil, one knew, the hair was lustrous. Her brow was high and clear, the eyes set not too widely apart, the slim nose straight. He longed to draw his finger across the arch of a dark eyebrow and down the delightful nose to touch her soft lips. He longed for her to kiss his fingers one by one; for her kiss upon his palm.

He wanted to lift her face and touch her closed eyes and their curl of dark lashes with his kiss, then claim her mouth with his. She would sigh into his mouth and reach to draw him against her sweet body, urge him touch her gentle limbs, full breasts, and small tight waist. His intoxication complete, she would press herself against him with an invitation for him to lift and pull her hard against his eager manhood.

The priest gripped the railing before him, stilling in his chest an involuntary groan of passion, willing away the already intense response of his body.

His heart beat with furious desire, yet he admitted Cathryn had not entrapped him with her beauty alone. It was far more than her simple appeal to his eye that had seduced him and stirred this vile lust. She had attached to and woven herself into the fabric of his soul. Her presence in his life had given him more than music to live for. With artful guile she had posed as a woman of gentle spirit, tenderness, intellect, and wit, and in this disguise, she had won his heart.

Father Vittorio frowned at the art of Cathryn's very skillful seduction. As a priest, he should have been alert and immune to all her wiles—that she had come so easily to the joys of the flesh should have alerted him instantly to her real identity. Instead it only served to damn him further, enlarging upon his sin of lust with the sin of pride.

No simple fool, the carefully schooled priest knew well but ignored that no woman as pure as Cathryn appeared to be could be brought so easily to ecstasy. The truth could only be that he had been bewitched by Cathryn. If not, he reasoned, he would have seen the danger and renounced her.

Father Vittorio closed his eyes. Why did he have so much difficulty accepting the obvious? Satan often wrests souls from God's keeping. Why not his own?

As the liturgy of the Mass continued, Father Vittorio opened his eyes and let them wander over the other worshipers. He surveyed each bowed head and wondered who present could have warned him against the Witch Cathryn Godwyne. Who had known of her deceit? Obviously not the signorinas. Obviously not her young charges or her friends. Even the worldly Simone Barbera still appeared to be ignorant.

Father Vittorio's gaze fell upon Cathryn again, and in spite of his renunciation and grave doubts, his blood warmed at the sight of her. As the voices in the Mass droned on, he stared at her. To look on her, who would dream that she was an instrument of Satan?

When Father Vittorio next looked up, Father Umberto looked down at him from before the altar in a way that made Father Vittorio wonder if Father Umberto addressed him in particular.

"Satan knows a soul's every weakness," Father Umberto announced. "He seeks entry into our hearts by preying upon our vulnerabilities, seducing the sinful with offerings that we most desire. Satan knows not our Christian names. He knows us by our vile appetites."

As Father Umberto continued, he did not take his eyes from Father Vittorio.

"One might think a priest would have reached a station where he might for an instant let down his guard, but Satan wages an unremitting war for souls. As long as one lives, no soul is invulnerable, not even a priest's.

"From the beginning, from the moment God created man, Satan has plotted man's ruin, and, selecting the most corrupt of God's creatures to aid him in man's downfall, Satan chose woman as his most likely ally.

"Reflect that without the temptation of Eve, God might have anointed Adam His holy priest. Realize the punishment God chose for Adam's wicked disobedience was the constant torment of lust. Not a day passes that a man is free of this torment. Not a day passes that a woman is not vulnerable to the summons of Satan—the call for her to submit herself to a man's lust."

At last Father Umberto removed his stare from Father Vittorio and with harshness gazed down upon the congregation, predominantly schoolgirls.

"Know that a maiden has a choice. With God's support, through strict devotion, a woman can withstand the overwhelming urge to sin, to offend God, who loves virgins above all other creatures.

"And though a virgin, a woman must be ever diligent. Because of her natural inclination to evil, never for a moment must she let the whispers of Satan's demons penetrate her ears.

"A married woman must submit her body to her husband for the purposes of God: the procreation of souls by a reprehensible act which would not exist but for the Fall of Man through the wickedness of the woman Eve. Any pleasure she receives is but a sign she is unworthy of God's love; her pain in delivering the issue of the union just punishment for her sin and her mother's sin, in the garden.

"The soul is forever under seige from Satan. Only through ceaseless obedience to God's will and through the sacraments of His Church can one obtain grace and life everlasting. Amen."

"Amen," replied the rapt congregation of schoolgirls and their attendants, their hearts recommitted to purity by the inspired sermon.

"Amen," whispered a chastised priest, and after the rite of dismissal, Father Vittorio lingered in the chapel. He intended to pray but could not help but wonder whether the example of Father Umberto's sermon was mere coincidence, or did the senior priest aim his sermon directly at him? Did Father Umberto know of the sins he had committed under Cathryn's influence, sins that were among the most serious offenses imaginable for a priest?

Vittorio kneeled before God in misery. Was he not as guilty as she? In truth, how difficult had it been for Cathryn to trap him, to snare his soul? Had he not made his vows reluctantly? Was he not especially vulnerable to temptation?

Father Vittorio sighed. He had no reason to argue Cathryn's innocence. He had only to recall the nights with her to know how willfully depraved she was. To bare her body completely as she did so willingly was damning evidence enough of her depravity. Furthermore, she admitted she enjoyed his nakedness and took pleasure in inciting his flesh to incredible heights of passion. She urged him to explore and enjoy all manner of forbidden acts. How perverse it was, but at the time of commission their lovemaking had even seemed a form of worship; a means of glorifying God.

His mind swayed by the power of his love for Cathryn, the erring priest had even questioned the Holy Church's rabid opposition to behavior that God Himself had ordained for man. For had God Himself not created the desires of men and women for each other—the need to become one through an act of passion? Did not the Church's attitude regarding sex suggest that God had made a terrible error in His creation of male and female?

In a more rational moment, Father Vittorio knew that this reasoning was simply further proof that he had been easy prey for Cathryn, a willing victim of her evil.

From an early age, from stern and devoted priests, Vittorio had heard that lust was God's punishment and the devil's doing. "The love of a man for a woman is lust, and for a man to love his wife is a sin worse than adultery!" *Omnes ardentior amator propriae uxoris adulter est.*

When Father Vittorio had the occasion to take the place of an ill priest in a church outside the walls of degli Innocenti, and heard the confessions of women who lived quite ordinary lives, he knew just what to say to women who held affection for their husbands. Theirs was an overwhelming burden: the curse of warmth and kindness; the curse of tenderness and of wanting to ease the burden of a man's body; of knowing pleasure in a husband's arms. "Forgive my love for my husband; forgive my lust."

Sure of himself, knowing the Church was infallible, young

Father Vittorio issued harsh penance to the despairing women. There was no room in marriage for love, the sole purpose of which was procreation.

When he listened to the part of his mind that without challenge had memorized the Church's precepts, Father Vittorio knew with certainty right from wrong. But when he considered Cathryn Godwyne, he became utterly confused.

He felt his heart lurch and struggled to remember that Cathryn was a Witch sent by Satan, and although he had discovered her nature, it would take all of his strength to combat her wiles.

"Father, forgive me, for I have sinned. I am guilty of the sin of lust," Cathryn whispered to him in confession. "I love you. I will always love you. I am unable to help myself."

The man inclined to her with adoration, but the priest hardened his heart. It was impossible to save her soul. "All Witchcraft comes from carnal lust, which is in women insatiable," stated the learned men of the Church. In her confession, Cathryn had all but admitted to being the Devil's Woman.

Fearing eternal damnation, Father Vittorio mourned his love for Cathryn Godwyne. His duty was to God. He should renounce her to save others from iniquity

But betraying Cathryn for what she was was a feat beyond the priest for without a doubt, he knew her inquisition would destroy him.

Chapter 18

The Church taught that the Devil's work on earth is done by means of Witchcraft. Born in sin, a man's flesh is weak, making him prey to Witches, who, because of their easily corruptible natures, are mostly women. Every woman, without exception, inherits Eve's inclination to evil.

Father Vittorio knew this, and yet, as if he were an ignorant savage, in the time it took for Cathryn to fan her eyelashes upon soft cheeks, he could forget what constituted sin and the penalties involved. All that he knew was gladly set aside for an hour in Cathryn's arms.

As if he were a pagan, the dark priest had no control over his attraction to Cathryn, his lusts inflamed the instant it took for her to catch his eye. Then, readily, he bowed down to her, seeming to have no memory that carnal pleasure was a sin. He was joyful beyond his wildest dreams, her passionate desires his, his ready downfall simple proof of Cathryn's unholy pact.

Remembering nothing, he reveled in the pleasures of his body and in hers, forgetting absolutely that as a woman she was nothing but "*saccus stercoris*," a sack of filth, contaminated in the Church's eyes by the functioning of her body; damned as the receptacle of lust; made foul by the brutal, bloody process of giving life to the souls the Church required for its survival—her only reason for existence and just punishment for her sins.

Enamored, Vittorio found Cathryn only delightful, a pleasure to all his senses while he devoured her with kisses and excited her to shattering ecstasy. Against the exacting laws and edicts, he relished his nakedness and exhilarated in her knowledge of his every vulnerability. Above all he was grateful for her willingness to bring him the extremes of gratification, knowing his penchants and committing herself to his rapture without his having to beg.

She rose from him and lay on her side against him, propping her head on her hand. She gazed down at him and enjoyed the ecstasy-softened serenity of his face. She rested her other hand on his chest and felt the thudding of his heartbeat.

Vittorio smiled at Cathryn with love, and she savored his gaze. "I am your slave," he whispered. His breathing was still ragged, yet he began to tease. "You have but to command. Tell me what your heart desires."

Cathryn laughed softly and laid her head upon his shoulder. "I only wish I had the power you impute to me. *I* am the slave, not you." Cathryn sat up again and pulled her hair back severely from her face, then drew several long strands across her upper lip. "I'm a very good slave, don't you agree? Perhaps I could even disguise myself as your servant. I could pass for Issaco, don't you think?"

Vittorio touched a breast fondly. "You would fool no one," he said, and drew her against him again. Cathryn nestled with him, slipping a shapely leg between his thighs.

Vittorio closed his eyes and wrapped her in his arms. He held her to him and tried to memorize forever the delicious sensation of having her warm inviting body pressed against his. He wanted to remember for all time the feeling of love her tender presence radiated to his soul. "I dream of dying in your arms." He sighed. "It would be a death close to ecstasy."

"I fear death is rarely bliss."

"You enchant me and distort my reason." He raised himself above her, gathering her face in his hands, planting gentle kisses on her mouth. "Sometimes, especially in the afterglow of my enchantment, I wonder if perhaps your mother was a gypsy Witch whose daughter now follows in her wake to spell-bind foolish men." He caused her to close her eyes and outlined the shape of each. "Yes," he whispered, "a beautiful Witch who came to Venice on the east wind."

"You're quite mad," she scoffed, and pinched him, wriggling from beneath him and sitting up. "But sometimes I also wonder about my mother."

"Your mother was a beguiling witch from the Orient, sent to seduce men's souls and render them useless shells, unless they did her treacherous bidding."

Cathryn pushed Vittorio back against the pillows. She frowned, hoping to make an impression on him. "I shall leave you to rave yourself to sleep," she said. "You grow tedious with your teasing about Witches and spells. It's no laughing matter to contemplate the rack!"

Vittorio held her arm, preventing her from moving away. "You're safe with me, I promise," he whispered in an urgent voice. "I'm hopelessly enthralled. In fact, I relish your spells and the acts of lust you think of to persuade me to do your bidding."

"How do you dare make such an accusation when your imagination far surpasses mine!"

"It shall be your word, beautiful seductress, against mine, a humble priest." His voice was convincingly modest.

"Humble?" Cathryn protested.

"Modest and self-effacing."

"If your defense, Father, is based solely on humility, I shall be able to prove my innocence with ease," she countered, then turned grave with speculation. "I wonder, troubled priest, would you renounce me to save your miserable soul?"

"How can I when there is nothing left of my soul to save?"

The light from the candle at his bedside dimmed, but Cathryn did not have to strain to see the pain in his beautiful but manly face. She touched his lips with the fingers of one hand, and he kissed them softly. "I will love you forever," he swore.

"I love you, too," she answered sadly, and sighed. "If that is evil, then I am all you say and have lured you from your sacred vow of purity. If not, then what you've spent a lifetime learning is wrong." She bent to kiss his mouth. The kiss was long and gentle. It was hard to pull away. "Tell me now," she whispered, "of the evil of my tender kiss. While your heart still leaps against my hand, say that God is offended by love. . . . Perhaps, Father, we have only been taught to be ashamed."

"I love you. I will always love you," he pledged.

"You fear me more than love me, priest. The pity for us both."

While she dressed, not daring an answer, Vittorio wondered at Cathryn's insight and gazed at her in silent speculation. Her motions now were as seductive to his senses as when she had removed her clothes, but his yearning went far beyond the body to the heart.

Cathryn left Vittorio then, and returned to her bedchamber, a future of sorrow and guilt looming and wedged between the lovers. The spell of love was broken, though as a rule, with her challenge, Father Vittorio refrained from taunting Cathryn with his accusations of Witchcraft to excuse his passion.

He grew moody and distant, as remote as any priest who was steadfast in his vows. At other times, Vittorio's desire to be with Cathryn seemed to stimulate his imagination excessively.

Inspired, sometimes Vittorio and Cathryn stole away together in the night disguised by elaborate masks used commonly by noblemen and merchant princes to attend notorious Venetian gambling parties. On those cold but delicious nights, the lovers strolled idly in the streets as though, like other masquerading couples, they belonged together. They gazed at the stars and mingled with others in the Republic's squares. The added danger of discovery and the illusion of freedom made the nights intoxicating and magical.

But in the glare of daylight, all magic faded. Tormented by the reality of her departure and his loss, and by the knowledge of his sins, Father Vittorio began to blame Cathryn again. "*Strega bella!*" he gasped, breathless and ecstatic in her arms.

At first Cathryn accepted his cry of "Beautiful witch!" as one of ecstasy; however, soon his voice became less blissful and his disturbing accusations increased. When he called her "*la donna del diavolo*," Cathryn rose above him, eyes flashing with anger and malice. "How dare you call me the Devil's Woman?"

Obvious pleasure evaporated from Vittorio's eyes. "Do you deny your joy?" he panted. "Or the way you encourage me in this unnatural way?"

Cathryn seethed, her voice as bitter as it was strident. "Is not every loving gesture *unnatural*, Father, and every act of *love* forbidden?"

His breath still short, the priest's eyes widened.

Cathryn deliberately softened her voice. "I've learned to take pleasure in your body; in your every caress. Your joy, when I hold you in my mouth, pleases and excites me, and, you must confess, there's nothing you crave more."

Vittorio's face registered his shock and anger at Cathryn for being so bold as to speak aloud of his perverse pleasures and of hers.

"Your heart desires me to perform this unnatural act, as you describe it, and then condemns me for obedience," she berated him, "which, Father, makes you both a sinner *and* a hypocrite."

Vittorio's reply was to slap her face.

Tears sprang to Cathryn's eyes, and without thinking, she slapped him back, starting something neither of them had power to control.

Vittorio shoved Cathryn back onto the bed. She struggled to leap up.

He pushed her down again and threw himself upon her.

Hurt and blind with fury, Cathryn struggled desperately, her motions creating enormous excitement in the naked priest. He pressed himself against her, demanding her acceptance, and bent his mouth to hers. He was an animal, brutish.

She pulled her mouth away. "You have no right to make love to me like this," she cried, "or to accuse *me* of evil!" She beat at him with her fists.

"I've every right. You use all your powers against me, and at your every whimper, I come forward to gladly disobey the laws of God. Endlessly I crave the forbidden pleasures that you offer.''

"Then you must be the Devil himself," she cried, "for *you* have created *me*."

At her rejoinder, Cathryn watched Vittorio's face change from distraught anger to uncertainty; she felt the already tremendous tension of his body multiply. For several moments he stared as if he despised her, then planted searing kisses on her lips, making plain his passion for her regardless of its source; her daring acts and fearless challenge excited him anew.

Consumed by their whirling emotions of anger, guilt, and love, the lovers submitted to the fire of passion, and in the end, unable to resist him, Cathryn forgave Vittorio. He was troubled and she loved him: his grief in the face of losing her was at least as tremendous as his guilt.

Chapter 19

Perdita waved a letter as she burst into the music salon. "I've just received word *Il Vento* has returned to Venice," Perdita announced to Cathryn, referring to the ship on which she would sail from Venice in three short weeks. "You will share your cabin on the voyage with Contessa Dansette, who has been in Venice visiting her sister, but now must return to Versailles due to her husband's grave illness," Perdita reported from a note from *Il Vento*'s captain. "Capitano Salvadori says he will call, but I think we should take a stroll and get a glimpse of the vessel before then. Perhaps tomorrow?"

Cathryn sighed inwardly and nodded, annoyed by her foster mother's second interruption of the morning.

Now that Cathryn's departure was only three weeks away, Perdita was determined to spend every spare moment with her dearest child. Whenever it was convenient for Perdita to join Cathryn, Perdita interrupted whatever Cathryn was doing to be with her.

Not only were her interruptions sometimes awkward, they caused Cathryn to dwell on her departure more than she cared to. Perdita gave advice and voiced endless questions about Cathryn's future, her travel arrangements, the wisdom of packing this garment or that. Would Cathryn be able to keep her rosary in a Protestant household? How many fans would be a necessity? Where would Cathryn come by a violin in Suffolk, England? How many other passengers would there be aboard *Il Vento*?

When very early one morning a trunk was delivered to Cathryn's room, she objected. "It's far too soon."

"I fear not," Perdita said, going immediately to Cathryn's wardrobe. "You know you can't take everything and we must decide."

Still sleepy, Cathryn stood in her nightgown. She poured water into a basin and splashed some on her face.

"I've ordered you another traveling gown. It's quite plain and shall suit your needs in Puritan England," Perdita said, inspecting the hems of Cathryn's gowns. "This gown needs mending, bodice too bright for dour Puritans." She separated the dress from the rest and tossed it aside.

"Please, Dita, I cannot bear to consider my future this early in the day."

"I'm certain you would rather be out bounding in the lanes, arriving barely in time for Mass," Perdita huffed, "but I arrived early enough this time to catch you still in bed."

Cathryn went behind a damask screen and pulled her nightgown over her head, glad she had arrived early enough from a night of masquerading with Father Vittorio to have Perdita find her in bed—alone.

When she opened her eyes this morning and saw Perdita standing by her bed, Cathryn knew instantly that there would be no more nights shared with Father Vittorio, whether in the streets or in her bed. There would likely be very few more encounters of any kind with her lover until she left Venice.

Cathryn sighed and closed her eyes, pressing her petticoats against bare breasts. She felt both physically and emotionally exhausted—almost at the point of admitting to being weary of love.

Far too often, Father Vittorio seemed to want to believe she was a Witch, and she feared the love he had proclaimed was mainly lust. Yet when Cathryn held him in her arms or heard him sigh, or heard the glorious music he wrote for her, or stared into his unmasked eyes, she had no doubt that what he felt for her was more than lust.

Cathryn opened her eyes. She felt light-headed—from lack of sleep, she reasoned. But if her dizziness proved to be illness, she decided, instead of her usual terrified bargains with God for recovery, she would pray for death—a lingering, dramatic death in Venice—with Father Vittorio weeping at her bedside. Cathryn raised her eyes to heaven, afraid it was definitely too much to ask for.

"Cathryn!"

Startled, Cathryn turned in Perdita's direction.

"You've not been paying attention to a thing I've said. I'm now considering your calicoes. Do you wish to carry them with you to England?"

"I suppose the sun sometimes shines there, too, don't you?"

"I imagine. Besides I'd like for you to have them—they become you. Didn't Father Vittorio buy the bolt for this one for your birthday—such pretty shades of blue," Perdita said, holding up one dress in particular to the lamp. "I didn't think he cared for anything but music, but I suppose, raised in a family of shrewd mariner merchants, he might have learned to judge good cloth."

Cathryn stared at Perdita, surprised to hear her admit Father Vittorio was anything but holy and separate from ordinary men. Her acknowledgment that he came from a human family and was not delivered directly from the hand of God was a remarkable revelation. "I suppose he might have learned something from his brothers," Cathryn muttered, but Perdita did not seem to hear.

Certainly, Cathryn feared, from his family the priest had learned too much respect for the opinion of his older brothers, for on their word alone, Vittorio had come to fear and doubt her. The night they had renounced her had brought about the change in him. From the moment Piero cried Witch, nothing had been the same.

How could one word cast so much doubt? How could one word destroy love—unless, as the world and the Church wanted to believe, love was nothing more than evil lust disguised.

Cathryn trembled from head to toe. She closed her eyes and explored their shape with gentle fingers. "Gypsy Witch's eyes," the panting priest had called them.

Cathryn Godwyne bowed her head to pray that she would never hear the word "Witch" again.

Chapter 20

"Remember, this life is but preparation for the next," Perdita counseled.

Cathryn nodded. "Promise me the next will be an improvement over this one."

"That's up to you, *angelica*."

Cathryn smiled though she despaired.

Her trunk and other baggage were carried down three flights of stairs and positioned by the outside door, coming to rest on the flooring with a thud that sent an echo throughout the palace. A silence followed, and in the stillness, Cathryn handed over her precious Amati for Perdita to pack.

Signorina Fabiani stroked the varnished back, tracing the graceful pattern of the grain, then gently wrapped the shining instrument in deep velvet. "I need not warn you to take care."

"Of course not. It's my most cherished possession—one I never expected to own."

Perdita smiled. "I know you feel Father Vittorio is quite indifferent to your departure, but after all, *angelica*, there are limited ways for the priest to show his fondness. Surely this gift more than expresses the strength of his affection."

Cathryn blushed crimson.

"It's right you should blush. You've been much too occupied with your own misery to notice the misery of others."

Cathryn turned away from Perdita, glad no one seemed to observe the real extent of her misery. The priest's gift of the Amati had taken Cathryn by complete surprise.

Over the last weeks, with Perdita bobbing in and out of

Cathryn's presence, there had been precious few occasions for
her to be alone with Vittorio, but the situation had seemed to suit
the priest's temper. During the last weeks when they were
together, he was unusually silent and rarely touched her. His
brooding seemed only to reflect his change of heart, his silences
almost more painful than his earlier taunts of witchcraft.

As the day of her departure neared, Cathryn took to retiring to
her bedchamber early and never expected to have him come
knocking at her door with the Amati in hand.

She let him in and stood expectantly, waiting for him to
speak. She saw a sadness and a distance in his eyes.

"Perhaps you didn't know, but this instrument is mine," he
said, holding the violin before him. "I'd like to give it to you,
with all my love." He offered her the violin that had become
almost an extension of herself, another limb.

She reached for the Amati instinctively. Occupied with so
many other losses, Cathryn had not yet begun to mourn its
loss. "I was saving my grief over my violin for later," she
she said, stunned by his gift. "But whyever would you part
with it?"

"Once it was my heart, but now it's more a part of you than
me."

Cathryn hugged the violin against her. She smiled up at him,
beginning to fear she would once again drown in his now warm
gaze. "Thank you, Father," she whispered. "You've been so
silent, so remote, I feared you no longer loved me."

As though suddenly embarrassed, Father Vittorio hastily looked
away from Cathryn, torn in two by his love for her and his
recovered sense of duty. He regretted every unkind accusation he
had made, yet could justify the passion he felt for her no
other way. Even now as he beheld her, he felt the possessive pull
she had on him, God help him, a stronger pull than he felt for
the Church! By everything he had been taught, his sentiment was
a disgrace; the pull satanic.

In the growing silence Cathryn's eyes filled with unshed tears.
She laid the Amati on her bed. "I am mistaken. This is no token
of love. It only represents your guilt."

"No! I love you—I fear I shall always love you!" he
cried, the tangle of his emotions evident in his voice and
face.

Cathryn managed a soft but bitter laugh. "You mean you loved the pleasure my body gave you!"

"No, Cathryn!"

"It is easier on the soul to think it was only vile lust between us, Father," she sneered.

Father Vittorio reached for Cathryn and pulled her close but he did not take her in his arms. "How I wish lust was all that existed between us! But our forced parting is fitting penance; our only hope for salvation is to repent what we know to be sin. Repent as I have, Cathryn. Repent our love to save your soul!" Tears welled in Vittorio's eyes.

"God would know my lie, Father," she whispered. "Loving you is a sin I shall never repent."

With a groan of despair and resignation, Vittorio pulled Cathryn against him. "Our separation will be perpetual fire. By comparison, the stake would be brief agony."

Cathryn felt Vittorio melt against her and for a moment experienced a feeling of bliss she had known so many times before. "Find some way to follow me," she begged.

The priest sighed. "I was mistaken—you're not a Witch at all." He smiled down at her. "Only still a child—believing in your power above the will of God." He gave her lips a light, brief kiss. "It is not ordained that I should follow you. We shall be separated forever."

"Why should God want to destroy us?" Cathryn demanded, and wrenched herself away from him, the tears she had fought until this moment flooding her eyes. "Why does He hate us?" she cried.

"Through sin we have fallen from grace."

Cathryn covered her face to hide a torrent of tears.

Then suddenly her tears stopped falling. She fell to her knees before him and reached for his hand, pressing it to her cheek. She bowed her head and clung to him. "Father, forgive me, for I have sinned. I have loved a man who is a priest and with that love have been granted breathtaking ecstasy—and torment that far surpasses all my fantasies of Hell. I humbly accept your punishment of my sin. I accept my exile to England, where I will dwell without him, banished like a leper from his presence, as fitting penance."

Cathryn lifted her face to see anguish in his eyes. "No!" she cried, and defiantly pushed away the hand she clung to. "No! Never!" She rose from her knees. "God knows better than to believe me, if you don't!"

Father Vittorio stared silently at Cathryn.

"I may come to curse the day I ever loved you," she whispered, "but if loving you is sin, then I am willing to pay."

"Many would say only a fool, or a Witch, would take such a stance."

Cathryn sighed and slowly turned her back on the priest. "I know already what you believe, Father."

Defeated, she felt her shoulders droop. Then with a gesture that seemed to require herculean strength, Cathryn stood erect and turned again to face him. "Farewell, Vittorio," she said, and coolly dismissed him.

PART TWO

Suffolk, England
1687–1691

The
Sowing

O God with horns,
come back.
O unicorn in captivity,
come lead us out
of our willful darkness!

Come skewer the sun
with your pointed horns
& make the cave, the skull, the pelvic arch
once more
a place of light.

from "To the Horned God"
by Erica Jong

Chapter 21

Cathryn sat on the edge of her narrow bunk and dared to consider the risk of eating something substantial. There had been many moments during the last seven days when she had been positive she would not survive the sea journey to England and had turned down even water, but at last, her stomach was not in violent convulsions.

For the first few days at sea, Cathryn worried that *mal di mare* was the least of her concerns but within the week was reassured to find that she was not pregnant.

Surely it had to be more than a week since she left Venice, Cathryn thought, yet at the moment, her memory of degli Innocenti seemed vague, almost a dream. In recent days, she had been occupied more with *mal di mare* than with her memories.

Il Vento's master, Capitano Giuseppe Salvadori, had promised Cathryn the seasickness would pass; however, his words rang hollow as the days and nights ran together in an endless haze of nausea and violent retching.

Rising now from her uncomfortable bunk, Cathryn dipped a damp cloth into a small porcelain basin filled with water. It seemed to her she had bathed her face a thousand times since daybreak, but it was the only means at hand for soothing her misery.

Cathryn swirled the cloth in the water, anticipating its welcome chill. She was certain she did not have a fever, and now that it seemed a distinct possibility she would survive, she supposed she should be grateful.

As Cathryn pressed the cool cloth to her forehead, the door to the cabin opened and Comtesse Dansette entered in her usual abrupt and cheerful way. "Darling Cathryn, you are up at last!"

"I'm even hungry."

Teresa smiled. "A good sign. I shall inform Capitano Salvadori you shall be joining us for supper,'' she said as she turned on her heel and went out again.

Cathryn's companion and chaperone on the voyage to England was Comtesse Teresa Dansette, a Frenchwoman of middle age, about whom Cathryn already had learned a great deal—including her fortune of a robust constitution. ''If I were a man, I'd be the captain of a ship, or perhaps a general gathering glory for my king.''

From the countess, who seemed to Cathryn to talk without stopping from morning until she finally mumbled her last word nodding off to sleep, Cathryn had learned more details than she cared to know about life in Louis XIV's court at Versailles. While life in the king's favor sounded fascinating, in her unseaworthy condition, Cathryn would have preferred quiet. Once she almost was driven to leap off her bunk to beg to die in silence, but before she could summon the required energy, Teresa was off for some exercise on deck.

''Thank God!'' Cathryn had cried aloud. The only salvation in the circumstances was that the countess despised the confinement of their quarters and prowled about the decks, welcome or not. She was used, she said, to dancing and riding and brisk country walks. ''Idling about ruins my disposition,'' she complained, so she fled from their cabin as often as possible, earning Cathryn's eternal gratitude.

Now that Cathryn was feeling better, she even had strength to wonder where *Il Vento* sailed and estimated the current course to be somewhere in the Ionian Sea. At the start of the voyage, she had followed the ship's progress with interest as they sailed along the Venetian coastline. However, within a few hours of their departure, she had lost all fascination with the ship's course, at times wishing the unremarkable ship would sink immediately to the bottom of the Adriatic Sea.

''May this be the first and last time I must board a ship!'' she prayed. Though arduous, slow, and often treacherous, a land journey, she imagined, must be pleasant by comparison.

Cathryn bathed her face with cool water one last time and patted her skin with soft linen, fearing she looked much the worse for the journey. She ached from bouts of seasickness, and where it should have fit closely, her silk chemise draped loosely beneath her breasts. When he saw her, she imagined her guardian would think the money that had been provided for her sustenance had been spent on something other than food.

Reaching for a gown that lay folded with care at the foot of her bunk, Cathryn unfastened its bodice and tried to focus her mind on the dark rich fabric and small-faceted jet buttons that glistened like jewels in the light.

The style of the gown was severe and modest, in keeping with the demand of the Puritan community she would enter: its collar was high upon the throat; the color, deepest black. But within the restrictions of Puritan dress, the gown was elegant. In fact, nothing in Cathryn's wardrobe suggested she was an orphan, and nothing in her carriage or countenance summoned pity from the observer. Though she was thinner than when she boarded *Il Vento*, her beauty ravished the eye.

"For one so ill, you are still quite lovely," Comtesse Dansette remarked one night when she tucked Cathryn into her bunk again. "I only hope I'm half as lovely on my deathbed! I promise, dear, you shall live to laugh at this nightmare."

Cathryn unfastened the buttons of her bodice, and remembered she had been sure that she indeed lay near death. Now she looked around at the meager quarters and was grateful not to have died in such a bed.

The quarters were horribly cramped, and traveling with the extravagant Comtesse Dansette, who was used to luxury, made the space seem especially tight. Both women were provided a short, narrow bunk with a mattress stuffed with musty wool: a far cry from the featherbed she in error had called her own at degli Innocenti. The accommodations were an outrage by Comtesse Dansette's standards.

"Why, if I'd known the cabin to be so crude, I should have never come aboard! I was assured, and Capitano Salvadori promised, and I suppose Henri should like to see me if he's going to die. . . ."

Cathryn sighed. She suspected her new home would not offer much better than this lowly cabin. She might not even be well fed. The English had a reputation for gluttony, but it did not apply to every household. Probably England would never *feel* like home, Cathryn sighed, her morbid thoughts accompanied with a familiar stab of fear.

"It is best *not* to think, *not* to feel anything," she whispered to herself. And most of all, it was best not to remember the past.

Until now, Cathryn had forced all thoughts of her leavetaking from Venice from her mind, an easy task when she was preoccupied with illness, but now she was able to recall the occasion with bitter clarity.

While her friends shed copious tears as they stood with her in the school's speckled-marble entryway, Cathryn had accepted the loving embraces of friends and caretakers, feeling as if she merely watched; as if, perhaps, she were not present. She was barely aware of the touching of lips to her cheek; of hands pressing hers; of arms thrown around her. She appeared unfeeling, but her seeming calm was due more to her disbelief over Father Vittorio's absence than to calm acceptance of her fate.

Cathryn had not seen Father Vittorio since she had dismissed him so coolly two nights before, but she had never dreamed he would fail to bid her a public good-bye.

Her pain at being ignored by the priest was so intense, Cathryn at first felt numb, as though he had wounded her with such a furious blow that the injured part of her had lost all sense of feeling.

How could he not come forward to bid her good-bye, as if she had never meant anything to him? As though he had never loved her.

According to Perdita, who dismissed his absence with a light tone, the priest had been called away, something not uncommon for a priest.

But not the priest in question, Cathryn knew. He was not a village servant, summoned for all manner of consultation. He might say Mass and hear confessions and perform Church rituals. For a short time, he might replace an ill brother-priest outside degli Innocenti, but how dare he absent himself from her departure!

Aboard *Il Vento*, Cathryn warmed with her anger, but at the time she had been so stunned she could only nod in acquiescence to his slight. Now, a good distance away, Cathryn judged all his vows of love as lies. Just as she had prophesied, she realized Father Vittorio had forgotten her almost before she left his bed!

Cathryn grew furious. The priest no doubt had cleansed himself of sin through explicit confession! She could see him now, humbled before Father Umberto. He would bow his head and manfully beg forgiveness. He would be sincere. He would be contrite. He would forget her!

Cathryn seethed.

She crumpled her dress and threw it down upon the bunk and slammed her fists against the fabric. She felt a new emotion for Vittorio—pure and simple hatred!

If she were only the Witch he accused her of being! she raged silently. She would put a curse on him and make him remorseful through all eternity!

A wicked gleam flickered in Cathryn's eyes as she tried to shake the newly made wrinkles from her gown.

Perhaps the priest would not forget her after all. He might confess his sins, but she felt sure he would not entirely forget her. Vittorio could not help but dream of her—just as she could expect to dream of him.

Yes, Father Vittorio would suffer her absence.

Perhaps, for once, Cathryn imagined, the angels had sided with her—and for the moment at least, Cathryn Godwyne did not care from which world the angels came.

Chapter 22

From his end of the table, set with heavy gold candelabrum and tableware, Capitano Giuseppe Salvadori regarded his guests. His small black eyes were half-closed, the lids weighted by new red wine and speculation.

In Comtesse Dansette, the captain saw a charming, widely experienced woman of the world, used to the excesses and luxury of the French court. In Mistress Godwyne he saw such beauty and innocence he wanted to weep, his initial instinct to protect. Yet she also stirred other baser instincts. He smiled to himself; for this journey, at least, he was glad to have been forced by economic necessity to board passengers.

His ship, *Il Vento,* a small but proven bark, plied the western oceans in commerce, and it was a degrading notion for her captain to have to contemplate regular passenger trade. In the past, his usual cargo of malmsey, that rich sweet wine, carted to

England from Madeira in exchange for wool traded to Flemish agents for bolts of excellent finished fabric destined for Venetian merchants, was lucrative enough. However, increasing restrictions and duties imposed on foreigners, in particular those imposed by James the Second of England to insure profitable commerce for English mariners, decreased Venetian Giuseppe Salvadori's income to the point that to continue what was his life work and his only love obliged the captain to seek passenger trade.

The passengers he carried this trip more than suited his requirements for any trouble he might encounter. The countess's fare had been negotiated shrewdly, but he had collected an especially agreeable sum for the young woman who was on her way to England. What she offered for the eye was a decided bonus adding to the pleasure of his profit.

Giuseppe leaned into his chair to better study Cathryn Godwyne over the hooked angle of his nose. She was a distraction, one he could ill afford on a regular basis, but passengers of her quality would not often come aboard, he knew.

She seemed more like the cloistered child of royalty than an orphan. It was obvious she was not a commoner, and though she bore no title, she had a more regal air about her than the Comtesse Dansette. For a moment, Capitano Salvadori regretted not having made the passengers' accommodations more splendid, and he smiled at Cathryn, hoping to evoke a smile from her.

The weather this voyage had been monstrous for this time of year, and Giuseppe had been allowed little time to concern himself with their presence or absence from his table, but now he vowed to make up for his indifference. As a rule, passengers did not share their meals with the captain and ate from a tray carried to their quarters or with the crew, but it was somehow unthinkable for either the countess or Mistress Godwyne to be exposed day after day to that kind of crudity. A plain man, not much more elevated in class than his sailors, Giuseppe Salvadori prided himself on his appreciation of the finer elements of life whenever he could afford them, and to have these obviously elegant women aboard brought forth in the captain a need to portray himself at his best. The linen and gold service reserved for entertaining agents and preferred merchants came from sea chests, and the ship's cook had been ordered to present only the freshest fare to his guests.

Tonight Giuseppe poured Cathryn more wine. "This is wonderful," she praised, but uneasy with the captain's frank stares, she consumed far less than either her smiling host or Comtesse Dansette.

Comtesse Dansette had warned Cathryn in advance that the captain would have trouble taking his eyes off her. "Dear, I should warn you about our captain, since I doubt you've had much experience with men at that precious school. He's the sort of man who hasn't learned not to drool over a woman in public. I'm sure his eyes will betray he should like to have you for his supper."

The countess's prediction proved quite accurate. Even when he did not stare, his eyes rarely seemed to leave Cathryn's face or form. Cathryn did her best to ignore him, and to her immense relief, the captain eventually regained his manners.

Cathryn believed both the captain and the countess as yet knew very little about her, though in their knowing she was to make her life in England, she felt they knew almost all there was to know.

Both were free with their opinions and advice, and when Cathryn shivered with a chill, the comtesse took the opportunity to advise, "If you are cold now, you should wait until you arrive in England. I am *not* exaggerating, am I, Captain, when I say England is not just cold in climate?" she said, looking to Giuseppe Salvadori for confirmation. "The English are shrewd and as cold as the waters that lap the country's shores."

Their advice and conversation ranged over many topics with regard to Cathryn's future in England, as if they were more worried than she. "James the Second is a Catholic, a friend of the Divine Louis of France, but except for the sovereign it is a crime in England to be of the Roman faith. Charles the First, James's father, you know, was beheaded and the son may yet lose his. Did you know, if discovered, a Catholic priest is certain to be hanged, drawn and quartered?"

Cathryn blanched.

"I should hide my rosary, dear," the countess counseled.

"The Blessed Virgin shall surely protect her," Capitano Salvadori offered.

Cathryn was not noticeably cheered. "I'm aware that I'll not be able to practice my faith, but I must confess that I don't understand how the English dare risk their immortal souls by observing a false religion.'' Cathryn made the sign of the cross. "Surely it is blasphemy.''

"In Suffolk, you shall be living among dissenters,'' Giuseppe informed her.

"My guardian is of the Puritan faith.''

"Dissenters. Puritans. It is all the same to you. Whatever their name, they wish to see the Church of England purified of any resemblance to the Roman church. They hate the Holy Father and all ordinary Catholics. But King James has no special love for the Puritans, I hear. Perhaps they shall lose their heads before he does.''

Cathryn shuddered.

"The English have their Puritans; we French our Huguenots, whom Louis finally cast out by revoking the promise to insure they could worship as they believed. Much like the English dissenters many have fled to America. Though I'm sure Louis was motivated more by his desire to have absolute control of France than by piety, I say good riddance. At best Protestants seem to be a rather dreary lot.''

Capitano Salvadori nodded. "Your beauty, signorina, shall be hidden.'' He motioned to the short rope of pearls at her throat that Vittorio had given her. "There shall be no jewels to adorn you, nor even lace.''

Cathryn touched the love knot that Vittorio had given her.

"You shall even have to hide your hair beneath a cap—else you offend God.'' Comtesse Dansette grimaced. "One and all the Puritans have no heart—no passion—except for God. It's a wonder they have souls!'' She sighed. "But Capitano, I fear we have already said enough to give this poor child bad dreams.''

The captain rose from the table. "I see you tremble, signorina, and to warm you I should like to present you with a sample of my trade.'' He opened a leather chest and produced two enormous shawls of exceptional Flemish wool. He gave one of soft white wool to Cathryn and another of pale gray to the countess. Cathryn's wrap was fringed with threads of gold and Comtesse Dansette's with silver.

Cathryn wound the warm but lightweight shawl around her.

"You'll need every layer of warmth where you go.''

"Please, Capitano,'' begged the comtesse. "We've already depressed her spirits enough this evening!''

"You speak as though I go to England by choice.''

"No?" the countess and the captain answered in unison, their curiosity piqued.

Cathryn shook her head. "Capitano, would you leave Venice forever of your own will?"

Giuseppe sighed. "You are *so young*." He sighed.

"I grow older by the moment," Cathryn answered.

"It is a pity you do not come to France instead!" said the countess.

Giuseppe poured them each another glass of new Bordeaux, not wishing to bid Cathryn good night. "Signorina, I understand you studied music while you were in Venice. Perhaps you would honor us with a song or two."

"Dearest Cathryn, please!" begged the countess.

"It would please me very much," urged the captain.

"Tomorrow, perhaps."

"Perhaps tonight," he replied, and lifted his glass, savoring the prospect.

"It's late," she appealed, feeling tired from her illness and a little forlorn by the evening's conversation.

"It is not so very late, signorina. The candles still burn brightly."

Though she was not the least in the mood to entertain anyone, Cathryn acquiesced and brought the Amati from her cabin. "Your generous portions of wine have made me unusually weary," she apologized. "You must excuse me if my performance tonight lacks vitality."

Giuseppe Salvadori knew well the reputation of La Casa delgi Innocenti for producing exceptional musicians, yet he was amazed by Cathryn's proficiency. He had a difficult time reconciling in his mind how a young woman of such grace and extraordinary beauty could be something more than a feast for the eyes and a promise of satisfaction for a man's other appetites.

The comtesse's ear was better trained than the captain's and she listened with greater musical interest, but at the back of her mind she too could not refrain from speculating about the beautiful Signorina Godwyne.

In performance Cathryn tried to raise her flagging spirits. She did not feel inclined or capable of performing anything elaborate and instead played exercises and songs she generally used to limber her fingers before practicing anything serious. It was a familiar ritual and she closed her eyes and dreamed herself in Venice.

Without effort she drifted from her exercises to other scores, almost unaware of the words of admiration the captain and the countess murmured each time she paused. When she finished, they applauded with great enthusiasm.

"I am astounded by your skill!" the captain said with deference.

"A gift from God!" cried the countess.

"I am often reminded," Cathryn answered.

"What a pity you go to live among heathens who will not appreciate you." The countess sighed.

"Perhaps my English charges will be blessed with much the same abilities as I."

Giuseppe's face changed expression. "Such a gift surely is not common, nor will your music be welcomed by the Puritans."

Cathryn took the captain's news with calm. "Perhaps it's just as well. Perhaps the past should be laid to rest," she said, cradling the shining Amati in her hands for closer examination. Her fingers traced the perfectly carved "f" holes. "My future does not lie in the past, it seems."

"Who but a sorcerer should know what lies ahead, dear Cathryn?" said Comtesse Dansette to comfort her, detecting the wistfulness of Cathryn's voice.

Cathryn looked into the countess's eyes. "It takes no special sense to know some things," she insisted in a quiet voice.

"God should not forgive you, signorina, if you renounced your gift."

"He already has much to forgive me," she answered. "I should wonder He would notice."

Hiding their smiles of disbelief, Capitano Salvadori and Comtesse Dansette looked at one another. "In any event, you must play a little something for us each evening," Comtesse Dansette insisted. "We do not care to be robbed of such pleasure while we can enjoy it."

"I shall be happy to play for you, Comtesse. Indeed, I have at least a little more to say before my voice is silenced forever."

Chapter 23

For a while each night after the evening meal, as Il Vento *sailed* the Mediterranean Sea, Cathryn entertained Comtesse Dansette and Capitano Salvadori with her magnificent Amati. It seemed a reasonable way to channel her increasing restlessness. She hoped, as she concentrated on her music in practice and performance, to direct her waking thoughts from paths that troubled her, for despite her resolve to destroy her memories of the priest, Cathryn longed for him.

During the day Cathryn tried to cultivate an interest in the path of *Il Vento*, and studied maps Capitano Salvadori displayed for her enlightenment. She also began to listen more attentively to the lively and endearing countess.

Yet in a lull of Teresa's chatter, Cathryn might look out to the seemingly endless stretch of gray sky and darker sea and feel her loneliness to her core. At dinner, Cathryn began to drink with relish the wine Capitano Salvadori provided, grateful for its eventual numbing properties. But before that effect relieved her, Cathryn suffered to the depth of her soul from her yearnings.

She hoped her music might relieve her and began to dwell on Father Vittorio's melodies, to perfect them to her memory of his exacting standards, and when she closed her eyes in concentration, her teacher seemed to stand before her as he had in Venice. She felt little surprise when she imagined hearing his voice and in her dreams at night succumbed with all too willing ease to his seduction.

In the light of day, Cathryn was of another mind. "He has forgotten me," she reminded herself in an angry voice, convinced she hated him for his betrayal.

"What was that you said, my dear?"

Cathryn blushed and said nothing.

"Ah, I see the captain and I have mistaken your look of innocence for one of ignorance, eh?" The countess eyed Cathryn in a new light. "But now I see you are very much a young woman and terribly desirable," she said, and stared in frank speculation.

"So, you leave a lover in Venice." Teresa sighed. "You are seventeen, yes . . . well, when I was your age I had two lovers and a husband! Do not despair, Cathryn, the lover you leave behind will not be your last, I promise."

Cathryn turned away from the countess.

Teresa Dansette laughed softly. "Oh, but I'm afraid you loved him with all of your tender young heart!" She sighed. "My dear, I can only imagine your life in that academy of music you've told me about. How dreary—if only you were coming with me to France, to Versailles and Louis's court, I should say you'd have the time of your life. You would forget your Venetian very quickly." She gazed at Cathryn's back. "There's nothing like the arms of a new lover to make one forget the last.

"Now who could your lover be—a patron of music?—the luthier's boy? Mmmm, you said all the children were girls. . . . Now, who could it have been?"

Cathryn pretended to ignore the countess and began to tend her bow in preparation to practice.

"You were cloistered in that school and chaperoned, and you said your teachers all were priests. . . ." Suddenly Teresa Dansette was silent. "Ah, *cherie*, your lover was a priest!"

Cathryn stiffened her back. "You make an outrageous accusation, Comtesse."

"Nevertheless, it is true."

"It is a sin to imagine a priest a man."

"And worse to seduce him."

"By far."

Still sitting in her bunk, dressed in a cream-colored silk nightgown with the deep V of the neckline edged in elaborate wide lace, and satin pillows she brought with her for the voyage piled behind her back, Comtesse Dansette smiled and rolled her eyes at her young companion. "I fear you take the Church and her men quite too seriously. Why, Cathryn, the priests and bishops and all the others are only ordinary men strutting or somnambulating, as the case may be, in cloth they've convinced everyone is holy; pretending to have the ear of God to separate the rich from their fortunes and—I swear, I have no notion what it is they want from the poor peasants."

Cathryn's own challenges of doctrine in Venice paled before the countess's outspoken thoughts.

"My dear, to listen to them on matters of love is utter foolishness. Indeed, I'm sure God hasn't spoken to most of them in years."

Teresa Dansette settled herself in a more upright position. "I suppose every one of us could stand to love God more, and be more kind and generous with our neighbor, but it escapes me why God would be in torment because of our interest in the most ordinary of desires. Surely He has more intriguing things to do than trouble Himself with all manner of almost boring human behavior. And isn't it reasonable that priests should sometimes serve themselves as well as God?" she asked, but did not wait for Cathryn to reply.

"If I were God, I should hope I could find something more enjoyable to do than make myself miserable contemplating who is doing what with whom. Perhaps if the flesh of His priests was satisfied, the clergy would be free to be more imaginative, and perhaps then the Church would refrain from depicting God as little more than a heavenly voyeur."

Cathryn was speechless and rather surprised that God did not strike the countess dead for thinking, not to mention uttering, what she did. However, Comtesse Dansette looked the picture of health—and quite seductive in her sheer silk bedgown, obviously much experienced with the "ordinary desires" of men. "I thought you were a Catholic," she said.

The comtesse laughed long and loudly. "Of course I am. It is a perversion to be otherwise, but you see, I am an iconoclast, and I do not always speak so openly."

Cathryn was not surprised.

"Well, Cathryn, you have had a priest, and I have had a bishop, and I say the clergy may pretend to be more rarefied, but I say they are nothing extraordinary and not one franc more refined—I, at least, don't remember anything particularly sanctified about the bishop. If anything, he was more single-minded than most."

Cathryn put her hand over her mouth and laughed out loud. If Comtesse Dansette had any morals, she, at least, had no inhibitions.

"That's better!" Teresa laughed, too.

"I cannot believe you have no feeling of guilt and are so frank in your contempt for the Church."

"In some ways the Church is nothing more than another powerful political entity, but for some unfathomable reason her aristocracy has chosen to deny their manhood—perhaps to appear more noble in their pursuit of power."

Cathryn shook her head at her companion. "You are the most remarkable woman I shall ever meet, I'm sure."

"I agree." She smiled. "Now, tell me all about your lover. I feel certain *he* was extraordinary."

"But I've never talked about him to anyone."

"No one? I gather, then, he did not acknowledge you."

Cathryn shook her head. "Our affair was mostly secret."

Cathryn's answer intrigued Teresa. "Mostly?"

"My lover appealed to his brothers to take me in, until he could arrange to leave the Church."

"And?"

"They renounced him and called me a whore." Cathryn's face turned scarlet with the memory of her shame, unable to tell the countess that Piero had called her much worse.

"Saints themselves, I'm sure," Comtesse Dansette sympathized. "How is it men have different standards for themselves than they do for us?"

Cathryn had no reply.

"I'm sure your lover was hopelessly seductive and manipulated you, sweet girl, for his own desires. You mustn't take the brothers' accusations so to heart. And to feel guilty is a waste of precious energy.

"Now, enough of men. Play something delicious for me. Let me imagine I am in the countryside with my young lover Francois. . . ." Comtesse Dansette lay back against her pillows and closed her eyes.

For several moments, Cathryn could only stare at her companion, unable to believe the woman's complete acceptance of the fact that Cathryn had seduced a priest. Perdita would have reacted rather differently. Cathryn winced. She was glad she was in the countess's presence and *not* Perdita's, and could not help but wonder how many other people in the world were so completely at ease with sin—with simply being human, as no doubt the countess would have said.

Chapter 24

"It is a good thing I am here to chaperone you, or I fear our capitano should have molested you by now."

Despite the countess's warning, Cathryn regarded the captain as a guardian for her journey from her home to a land and life unknown. She felt Comtesse Dansette took her situation as, in effect, her chaperone too seriously, though unconsciously Cathryn began to regard Capitano Salvadori somewhat warily. In general she found him kind and solicitous of her comfort aboard his less than splendid ship, judging he was close to forty years of age—an almost elderly man in Cathryn's view—and due her respect. She read empathy or admiration into his remarks where the more experienced countess suspected his real intentions.

While Teresa watched over her young companion, Cathryn worried only about controlling the sound of her violin, often so occupied with pained remembrances that she did not seem even to see the captain or hear his praise. Her concentration was limited to her music, to the compositions Vittorio had written under her inspiration.

She had memorized the notes and their inflections when first she heard them, for they were songs composed by one heart to be instantly recorded by the other. They were indelible, as much a part of Cathryn as the marrow of her bones, and when she played Vittorio's music, its passion was unmistakable.

Though untutored, Giuseppe Salvadori was not deaf, but it was not only the music that stirred him. Cathryn Godwyne intrigued and enraptured him. Never before had he known a woman like her. He was hopelessly besotted and often further intoxicated with malmsey. His elemental desires were raw with neglect.

He despaired of Comtesse Dansette's presence, and after supper one night when the countess took to her bed ill, despite the comtesse's discouragement, Cathryn lingered as usual to play her violin. "I won't be long," she promised Teresa. "Tonight I'm as much in need of music as the captain."

Her music was especially breathtaking. First came shimmering light passages that made the captain hold his breath; then the notes sang with pathos and turned his emotions dark. When Cathryn finally put her violin down, Capitano Salvadori took her hand in his. "You have enchanted me with your music, Mistress Godwyne. I am under your spell, quite bewitched," he said, and lifted her delicate hand to his lips.

Teresa's warnings sounding in her ears, Cathryn pulled her hand away, his choice of words offending her especially. "I do not have the power you suggest."

"Signorina, you are very wrong. In your presence I am reduced to a quivering youth, willing to do whatever you bid." He reached for her and pulled her against him. "But I am a man at the height of my powers," he said, and crushed her to him, seizing her mouth.

Stunned, Cathryn froze, Giuseppe's harsh wet kiss almost suffocating her. She suffered for air and began to struggle fiercely, the mildly unattractive man suddenly gross and ugly in her sight.

Built like a slab of marble, Giuseppe Salvadori's small stature was no advantage to Cathryn, but as she struggled, he suddenly let her go. "You seduce me every evening with your songs, *cara*, then leave me to suffer your absence. I'm no student of music, but I listen with great care, and I know of your deep passion."

"How dare you call me *cara*! How dare you touch me!" she hissed. "You've heard more than there is to hear!" Cathryn grabbed her violin and fled the captain's cabin, only feeling safe when she bolted her cabin door.

The lamp still lit, but already asleep, Comtesse Dansette awakened at the slamming of the bolt. "What has happened?" she demanded at the sight of Cathryn's obvious distress.

"You were correct about Capitano Salvadori, Comtesse." Cathryn shuddered. She wiped her mouth with the back of her hand, hoping to remove the lingering stain of his kiss. "He accuses me of being an enchantress, a bewitcher of men, and perhaps I am—I have been accused before of such evil."

Teresa Dansette guffawed and sat up. "You have lived too long with priests and old women, *cherie*. An appetite is about all a man needs to be encouraged and all men are born with hearty appetites.'' The countess smiled at Cathryn. "A woman needn't be a *sorcière,* or even half as beautiful as you are to have a man panting after her!"

"The Church calls it lust."

"'Which is in women insatiable.' I have heard that rot before, Cathryn. Because a woman can favor any number of men, while a man must spend some time recovering, does that make her insatiable? *Merde.*"

Cathryn wondered how long she would have to know Comtesse Dansette before she would not be shocked by her candor.

"As usual, my frankness startles you. Well, I would rather shock you than have you suffer from such idiocy."

"Is there any point on which you and the Church concur, Comtesse?"

"Not much, I imagine," she answered with a wry smile. "Please, if we are to be up, pour me some brandy to wash away the unpleasant taste in my mouth."

"I'm sorry. I quite forgot you were ill."

"I'm better now. I added some curing powder—which I obtained from a true sorceress—to my wine. I was promised, added to wine, the powder should cure almost any ailment—including the plague. Unfortunately, it tastes like dog dung—a not unlikely ingredient." She drank the swallow of brandy Cathryn offered. "A little more, please," she coaxed.

Cathryn complied. "Now, Cathryn, pour yourself a dose of this very excellent brandy. It shall help remove your unpleasant memory of the captain—but don't take so much that you forget entirely. Then next time you shall heed my warnings."

Gladly, Cathryn poured herself some of the countess's brandy, relieved to be in Teresa Dansette's protective company, her agitation diminishing as the moments passed.

"When I first set eyes on you, Cathryn, I knew you suffered from your upbringing in that convent."

"It wasn't a convent."

"Well, it might as well have been. You were cut off from the world with no experiences to counter the harsh teachings of addled priests and women with no interest in men. Now don't interrupt me," she cautioned.

"I am thoroughly alarmed by some of the things you say. You believe our wine-bloated captain when he says you bewitched him, and I'll wager all the remaining francs in my possession that your priest blamed you for his passions, twisting all that happened to make *you* guilty of *his* sins.''

Cathryn lowered her eyes in confirmation.

''Because a woman is tender and merciful, she is wicked. Don't you ever wonder, Cathryn, what sickness besets the men of the Church and makes them twist something good into something vile?''

''But Eve . . .''

''*Merde*. The first woman corrupted the first man and made him fall from grace. Don't you suppose it was a man who first invented that fable? It bores me—and suggests that men have not much more brains in their heads than beasts of burden—than asses, shall we say.''

A vision of a gallery of dark-robed churchmen turning scarlet at the comtesse's inquisition filled Cathryn's head, yet she could not suppress a smile over her companion's reasoning. ''I fear you could be accused of being a heretic or worse, Comtesse.''

''As a rule, I am discreet enough not to be burned at the stake.'' Teresa smiled at Cathryn. ''But I am enraged that women are persecuted for responding as they should to the nature of men. It is not just! It is madness!''

The countess grinned, then sighed. ''My husband thinks I am possessed—though he is not a religious man. He humors me, and for safety's sake, sends me to Venice to visit my sister for years at a time. He indulges his appetites quite freely while I am gone, and I doubt he accuses his mistresses of using Witchcraft to seduce him.''

Teresa Dansette continued to watch Cathryn as a silence grew between them. She extended her cup and Cathryn filled it with brandy.

''I suppose, Signorina Godwyne, that you also believe that a woman is no better than a bag of filth.''

''Our bodies are sometimes foul.''

''More so than a man's?''

Cathryn shrugged. ''I do not know much of men.''

''Well, I can assure you, as a rule, they are no better than we are.''

''But we bleed.''

''For their purposes. Is it not cruel and a little insane for them to damn us?''

Cathryn closed her eyes and took a deep breath. The upsetting events of the night, the brandy, and the countess's challenging conversation whirled in Cathryn's head.

Comtesse Dansette did not really expect an answer from the young woman who sat beside her. It had taken a lifetime of experience to hone her own philosophy that countered so dramatically with the prevailing notions of the time. A girl raised and sheltered as Cathryn had been, she realized, could only think a woman like herself quite mad—if not a heretical Witch.

Teresa Dansette sipped her brandy, glad for the rare opportunity to air her beliefs for someone to hear. She had recorded some of the ideas she had just expressed to Cathryn in her diaries, but it would take a more enlightened age, she knew, before such divergent opinions could be freely exchanged, especially by a woman. She would have to suffer silence and occasional banishment by a bewildered husband, but she consoled herself that eventually her ideas could not help but have their day.

Chapter 25

For several days following Capitano Salvadori's assault on Cathryn, the women dined alone in the captain's cabin, exchanging knowing glances when they were told the captain was too busy on deck to join them.

After a few days of absence from his own table, Capitano Salvadori joined the women again. "Please forgive me, signorina. I blame my behavior on your enchanting music and the Devil's brew."

"Blame your very nature instead, Capitano," interrupted Comtesse Dansette. "Regardless, until we dock in England, I shall not be letting Signorina Godwyne out of my sight."

Aware that soon she would abandon if not discard her instrument, an admission that brought Cathryn to the point of tears, she continued to practice and played her violin for the comtesse and the captain every night.

She concentrated on the tone of the beautiful Amati; on perfecting the notes of the last songs Vittorio wrote for her; on passages that reminded her of the passionate priest.

His music was very like his lovemaking—vigorous and emotional, with an incessant rhythm—at times driven and consumed by passion; at other moments overwhelming with its tenderness. She heard his music and knew he had given and wanted love.

Cathryn put the violin down. Perhaps it was best that soon she would be forced to give up her music, for playing Vittorio's songs only stirred her memory of love and made her forget that in the end her lover had betrayed her. Vittorio covered his body with his cassock and freed himself of guilt. "*Strega bella*," he breathed and, so saying, absolved himself of culpability.

Cathryn began to feel rather like a prisoner aboard *Il Vento*, which did not, as its name implied, travel at any noteworthy speed. The wind, too, Cathryn assumed, must not be in her favor.

Nor she in God's; she sighed, feeling remorse in spite of her frequent exposure to Comtesse Dansette's very liberal views.

The countess chided Cathryn for her guilt whenever she saw the young woman looking sad. "There shall be many lovers for one as charming as you, my dear Cathryn." But unlike Teresa Dansette, who had enjoyed many lovers in her life, Cathryn had no desire for another man. If love brought such misery as she now experienced, Cathryn reasoned, she would gladly do without.

At last, as Capitano Salvadori had promised, the coast of England was a night away, and on the final night aboard *Il Vento*, Cathryn lay awake, excited to think that in the morning the Venetian merchant would anchor at Ipswich, her English destination.

In the darkness, Cathryn forced away stray tears with stern resolve. Though everything she had heard about England and her people disenchanted Cathryn, she told herself nothing but misery and heartache lay behind in Venice.

Cathryn remembered that her English benefactor, Lord Ashley Godwyne, as portrayed by Perdita and Bianca Fabiani, had been a charitable man. He had found it in his heart to support an orphan, and she hoped he possessed a largesse of mind as well as spirit.

But what of her guardian, Master Gerald Seymour? Did he also hold sympathy for orphans? In his view, Cathryn knew she might be considered no better than a servant, and a foreign one at that. Foreigners might be curious and intriguing, but always they were held inferior, just as a commoner forever would be regarded a lesser form of humanity than someone of royal blood.

About to be thrust into a strange and Protestant world about which she knew little more than frightening tales, Cathryn turned the tables in self-defense and declared England foreign.

The violence of the country's history was unremarkable enough in an age of often sudden, if not bloody, death, but at the very least England's history was confusing to Cathryn. Venice was a republic with a doge elected for a lifetime, while England boasted a monarch who claimed divine right to rule. Yet the succession of kings did not seem a very stable order, and while there might be strife in connection with the election of the Venetian doge, it did not compare with England's struggle to enthrone a king. As Comtesse Dansette informed Cathryn, after beheading Charles the First and more than a decade of experiment with a government without a king, the English restored a Stuart king to power. But bliss did not arrive with the restoration of Charles the Second, nor did it follow with James the Second.

The lawful and established Church of England was Protestant, Cathryn was reminded, yet the current king, James the Second, was a professed Roman Catholic who, upon ascending to the English throne, had promised to abide by the laws that supported the Protestant Anglican church. At first, he had done as he promised, Cathryn learned, and in fact, in many an instance James was championed by the established Church.

But at the height of his power, Comtesse Dansette assumed, James the Second had second thoughts about his course of action and began to violate the laws he had given his oath to uphold. This change of conscience served only to inflame the English hatred of Roman Catholics. By breaking his oath, James did as the English feared all Catholics did, and soon, most Englishmen believed, by the pope's demand, James the Second would convert the nation to the Roman faith.

His Royal Majesty King James promoted unqualified persons; demanded a standing army and the necessary staggering support which required additional amounts and forms of taxes; resolved to abolish the Habeas Corpus Act; and, most damning, announced his intention to appoint whomever he pleased to office, ignoring a law that excluded all who dissented from the established Church of England from civil and military office.

Furthermore, James's second wife, Mary Beatrice of Modena, was a Catholic of exceptional devotion. Perhaps more dangerous from the English point of view, one of the king's most favored advisers, Edward Petre, was a loathsome Jesuit priest. In Comtesse Dansette's opinion these two facts only served to fuel the average Englishman's belief that James's ultimate goal was to restore the Roman Catholic church and the devastating power of the pope to England. Since the English believed with no uncertainty that a Roman Catholic would forsake all morality and do whatever he was told by the pope, whose foremost ambition was to increase the power and influence of his holy empire, the comtesse warned Cathryn she would be ill advised to cling to the Roman faith.

Cathryn knew that Master Seymour was a Puritan. To her this meant that he was a heretic and, by definition, possessed, or at minimum a little demented, regardless of the politics involved. But not only did Puritans dissent from the Roman Catholic tradition, they had mighty quarrels with the established church. It meant her guardian was at odds with, and was perhaps an enemy of, the Crown.

By order of her benefactor, Cathryn was not supposed to have been raised a Catholic, because the plan always had been for her to be sent to live in England, but for the sake of her soul, the Fabiani sisters had ignored Lord Godwyne's demand.

Lifelong warnings from her childhood guardians had prepared Cathryn for the fate of never being able to practice her religion in the open, but now Cathryn worried on an even more simple level. How, she wondered, would she manage in so hostile a world? To the simple dread of facing a new and foreign homeland was added a knot of fear for her very life.

In Venice she had been forced to choose between a man of God and God himself. In England she would face choosing a Protestant God or a Roman Catholic God. As inconceivable as it seemed to her by her own recent challenges to faith, perhaps she, along with thousands of others, would be called upon to die for the true, the Catholic, religion.

Cathryn shivered and the chill penetrated to the bone, but when the morning finally came, the cold became a welcome distraction as Cathryn began her final preparations for disembarking from *Il Vento*.

At the moment, above all else, she wanted to be warm.

From her trunk, Cathryn chose her warmest dress. Next she selected her heaviest cape, which though deep black wool possessed a scarlet satin lining. Without thinking, Cathryn opened the cloak and lifted the soft lining to her cheek, in an instant recalling a night spent with Vittorio when the shimmering satin rubbed soothingly against her flesh while it cushioned her beneath him. In the heat of passion, a touch of its cool surface felt welcome, but, she remembered now, it had fast warmed with the fire of the lovers' embrace.

Cathryn tossed the cloak onto her bunk. "One day, I *shall* forget," she promised herself, and tried to deny the sensations that rushed over her: the tingling of her skin, the swell of desire for Vittorio's adoring presence, his touch, his breathtaking kiss.

A tremor of passion passed through her. "I *will* forget!" she swore again, and slammed and latched the trunk. One day, she vowed, she might even come to truly hate him.

But could she? And even if her mind lost its memory, would her body ever forget?

And what were dreams that when waking left her reeling with delicious sensation, her soft cries of pleasure echoing in her ears, her body flooded with a glory of its own, convinced she lay rapturous in Vittorio's arms? Perhaps her dreams were his, traveling on the wings of night.

In Venice, they often had shared their dreams to discover that though they had been separate in body, in soul they had not been far apart. The dreams of one were filled with the presence of the other; with the same desire and passion.

With all her heart, Cathryn wanted to believe Vittorio someday would find a way to be with her, but not merely in his dreams. Then she would wake to find him truly joined with her, breathing helpless sighs of his own, and she would clutch something more delightful than an empty sheet.

Cathryn clenched her fists in resolution and forced herself to be rational. She would give up fantasy and this day in England, she would begin a new life free of memory.

Chapter 26

Waiting at the dock when Il Vento *arrived at Ipswich, county of* Suffolk, on the tidal estuary of the river Orwell, was a woman of small yet overall substantial size. She gave the initial impression of being all of the same color and would have blended into the gray horizon but for her glinting stare of disapproval.

The quaymaster boarded the ship and introduced Mistress Bridget Seymour to the captain, but she barely acknowledged him and completely ignored Comtesse Dansette's presence. Instead, her eyes were fixed on the young woman standing nearby, her cold gaze making Cathryn feel unwelcome.

Mistress Seymour disengaged her eyes from Cathryn only long enough to hand Capitano Salvadori an envelope. For a moment it seemed that Giuseppe might refuse the proferred item, but he pocketed the envelope, turning to introduce Cathryn. "Your guardian's sister, Mistress Bridget Seymour."

Cathryn hardly replied before Mistress Seymour instructed the captain to have Cathryn's baggage lowered at once to the dock. " 'Twill be a long journey to my brother's home. Good day," she dismissed him, and turned her back without another word, expecting Cathryn to follow obediently.

Cathryn's face betrayed her uncertainty, and Capitano Salvadori stepped forward to take her arm. "For once I regret a prompt arrival. May the Holy Virgin protect you," he whispered, kissing her hand. Giuseppe then led the way to the wharf below and handed Cathryn into a wagon that was little better than a cart.

A sense of dread overwhelmed Cathryn as she left the captain's protection. She sat upon her trunk feeling completely daunted by the prospects of her journey.

"*Addìo*," Capitano Salvadori called, and Comtesse Dansette blew a kiss. Cathryn replied with an apprehensive smile, finding it difficult to keep her tears at bay, but as the cart lurched into sudden motion, she occupied herself with keeping her seat.

She sat facing the driver's back, her knees almost touching Mistress Seymour's, her eyes square with those of the older woman. She tried to ignore her hostile stares and attended to the details of the crowded seaport town, noting in particular the towering church spires and numerous gabled houses built of a mixture of straw and twigs and whitewashed clay. Located on the left bank of the river Gipping in the eastern part of Suffolk County, Ipswich was well wooded, its streets irregular.

"The road worsens," Bridget warned as Cathryn was almost jolted from the cart.

Cathryn could not imagine worse conditions. How far she had come from Venice and its graceful gondolas!

"Be glad it isn't raining." Holding on for dear life with one hand, Mistress Seymour motioned to the rutted and sometimes mired dirt road as they traveled out of town.

Cathryn decided she was grateful for the dry weather as the two passengers were almost pitched out of the cart on more than one occasion. "How far do we have to travel?" she wondered after an hour had passed.

"We cannot journey after dark, and, with God's indulgence, we should arrive by then. My brother should have come for you, but at present, he is ill, and still needs nursing. God be praised, it doesn't seem to be plague."

The suggestion of plague, the most dreaded of the world's diseases, startled Cathryn.

"But we would accept God's will if it were," Bridget added, "and strive to discover His purpose; to learn the lessons of His perfect logic."

Thus began Cathryn's Puritan indoctrination.

As they continued their journey together, Bridget scrutinized Cathryn. Never had she been more carefully or more obviously observed. Her appearance did not meet with Mistress Seymour's approval. There was a rich and luxurious quality of fabric and of color that was lacking in the older woman's clothing, and the scarlet satin lining of Cathryn's cloak was especially offensive. Whenever a portion of the lining flashed into view during the jolting ride, Bridget's frown deepened.

"I should warn you, no popery shall be tolerated under our roof. My brother does not for a minute believe that you were raised outside the Roman church, coming as you do from a Catholic state."

Cathryn bristled under Bridget's glare. "Your sovereign is a Catholic, is he not, as are many of his closest advisers?"

Mistress Seymour nodded in assent, stopping herself just short of uttering an opinion tantamount to treason concerning the lawful king. "But that does not give you leave to practice your wolfish faith in my brother's house," she warned. "The law forbids Catholics to worship in public."

The older woman smiled in spite of her expectation that the young woman would be difficult. One look at Cathryn Godwyne revealed that she was stubborn and strong-willed. "However, in time, with suitable example, I am confident that you shall renounce your mistaken beliefs. We shall guide you to enlightenment and grace."

Bridget motioned to Cathryn's trunk and the case containing the violin. "You have brought a great deal with you. Have you no suitable clothing?"

"Am I not properly dressed?"

"We do not believe in ostentation of any kind."

With the exception of the lining of her cloak, Cathryn did not consider her dark garments remarkable. "You shall have to judge my wardrobe for yourself."

"For instance, the buttons on your bodice. They seem to be jewels."

"You are mistaken. They're not jewels."

"Nonetheless, they distract the eye. Such ornaments take the mind from God."

Cathryn ground her teeth. This was a worse beginning than she could have imagined, and she suspected that regardless of the circumstances, she would never be suitable in Mistress Seymour's eyes.

"I warned Gerald about bringing you here. Someone to supervise his children should be found amongst our own. I do not comprehend his pact with our half brother, Lord Godwyne. It seems irrational to me." She heaved a great sigh. "Since the Lord took my brother's good wife Phoebe, Gerald sometimes seems quite unsettled in his reasoning."

Bridget lapsed into silence leaving Cathryn to meditate alone. The particulars of her situation in England had not been given. She knew nothing beyond the explanation that her benefactor, Lord Godwyne, had arranged for a guardian for her upon his death, and that he had provided that she come to England to make her way in the world as befitted her unusual degree of education.

Cathryn wondered if her guardian would keep her in his household or send her out. She feared that there would not be many places she would be welcome. The best she could hope for was a position with the children of the gentry, with some responsibility for their education, but with the taint of her Roman Catholic religion hanging over her head, Cathryn feared she would be judged unsuitable in most households.

How much influence did Bridget Seymour have upon her brother? Cathryn wondered. From the depths of her sighs, perhaps not as much as the woman wished.

Daydreaming, Cathryn began to imagine herself forced to be a common servant, destroying the sensitivity of her musical fingers by scouring pots; being reduced to all manner of unpleasant tasks. In an unconscious gesture, Cathryn placed her hand on the case containing her Amati, a movement that caught Mistress Seymour's eye. "What do you have there?" she probed.

"A violin. I have played ever since I can remember."

"You should have left it behind."

Cathryn could not ignore the pleasure she saw in Mistress Seymour's face at her pronouncement. "Surely you glorify God with music?"

"We use no devices but our God-given voices to praise God," exclaimed Mistress Seymour. This young woman was even more corrupt than she had feared.

Bridget watched Cathryn grow wary and silent, and comforted herself that she was not deceived. Cathryn Godwyne, Bridget judged, was as steeped in sinful ways as she was beautiful.

What a curse to be born beautiful, Bridget reaffirmed in silent appraisal, but the burden of physical beauty God had given Cathryn was for a purpose, Bridget knew. Pleased by her remarkable perception of Cathryn's unwholesome nature, Mistress Seymour welcomed the challenge of bringing Cathryn to renounce her evil ways. Perhaps she might be converted to the Puritan ideal after all.

Yet Bridget had strong doubts about the prospect of saving Cathryn's soul. Of what Bridget had seen thus far in the young woman's countenance and bearing, there was nothing to suggest that she would ever share God's grace or be invited to enter the kingdom of heaven.

Chapter 27

The market town of Wollingham was ten miles northeast of Ipswich along the river Tar, and the Godwyne estate lay three miles beyond in a heavily wooded section due east. As they approached Wollingham, the rolling, forested hills at times gave way to open heaths where herds of sheep and cattle grazed.

Hoping to arrive before dark, Cathryn and her escort traveled at a steady pace all day making no stops. The roads were too terrible for nighttime journeys and even more perilous than in the day because of thieves.

Had the ride not been interspersed with unpredictable jolts and jars as the wheels of the cart revolved into holes and ruts, Cathryn would have fallen asleep from exhaustion as the afternoon advanced. Her companion looked equally fatigued and, to Cathryn's amazement, even dozed off from time to time.

At dusk, the cart turned down a narrow lane shaded by a dense stand of enormous trees. For several minutes they traveled on a path remarkable for its smoothness, in light so sparse that it could have been deepest night. Cathryn felt certain the giant shaggy cart horse plodded only from memory.

At last they departed the lane and entered a wide clearing, and Cathryn could not help but gasp at the sight beyond the trees. There, towering before them, stood the gutted remains of a great stone house, which covered the space of at least half an acre. The skeletal E shape of the structure was black from smoke and broken, the turrets and bays battered and deformed.

Cathryn remembered that Lord Ashley Godwyne had died as the result of a fire that had destroyed his house, but until now, she had considered the event on a small scale, and not in proportion to the grand house that lay before her in ruin.

The driver did not stop for her to gawk as Cathryn would have liked, but continued, making a wide half circle around one side of the still imposing structure, then entered another sheltered lane.

This passageway was shaded also, but by comparison to the first there was considerable light. Yet, not until the cart shuddered to a halt and the exhausted horse faltered did Cathryn see the woman who darted out to grab the horse's harness.

The driver had not uttered one word throughout the trip, but startled, and as frightened as his horse, straining to keep the animal from trampling the woman where she stood, he shouted, "Be ye the Devil or be ye mad?" at the small figure. Then he sat back, seeming unsure, as before them stood a grotesquely disfigured but strangely commanding woman of indeterminable age.

Without thinking, Cathryn made the sign of the cross, her eyes wide. Busy trying to steady herself, her companion did not see the gesture as she turned around to discover the reason for so abrupt a halt. Cathryn expected her to make some remark or take a stand, but instead Bridget Seymour composed herself and turned to face Cathryn again. Silence fell over the scene as the stranger released the animal and walked toward Cathryn.

For what seemed an eternity, the woman stared at Cathryn, and, helpless, Cathryn stared back, repelled but fascinated, her eyes drawn to the scar that disfigured the right side of the woman's face.

The scar was the shape of an inverted cross, the short arm of which traversed the jawline, the longer arm traveling past and engulfing the eye. The remaining skin on her face seemed perfect, clear and smooth, and if it had not been for the mass of her disheveled white hair, which fell down her back almost the length of the black, ground-skimming cloak she wore, Cathryn would have guessed the woman still to be quite young.

The woman's good eye was bright and an intelligent light shone from it as she observed Cathryn. She did not speak nor give any other sign, but it was clear she was neither the Devil nor mad, as the driver had feared. When she had a long look at Cathryn, she stepped back and waved the driver on.

When the driver started up again, and the woman could no longer be seen in the dim light, Bridget found her tongue, all but hissing as she spoke. "She should be banished! It escapes me why Gerald, against my counsel, continues to tolerate that evil woman's presence on his property."

"Who is she?"

"More than a nuisance, I fear," Mistress Seymour snapped, refusing to elaborate.

Cathryn had little time to dwell on the woman as the Seymour house came into view. The house, a large two-story brick structure, seemed to be of very modest proportions in contrast to the charred behemoth that lay behind them, but it looked to have been built by an able mason. It was constructed all at once, Cathryn guessed, since it lacked obvious additions and the roof was straight. In addition there were several outbuildings a short distance away that, in the dark, were now almost invisible.

As the cart lumbered to a halt, three children slipped past the entry door and, in silence, huddled together in the lantern light, observing Mistress Seymour's and, especially, Cathryn's arrival.

Cathryn was as curious about the children as they were about her, but when she smiled at them, they let their gazes fall.

All at once, Cathryn felt more tired and hungry than curious, and she followed Mistress Seymour, the children, and a servant with the lantern into the house without a word.

"Father is asleep, but he is improved today," the oldest, a boy, offered.

"Prudence is feverish and in bed without supper," said the oldest of the two girls present.

If she was concerned, Mistress Seymour did not show it, wishing to have the introduction of Cathryn to the household concluded as soon as possible. "Children, this is Cathryn Godwyne. She is here to help me look after you. She comes from a Catholic country, but we shall endeavor to sway her from her pagan beliefs and enlighten her, so that she may come into the perfect grace of God. We presume she is capable of caring for your more worldly needs and shall teach you at least a few useful things."

Beginning with the eldest child, Cathryn met Jacob, who informed her he was a manly eight years of age. He was dressed like the others, in sober gray wool, in a style that imitated adult Puritan dress. His hair, a medium brown, was cropped below his ears. The pupils of his eyes, a lively bright blue, were set incongruously in a dull, expressionless face.

Comfort, the eldest girl, was seven. "You'll sleep in my bed," she announced as pink splotches of embarrassment suffused her cheeks. She began to fidget with the dark blond braids that were wound tightly around her head.

"Why is your hair not covered?" Bridget demanded.

Comfort turned scarlet and without answering fled upstairs.

Bridget sighed. "I warn you, she is very willful," she counseled Cathryn, who felt immediate sympathy for the child.

"And this is Diligence. She's five and as steady as her name." Bridget gave a genuine smile that touched the whole of her face and surprised Cathryn, who had begun to think the simple feat impossible. Regarding the child with suspicion, Cathryn wondered how unpleasant Diligence had to be to win her aunt's obvious approval. The child, in turn, gave Cathryn a sour look.

"Prudence, as you know, is not well. We should look in on her, and afterwards have supper to revive our spirits." Prudence, Cathryn learned, had just turned three and had not been weaned when her mother, Phoebe, had died delivering a stillborn baby.

In all, there had been seven children born to Phoebe and Gerald Seymour in as many years, but only four survived, the loss of almost half their brood taking its toll on both husband and wife. According to Puritan belief, the death of a child was one of God's methods of punishing sinfulness, but even at their first meeting, Cathryn wondered if survival in the Seymour house was greater punishment than death.

Chapter 28

Cathryn was led upstairs to the children's bedchamber, a room of modest size, severe but clean, accommodating two low, wide beds and a large cradle. Between the beds and cradle were candle stands, and at the end of each bed leather trunks for storage. There was also a large, unadorned wooden cupboard, which was full of the children's belongings. For the time being Cathryn was forced to rely on her own trunk for storage. The only comforting concession of the room's utilitarian decor was a small mother's rocking chair that was provided with a turkey wool work cushion.

Once in the bedchamber, Mistress Seymour displayed more obvious concern for her youngest niece's condition than she had at first. She stooped over the cradle to feel the temperature of the child's body, noting her pallor and overly bright eyes. Bridget's mouth became set with a grim tightness.

"She's refused the barley milk all afternoon," Comfort told her aunt.

"Then she must be forced," she said, and lifted Prudence, handing her to Cathryn.

Prudence's lassitude turned to loud protests when Cathryn took her in her arms.

"This will be a good introduction to your duties in my brother's household," Bridget said. "Make the child take the barley milk, while I see to my brother's condition," she ordered.

Cathryn was nothing short of terrified. She had little more than her own limited experience with illness on which to draw, and Prudence's strident shrieks gave her no confidence at all.

Stiff with uncertainty and appalled by the heat radiating from the baby's small body, she instinctively began to pace the room under Comfort's watchful eye. Cathryn held the unhappy child to her breast and felt her own body temperature gradually begin to rise.

After several minutes, unable to console the crying child, Cathryn sat down in the armless wooden rocker. Miraculously, Prudence quieted and Cathryn relaxed a little herself, settling on a slow but steady rhythm of rocking.

Comfort held out the cup of barley milk to Cathryn. "She's very parched."

"I've no doubt you know more about this than I do," Cathryn lamented, taking the proferred cup and raising it to Prudence's lips. The frail weight of the quiet child in her arms did nothing to reassure Cathryn.

Prudence objected, turning her mouth away, and began to wriggle, causing Cathryn to almost drop her. The milk sloshed in the cup, splashing both nurse and baby with the stale-smelling liquid.

Comfort saved the cup from falling on the floor while Cathryn righted herself and Prudence. She took a deep breath and tried again. This time, if only from exhaustion, Prudence did not resist. With extreme patience, over what seemed an eternity in time, Cathryn fed the child, then rocked her to sleep.

Prudence felt no cooler to Cathryn when she laid her down, and for several minutes she stood above the cradle and watched her. For the first time in a long while, Cathryn worried not what her own fate would be. Suddenly she had someone else, something more than herself to occupy her mind, and it was an odd relief.

Cathryn realized she would have responsibilities for the Seymour children for which she was ill prepared. And doubtless the blame, in the event something went wrong. Her thoughts were interrupted by Jacob, who came upstairs to announce, "Supper is waiting."

Obeying the summons, Cathryn joined the children and their aunt for the evening meal. A long prayer given by Bridget introduced a supper of cold lamb, bread, and cheese. Everyone but Diligence drank a warm ale with the food. Diligence had milk, which explained the child's chronic pained expression, Cathryn thought, and smiled.

"What amuses you, Cathryn Godwyne?" Bridget demanded, interrupting the heretofore silent meal.

Cathryn was startled. "Am I forbidden to smile?"

"Disrespect to elders sets a bad example for my brother's children," Bridget snapped.

"I didn't realize that asking a question was disrespectful. In fact, I have been told that questioning, or examining, is a vital part of Puritan faith."

Bridget glowered at Cathryn, and the children watched their exchange with intense interest.

"Much you have learned that will need to be amended. Firstly, in addition to unlearning your Catholic ways, remember, in this house, you are little better than a servant. Your talent for papist music is of no import."

All eyes now focused on her, Cathryn felt her stomach knot, aware of how effectively she had been put in her place.

"My brother asks me to welcome you," Bridget added, leaving no doubt in anyone's mind that she did so with reluctance.

"I have no wish to influence the children to be disrespectful," Cathryn replied, vowing that she would never knowingly do anything that would cause the Seymour children to receive their elders' disapprobation. As she looked into the children's faces, however, she realized that it would be a difficult promise to keep and wondered if there was any hope that they would ever achieve friendly terms.

As Cathryn had expected, there was a definite chill in the air in Wollingham, and the children, who regarded Cathryn with cool stares, gave her little hope that there would ever be much warmth in which to bask.

Chapter 29

*Soon after Cathryn retired on the first night, Prudence's breath-*ing grew labored and she could breathe with ease only if held or propped upright. As the children's nurse, Cathryn was elected to provide whatever was needed for Prudence's benefit, at once becoming familiar with the contours and creaks of the wooden mother's rocker.

To Cathryn's surprise the young child seemed to be soothed easily enough, but she cried and fretted whenever Cathryn tried to put her down. At last, when from exhaustion Cathryn could not pace the room or sit and rock another moment, she lay in the bed next to Comfort, propped with pillows behind her head. For the remainder of the night, the baby lay very heavy upon Cathryn's chest.

The next morning Cathryn ached all over. Her arms were leaden from holding Prudence and what would be a very demanding day had just begun. The other children were slow to rise, and were soon in bed again as fever forced them down one by one. Throughout the day, no one but Cathryn had an appetite and she ate her meals hurriedly from a tray brought to the nursery, scarcely leaving the children's sight.

A vat of vinegar was boiled in the wide fireplace downstairs and carried upstairs to purify the air. The wooden floors were scrubbed and the small windows in the room latched tight to prevent any bad air from circulating. The children's chests and foreheads were slathered with a vile-smelling unguent that made Cathryn's eyes water and discouraged the remnants of her appetite.

She still had a thirst and comforted herself from time to time with sips of warm hyssop tea, the drink meant to cure fever, brought upstairs for the children's benefit. "You should drink this, also," Mistress Seymour suggested in a solicitous voice that took Cathryn by surprise. "It is good for the ague, and perhaps it will help you keep your vigor."

The only relief she had was late in the morning when Bridget summoned her downstairs, sending a servant to the children's bedside. "You will have other duties here besides looking to the children," she stressed, as if their care thus far had allowed Cathryn an idle moment.

Bridget led Cathryn to a plot of land near the house on which grew an unimpressive collection of vegetables and herbs. "Seeing to the kitchen garden is your duty. The children will help. And the chickens will also be your worry, as will their enemies: the foxes, skunks, and weasels, who poach a goodly number. And I'll be glad to have you do the children's sewing. You have the skill, don't you?"

Cathryn shook her head.

Bridget frowned and sighed. Whatever made Gerald think this Roman Catholic would be a helping hand escaped her. "Did you not learn one useful thing in Venice? I suppose you don't know anything about caring for a garden, either."

"There was a garden on one of the sunny terraces at the palace. I often spent time working in it."

"The palace? It's no wonder you have airs!"

Cathryn started to deny the accusation but stopped, sensing nothing she could say would ever alter Mistress Seymour's opinions.

"The garden will require constant attention. And with all, as you can see, you'll have few spare moments. And those you do shall not be truly idle. Even my brother agrees no Roman Catholic shall lodge with us for long. You shall be required to study our faith in earnest. You shall forswear your faith soon enough."

Bridget's arrogance galled Cathryn, but she forced herself to bite back a scathing retort. In her new life in the Seymour home, there would be no escape from the campaign to save her soul, just as there had been no escape from her journey to England. Cathryn sighed. She supposed it was fitting punishment for all the joys she had taken for granted in her former life—the music, her friends, the Fabiani sisters, the affection of Father Vittorio. For too long, Cathryn knew, she had assumed she was entitled to the riches she enjoyed, and now she had to pay for the folly of ingratitude.

"I expected to help the children with their books," Cathryn said. "In that I have experience."

"That you'll do, in time—under my brother's close scrutiny, of course. The only purpose of the children's study is their enlightenment, the sole reason for life. They apply themselves to make their souls acceptable to God, which you cannot encourage until you have proven your own worthiness."

It was an immense relief to Cathryn to hear that Bridget would not be the one to supervise her in the matter of the children's education. She could not imagine anyone more difficult to please than Mistress Seymour. "About Master Seymour. Is his health improved?"

Bridget led the way back to the house. "God has spared him," she said. "I have reported your arrival. My brother is most curious to see you."

Cathryn feared Mistress Seymour's report had not been in her favor.

"He is most eager to assist in your conversion."

Trailing behind the older woman, Bridget did not see Cathryn flinch. At the moment Cathryn felt as if the survival of the Roman Catholic faith in England rested with her. Protestants were held to be devils by the Catholic faithful, and Cathryn trembled at the prospect of even an outward show of conversion to the dreaded Protestant camp.

She had been amply warned of the dangers of resistance. "It would be less dangerous if you were an infidel," Comtesse Dansette had warned her with a sigh.

"His Majesty King James encourages Catholic priests and followers to worship in the open, but I, for one, would not take his advice," Capitano Salvadori cautioned.

"No, Cathryn, open defiance would be utter stupidity. Pretend whatever is necessary. Your heart need not be changed. Play their foolish games, my dear," the countess had urged.

Both the captain and the countess had urged Cathryn to abjure her faith, like hundreds of others in rabidly Protestant England had, and though she listened to their well-meaning advice, she worried that God would misunderstand and see fit to punish her for being a faithless coward.

Cathryn now stared at Mistress Seymour's back, convinced the woman would know her ruse. It seemed to Cathryn that Bridget Seymour's penetrating gaze could easily slide beneath her bones and read the secrets of her heart. Cathryn did not for a moment doubt that Bridget would not hesitate to eavesdrop against the bedchamber door and overhear Cathryn whisper for God's blessing on King James the Second.

No matter what he had sworn, the English Protestants knew that if it was within his power, the Stuart king would have England Catholic once again. There was hardly an Englishman who did not believe that every Catholic was the puppet of the pope, imagining every Catholic eager and available to break all moral and civil laws for the purpose of uniting Christendom under Rome.

"James's loyalty to France's Catholic king does not serve him well, I fear," Comtesse Dansette had told Cathryn, and from her history lessons, Cathryn could understand the average Englishman's lack of ease. Over the centuries England had fought long and hard to win and preserve her independence from Catholic Europe.

Cathryn cared nothing about English politics, but, like the reigning king of England, she did care to survive, and as she followed Bridget Seymour into the house, she resigned herself to bending to the will of the Protestants. But, she vowed, they need never know the secrets of her heart.

Chapter 30

Cathryn had little rest in the first week at the Godwyne estate.
Prudence occupied most of her time, but the other children, who
one after the other went to bed with fever, also demanded her
attention. Soon it seemed the sound of someone coughing would
never cease. Cathryn swore she heard coughing even in her
dreams.

Except for the first night, Cathryn wore her daytime clothes to
bed, for to her utter disbelief, she discovered that caring for four
sick children took an unimaginable amount of time, enough that
she was often too exhausted to change into a nightdress.

On the first night Cathryn had a full night's sleep, both
Prudence and Comfort shared her bed, but she was far too
exhausted to care how many others crowded in beside her. She
was grateful only that the children at last slept through the night.

Cathryn woke the following morning when daylight filtered
through the nursery windows. She felt drugged and numb, and
for a long while dared not rise for fear of waking her slumbering
patients.

Though the children would lie in their beds for at least several
more days, everyone was definitely on the mend. Not so everyone in the Wollingham district, which Mistress Seymour reported at every opportunity. She remarked on every death well
within the children's hearing, which Cathryn regretted, for it
frightened them, provoked more coughing, and seemed to cause
their breathing to be more labored.

Mistress Seymour told Cathryn that she wanted her brother's
children to be prepared to meet their Creator and urged them,
especially in their illness, to pray without ceasing; to be ready
should God call for them to join Him.

"They're not baptized," the aunt informed Cathryn, "but are
by birthright members of the Puritan church, which thereby
makes them the select of God.

"At least if the Lord God calls any of these children to His side, they shall be free to go to Him. They are not cursed by holding to a pagan religion, such as you and our sovereign do."

Cathryn's face grew red with anger, but Mistress Seymour might have been blind for all the notice she took. Cathryn ached to contradict her but recalled her vow.

Life on earth was brief; the length of time uncertain; Cathryn quite understood the need to be ever ready to God's call. But listening to the children's aunt, she also wondered if one's stay on earth might be considerably shortened, certain she would have withered away by now if, like the children, she had been subjected to long years of Bridget Seymour's unloving care.

After her first night of full rest, Cathryn stole from under the bedcovers without disturbing either child who lay beside her. Silently and quickly she bathed and changed her clothes, then gathered her rosary and knelt to pray.

"Hear my prayers, I beseech You," she whispered, and wondered if God would listen to her knowing she intended to disavow her faith. "Do not despise me, and forgive me if I err. Grant me strength against my enemies," she began, and ended with a prayer for her charges. "Bless and preserve the children, though they are misguided in their faith. Heal their afflictions. Grant us wisdom to understand one another."

When her prayers were finished, she stood beside each sleeping child. Though their fevers might be gone, Cathryn did not expect them to look robust, for even before they'd fallen ill, they'd seemed a little parched and winced, almost starved. There was no obvious want of food, and upon reflection, Cathryn wondered if it was Bridget's influence that made the children fail to thrive. She remembered Bridget's garden. It, too, looked in want of proper care. Perhaps, Cathryn reasoned, it was the English soil or the English climate or, in the case of the Seymour children, the English temper.

In Cathryn's memory, the gardens and the orphans of Venice seemed to thrive compared to their English counterparts. Certainly the feeling at degli Innocenti was warmer than the chill of the Seymour house. But here, there was something else lacking, and though she was at a loss to name it, she sensed it in her heart.

While the children slept on, Cathryn stole downstairs to the buttery, ravenous after a good night's sleep. She hoped a hearty breakfast was in store and was not disappointed as a servant, Ruth, led Cathryn to the dining parlor and served a large meal of oatmeal porridge and cream, eggs, cold lamb, bread and butter. A bowl of sliced oranges was available to quench her thirst, and because there was sickness in the house, a pot of China tea.

Afterward, Cathryn would have loved to slip upstairs and into bed again, but instead, while the children slept on, she stole into the garden.

She discovered a good assortment of vegetables, pulling up a carrot and snipping a tender spinach leaf. There were beetroots, parsnips, beans, peas, lettuce, artichokes, and many others besides the usual collection of cooking and medicinal herbs. She crushed a bit of rosemary in her fingers and inhaled the delightful fragrance, then selected some lavender for tea. She garnered sweet woodruff to rinse her hair.

Though there was a good variety of vegetables and herbs, not a plant truly thrived. Cathryn wondered what she could do to make the garden flourish.

She pulled her shawl around her shoulders. Perhaps it was the air in England that accounted for the difference between this garden and the ones she remembered in Venice. The soil was a different color and texture, too. But whatever the reason, she would have to toil long and hard to make this English garden thrive.

A small orchard Cathryn had not examined lay several yards behind the garden plot, and glancing at the house and to the window of the children's room, she moved toward the bounty of apple, pear, and plum trees.

Cathryn pulled an inviting apple from the tree and bit into it, then spat the fruit out, though she missed the worm. She used the back of her hand to wipe away the last traces of the fruit from her lips. "Is there nothing about this place that is not in some way spoiled?"

Cathryn walked a little farther beyond the orchard and looked around her. Well beyond the barn and outbuildings, she had a better view of the surroundings. Flocks of sheep grazed in the distance, and beyond gentle hills lay yet another stand of trees. What were the boundaries of the Godwyne estate? she wondered. Who owned this land? That first day, upon seeing the charred rubble, the remains of the great stone house, she had concluded that this was Godwyne land. But Mistress Seymour had said the land was her brother's property.

Cathryn turned back into the orchard and admitted she was growing almost anxious to meet Gerald Seymour. Which of his children most resembled him? she wondered. Were his eyes the piercing blue of Jacob's or sullen and gray like Diligence's? Could baby Prudence have taken her hair, the color of moonbeams, from her father?

Perhaps he would not prove as unpleasant as his sister, Cathryn daydreamed. But when she had the house in sight again she acknowledged there was nothing on which to rest her hopes and gave up the notion entirely.

Bridget stood in the garden yard. "My brother wants to see you," she called.

"Did you notice how much better the children seem today?" Cathryn asked, trying to be cheerful when she met Bridget in the yard.

"They're hungry."

"I'll take them something right away," Cathryn answered, feeling as though she had been neglectful.

"Ruth shall take that obligation for you this morning. My brother is waiting." Bridget led the way to a downstairs door and knocked. She waited for an answer, then entered, beckoning for Cathryn to follow.

Before them seated at a table covered with account books was a much younger, more attractive man than Cathryn had expected. Her hopes were revived.

Though he looked pale, confirming he had not been well, Gerald Seymour gave the appearance of a man who had an inner strength that would carry him through any hardships and trials to come. He scrutinized Cathryn with penetrating blue eyes that reminded Cathryn of his son's. His light brown hair and beard, though trimmed, seemed a bit unruly, due to their inclination to curl.

Cathryn stood in silence for several minutes while Master Seymour surveyed every inch of her. At first she looked at him directly, locking deep brown eyes with ice-blue ones. As his scrutiny lengthened, Cathryn began to have the eerie feeling that he had the power to read her thoughts, and she dropped her gaze. Her long black lashes swept against her cheeks, now suffused with pink, and she stared at the multitude of books that covered Gerald's desk in stacks.

"You have come a long way to join us, only to be introduced under difficult circumstances, Cathryn Godwyne," Gerald said, his tone devoid of any warmth. "I hear you have taken to your new obligations with energy and with remarkable devotion."

Uncertain, Cathryn smiled, for a moment imagining she was being praised, startled to think that Bridget could have given a favorable report.

"I've visited with my children this morning. They are fast to praise you."

"They deserve my best efforts."

"And you, ours," Gerald said. "Mistress Seymour informs me that you, contrary to Lord Godwyne's precise instructions, have been reared a Roman Catholic."

Cathryn remained silent and waited for him to resume.

Master Seymour rose from his chair and went to a cupboard to retrieve from a small locked drawer what Cathryn recognized as her ebony-and-ivory rosary.

Gerald dangled the attached gold crucifix with irreverence. "You neglected to put this away before you came downstairs this morning. I cannot allow you to leave such idolatrous symbols lying about in the children's view. Further, I demand that you promise not to corrupt my children with your damning Catholic beliefs."

Cathryn's pink blush turned crimson. "I do not intend to interfere."

"Other dangerous items have been removed from your possession," Bridget informed Cathryn.

"What items?" Cathryn demanded.

Gerald interrupted in a stern voice. "Your tone disturbs me, Cathryn." He frowned. "Because of the newness of your station, I forgive your lapse of respect, but do not misinterpret my kindness. Lord Godwyne erred in permitting the kind and degree of your education. It has given you a false impression of your worth."

He glared at Cathryn, not failing to notice the ripeness of the young woman's body as she stood proud and erect.

"About your belongings," he continued, forcing his eyes from her curvaceous form. "I have confiscated your prayer book and the pagan images Mistress Seymour found. For now, I shall keep them under lock and key.''

Cathryn felt violated by his decision. ''You have no right!''

''I have every right to protect my home and children from idolatry.''

Cathryn lifted her chin in defiance, but Gerald ignored her.

''Though it was a pitiful waste of money all these years, I understand you were an able student. Perhaps it is a quality that shall serve you now.'' He lifted a small leather-bound notebook from the desk and gave it to Cathryn. ''You must begin in earnest to learn the error of your religion. Each day I shall instruct you in the Puritan faith. I shall guide you to discover whether God has elected you as one of His chosen, and you will use this book to record your progress. Until you are familiar with the Puritan doctrine, you will not be fit to instruct my children.''

Cathryn was speechless as she examined the leather exterior of the book Gerald handed her.

''For the time being, I will allow you to keep the musical instrument you brought with you in your possession. My sister has warned you that pagan music is forbidden, has she not?''

Cathryn barely nodded, looking back at Bridget, whom she had forgotten was in the room.

''But you must give your word never to play the instrument under my roof.''

Crestfallen, Cathryn answered, ''Yes, I promise.'' All the weariness of the last days and weeks caught up with her as she gave her word to the children's father. She felt unsteady on her feet, as if all blood had been drained from her body.

Satisfied, Gerald smiled, then dismissed her. ''After dinner, we will commence your lessons in our faith.''

Cathryn seemed rooted in place, forcing Bridget to nudge Cathryn's elbow to make her move.

As she ascended the stairs to the children's bedchamber again, Cathryn looked ill. Her face was splotched with color and her breathing was strained. Her dark eyes were moist and feverishly bright. Her lower lip trembled as she clutched what soon would be a diary of her newfound faith, the proof of one pilgrim's progress.

Master Gerald Seymour could do many things. He could steal from her as he already had done and force her to pretend to be a Puritan. He could forbid her the solace of her music, and, as she must, she would bow to his wishes in the care of his children. But as long as she lived, Cathryn swore, Master Seymour would never truly subdue her in the way she sensed he wished. Her surrender to him would be a lie, and not for the promise of eternal salvation would Cathryn allow the tears that now threatened to fall.

Chapter 31

"You've made too late a start on your garden," Bridget warned Cathryn, not for the first time.

"It seems to be faring well in spite of the delay," Cathryn answered, feeling rather satisfied, in spite of Mistress Seymour's constant denigration.

"I'd say you have an aptitude for growing things," Gerald remarked, ignoring his sister's appraisal. He was impressed with the neat rows of vegetables and herbs that had been grouped to obvious advantage, with such as coriander, chevril, mallow, and dill planted next to each other; sweet basil and rue kept far apart. At the corners and along the perimeter of the garden, wormwood and mugwort were cultivated to discourage adders.

"Do you know the use of all of these?" he asked, gesturing to various plants.

Cathryn nodded. "I know most."

On the day Gerald Seymour had first surveyed her garden, Cathryn had had no praise from Bridget, but Cathryn remained hopeful that she might yet win the woman's favor. Perhaps Mistress Seymour was ashamed in view of the failure of her own efforts; Cathryn sighed, putting down the trowel to wipe away the perspiration collecting on her brow. She pulled at her collar and the cuffs of her sleeves to encourage even a small draft of air to circulate beneath her gown. Though it was still early in the day, she already felt uncomfortably warm.

She would be more comfortable, she knew, if only she could wear one of her India cotton dresses instead of the high-necked woolen one she wore, but her calicoes had been confiscated by Master Seymour along with the symbols of her errant faith.

"I should like to have my calicoes," Cathryn had ventured of her guardian only the day before. "Otherwise I shall perish in this heat."

"It is unlawful to use or wear any fabric but wool and, in this matter, I am in full support of the Crown. You must know it is better for the humors to wear wool," Gerald explained.

In spite of his argument, Cathryn understood that as a wool grower and merchant, Gerald Seymour stood to profit from the restrictive English trade laws.

"You do not deserve special favor, Cathryn Godwyne, and like the rest of us, you shall wear wool. And when you die, your body shall be wrapped in wool."

When the heat was almost unbearable, Cathryn was certain it would not be long before she would need a shroud, fearing she certainly would die as a result of Gerald's steadfast obedience of the law, if not from disease. Knowledge that simple relief was available to her in the form of cotton garments only made her suffering more intense.

In order to minimize the effects of the heat, Cathryn went into her garden as soon as it was light. "No wonder the English have an unnatural dread of sunshine," Cathryn muttered, and scratched at the wool sleeve clinging to her arm. She gave her morning's efforts a final survey and smiled to see her garden flourish at last.

In other matters, however, Cathryn felt a sense of failure.

Her gaze fell on the house and she worried how long she could continue to convince everyone she was receptive to the Protestant heresies and on the verge of renouncing her Catholic faith. Just as she had imagined her friends and loved ones in Venice would know of her passion for the priest, Cathryn imagined the Seymours and others in the Puritan community would know the falseness of her heart.

Without protest Cathryn attended the twice-weekly Puritan meetings, managing thus far to stay alert throughout the lengthy lectures. At first she was aghast at the Puritan service, a simple ceremony that seemed to lack holiness and proper respect. The very idea that a person could pray to God directly was an abomination that made Cathryn's insides quake each time she mouthed Puritan prayers. The absence of grand sacred music during the service made the proceedings seem irreligious and made her feel desperate with loneliness.

In moments of silence, Cathryn would close her eyes and wait for the sound of flutes, violins, and mournful oboes; to hear a glorious new composition by the master, Father Vittorio. She waited to be inspired by a chorus of angelic voices, only to be startled into the present by psalms in English translation, sung by an almost unmusical but earnest congregation of Puritans.

Gerald Seymour accepted Cathryn's efforts toward conversion, pleased by her progress, but he realized he needed to keep a steady eye on her efforts to accept the errors of her Catholic ways. "In truth, a believer works his lifetime to assure himself of God's grace."

He was confident enough of Cathryn's earnestness, however, to relax a little with her supervision of his children.

Cathryn raised her eyes to the children's windows from the roses in her garden, pleased that she had made at least one convert of her own. Prudence had been on Cathryn's side from the moment of her recovery—perhaps even before then.

When ill, Prudence had clung to Cathryn in feverish desperation whenever strength permitted, and when recovered she had gone to her cradle with great reluctance, to sneak into Cathryn's bed as soon as she was certain Cathryn was sound asleep. Comfort protested the intrusion. The bed, after all, was small, but with a child tucked under each arm, even Cathryn managed to sleep.

Though hesitant, Comfort, too, came Cathryn's way, openly envious of her youngest sister's ease at catching Cathryn's eye, but Diligence and Jacob were another matter. Cathryn sighed and lowered her gaze from the children's window. She pulled the petals from an almost spent fragrant red rose. Diligence was nothing like her sisters, and Cathryn imagined it would be only a matter of time before the English heat would dry the child into a replica of her Aunt Bridget, just as the sun would dry the center of the rose whose petals she now placed in her basket.

Cathryn doubted she could do anything to prevent Diligence's withering, but she might prevent her own, she concluded, gathering her full baskets of vegetables and herbs, intending to escape the sun inside the house. But Cathryn halted in her tracks when she caught a glimpse of the figure of a woman out of the corner of her eye.

She turned her head quickly but, as usual, saw nothing. Was someone there? Or was what she saw almost every day in the corner of her eye merely some trick of vision?

This time Cathryn was certain she had seen someone; she threw down her baskets and, lifting the hem of her skirt high, ran toward the orchards. She was breathless by the time she reached the final row of fruit trees, and just as Cathryn saw what she had hoped to see, the woman disappeared into the trees beyond the heath.

Cathryn lost no time in following, feeling her blood race, discovering how it must feel to be a fox in pursuit of its prey. She ran, making nimble jumps over stumps and brush in her path, and as she crossed its path, she forced a startled rabbit to suddenly reverse its course.

Once inside the woods where the woman had vanished, Cathryn also knew how it felt to be outrun.

The woods were dark and deep, and the woman she chased had vanished. "Wait! Please, wait for me!" Cathryn cried.

Cathryn looked back the way she had come and considered a retreat; then, ignoring a voice inside her head that warned her against foolhardiness, she wove her way more deeply into the woods, going wherever there was a likely path. At last, Cathryn admitted she was lost.

No longer overheated in her woolen dress, Cathryn shivered and worried about fierce animals and outlaws whom everyone knew abounded in forests.

At this very minute, Cathryn realized, she should be sitting at the Seymour table, having endured the morning prayer. If she had been prudent, she would now be eating breakfast with the children and their aunt. Instead, Cathryn's stomach grumbled and her heart thumped loudly in her chest.

Cathryn took a deep breath, then went on.

"One tree looks terribly like another," she muttered, the smaller plants and vines below the trees never offering her a clue whether she had been this way before. "The woods only *seem* to go on forever," she tried to reassure herself.

Cathryn stopped and looked up through a web of tree limbs in search of sky. There was none to see. Suddenly she felt frightened, but she was too exhausted to cry.

For several minutes, Cathryn stood in blank despair, listening to the calls of birds and insects, and to the rustling of leaves.

Then, intermingled with the other sounds, she recognized one, at once hopeful as it came clear.

She heard the sound of running water and followed her ear until she found a stream. She refreshed herself with several quick gulps of water, then hurried along the shallow bank of the stream a good distance until she came into a clearing several acres wide.

At one side of the clearing stood a small cottage. The structure was solid and maintained with scrupulous care, its thatched roof sprinkled with green fleshy cabbage rosettes. Several raised garden beds lay near one side of the cottage, and a variety of small animals milled within a large pen on another side.

Suddenly a dog reared from behind the cottage window. He growled, then began to bark, forcing Cathryn to cease her appraisal of the scene.

Frozen with fear, Cathryn stood at the edge of the clearing as the cottage door opened and an enormous white dog bounded in her direction. He stopped a few feet from her and positioned himself in a menacing crouch, a low growl sounding in his throat. Her stare fixed on the dog's golden eyes, Cathryn was unaware of the approach of another human being until she saw the hem of a woman's gown rustle against the dog's coat.

"Silence!" the woman commanded the beast, whereupon the dog leisurely stretched himself, then lay down. Only when he appeared friendly did Cathryn take her eyes off the dog to look up into his mistress's face.

Cathryn sucked in her breath as she recognized the disfigured woman she first had seen on the day of her arrival. The possibility that the watcher could be the same woman who had halted the cart that day had occurred to Cathryn, yet the scar on the woman's face was so terrible that Cathryn could not manage to conceal her shock.

"You needn't be afraid."

"You're the one who watches me! Why?" Cathryn demanded as though she were not the least fearful.

"What makes you think I'm watching you?"

Cathryn hesitated. "I've often seen you."

"Perhaps you imagine so. Or perhaps you have been listening to tales."

"What tales?"

"You've been given no warnings?"

Cathryn shook her head.

The woman smiled. "I'm astounded." She laughed. "Well, no matter. You should not have come here. You must leave." She turned to lead Cathryn toward her cottage.

"Please, tell me, who are you?" Cathryn inquired with a more polite note to her voice.

"You must ask your guardian, though perhaps you will not like his answers." She gazed into Cathryn's dark eyes and reached to tuck a wayward strand of Cathryn's hair back under her Puritan cap.

At first, Cathryn shied away from the woman's hand, then she allowed her touch.

"You've missed your morning meal following me. Before you go, would you like something to eat?"

Cathryn nodded, feeling her thirst more than her hunger.

"Sit here." The woman motioned to a brick-and-mortar bench under the shade of a tree.

Cathryn seated herself gladly and while waiting noted the plants that bordered the cottage: flowers that looked a great deal like roses but were not—delicate red, white, and variegated pink blooms on long green stalks. Nearby, beds of plants contained herbs that Cathryn knew well and many she did not.

Cathryn investigated the plot, dipping her hand into the soil, rubbing the texture between her fingers, lifting it to her nostrils to test its sweetness. The woman with the scar had an extraordinary ability; Cathryn's pride in her garden was unwarranted by contrast. She pulled a leaf of rosemary, crushing the succulent bit between her fingers. The aroma was pungent and hearty. The rosemary that Cathryn grew was lame in comparison.

"Would you like some cuttings to take with you?"

"Thank you, I would," Cathryn answered, startled, not having heard the woman approach. "Obviously you know the secrets of the soil." She sighed with envy. "You must have planted early."

"Earlier than you did," she replied, handing Cathryn a mug of spiced tea.

Cathryn did not conceal a small smile of satisfaction.

"Yes, I am the one who has been watching you," the woman yielded.

"But why?"

"Curiosity, or perhaps from lack of something to do."

Cathryn raised an eyebrow, surveying the immaculate yard and animals with a sweeping gaze.

"Or perhaps, as it is judged, it is because I am only a useless old woman, and lonely for the company of others."

Cathryn lowered her gaze. Someone as disfigured as the woman was would have difficulty attracting anyone to her door, she supposed, and wondered how long the woman had had her scar; if she had children; if she had ever had a husband. But aloud Cathryn inquired, "Have you no friends?"

The woman smiled, one-half of her face immobile and distorted, the other full of life. "Sometimes it is not easy to find friends in this country, even when one is as beautiful as you are. But you have met many people at Puritan meetings and at market, and you have made friends with the Seymour children."

Cathryn sighed. "I have met many people in the district, but I have no friends."

The woman nodded and Cathryn began to eat the seasoned bun and drink fragrant tea. She sighed with pleasure at the taste of the food and drink, thinking she had never eaten anything so wonderful.

"You must go now," the woman urged, seeming anxious, when Cathryn drained the cup. "You will be missed."

"But I don't know the way," Cathryn protested.

"Zephyrus will lead you."

At his name the great white dog stood, eager and obedient. The woman gave a signal with her hand and Zephyrus bounded out across the yard toward the trees. He looked back at Cathryn as if he knew she needed to follow.

Cathryn handed the disfigured woman her empty cup. "Shall I see you again?"

"Perhaps," the woman answered. "Perhaps."

Chapter 32

Missed almost at once when she did not appear for the morning meal, Comfort and Prudence went to look for Cathryn. They found her baskets of vegetables, herbs, and flowers, and returned to the house alarmed.

"Cathryn has been carried off!" the girls wailed.

Bridget rebuked them for their noise and for their imaginations, but Gerald was grim-faced when informed of Cathryn's mysterious disappearance and troubled himself to spend the morning looking for her. When he came to the heath, he went no farther, frowning deeply, certain of the direction the girl had gone.

When Cathryn returned at midday, he rebuked her for wandering off.

"I'm sorry. I wandered too far and became lost."

"I forbid you to go into the woods alone. There are animals . . . and other dangers. A Witches' coven convenes nearby."

Cathryn's eyes widened with interest, and Gerald Seymour wondered what she had already seen. "In this life, evil surrounds us at every turn. We must keep from its path and be on constant guard. The charred remains of the great house you see not many yards away is the direct result of their evil deeds."

"I thought, perhaps, Lord Godwyne . . . had . . . died there," she stammered.

"Indeed he did. That is, his injuries occurred there. His death was but one result."

Cathryn wanted to know more, but Gerald would not continue in that vein. "I forbid you to journey beyond the heath. Even then, be mindful of danger surrounding us. I wear a paper with the Lord's Prayer written on it in my boot for protection. You ought to do the same. Above all, speak to no one you do not know."

Cathryn felt terrible loneliness, at once understanding how

being lonely might drive one person to spy on another. She thought of the disfigured woman whose age and scarred face would not improve her chances for acceptance in an unaccepting world. How cruel we are, Cathryn reflected as Gerald continued to scold. And how often we disobey Christ's command to love one another. Puritans only loved others like themselves and kept a very watchful eye on each other to be sure those they loved continued to merit love. Did Catholics love one another more easily? Did God intend us to love the world? Or just the faithful?

Cathryn sighed. Loving one another does not come easily, she admitted as she stared at her disapproving guardian.

In the private company of the Seymour children, Cathryn began to sense that if she was not loved, she at least was respected. Each day as she and the four children labored side by side, whether in the garden or over readings meant to instruct and uplift their minds and souls to God's designs, they worked together in harmony, learning both trivial and important things; at minimum learning respect for each other.

The four children all took an interest in the garden, especially as Cathryn revealed something of what she knew of the medicinal and magic properties of herbs. "Surely you know magic is different from Witchcraft. Black magic is used by Satan's disciples, but everyone, including your father, uses white magic—if only to ward off the evil of Witches," she counseled.

"Now . . ." Cathryn pointed to the plant. "Angelica won't bloom until late in summer, and it likes moisture, so we must see it's well watered. All of the plant is used, one way or another, as a remedy for plague. Its new shoots are good in salads. Boiled down, it's good for the stomach. We can even dry and hang the flower sprigs to ward off and break the spell of Witches."

"We shall have to give a bunch to Aunt Bridget when the flowers come into their bravery," said Comfort.

Cathryn nodded. "I'll leave you to remember to collect it when it's ready," Cathryn told her, hoping the woman's gloomy temper to be only a Witch's spell. "As for basil . . . did you know you have to put a curse on it before it will grow—something your aunt obviously didn't know. It's delicious in soups and salads and stews."

The children looked at one another. "Tell us the curse, please," Jacob implored.

Cathryn laughed mischievously. "It's a secret," she said with narrowed eyes, "that I share only with my friends. Someday, Jacob, maybe you shall be my friend. Then I shall reveal my secrets to you," she teased with kind intentions.

Cathryn pointed to another delicate green plant. "Dill is good luck as well as tasty," she said, then singled out an oatmeal-colored plant with fernlike fronds containing hundreds of tiny leaves. "When the time comes, Comfort, we'll dry some of these yarrow flowers to put under your pillow so that you will dream of the man you shall marry."

Comfort blushed.

"We can make a tea of the leaves and flowers for aches and coughs. I should have brewed some when you were ill, but then I didn't know it grew in our garden," she said. "Macerated and held in the mouth, it is good for toothaches, which I hope, Comfort, you'll not need—I should hate to see you a toothless bride," she said, and the children laughed.

But in their father's or Bridget's presence, everyone, including Prudence, grew distant and cold.

The tangible chill baffled and disturbed Cathryn, and made her fear that she would always be a stranger in their midst. Their ambivalence made her loneliness acute at times and caused her mind to flood with memories.

Before Cathryn met the Seymour children, she believed even the simple miseries of childhood could be cured by having a family of one's own. And now, Cathryn constantly recalled the orphans of Venice as happier, less fearful, less somber, more loving by nature than the Seymour children, who had always had a home. To her utter amazement, Cathryn discovered unhappiness could grow in hearts sheltered by a family as well as in the hearts of those who had no kin.

There were, she learned, always conditions to love in the Seymour house. Parental love was obtained only by strict obedience to God, and, Cathryn was advised, only Puritans were truly obedient.

Clearly, God did not love Catholics, who fell even further from grace through ignorance of God's Word.

"Even Catholics are aware that all men come into this world as wretched sinful creatures almost unworthy of nurture," Gerald informed Cathryn, his captive Catholic. "The only reason to breed and foster life is for the salvation of souls.

"The very event of birth is the culmination of a loathsome act, a sinful association of a man and woman brought about by Original Sin and man's willful disobedience of the Lord,'' Gerald seemed to take pleasure in advising Cathryn. ''Women continue to this day to lure men's hearts from God, but for the sake of bringing souls into the world, this vile association is tolerated.

''Once on earth, a man's or woman's only hope is to obtain grace, which, contrary to the deluded beliefs of Catholics, does not come from pagan sacraments. Grace is not conferred by a pope, or bishops, or priests, but only by the Lord to those repentant souls He has chosen for redemption.''

Gerald further assured Cathryn that the select of God do not fall from grace and do not rely on the sacraments to keep them in God's favor. They proved their state of grace by a life of devotion and obedience to God's Word and through good works. ''The goodness of one's behavior reflects God's grace and one's salvation. Each of us must search his soul to know the will of God, and if it is His will, Cathryn, you, too, might be among the number of His chosen.''

Cathryn regarded Puritan philosophy confusing at best and had no doubt at all that it was heresy. The idea that everyone was a godless sinner from birth whom God despised was nothing new to Cathryn, but like all Protestants, the Puritans rejected as necessary all but two of the seven sacraments: baptism and Holy Communion. Like other Christians, they believed that only through faith in Christ was man redeemed from sin, but that faith was a gift of God to man—and true faith was available only to His chosen: the Puritans. They further dared not to believe in transubstantiation: that the bread and wine of communion were in fact transformed to Christ's actual body and blood.

To Cathryn the notion that a believer could obtain salvation through God's grace without the intervention of the Church was unthinkable. She was astonished to learn that the Puritans believed any man could be a valid minister of God without necessity of ordination by a bishop. She could hardly sit still to hear Gerald Seymour scoff at the pope, whom Cathryn knew to be infallible and the primary link of man with God.

Yet Cathryn saw no reasonable course but to feign the contemplation of her soul, and while Gerald sat satisfied with her seeming willingness to study Scripture and explore God's acceptance of her soul, she held on to her Catholic faith and vowed to be as independent of his stern influence as she could manage.

She plotted in secret to withstand his obvious desires to dominate her thinking on all matters and defied him at every opportunity by whatever means she could.

Cathryn sat apparently obedient to her guardian's will, studied the Scriptures, and contemplated God's Word, learning there could be but one interpretation—the Puritan. "All others who glean something contrary are godless men and women," instructed Gerald.

Beneath her meditating brow, Cathryn forswore Gerald Seymour's demands for her devotion and continued to think exactly as she pleased.

She also plotted to circumvent Master Seymour's requirements for her strict obedience, knowing someday soon she would make another excursion into the forbidden, ever-inviting woods. And she would be happy to become acquainted with anyone upon whom she might happen there—especially the Witches that Gerald Seymour feared.

Chapter 33

Cathryn lifted her head from the English translation of the Bible. It was time to contemplate. Instead, she looked around the table at the children's faces. They had listened to her read, and after mulling over the passages for a few minutes, the two oldest children would record their interpretation in diaries for later discussion with their father. A devout Puritan would spend his life recording his thoughts on and understanding of the Scripture, and would record the incidents of his life that gave the world visible proof of God's grace.

Cathryn glanced at Jacob, who, so stern a copy of Gerald Seymour, appeared years older than his actual age. Although all children were regarded as miniature adults from the time they were four, the Seymour children often seemed to Cathryn to have advanced to old age before enjoying youth.

Comfort, an earnest, eager student of the Scriptures, had

greater intelligence than Jacob, and on occasion forced her father to overpower her gentle reasoning with long-winded explanations that in the end silenced the child by sheer exhaustion.

True to her name, Diligence struggled valiantly with her penmanship in copying the passages for the day. She would rephrase simple verses in her own words, sometimes quite innocently missing the point.

To Cathryn's surprise, Gerald was patient with his child.

He was less magnanimous with Cathryn, dogged and determined in his effort to save her soul, to see she became one of the elect of God. Cathryn became the target of his most ardent sermons, which only fostered her fierce resentment. For one thing, it forced her to be more attentive to the Puritan doctrine than she liked. For another, she knew her efforts would eventually lead her to public renunciation of her Catholic faith, an act she believed would condemn her to everlasting Hell.

Gerald Seymour claimed to be in direct communication with God, a thoroughly unnerving notion for a Roman Catholic who was used to the intercession of saints and priests, and Cathryn suspected Gerald believed his Protestant God had made him alone responsible for Cathryn's renunciation of her Catholic faith.

She felt the pressure of Gerald's determination, and she noticed his growing interest in everything she did. Often she would look up from her reading only to discover his eyes on her. His scrutiny unnerved her and sometimes made her embarrassingly clumsy, which even the children noticed.

She felt guilty about pretending to do and think as her employer wished. But what other choice did she have than to appear to follow his reasoning? There was no freedom to do or think otherwise in the Seymour household. Anyone who questioned Puritan doctrine was a godless heretic.

Cathryn remembered she had not been free to question the teachings of the Catholic religion, but to compensate, she had felt some warmth connected with her faith and childhood. There had not been so much emphasis on reasoning or upon self-control, or such absolute sobriety and suppression of emotion. There was no heart in the Puritan religion that Cathryn could see.

God might grant faith and mercy to His chosen, but His way was terribly harsh. The Puritans even forbade music to honor God.

How could God be offended by glorious music created to honor Him? Cathryn wondered, haunted by the compositions that filled her brain. She had spent her life humming and singing. Now she had to bite her tongue to prevent melodies escaping from her throat.

Cathryn looked at her fingers resting on the edges of the open pages of the Bible. How they ached to touch her violin. And how they needed practice! One either practiced every day or lost agility. If she could play for Father Vittorio today, she would see his agonized face, and his reprimands would burn her ears.

Though she continued to insist she would forget him, Cathryn thought of Father Vittorio with fondness and more often than she did of anyone else. She had letters from the Fabiani sisters and from Simone. Perdita said Father Alberto sent his love, but she received no word from Father Vittorio.

Fool, Cathryn chastised herself. This is my punishment. This is the Hell I've heard so much about! In despair she reasoned that God had abandoned her to the Protestants for her numerous sins with the priest.

Cathryn sometimes woke in a fevered state, dreams of Vittorio still fresh, her body betraying the secret longings she insisted she no longer had. Awake, she sometimes succeeded in producing a convincing frown when her wayward thoughts wandered to him, but the first response of her body was to warm and thrill.

She could recall him as vividly as she did in the days and nights she had lain with him. His features, the contours of his body, the textures and fragrance of his skin were clearly remembered. His touch, his taste, left a vibrant memory, and there were times when she thought she would die without him. He had seemed to have life-giving ability in his hands. She felt more alive in his arms than ever she had before or since. His simple touch could revive her and bring her a new awareness of and gratitude for being alive. One kiss from his succulent mouth and she forgot the flesh was but a prison of the soul and life itself exile from God.

The idea that all sin originated from disobedience to God Cathryn could comprehend. However, the fact that the punishment He ordained for man for His fall involved indescribable pleasure was not entirely reasonable. Even Gerald Seymour would be hard-pressed to explain that sort of punishment by any logic.

It suggested God had made a stupid mistake in creating men and women the way He did!

As often as possible, Cathryn escaped Master Seymour's logic by daydreaming. She bowed her head over her lessons, but her heart and mind drifted to Venice—to the lessons she learned there from her first tutor, her priest.

In spite of her pledges to hate and forget him, and her anger over his final rejection, Cathryn's loneliness drove her to dwell on that part of memory which consoled her—the memory of Vittorio's love. Her resolve to hate him quickly crumbled with her recollection of his passionate embrace.

Instead of the printed Scripture before her, Cathryn dreamed she saw Vittorio open the door to the music salon as he had every day in Venice. He entered and stood silent while she completed a passage on her violin.

"My most excellent student," he said when she finished, "soon you will surpass your teacher." He took the violin and laid it aside, then gathered her into his arms.

"Have you taught me all you know?" she teased, enjoying the delicious feel of his body pressed against hers.

"You, my love, need no instruction in some matters." He smiled and sought her tender lips with his. The fire of passion flared almost at once. One touch, one look was all that was necessary.

"Each moment we're separate seems an eternity," he whispered, enfolding her, each loving touch made more exquisite with the knowledge that a true eternity loomed before them. "I didn't hear half of what was said at confession for thinking of you."

Cathryn pulled away from him a little and touched his forehead. "I absolve you of your sins, Father," she mimicked, then teased his lips again with hers, nibbling lightly.

"How can you?" he asked, replying in kind to her playful kisses. "*You* are my sin." With that accusation he pulled her hard against him, letting her know how urgently he needed her. "*Angelica*," he murmured, as he began to move his hands over her curvaceous body, his mouth almost brutal with its insistence. "I'm forever hungry for your touch." Vittorio raised his cassock and urged her to fondle him.

Cathryn smiled her consent, full of her own desire, knowing what pleased him, caressing his rigid manhood with eager fingers.

The rhythm of his breathing was subject to her whim, to the pressure of her touch. Softly he moaned his pleasure into her mouth, kissing her with an undeniable and growing passion. He unbuttoned her bodice and untied her silk chemise with haste. He reached for her warm breasts, both nipples hard and throbbing, aching in response to Vittorio's heat. She pulled her hands from him and placed them lightly on his while gently he caressed the sensitive tips of her breasts. She closed her eyes and clung to him, soaring. . . .

In England, hundreds of miles from Father Vittorio, Cathryn knew what it was to be damned by too fresh memory and, worse, by the knowledge that she would never again hold her lover in her arms.

The proof that the pleasure enjoyed between a man and a woman was true punishment was evidenced by the torment to which she was now subjected. Remaining a virgin—ignorant— would have made her life more tolerable. To remember, in truth, was torture.

Cathryn recalled Teresa Dansette's derisive laugh when she had tried to argue with the countess's very liberal point of view on sex, but the lessons Cathryn had learned in childhood were reaffirmed by the religion she now pretended to adopt in England. Both Catholic and Protestant doctrines declared that if it had not been for a woman, Eve, man would still be in God's favor. It was *she* whom Satan corrupted; *she* who poisoned Adam and made him fall from grace. The fall of man was Eve's doing, and all of her sisters, every woman, must share the blame and do penance forever.

Surely God did not love man. And especially not *woman*.

Cathryn was raised to believe the holiest of men forswear even touching a woman. If a man makes love to a woman, she contaminates him. If their union seems a natural act, it only proves the act more sinful, for all things of the natural world keep man from a state of grace, keep man from his God.

Cathryn glanced up from the reading she was supposed to be doing. Poor Vittorio. How much he gave up to love me. He will never live long enough to do full penance for the depth of his passion.

Nor will I.

What was worse, she admitted in her heart of hearts, she was not truly sorry, though she knew she should be. "I am a sinner," she muttered.

"What was that you said, Cathryn?"

Cathryn jumped visibly in her chair. She had not seen Gerald enter the room. Her face filled with color. "I said, I am a sinner."

Gerald Seymour smiled. "It pleases the Lord to hear you say so."

Cathryn stared at Gerald Seymour. "I'm certain that it does," she said. And *you* are *twice* as pleased, she thought, all but glaring at him—and, at the same time, she wondered if pride was not a Protestant sin, also.

Chapter 34

From the moment of her arrival at Wollingham, Gerald Seymour burned with his desire to be instrumental in redeeming Cathryn Godwyne's soul. He expected to lead her through knowledge of the Scriptures to enlightenment and, ultimately, with God's blessing to salvation. When he gave his word to look after Cathryn's affairs, to oversee her inheritance; of which hardly anyone, including Cathryn, was aware, in exchange for the settlement of his own considerable debts, Gerald's first thought had been that his half brother, Ashley, had been naive to imagine his instructions about her religion had been obeyed.

Though Lord Ashley Godwyne claimed to be a defender of the Church of England, Gerald doubted he could have quoted more than the most obvious doctrines in opposition to the Church of Rome. The name Godwyne might mean "friend of God" in the ancient English tongue, but Ashley had been a worldly man, not a pious one.

Gerald smiled to himself about Cathryn's progress with the Puritan faith. He had been advised by the Fabiani woman that Cathryn an able student. To his surprise, she proved to be less argumentative than his own child, Comfort, who seemed always to challenge doctrine to the point that one might be driven to suspect she, instead of Cathryn, had been raised by papists.

In England there were plenty of men who claimed to be Protestant who in fact bowed to the pope. Gerald suspected a few men of his own acquaintance to be guilty of such duplicity. Uncomfortable, Gerald shifted his weight in his chair. If Comfort's questions were entertained in public, even he might be accused of being loyal to Rome.

For a time Gerald had been quite patient with Comfort. He had wished to encourage the intellectual turn of mind so necessary for obtaining insight and regeneration of the soul. But there was a limit to tolerance, and when Cathryn arrived, Gerald decided to be more strict. He did not want Cathryn to think she could poison his family with Catholic doctrine.

His decision had been the right one: Comfort ceased to be so argumentative in their discussions, while Cathryn seemed to comprehend the Puritan point of view and had few questions.

Gerald Seymour's heart beat with new hope. If he could be instrumental in Cathryn's conversion, if he could bring her to renounce her false religion before his friends and fellow believers, it would be to his everlasting credit. Moreover, Cathryn's conversion would be public witness to Gerald's own firm standing as one of the chosen of God. Her conversion would serve to make him a more visible saint.

When Gerald Seymour had bargained with Lord Ashley to look after Cathryn's interests, and to collect the rents and fees of the sizeable proprietorship, agreeing to bring her to England, to find her a suitable place or marriage, Gerald had at first planned to do the latter with all possible haste and be done with his obligation.

To Gerald, the stipulation that Cathryn be brought from the school in Venice no sooner than her seventeenth birthday squandered the profits of the estate, but he'd had no choice but to agree, and was now honor bound to fulfill his obligation, for he had given his solemn oath.

Gerald frowned. He regretted having been in the position to contract with his half brother, but at the time of Ashley's death, Gerald had had no recourse but to take his brother's offer. The wool trade was as precarious as it had ever been, and the king was forever finding new schemes of taxation—no doubt for the ultimate purpose of destroying the Protestants and realigning England with Rome.

Sitting in comfort in what used to be Ashley's study, surrounded by extravagant furniture imported from Lisbon, the rage of fashionable gentlemen during the Restoration, and by many volumes of books, kept for their value and not for their content, Gerald reflected how peculiar he had thought it for Ashley to request his presence after their many years of separation.

Gerald had been aware of the fire that had left His Lordship unsteady and had destroyed the famous Godwyne house. With friends in high places, even London had heard of the conflagration that left Ashley's home and health in ruin, but Gerald had little memory of his half brother; their relationship had been severed when Gerald was very young and Ashley left his mother's home to claim his birthright as the Godwyne heir.

Ashley was the only child of their mother's first marriage to Lord John Godwyne. From the beginning, Glenna Sheridan's union with John was opposed by John's father, Fraser Godwyne, and when John died before Ashley's birth, she was turned out. Disgraced, heavy with child, Glenna was not welcomed by her own family again with much eagerness, but until Gerald's father, Cedric Seymour, married her, she at least found shelter there.

A man by the day's standards, Ashley was thirteen years old when Gerald was born. Ashley continued to live with his mother and her second husband until the elder Lord Fraser Godwyne reversed his earlier decision against his son's wife and named Ashley his heir. For the sake of her son, Glenna put her bitterness aside, but Gerald remembered that her charity gained her nothing but the loss of her firstborn son, whom she never saw again.

Glenna forgave Ashley's obvious scorn, a remarkable gesture in Gerald's view. Forgiveness was a trait of a good Christian, Gerald admitted, and a gesture that, in God's eyes, would be in his mother's favor, yet Gerald knew he could never forgive a son that kind of treatment.

When Ashley had first summoned Gerald, calling him "brother," Gerald had turned his proposition down. However, after deliberation, he'd realized that the opportunity Ashley offered could not have come at a more fortunate time. Financially, Gerald was at the brink of ruin and Ashley proposed an arrangement that would eliminate Gerald's debts and provide for his future. What greater proof could there be of God's favoring him? he had finally reasoned.

His good fortune elevated him in the eyes of the Puritan community, where, as long as it was accompanied by a life dedicated to fulfilling God's commandments, a man was free to claim all the material blessings that this life offered.

God worked in mysterious ways.

Indeed, as Gerald Seymour deliberated on his plans for Cathryn, he was convinced again that God's purpose could be seen in all things.

Originally, to be quickly rid of the burden of his duties as guardian, Gerald had intended to marry Cathryn to any man who would have her. However, Gerald's children now were fond of her and her Catholic soul appeared redeemable. Suddenly, Cathryn Godwyne seemed too desirable a prospective wife to be handed to just anyone.

In the Puritan belief, marriage was more than a state ordained by God for the purpose of avoiding the sin of fornication, or for the purpose of the procreation of souls. It was not for the purpose of pleasure, which was sin, but the physical union of man and wife was for the communion of spirits united in the Lord.

Until now, in spite of God's command to marry and fill the earth, Gerald had regarded marriage as an impediment to living a truly Christian life. Like the Apostle Paul, Gerald believed a man should not burden himself with a wife unless it was to avoid sin, and upon his first wife's death, he had declined a second marriage. However, in view of Cathryn Godwyne's conversion, it seemed to Gerald Seymour that she would be worthy of his efforts as a husband. No one would think to forbid their marriage on the grounds they would be breaking the laws of both God and man, Gerald reflected, for no one knew Cathryn was his brother's daughter.

She had yet to prove her virtues, of course, or begin to approach Phoebe's good qualities, but she seemed of good mettle and, likewise, malleable. She was foreign in both appearance and manner, but she had not polluted his house with her Catholicism and seemed to give up her beads without much resistance. Intelligent, she appeared to study with rapt attention the new faith outlined to her.

Intelligence was important, but in addition, a wife must be thrifty, faithful, patient, and devoted. Fertility, in conjunction with God's command to multiply and fill the earth, was also to be considered, and Cathryn was young and healthy. She had survived the recent ague with nothing more than weariness from caring for others.

A few shadows could still be seen under her eyes, which, Gerald thought, only added to her appeal. He judged her rather pretty as he overcame his distaste for her dark, foreign look. Other men in the district often paused at meeting or market to admire her, and he had taken notice of the number of unmarried men who would likely wish to pay Cathryn court if he would but allow it. From their frank stares it was obvious they were quite willing to overlook Cathryn's exotic appearance.

The blackness of her hair, the deep color of her brown eyes, the olivander of her skin, in all, were not displeasing. Cathryn Godwyne could make a man warm. She could make a man who served God happy.

She might even be regarded as one of his rewards.

Chapter 35

Cathryn was startled to learn that the addition to the house, which was almost complete, would be her room when it was finished. She was delighted with the prospect of having a private bedchamber once more, not to mention her very own bed; however, there were disadvantages. The room was downstairs a good distance from the children's room, as well as from the other bedchambers. She would have no idea when the children needed her at night, unless one of them came to her.

Prudence, who curled herself against Cathryn in bed every night, was also surprised to learn that her "Cat" soon would be sleeping by herself. "But where's my pillow?" Prudence demanded.

"In your bed upstairs, where it belongs," Bridget answered.

"But I sleep with Cat," Prudence insisted, tears welling, then spilling.

"No more," Bridget answered in a stern voice.

Prudence's wail stopped all further conversation.

Cathryn would not quite miss the tight embrace of the slumbering child, but she would miss her warmth and the communication of affection that her closeness conveyed. "Perhaps, for a few nights, she can fall asleep in my bed. Then I'll carry her upstairs," Cathryn suggested.

"I do not believe my brother will approve."

Probably not, thought Cathryn, saying nothing more to Bridget, nor discussing her plans with the children's father. In private, however, she spoke to Prudence. "I think we might do just what I said to Aunt Bridget. Only we won't tell anyone. It shall be our secret."

"I want to sleep with you," Prudence insisted, not wanting to compromise and threatening another storm of tears.

"Your father won't permit it," Cathryn counseled, and the child's tears began to fall, quietly at first for lack of air, then loudly, when Prudence caught her breath.

After a while there was silence. "Shall we try it?" Cathryn asked.

Prudence nodded. "But Father always has his way," she replied, pouting.

Cathryn supposed he did, and there was no room for compromise with Gerald. The children feared more than loved him, but Cathryn granted it might be the way of children and fathers. She had been impressed by Gerald's insistence that one must first *fear* God the Father and his inference that one must fear one's earthly father as well.

I'd rather be an orphan, Cathryn said to herself, than have Gerald Seymour as a parent. Her imaginings and longings for a parent suffered in light of having Gerald Seymour as the only model for her image of a father.

Sometimes Cathryn regarded Gerald in silence as she pretended to be engrossed by the study of religion and the contemplation of her soul. In all, Gerald Seymour was not an unattractive man. He was of medium height, with intense blue eyes, and

light brown curly hair. Often he looked benign, but Cathryn
wondered what truly lurked within his heart.

Though she often disagreed with him, Cathryn discovered
Gerald Seymour had a keen intellect. He had not been university
educated, she knew, but suspected he had read many of the
volumes in his library; at other times, she was convinced that all
Gerald read was the English Bible.

It startled her to be presented with the King James Bible to
read and astounded her to be expected to ferret out the meaning
of the Scriptures for herself. Of course, if her understanding
varied with Puritan doctrine, she was instantly corrected, but a
Catholic never dreamed of such a requisite. The Scriptures were
read and interpreted by priests and other holy men. The notion of
coming to God through one's personal understanding of Scripture, which was a primary tenet of the Puritan faith, was a
staggering concept.

Her utter amazement caused Cathryn to explore the English
Bible with great curiosity at first, and Gerald Seymour was
encouraged by this, imagining that this Catholic might be a
Puritan saint, as all Puritan chosen were considered to be.

In chapter ten of Saint Matthew, verses thirty-four through
thirty-nine, Cathryn read:

> Think not that I am come to send peace on earth: I came
> not to send peace, but a sword.
>
> For I am come to set a man at variance against his father,
> and the daughter against her mother, and the daughter in
> law against her mother in law.
>
> And a man's foes *shall be they* of his own household.
>
> He that loveth father or mother more than Me is not
> worthy of me; and he that loveth son or daughter more than
> Me is not worthy of Me.
>
> And he that taketh not his cross, and followeth after Me,
> is not worthy of Me.
>
> He that findeth his life shall lose it: and he that loseth
> his life for My sake shall find it.

Cathryn thought she understood Gerald Seymour's attitude
toward his children better from these verses and wrote in her
diary:

Jesus commands us to love Him and follow His Word, though it means we are forced to defy the wishes of our parents. A man must not love his children, or a child his parents above God. We must live by God's Word and do His will though it means others despise us. Perhaps following Him will bring us to the Cross. All men die, but only those who follow His Word will find salvation.

Cathryn's Catholic notions were not disturbed by this particular reading of the Scripture, and from the reading of Scripture she felt a measure of enlightenment, but she knew not to trust the Protestant translation of the Bible. For example, in chapter six of Mark, verse three, one of the first passages her guardian instructed her to read, the King James Bible said that Christ had sisters and brothers, while the Catholic Church declared the Mother of God to be perpetually virgin; there was never any mention of Jesus having any near kin, and Cathryn had no doubt there were other gross inaccuracies in the Protestant text. She was thereby forced to reject the Puritan Bible as the Word of God, steadfast in her decision to secretly retain her Catholic faith.

"You shall one day be among the select of God," Gerald said in praise of her diary, which falsified Cathryn's true feelings.

"I'm flattered by your confidence," Cathryn replied, feeling a traitor, vividly recalling the tortures of Catholics that Capitano Salvadori had recited for her.

She felt the target of Gerald Seymour's energies and knew he would not give up until convinced she was converted. The strength of his determination gave Cathryn a sick feeling no herbal cure could possibly relieve. There would be no persuading Gerald Seymour that God simply had not chosen her as He so obviously had chosen him.

Doomed to be apparently converted, Cathryn was overcome with a sudden sense of dread. She felt Master Seymour always watching her and one night while carrying Prudence upstairs to bed Cathryn was, not surprised to meet him in the dark hallway outside her bedchamber. Yet an instinctual chill of fear shuddered through her body and she pulled the sleeping child against her in a fierce embrace.

"Why is Prudence with you?" Gerald challenged, quite furious.

"She—she couldn't sleep," Cathryn stammered.

"I forbid you to take her to your bed again!" he demanded, taking the sleeping child into his arms.

Shaken, Cathryn defied Gerald's explicit order and returned to her room. She continued to harbor Prudence in her bed early almost every night; certain a day of reckoning soon would be at hand.

Chapter 36

In Venice, Cathryn had led the life of a cosseted student free of responsibility for anything but the perfection of her musical gift, her needs met sometimes before she became aware of them. In England, however, the needs of the Seymour children were her first concern. They were her worry night and day. She came to think of the children before herself.

Cathryn would have been even more lavish in her regard and affection for the children, but the restrictions of the Puritan household imposed restraints on Cathryn's nature. She was aware not only of the harsh scrutiny of Bridget and Gerald Seymour, but of the wrathful judgment of the Puritan God.

Cathryn lent a hand to any task requested of her, for it was her nature to try to please her masters, toiling diligently whether in the nursery, in the garden, or in the kitchen preparing decoctions or drying herbs. But of all the tasks in which Cathryn engaged, she judged the laundry to be the most profoundly shocking to her sensibilities, suspecting Gerald Seymour would say that bending over a vat and inhaling vile and noxious odors, when before she had avoided all such distasteful fumes, was nothing less than retribution for sins committed that had offended God's own senses. It was so unpleasant a task that Cathryn was on the verge of agreeing with this interpretation.

One batch of laundry, which involved many days of unpleasant and laborious effort, was a quite unnerving process involving coating, soaking, rinsing, and drying the linen several times, and used such nauseating ingredients as cattle dung and fresh urine.

In Venice she had been sheltered from most mundane functions of the household, except for gardening, which had seemed more a treat than labor. As for the laundry, Cathryn had never dreamed what was involved.

Perhaps, if she had known what was required from the beginning, as Comfort did, her current laundry duties might not seem so awful, she reasoned. However, as Cathryn stood stirring the boiling laundry, she doubted she would ever become used to the process.

She far preferred toiling in her garden and leaned a moment against the stirring paddle to consider its progress. On the whole, the garden was reasonably productive but in particular, every one of the new plants was thriving, the additions mysterious gifts to the gardener.

Almost daily in recent weeks, Cathryn began to find a small bundle of cuttings packed in moss lying at the corner of the garden where Cathryn began her gardening tasks each day from habit. Just this morning there had been another mossy bundle tied with straw waiting for her when she arrived at sunup. She was certain that of the several people in the district she knew, the only possible donor was the disfigured woman who had admitted spying on her, though since the day of their encounter, Cathryn had never seen the woman again.

Twice Jacob reported seeing someone from the orchard. "There she is! I'm sure of it," he cried one morning when they were gathering the ready fruit. He pointed in the direction of the woods. "I saw her last week, too. Father will be furious. I shall report it at once." He spoke mainly to Comfort.

"How can you be so sure?" Comfort demanded.

"I could see her ugly scar."

"You're lying, Jacob. You can't see anything of that nature from here."

"The light around her is different."

"That's your imagination, also."

"It is not. You know that—"

"You should be silent," Comfort cautioned, nodding in Cathryn's direction.

"She sometimes changes herself into animals to better do the Devil's work. Haven't you seen the white dog of hers—her magical servant?"

"I said you should be *silent*!" Comfort glared at Jacob.

Cathryn tried to pry more information from Jacob, but it was useless. The boy still did not accept her. She had more acceptance from the general countryside than she had from Jacob. She was a foreign interloper in his eyes, even if his father judged she should remain.

Cathryn stopped daydreaming and stirred the laundry once more. Thinking of the incident with Jacob reminded Cathryn of Bridget's close-mouthed behavior on the day of her arrival. Upon reflection, Mistress Seymour's silence that first day surprised Cathryn, since as a rule, Bridget Seymour had advice or opinions to spare on almost every subject. Everyone seemed to want to keep the woman a mystery, and Cathryn wondered why.

She also wondered about some of the gift plants the disfigured woman had been leaving behind: about their uses—which plants were medicinal, which were magical, and which were for cooking. Before harvesting any of them, Cathryn would have to know their properties, else they might be dangerous. Often only quantity prevented a plant from being poisonous.

Cathryn liked best the first plant the woman left for her. From the leaves, she recognized it as the beautiful flowering shrub that grew all around the disfigured woman's cottage. "Peonies," she remembered the woman said when Cathryn had finally inquired. The seeds, which shine at night, were a talisman against evil, and the root was valued as a remedy for falling sickness. Drunk in wine the powdered seed purifies the womb, but Cathryn wondered if it had other, more powerful properties of which she was not aware, for the scarred woman grew it in great quantity.

Now that Cathryn had so many responsibilities that took her from the house and sometimes kept her from going twice weekly to market, she realized it would be quite easy to slip away without notice from the Seymour house—as long as she did not get lost.

She would not get lost again, Cathryn was certain, for when she had followed the woman's great white dog home, she had marked the trail with small piles of stones and twigs stabbed into the earth.

Cathryn longed to venture into the woods again in search of the woman's cottage, but she puzzled over what Jacob had meant when he'd said "the light" around the woman from the woods was "different." Practical Comfort had suggested it was Jacob's imagination playing tricks on him, but Cathryn did not find him quite clever enough to be so inventive, although she admitted her judgment might be overly harsh—Jacob reminded Cathryn too much of his father to invite her charity.

As each day passed, Cathryn grew less easy with her feelings about the children's father, further annoyed and angered that it never appeared to occur to Master Seymour she might be unworthy of election to the Puritan faith. Why was he so determined for God to cast his blessing upon her?

It also troubled Cathryn that though she continued to shelter Prudence in her bed early at night, Master Seymour had not spoken to her about the matter. She expected at least a reprimand. Cathryn knew her guardian had not said anything to Bridget, for Mistress Seymour would not have lost such a perfect opportunity to upbraid her.

Sometimes, when Cathryn climbed the stairs with Prudence asleep in her arms, the hairs on the back of her neck stood up and she had the eerie feeling she was being watched. But when she turned around, there was nothing exceptional to be seen, and she convinced herself that it was only a draft of night air that disturbed her.

Since Cathryn began sleeping in her separate bedchamber, she awakened several times thinking someone was in her room; she would call one of the children's names, only to realize that she had been dreaming. To her surprise, Cathryn was lonely in the room that was so far from the children and the rest of the house. The advantages of privacy and a bed of her own did not outweigh the isolation.

Her employer's growing interest in her did little to make Cathryn feel welcome. She continued to feel very much the intruder and, more than ever, longed for Venice . . . and the sheltering arms of someone who loved her. When she dared to be truthful, Cathryn admitted it was not of Perdita's motherly embrace that Cathryn dreamed, but rather of her dark priest—especially when she woke thinking she heard someone in her room.

Sometimes she awakened with the name "Vittorio" on her lips, surprised and disappointed to discover that she did not wake in Venice where she almost surely would have found comfort—in Father Vittorio's arms.

Her desire troubled Cathryn, thinking she should despise the priest for the way he had treated her, but in the deep of night, it did not matter to Cathryn's unconscious memory that Father Vittorio had rejected and then forgotten her.

In reverie, Cathryn recalled only that she felt completely safe in her lover's embrace. His shelter and his love had made her feel invulnerable. In memory it was so, and she could overlook the disappointing truth and fall asleep again with her heart flooded with love and a sense of peace.

Chapter 37

Soft and warm, the gentle night brought welcome dreams. Of seductive Venice. Of the light touch of Vittorio's lips coaxing her from sleep to nestle in his arms and be renewed by love.

Now half-awake, she sighed and turned as if to face her lover and moved her body in the direction of her dreams. The kiss at first was gentle, then deepened until she grew desperate for air.

No longer sleeping, Cathryn woke to struggle for breath and life, her tender dream turned into a nightmare. The disorienting darkness of the room intensified her terror as a man's strong arms crushed her against his naked body. He held her immobile, then freed her lips a moment while, helpless, she gasped for air.

He seized her mouth once more and pried her lips with a rough, insistent tongue, his breathing labored, his motions verging on the frantic as he pressed himself down heavily against her belly, trying to push himself between her legs.

In the luxury of privacy, alone, Cathryn sometimes slept with her nightgown folded beneath her pillow, and tonight it was to the intruder's distinct advantage, for he had no clothing to struggle with, only large perfect breasts to try to capture. Weighing her down, sounding like an animal, the man groaned in appreciation as he reached for them, bruising her with his violent touch.

Cathryn struggled but feared there would be no escaping him, her strength ebbing, her every ounce of energy consumed by the physical battle. Finding her voice, she screamed in protest when he bent his mouth to her nipples, her fury and her terror rising.

In defense, he pulled his mouth away from her breasts. "No one can hear you." He laughed, then secured her silence by pressing his lips to hers again.

Cathryn clawed at him for freedom. "Whore!" he answered, "It will take more than a scratch to dissuade me," he promised, slapping her face. "Did you know that you cry out for your lover in your sleep?" he demanded, then resumed his feast at her breast.

Cathryn writhed beneath his sucking mouth and, stunned, recognized his voice. "Let me go!" she begged, tears streaming from her eyes. "Please! How can you do this? Your God shall never forgive you!"

He slapped her again, then covered her mouth and nose with one hand to pursue his goal. Cathryn tried kicking, but to no avail. Then she held her thighs together defensively.

"Open yourself," he demanded, and forced his hand between her legs. She was no match for him as his fingers found the softness he was seeking.

With the last of her strength summoned for the final battle, Cathryn resisted him, causing him to hurt her, and brutally he lowered himself and tried to penetrate her, ejaculating before he could succeed.

"Damn you, whore!" he swore as he fell with his full weight upon her.

Cathryn felt defiled. She tried to hold back tears, but soon her body was racked with sobs. The man who lay on top of her did not budge, and for an instant of utter panic, for his lack of motion, she feared him dead. He deserved to die, she raged, then, terrified, she thought of being buried helpless beneath a dead man. She regained a sense of outrage to realize that even at the peak of her wildest imaginings she had not envisioned this would be her fate in Gerald Seymour's hands.

Cathryn tried to move beneath him, and though he was not massively larger than she, Cathryn could not budge, held captive by his full weight and the soft cushioning of her feather-and-wool-stuffed mattress.

Pious Gerald Seymour, who wanted nothing more than to save her soul for a Protestant God! Now she could read the looks he gave her for what they were: vile lust. How could he justify himself? And he dared to call her whore!

Cathryn shivered with revulsion. The devout man that he pretended to be did not make use of a woman in this way. A holy man did not foul himself in such a manner.

A holy man! Cathryn had had enough of holy men!

She knew how easily her priest had cleansed himself of his sins with her. He had scoured *his* soul with penance. But how did a Puritan cleanse himself? Or did the select of God have privileges that had not been revealed to her, a wretched Roman Catholic?

Cathryn began to pound Gerald with her fists in an effort to force him from her, but he only stirred to grab her wrists. "Be still!" he commanded. "How dare you strike me? You have strutted yourself before me, luring me these months, pretending a maiden's innocence. But I have heard your whispers as you pretend to sleep. I have studied you and watched you toss and turn and cry out his name with breathless desire."

Cathryn burned with fury.

"I know who he was, this lover of yours. I know his name. You're a creature who lures a man from his devotion to God."

Cathryn jolted in his grasp.

"I thought you cloistered and protected; perhaps pure enough despite the teachings of your despicable religion to be one of us. But your lover was a Roman Catholic priest. Tell me, Cathryn, of the pagan rites you and Father Vittorio performed?"

Cathryn tried to cover her ears, but Gerald pulled her hands away.

"Lord Godwyne spent his fortune keeping you, believing you perfected a talent ordained by God—only the talent you cultivated was not what my dear brother thought.

"You have definite gifts, though, don't you, dark and lovely Cathryn? Your look sears a man's soul, leaving his flesh to crave and think of naught but purging himself of lust—but it is folly for a man to believe that even then he can be done with you. At least I know I am not yet finished."

Cathryn felt the hardness of his erection against her thigh. Again she tried to prevent his invasion of her body. But she failed and Gerald drove himself into her, while Cathryn prayed that God would strike him dead.

Later, when she lay alone, sore and in despair, Cathryn recognized she did not have the proper influence with God to have Him act in her defense. She was an unredeemed Catholic and an unconvincing Protestant. She was neither chosen, as Gerald's God would say, nor, as any priest could confirm, fit to beg directly for God's mercy. Cathryn reasoned that it was useless to beg for help from either the Catholic or the Protestant God and knew she alone would have to save herself, if she were ever to be saved at all.

Chapter 38

Before first light, Cathryn fled the Seymour house with a lantern and without hesitation, entered the woods traveling the path Zephyrus had taken her many weeks before. At first she searched for her markers to confirm her direction, but with growing confidence, she soon abandoned that unnecessary effort.

Forced to stop and catch her breath, Cathryn stepped into a clearing and realized she had succeeded in finding her way. While she waited for her heart to stop pounding, she noticed the clearing was carved in an almost perfect circle, with the woman's cottage situated to one side. Tonight the moonlight accentuated a decorated border around the window, and its deftly painted though simple designs intrigued Cathryn.

Without thinking, Cathryn stepped nearer, discovering the painted symbols to be a series of designs depicting the phases of the moon; several poses of impressive stags and horned goats; seeds, plants, and haystacks; and completely mysterious sigils. She wondered how she had failed to notice the unusual edging the first time she saw the cottage. Then Cathryn remembered the great white dog who had taken her full attention that first morning. Was he the woman's *magistellus*, her familiar granted by Satan to serve her magically as Jacob said?

Cathryn glanced from shadow to shadow in the clearing. The silence told Cathryn Zephyrus was nowhere near. There was no doubt that the dog was unusually responsive to his mistress's demands and at the least was a protective guardian.

The stillness of the glen suddenly made Cathryn feel even more lonely. "Why did I come here?" She wondered aloud.

She knew the answer, for despite her first frightening experience with the dog, whenever Cathryn thought of this glen, she felt at peace, almost as if she had come home. Aching for comfort after Gerald's assault, Cathryn's only thought of escape was to seek this place.

The seedling plants that had been left at her garden step could only have come in friendship from the woman who lived here, and if for no other reason, Cathryn wanted to believe she would be welcome.

Recalling Bridget Seymour's disgusted remarks about Gerald's tolerance of the disfigured woman's presence on his property, Cathryn realized if Gerald chose to pursue her, he could with impunity. To the world she was little better than his servant. Who would believe such a righteous man would lower and defile himself by touching her?

All at once, exhaustion caught up with Cathryn and she thought of trying the cottage door, but she hesitated and remembered the unmistakable aura of menace the disfigured woman could convey.

Feeling confused and disheartened, the events of the long night and her flight overcoming her, Cathryn slumped onto the stone bench, where she lay down and reclined on her side, drew up her legs, pillowed her head on her arm, and fell asleep. Much later, she opened her eyes, startled to discover daylight and, standing above her, the disfigured woman whose glen it was.

The strange woman stood immobile, covered by an enormous black cape, its hood down behind her head, her long white hair trapped beneath. Torn from sound sleep, frightened, Cathryn bolted upright, at a loss for words. She at first thought herself observed by a pagan priestess and her heart leaped in terror beneath her ribs.

"Please, do not disturb yourself," the woman urged Cathryn too late, and, receiving no reply, the disfigured woman reached gently to assist Cathryn to be seated again. "Why have you come here? It's barely light," she said, discerning the young woman's wild look was more than simple fright. "What troubles you, child?"

Cathryn answered with tears that welled and stole her voice, then trickled, and at last began to flow with force. Cathryn covered her face with her hands.

The woman touched Cathryn's head in a gesture of comfort, stroking her soft, sleep-tangled hair.

Cathryn gasped for air. "Come," the woman said, and led Cathryn inside the cottage.

Using a glowing ember from the fireplace, the woman lit a taper and secured it in a large brass holder. "Sit here," she said, motioning to the only chair in the room. The chair was large, almost thronelike, with ornate scrolling on the back and arms. It held a worn but thick, gold-fringed, purple velvet cushion.

Gladly, Cathryn accepted the chair, feeling more drained than she had when she first arrived.

As she watched Cathryn seat herself, the woman removed her cloak, revealing an exquisite white robe beneath. Even in the dim candlelight, Cathryn was aware of the purity and expense of the garment's luxurious brocaded satin fabric. The robe's neckline, hem, and long, wide sleeves were embroidered with strange gold symbols.

"Something dreadful has befallen you," the woman suggested, drawing Cathryn's attention from her elaborate dress.

Cathryn only nodded.

"You cannot talk of it yet."

Cathryn nodded again and lowered her eyes from the woman's steady inquiring gaze.

"You've come here thinking you'd be safe."

Cathryn looked up in hope.

The friendly visage changed. "You are no safer here," she cautioned, then felt Cathryn's acute distress. "You've nothing to fear from me," she assured her, "but I cannot harbor you forever. If it suits him, your master will come to fetch you. I remain here out of Gerald Seymour's, shall I say, charity and, more than likely, his fear."

Cathryn did not understand, comprehending only that she had misread the woman's interest and her small acts of friendship. "But he has assaulted me," she said in helpless protest.

Frowning, the woman nodded her head in silence. "If you intend to accuse him, you will be humiliated and punished. No one would ever believe you."

Cathryn had not for a moment thought otherwise. "I don't intend to accuse him in public. If nothing else, I am a foreigner."

"Yes, I know."

"How could you know?"

"Perhaps from your accent"—she smiled—"or from your appearance?"

Cathryn was curious. "What else do you know?"

"Not much more."

"But what?"

"Nothing that the eye can't see—that you have left your heart elsewhere."

"How are you so wise?"

"I am blind only in one eye."

"You've been giving me cuttings and seeds from your garden. I took it as a gesture of friendship."

"You were correct to do so."

"Then, please, let me hide here," Cathryn begged.

"I cannot," her hostess said with a finality that even in her desperate mood Cathryn could not fail to recognize.

Cathryn stared for a long moment at the woman. Though much older than Cathryn, and in spite of her scar, the woman was graceful, even strangely beautiful. "At least tell me your name," Cathryn ventured.

"Vanya. Vanya Russo."

"I'm right in thinking you're a foreigner, also?"

Vanya nodded.

"From where, exactly?"

"Places whose names would mean nothing to you."

"I know a little of geography."

Vanya smiled. "And, no doubt, have seen dozens of maps."

Cathryn nodded.

"Where I come from there are no maps, no charts. I come from a world away."

"And speak in riddles."

"And speak in riddles," Vanya acknowledged calmly, returning Cathryn's stare. The young woman who came seeking refuge suddenly seemed not so very young. "I cannot reveal how, but I promise, someday, Gerald Seymour shall pay dearly for his ill use of you. But for now you must go on as if what he has done has not happened."

"How can I?" Cathryn implored.

"I promise, in time, I shall give you a means to deal with him."

"Why not now?!" Cathryn demanded, desperate at the thought of returning to her guardian, compelling her to risk more familiarity with the woman than she would otherwise. "Bridget Seymour called you a Witch. Could you work some sort of spell against him?"

Vanya Russo smiled, but so brightly it seemed to influence even her clouded eye. "I cannot help you."

The woman's decline to use powers from another realm devastated Cathryn, her state leaving her quite prepared to conspire with Witches to punish Gerald Seymour.

Vanya Russo took Cathryn's hand. "Come. Eat something with me, now," she suggested as she smoothed a few stray curls from Cathryn's face. "Then you shall rest, but later you must go back to your master. You shall endure, in spite of him, I promise."

Chapter 39

Surely, Cathryn thought, Gerald Seymour could feel her hatred, yet he returned to her bed night after night. She prayed for God to give her the strength to protect herself and began to wear her daytime clothes to bed in an effort to make his use of her more difficult.

There were no locks on bedchamber doors and no furniture of sufficient weight to impede his entry to her room and when he confronted her, whether she struggled or reasoned or begged, nothing she did to try to defend herself made a difference.

Every morning after he invaded her room, Cathryn discovered fresh bruises on her body, though Gerald did not know of her discolored skin. He cursed the darkness and wished aloud for enough light to take in her beauty with his eyes, yet he never allowed a candle to illuminate them, as if the darkness rendered him innocent of his crime.

At first, Cathryn could not bear to look at Gerald in the light of day, and when she did, sparks of anger and loathing seemed to fly from her. She was curt and barely civil, but as far as she could tell, he ignored her rebuffs. He was aloof and in no way changed.

If Gerald failed to notice the distinct change in Cathryn's behavior, others did not. "Your moods offend my brother and me," Bridget complained to Cathryn, who made no reply to defend herself; nor did she alter her surly manner.

Bridget went to Gerald then. "I thought you would find a husband for the girl," she pressed.

"It seems an undesirable solution now," he replied, and Bridget knew her own place better than to pursue the matter further.

Gerald now loathed to consider Cathryn's marriage and departure from his home, his disposition due as much to greed as to lust. Every day he pored over his accounts and prayed for salvation, and over and over again, the answer to these and other unadmitted prayers was "Cathryn."

Gerald had no legal claim to the land on which he now lived or upon the other holdings of his brother Ashley's estate, except as Cathryn's guardian, and despite the settlement made on him when Cathryn Godwyne arrived in England, his finances were in shocking disarray. The wool trade continued to be depressed, and though the cloth he traded remained in demand, the prices offered would, he imagined, soon bring him to ruin.

As a respected citizen of Wollingham, the authorities would not dare to question his utilization of Cathryn's assets. He could spend her fortune almost without notice, though to spend it was not his intent. He intended to make use of it for his own gain—to siphon what he could into his own accounts.

While Cathryn lived under Gerald's roof, there would be no questions asked, for under English law, a female was an incompetent in need of a husband or a male guardian to oversee and handle her legal and financial affairs, and Gerald Seymour was in no hurry now to marry Cathryn off and deprive himself of her assets—nor was he eager, now, to be free of her person.

In addition to his worries over the state of his finances, Gerald was gravely concerned about Vanya Russo—"Ashley's whore," as he described her in private. Though now an ugly crone and sly, she once had been indescribably beautiful. To Gerald her beauty was the only thing that explained her successful seduction and possession of Ashley.

Ashley had been her slave to his last breath and had even provided for her in his will, leaving her a large settlement of forested land which was to be available for her use as long as she lived. While still alive, he had seen to the building of a house, albeit of modest structure, even seeing to its construction before the start of his own, and had lived with her in her cottage for a time.

Ashley had confessed to Gerald that many times he had begged Vanya to marry him, but she had refused, a fact that astounded Gerald even more than Ashley's revelation that he loved the whore. How could a man love a woman like Vanya Russo? Gerald puzzled. Unless, of course, Ashley had been under a demonic spell.

Before Ashley's death there had been bountiful gossip in the district about this dark and foreign woman, but due to Ashley's wealth and favor with the Crown, his mistress had been almost untouched by wagging peasant tongues—a man influential with the king had guarantees the lower classes did not.

Gerald strummed the table in front of him. To his immense regret, he had given his solemn oath not to disturb Vanya Russo in any way. However, the woman knew far too many secrets for him to accomplish what he currently had in mind. As long as Vanya Russo remained alive, he could never marry Cathryn Godwyne.

The Witch, Vanya Russo, Gerald decided, would have to be destroyed.

Chapter 40

Gerald Seymour had no conscience when it came to his lust for Cathryn. She cried, she begged, and she struggled, which often brought her more pain than if she had lain still, and still his interest in her did not wane. Then, because she bled, he was repulsed.

A perverse blessing, Cathryn began to bleed long, and at unpredictable intervals.

As additional defense, over Bridget Seymour's loud objections, Cathryn began to sleep with her charges again. "Here we've gone to the expense and considerable inconvenience for your comfort, as if you were better than you are, and you show my brother gratitude by huddling nights in the children's room, as if you were afraid of the dark," she badgered Cathryn.

Cathryn also defied Gerald by frequent absences from the house. Whenever the weather was fair, she spent the day outdoors and sometimes disappeared for long periods of time.

Bridget seethed when Gerald did not punish his wayward servant, but some sixth sense prevented her from challenging Cathryn's behavior before speaking to Gerald in private.

"Is she neglectful of the children? Does her garden fail?" he questioned with obvious lack of interest.

"In truth, no," Bridget forced herself to answer.

"Then do not disturb me," Gerald cautioned.

Bridget's hackles rose, glad she had not reprimanded Cathryn only to have her brother shrug off the young woman's absences as not worthy of his concern. Gerald's attitude silenced Bridget; however, she made note of Cathryn's comings and goings and, on occasion, even tried to follow her, always forced to give up when Cathryn's trail disappeared just as surely as she did. Mistress Seymour considered whom and where Cathryn might visit, but she had no proof, and Cathryn refused to say. Bridget had an eerie sense about the girl and about her brother as well, though her thoughts strayed in a very different direction from the truth.

From time to time, since Phoebe Seymour's death, Bridget had doubts about the state of Gerald's mind. His decisions with regard to Cathryn now made Bridget more conscious of her worries. She knew Cathryn's insolence deserved to be punished, but never imagined punishment had been meted out in advance.

Carthyn sought solace for her abuse where she imagined it available, though Vanya offered her only grudging welcome at first. Soon, however, Cathryn was greeted with apparent warmth, her every arrival anticipated with enthusiasm.

Many of the hours the women spent together were passed in companionable silence, working side by side in Vanya's garden, where Cathryn learned countless things by observation alone. Sometimes Vanya seemed distant, withdrawn, preoccupied. Other times she chatted amiably about her world or, little by little, without Cathryn even being aware, drew out Cathryn's secrets.

In a soft voice, Vanya sometimes sang strange haunting melodies in a tongue strongly familiar yet quite foreign. In Venice, a major crossroad of the world, the *piazzas* and alleys had always been filled with passersby speaking foreign languages; still, Cathryn could not place what Vanya only explained was her native tongue.

Vanya Russo's cottage was of sound English exposed-timber construction, a one-room house with a buttery to the side of the fireplace and, in the bare rafters, a cockloft that could be reached only by ladder. The unusual furnishings revealed Vanya's foreign origin; the chair she had offered to Cathryn on the morning of her escape from Gerald was the only one she had. While the number of chairs one had in one's house was usually a clue to one's wealth, in Vanya's cottage it signified her distaste for Western habits.

Cathryn learned the one chair in Vanya's possession was a keepsake, left from the time when Ashley Godwyne was alive, a concession she had made to his disabilities after the fire. Vanya preferred her once vibrant-colored cushions and rugs to sit upon, though they now were faded and diminished by years of use. The colors of blood red, orange, deep purple, and blue, and the weaving of gold threads spoke of an Eastern, not an English or European tradition. Ashley had joined her on the carpet-cushioned floor to sleep, she said. This was her home, to be furnished as she pleased. "He did not suffer with me," she replied, in answer to Cathryn's questioning look. "You have slept in comfort here, have you not?"

Cathryn could only nod in affirmation and wonder about the English lord and his foreign mistress, for Vanya was not just strange, but intensely secretive. Cathryn could understand how Bridget feared her, though she herself had grown to trust the disfigured woman.

Where had Vanya come from and how had she and Lord Godwyne met? Her questions were not answered. Perhaps in Venice?

"Perhaps."

While she avoided personal revelations, Vanya freely shared her knowledge of plants—simples and worts—medicinal and magic plants and herbs. Cathryn was staggered by the vast store of secrets Vanya held about what would heal and what would kill. Together they often ventured beyond the glen into the open meadows to collect plants that Vanya did not cultivate within her garden, returning with baskets and armfuls of vegetation.

Often, people Cathryn had never seen before abruptly appeared in Vanya's glen seeking remedies for myriad ailments, and always Vanya sent them away with something to work a cure—a paste of elecampane for a hacking cough; feverfew tea made with the flowers and leaves of the plant to cool a fever; an oil of seven herbs to anoint a lovesick girl; a comfrey poultice for the painful, engorged breasts of a new mother; rainwater to bathe sore eyes; a sweet electuary of bugloss for a wet lung; ale hoofe to be added to ale for worms of the brain; a charm for warts—all kindly dispensed.

"How do they know to come to you?" asked Cathryn.

"An herbwoman gains a reputation—or perhaps God sends them to my door," she answered, startling Cathryn, who in spite of herself had fallen victim to Bridget's rumors that the woman was a Witch.

One afternoon a woman of about Cathryn's age surprised her as she worked in Vanya's garden, mistaking her for the herbwoman. "Mistress, I need your help," she implored. "Please give me a spell or charm, for I am barren."

"I can't help you, but—"

"But you must! I am desperate. I've come from miles away. Your reputation as a wisewoman has traveled well beyond the district."

"You don't understand. . . ."

"Please!" The woman rushed forward as Cathryn stood up. She grabbed Cathryn's arm. "I can pay you handsomely. My husband threatens to divorce me if I do not produce an heir. I came here because . . ." Her voice faltered with her tears.

The woman was dressed handsomely, her right hand weighted with a large ruby-and-diamond ring. Cathryn put her hand over the hand that gripped her arm, causing the woman to relax her tight grip.

"I'm sorry if I hurt you," she said, "but I am desperate. I don't know what I shall do if I am unable to have a child."

"Come with me," Cathryn answered, and led her inside Vanya's cottage. "This is the woman you seek," she said.

Coloring, the woman cried, "Forgive me," as Vanya turned

around. It was obvious no one had warned her of Vanya's disfigurement, for on seeing Vanya, the woman's eyes widened and suddenly she was speechless.

"She is childless and comes to be healed," Cathryn explained.

"So you wish a child and cannot have one?" Vanya inquired, putting down a bunch of tansy she was tying with straw to hang and dry.

The woman nodded.

"Mandrake shall work the cure," Vanya promised, and led the way back to the garden to uproot a smooth-leafed plant with a few small yellow apples dangling on weak stalks. The plant was supported by a long, plump turberous root that divided into three parts at the end. "Mandrake, Cathryn, for its resemblance to a man or, sometimes, a woman, is uncommonly good for potency in either sex, for inducing sleep, for easing pain, and for drying abscesses." Vanya rubbed off some of the soil from the tuber. "This is a perfect specimen, mistress. Keep it near your body for a week; then boil it for the juice. Add a spoonful to your wine each night."

The woman clutched the root. "Thank you," she said, then briefly kneeled before Vanya and kissed her hand. When she rose to her feet she gave Vanya a small pouch of coins and hurried away.

Cathryn and Vanya barely had time to return to work when someone else appeared in the clearing. This time a man who walked with a decided limp moved slowly toward the cottage.

Cathryn summoned Vanya.

"You should not have waited so long to come for help," Vanya said as she examined the man's badly burned leg, then applied a poultice using leaves of strawberries, bitter aloes, and moldy bread. "Use this until the wound is healed," Vanya advised, and gave the man a generous quantity of paste. "Do not hesitate to return, if you need more."

"The pain is nearly gone," the man insisted within a few minutes. "I am very grateful," he said when he turned to leave.

The women watched the man disappear into the woods again. "Come, let's have some tea," Vanya urged, "and, also, I've a cure to dispense to you."

"A cure? But I'm not ill."

"And I hope you will not be. I should have thought of it sooner," she apologized as she gave Cathryn a bottle filled with a clear amber-colored liquid. "This decoction of rue shall destroy your ability to get children for as long as you use it. A spoonful in the morning and at night should be sufficient."

"I prefer a poison for Master Seymour," Cathryn insisted, "a Witch's curse."

"Soon, just as I promised." Vanya pledged. "You must be patient."

Cathryn wanted to fall on her knees before Vanya and beg her to summon whatever power she could for use against Gerald Seymour. Vanya seemed to have the ability and willingness to work cures for others, why not for her? Had not Cathryn revealed almost all there was to tell about herself to Vanya? She knew about her life in Venice, about her music, of being forced to come to England, of her brutal guardian. Why did Vanya Russo not help her?

Growing increasingly desperate, Cathryn saw no evil in defending herself by whatever means necessary to render her guardian impotent. She would use medicine or magic—even Witchcraft. In moments of unthinking rage, murdering Gerald had more than once crossed Cathryn's mind. To take a life as revenge was as immoral as it was criminal, yet from time to time, Cathryn seriously deliberated poisoning Gerald Seymour.

Vanya's garden, if not her own, contained a bounty of killing herbs, but the ones she secretly investigated smelled so vile that she could not imagine successfully inducing Gerald to eat or drink anything in which the poison was an ingredient. Also, would he not be suspicious if suddenly she offered him something to eat that she did not offer to others? The notion of killing Gerald was one thing; the thought of murdering the children as well was quite another.

Cathryn sat with Vanya Russo and drank rosemary tea. The silence between the women deepened. Cathryn eyed the now familiar cottage and realized she had never seen a Bible, but Vanya was not a likely Protestant and probably, like most women, could not read. Neither had Cathryn seen a rosary or crucifix in the cottage, only symbols whose meaning she did not know.

In a small alcove stood a low, lustrous ebony table with strange symbols carved throughout. A narrow cushion in place before the table invited one to kneel, as if the table were an altar, and always on the table on immaculate squares of white linen sat a censer containing burning incense, a dish of salt, a silver chalice brimming with water, a lighted candle, and a small engraved knife. There was also a golden sword with a slender blade. None of the objects spoke of any religion of which Cathryn knew. All signs suggested Vanya was a pagan.

Cathryn shuddered at the thought of involving herself with the powers and potions of the underworld, yet her agony at her guardian's hands began to outweigh her terror of the craft.

"Pray to your God for deliverance, Cathryn," Vanya urged.

Cathryn had prayed but had received no solace. In England God obviously did not care to rescue Catholics.

"While I cannot yet help you in the manner you wish, in the meantime I have something that will at least amuse you," Vanya said, and produced an ancient-looking, half-pear-shaped, bent-necked instrument.

"A lute!" Cathryn cried. "Where did it come from?"

"It came from Persia—handed down from mother to daughter since time began."

With reverence, Cathryn touched the magnificent seven-stringed instrument. It appeared to be in perfect condition. "Play for me, please!" Cathryn pleaded.

Vanya consented, thrilling Cathryn with her apparent skill. Cathryn knew how to play a lute but had learned on a larger, more modern instrument, using bare fingers instead of the quill plectrums Vanya used to pluck the strings.

As she entertained her visitor, Vanya could see the young musician longed to play the instrument herself. "Here, I will teach you what I know," she said, showing Cathryn how to use the picks, and listened while Cathryn tried to master the ancient instrument.

Quickly, Cathryn felt quite secure with Vanya's instrument and adapted a dance Vittorio had written for a lute of larger size and different tuning.

When she concluded the gay song, Vanya sighed. "It was not foolish to have left you in Venice."

"What do you mean?"

"I mean, you were meant to study music those long years."

"What use was all my effort? I'm forbidden to play. Master Seymour believes my music an insult to God—and he hasn't even heard me play!"

"You can bring your violin to me. Master Seymour will not follow to be offended."

For the moment Cathryn forgot her troubles as she dreamed of playing her Amati again. She smiled at Vanya and promised to find a way to bring the violin to Vanya's glen—under Gerald Seymour's very nose, if need be.

Chapter 41

"I know where you go," Gerald whispered as he pinioned her beneath him. "You think I don't, but I do. She is evil."

"She is *not*."

"She has the stench of death. She shall destroy you."

"And what do you do for me?"

"I bring you salvation."

"*This* is salvation? Surely, for all eternity, the Lord shall punish you for touching me." Cathryn made another desperate attempt to force Gerald to free her.

But Gerald ignored her as he always did when she challenged him. He seemed deaf to her logic as if he did not hear, and above her fury for his brutal use of her, she was baffled by his lack of simple reasoning.

It was as if, at night, when he preyed on her, he became a different man. There was a quality of madness and passion as he struggled with her of which she would never have guessed him capable. If he had been her lover and she in love with him, she might have imagined him obsessed by love for her.

But Cathryn despised Gerald Seymour. He was her assailant, and each touch, each sound he made in the rough ritual of possession, came as a blow to Cathryn's body and to her soul.

At times, when he left her bed at last, she lay numb, and at others, once certain she was alone, she wept. Often she reflected that it was she who had gone mad, a madness made worse by the knowledge that no one would believe a man of Gerald Seymour's piety could commit this kind of crime.

"You're a pagan Catholic whom God despises. No need to offer your Roman prayers, for He shall not hear you," Gerald whispered in the dark.

"But *you* are *not* a pagan!" Cathryn argued beneath him.

"You are of no consequence. Nor is my behavior toward you of God's concern," he answered, his logic twisted. In his mind it was not a crime to abuse a Catholic. "I am immune from ordinary punishment."

"How I hate you!" she screamed. "I wish you dead." In her rage, Cathryn felt something twist inside herself and vowed she would find a way to take revenge.

In the meantime, Cathryn wooed away Gerald Seymour's children. Jacob, and even Diligence, succumbed. She stole them not by design so much as by winning them with patience and tender regard. She considered them before all her other duties. She listened to them in the dark and in the light. With ordinary and unusual medicine, she healed their bodies when they were sick, and their spirits with love when they were sad. She forced herself to dwell on them, and whenever she was with them, she forgot her misery.

She did forbidden things. She lured the children away from the house and told them stories. They laughed and engaged in games, playing leapfrog, Chuck Farthing, pitch and hustle, and hot cockles until they collapsed. She taught them songs and rhymes she remembered from a chapbook Father Alberto had given her long ago.

Old Mother Goose, when she wanted to wander,
Would ride through the air on a very fine gander.
Mother Goose had a house, 'twas built in a wood,
Where an owl at the door for a sentinel stood.

"Just like the Witch in our wood," Jacob said.

" 'Tis wicked to gossip," Diligence reminded him, before Cathryn could pursue the matter.

Mother, may I go out to swim?
Yes, my darling daughter,
Hang your clothes on a hickory limb,
But don't go near the water.

She taught them rhymes they had never heard before.

Hector Protector was dressed all in green;
Hector Protector was sent to the queen;
The queen did not like him,
No more did the king;
So Hector Protector was sent back again.

"Who could that be?" Cathryn asked the children. "Who but Oliver Cromwell, the Puritan who killed Charles."

"You mustn't tell our father that rhyme," Comfort warned her.

"I promise," Cathryn promised.

It became almost impossible now for Cathryn to keep her disdain of the Puritan religion private and she could not force herself to make any further effort toward conversion, which made a mockery of Gerald's private reasoning about her future as his wife. She was cautious with her contempt for the children's sake, but they noticed she was something less than pious. At the very least, they knew she was bored.

On occasion Gerald grew red-faced with her inadequate replies to his inquiries. "You have overlooked the obvious, Master Seymour. Our Lord has not elected me. He chooses souls of your character to be Protestant and rejects lost souls like mine."

Alone with her at night, he exacted cruel payment for her insolence, inflicting intense humiliation and pain on Cathryn's soft flesh.

Cathryn prayed for Bridget to discover her brother in her bed but knew it was a hopeless supplication. The woman slept like the dead. Besides, she was an unlikely champion, Cathryn reasoned. Even if Bridget were witness to his raping her, Cathryn was convinced Gerald somehow would escape his sister's wrath, and Cathryn would be made the guilty party.

Eventually Cathryn began to dream in earnest of killing Gerald. At first, as was just, she imagined God striking Gerald dead. She felt his full weight upon her and woke panting, in the midst of throwing off the covers from the bed. Soon Cathryn's panic would give way to relief, then terrible grief at the knowledge that Gerald Seymour was still alive.

When God failed to strike him dead, in Cathryn's dreams, she became the aggressor, avenging herself with the engraved knife she had seen at Vanya's. In Cathryn's dream there was no blood, but on Gerald's face was a look of complete surprise as she plunged the knife. The dream continued, and as she feared, she was left alone to defend herself against her guardian's murder. No one believed that he had harmed her.

The voices raised against her were loud, including Bridget's and those of people she did not know.

Father Vittorio was present at her inquisition. He did not look at her, and, silent, he did not defend her, even when she begged. Who would believe her when the only man she'd ever loved denied her?

Often with this nightmare, Cathryn awakened crying, afraid her dream was prophecy as much as fantasy, and when her tears subsided, she dwelled on how the priest denied her. She saw the cold indifference of his eyes—or was it hatred?

Cathryn reflected on the priest who had sworn he loved her but begged she understand the torment of his soul. Without him, without the grace of his love, Cathryn felt utterly alone—and feared alone was what she would always be.

Chapter 42

Cathryn's dreams terrified her, but she feared both the outcome of doing what she dreamed and failing to accomplish Gerald's death. The only relief she had from the torture of her fears was the time she spent at Vanya's.

She longed to bring the children with her, but even though they trusted her, Cathryn knew it could never be, for if Comfort was out of earshot, Jacob and Diligence succeeded in telling Cathryn wild tales of the Witch who inhabited their dead uncle's estate.

"Lord Godwyne was the Witch's familiar. He carried out her spells," Jacob assured her. "Sometimes I see her riding the night mare from the nursery."

"You cannot!" Diligence insisted, annoyed that Jacob had told Cathryn a story she had once invented.

"Yes, I can," he countered. "I'll wager Father has seen her, too. Perhaps that's why he's often gone from his room in the middle of the night."

"What makes you think that?" Cathryn wondered, concealing her horror that one of the children might know where Gerald spent the time he was absent from his bed.

"I've been to his room, and he's often not there."

"That doesn't mean he's seen the Witch," Diligence countered.

"Maybe not."

"Maybe she uses *him*," Diligence suggested with an almost gleeful speculative smile.

"God protects him, fool."

"I am not a fool!"

"Children," Cathryn interrupted, glad their conversation strayed from their father to petty rivalries. "Let's be on our way," she said, and led the way back to the house.

If the children only knew how impatient I am to steal to the Witch's cottage; how eager I am to see her and play my violin, Cathryn thought, smiling.

To her surprise, it had almost been easy to carry the Amati to Vanya's, but she had been dismayed to find the gut strings broken. For the present the broken strings were replaced by others she had brought with her from Venice, but she worried that the replacements would not last forever, just as the agility of her fingers had not.

In the past, Cathryn had taken her limber fingers for granted, but she would never be so foolish again. At first, the Amati squeaked pitifully, and in her mind's eye, she could see her priest cover his ears in self-defense, his expression pained. Cathryn smiled at the vision of his playful grimace.

Cathryn closed her eyes to concentrate and drilled her clumsy fingers with scales until they ached. She promised to find a way to come to Vanya's and practice every day.

Cathryn tried a melody that haunted her and imagined again she saw her lover frown. "God spare me this indignity!" he cried, and in her head she could hear the way it should be played. "Now try again. But this time, have some regard for my tender ears."

Later he conceded, "Better. But you have *much* to improve!"

Cathryn agreed and played the song over and over until he called, *"Meraviglioso!"*

Cathryn smiled and set her fiddle down.

Vanya sat before her upon cushions whose colors were shaded by the darkness of the room, and beside her lay the great white dog. In the hearth a fire burned behind their backs.

"I decree it is a mortal sin for Gerald to forbid you to play," Vanya said, smiling, when Cathryn stopped her practice, then poured her a cup of steaming lavender tea. Her smile conveyed the unspoken affection that flowed between them.

Cathryn sighed. "His notion of sin is variable," she said with obvious bitterness. She drank several sips of the hot beverage sweetened with dark honey. "You promised to help me find a way to take revenge on Gerald Seymour," Cathryn pressed. "I want to know how? And when?"

"Bring me several strands of Gerald Seymour's hair."

"Why?"

"Soon you shall know."

Cathryn's voice rose. "Why not now?" she demanded. "If you don't help me, I fear I shall fall irretrievably into madness."

"I've given my word to help you, Cathryn," Vanya said calmly to Cathryn's near hysteria. "I wait now only for the right moment in time, for all of heaven's signs to be favorable—for the proper season."

Cathryn fell silent, her eyes dark with rage. "Life for me is hell, with no salvation I am sure of. Gerald Seymour proclaims himself a saint, and I am forced to wonder if all holy men are as depraved as he."

"There must be a few good men in the world."

"Have you known any?"

Vanya nodded.

"Was Ashley Godwyne a saint?"

Vanya smiled. "He was very much a man, and I came to England only because I did not want to live without him, but perhaps you do not yet understand the sentiment of love between a woman and a man." Vanya gazed at Cathryn. "I abandoned everything and everyone to follow my lover to this inhospitable land. But at last I have found my place. My soul now abides comfortably here."

"I doubt mine ever shall." Cathryn's voice betrayed a threat of tears. "You are mistaken—I do understand the sentiment of love—and its sorrows, as well. But unlike you, I am denied my love. Sometimes I feel as though I shall die without him.'' Cathryn choked back tears. "What I *don't* understand is why I haven't died.''

Vanya sighed. "Perhaps your fate is to live and learn more from life.''

"Or perhaps I am being punished for loving a man God would rather I did not.''

"Why is God always imagined to be so cruel?'' Vanya asked.

Cathryn had no reply to Vanya's simple question.

"I continue to defy God by dreaming my lover still loves me. I dream that someday I shall open Gerald Seymour's door and find my lover standing before me.''

Cathryn lowered her eyes and withheld the rest of her vision. In this recurring dream, Vittorio stepped forward to give Cathryn a kiss of pure delight, and when it ended, they lay together in Venice, having enjoyed the deepest pleasures of the flesh.

Cathryn stared beyond Vanya and beyond the fire. She closed her eyes and in the dark silence that ensued allowed her senses to wander from the cottage into the ether that surrounded them. Her anger and her pain seemed to drift away and exposed the true emotions of her heart. She had been wounded; she had known pain; but beyond her bitter words, Cathryn Godwyne knew she would love Vittorio forever.

Chapter 43

Cathryn felt she could not wait much longer for Vanya's aid, and daily feared she would soon be forced to desperate means.

In his attraction to her, Gerald Seymour grew careless in his approach. Sometimes with others barely out of sight or earshot he was grossly familiar, trying to kiss her or touch an inviting breast. In absolute horror, Cathryn succeeded each time in wriggling away and writhed inside each time she thought of him. She begged the saints to send Vittorio or some avenging angel.

At times Cathryn sincerely doubted that God was a Catholic—at least in England, for there now appeared to be no hope that England would ever be rescued from the Protestants. James II was no longer king, having fled to Europe behind his Catholic wife, and had been succeeded by a pair of Protestants, William of Orange and Mary.

How clever of Mary Stuart to refuse to reign without her husband at her side! Cathryn thought, and how she envied the queen, who would for all time have her beloved prince at her side. But Cathryn wondered if William deserved the queen's devotion. General rumor was that he did not.

But in this world, Cathryn was aware, most women were doomed to fall like adoring puppets at the feet of men, deserving or not. Cathryn supposed she should not have been so surprised by Gerald Seymour's logic and his expectation that the lure of becoming his wife would change her attitude toward him.

Quite boldly one night after the children had been put to bed, he came to her chamber at an hour before she was accustomed to retiring. "I've decided it prudent for me to marry you," he said matter-of-factly and watched the color drain from Cathryn's face.

"I shall never consent!"

"Come, Cathryn. There is no need to pretend. I need not court you any longer. The bargain is made," he said, and reached to touch her.

Cathryn retreated. "Are you so demented that you don't realize I'd flee if there were any place for me to go?"

"But there is no place, is there, Cathryn?" he gloated. "You're a prisoner to the bargain, just as I am."

"You're mad!" she cried, and tried to push his hands away as he seized her.

"Quite." Gerald held Cathryn firmly in a cruel embrace. "If you insist on being difficult, I promise I shall punish my children for your ingratitude. I shall send them all away."

Tears glistened in Cathryn's eyes. Gerald laughed with satisfaction at the look of grief that crossed her face. He had discovered his only possible means of manipulating her. Despite his madness, Gerald had seen clearly that Cathryn loved his children and cleaved to them protectively.

"I understand now that you shall never renounce your pagan faith, but you shall do whatever I propose, if you want to keep my children by your side."

Suddenly Gerald pushed Cathryn away. "Tonight I want the pleasure of seeing you in the light, naked, just as the Devil made you," he said, though he usually insisted on darkness. "Remove your gown and let me look at you."

"I will not!" Cathryn insisted, and felt before she saw his open-handed blow.

"In my house I am lord!" Gerald screamed. "You shall obey my every command!"

Cathryn regained her balance. "Are you not afraid someone will hear us?"

"It is your only hope." Gerald laughed, the madness in his eyes frightening and quite clear.

Cathryn stood immobile.

Again Gerald slapped her viciously. "Satan did not make you deaf! Undress."

Then his look softened and he laughed. "Of course, your pleasure is perverse." He struck her again, making Cathryn cry out and her lip bleed from violent contact with her teeth. She felt dizzy but struggled as Gerald began to strip her of her gown. Small fastening buttons flew from her dress. "Leave me alone!" she screamed.

"Cry out," he urged her. "I love the sound of your distress and the wild struggle required to take you!"

Cathryn's heart sank. Even her attempts to protect herself against his attacks excited his lust. Stripped almost naked, she managed to tear away from him. She retreated to the far side of the bed. "Where in Scripture do you find permission to use me this way?"

Gerald gave a derisive laugh. "It is much too late for reason— the bargain has already been struck—and you, Cathryn, are my prize. I did not ask for gold. I only wanted you—all I needed do was ask and Satan provided."

Gerald tore away the last of her clothing and stared at Cathryn. "How does Satan make so perfect a creature?" he gasped in wonder. Except for a few purple bruises, Cathryn did not have a blemish on her that he could see.

Loathing his lustful scrutiny, and furious that Gerald would want light, Cathryn began to feel a madness of her own. Her heart beat wildly, yet she forced herself to appear calm. Could Gerald believe the devil had granted her to him?

When he reached for her, though her flesh recoiled, Cathryn stood indifferent as he kissed and fondled her, reasoning if Gerald preferred she struggle, then she would gladly die before giving him that satisfaction again. Tremendously excited, he pulled her hands to his erection, demonstrating the strength of the caress he wished of her. "Satan promised you would consent to whatever I asked."

The instant Gerald released his grip, Cathryn let her hands fall from him. Growling with displeasure, Gerald threw Cathryn down upon the bed.

She lay still as he probed every inch of her tender flesh with his hungry mouth and rough caresses. His anger with her passivity mounting. He gave special cruel attention to her nipples with his teeth.

A voice inside Cathryn's head raved in utter madness and revulsion, and nearly choking, she kept her own voice still. He inflicted pain but Cathryn was submissive, eyes closed, lying as if she had no feeling.

"No! This is not what I expect." Gerald rose above her. He slapped her face, forcing Cathryn's eyes open and tears to spring. "You render me useless!" he snarled, and rolled away from her.

Cathryn stared at his flaccid member and began to laugh as Gerald tried to rub life into the suddenly unwilling organ. "This is not the bargain I made with your master!"

Cathryn's pleasure in his obvious torment was almost greater than her relief. "You're such a fool you expect the devil to pay his due?" she badgered, unable to let the opportunity go by. "He has gained your soul and that is all that matters."

Gerald bellowed in outrage and struck her with his fists.

Cathryn lunged back at him and reached beyond him to the table by the bed for a dagger she had stolen from Vanya's just that morning. With every intention of killing him, Cathryn thrust the knife with vigor just below his ribs. In an instant, she pulled the knife free and thrust at him again.

In agonized and horrified surprise, before she could stab him a second time, Gerald grabbed Cathryn's knife-wielding wrist and with the other hand wrested the dagger away. He darted from her and, naked, crouched warily before her, a wounded animal, enraged.

"You dare?" he demanded with convincing disbelief as he grasped for his discarded clothing. "I'll see you burn for this!" he swore.

"It shall be better to be dead than have you touch me ever again," Cathryn answered with equal fury, and watched the blood surge slowly from his wound.

Gerald tried both to staunch his bleeding wound and to stumble into his clothes. He was frightened but aware the wound she had inflicted was not fatal. "Your own blood tells, Cathryn Godwyne," he grimaced as he pressed against his wound. He sucked in a breath. "You are not of this world, Cathryn, but come from a dark abode to perform miraculous acts of healing with electuaries and possets only a Witch could know."

"You are insane, Gerald Seymour," Cathryn spit back at him.

"No—Prudence would have died, but you arrived to stave off death and her union with God," he recounted. "Your garden yields like no other in the district. You tame the crows and rodents to eat in other fields. Even my children follow you like sheep. They quote you night and day. You enchant and mystify all four—they mock me with your praises."

Gerald waved Cathryn's weapon at her. "But children are too easily led—what I do not completely understand is your power over me. Tell me, Cathryn, for I have not been able to deduce it, when do you administer your nearly lethal potions?"

"If I had potions and spells to work on you, Gerald Seymour, I'd not for a moment make you vital!"

Gerald sprang at Cathryn and menaced her with the knife, tracing her jawline with the bloodied point, then circling a rosy nipple. His wound continued to bleed.

"You're so perfectly made," he whispered, distracted. "I knew from the first moment my eyes settled on you that you had been sent by Satan to test me. I thought my faith would prevail—that I was strong. But I did not reckon with Satan's power. I underestimated him in many things—not the least of which, his evil ability to create such purity of beauty. I stand in awe of his skill to render something as perfect as you. You exceed anything I have seen that God has made."

Gerald's eyes held an odd shine. "I should have heeded my sister's warning, but I let you go, and you went straight to your mother to learn the craft. Your mother is proud of you, no doubt."

Cathryn glared at Gerald.

"You needn't pretend, Cathryn Godwyne," he said as he pushed away from her. "You've known from the beginning, else why did you so quickly rush to her side?"

"What are you saying?"

"I say the Witch Vanya Russo is your mother, and that your sire was my brother Ashley—a fact that only multiplies the crimes we've committed in your bed," he said, gesturing violently with the knife.

Gerald weaved back toward the door. "Cathryn Godwyne, descended of Eve, Satan's tool for the destruction of men, the Devil's Woman," he said, and stumbled out the door.

Greatly stunned by Gerald's revelation, Cathryn sat trembling in the flickering candlelight. Frozen with confusion and fear, she waited an eternity before coming to her senses. Then she dressed, all the while expecting an uproar to ensue.

When she left the house, all was quiet, and a thought at once both horrible and gratifying crossed her mind: Perhaps the wound was worse than she at first believed and Gerald Seymour now lay dead!

For killing him, Cathryn supposed she deserved the punishment of death. But no one she had ever known or imagined more deserved to die than Gerald Seymour—and she doubted she would ever feel remorse.

Chapter 44

As was her habit in distress, Cathryn fled in the direction of Vanya Russo's cottage; however, she halted short of reaching the woman's door, held back by Gerald's eager revelations. She had been light-headed as he'd waved the dagger point at her and quite faint when he'd announced Vanya was her mother. Had she imagined it? Cathryn wondered now. Was it a fact—or a lie invented by a madman?

For a long while Cathryn puzzled in the dark woods just outside the clearing where Vanya's cottage stood. She had come to love the glen, a place where she felt at peace—the only peace she had known since arriving in England. It seemed a haven filled with all manner of fascinating knowledge, which in light of Gerald's accusations took on new meaning.

Though Vanya Russo had befriended her, Cathryn could not imagine the woman her mother. True, there was warmth in their regard for one another, but Cathryn had always sensed the existence of a cold barrier between them—something separate and distinct in Vanya's nature that Cathryn imagined no one could penetrate—not even a child of her body and blood. If she was the mother who had abandoned her, did Vanya Russo simply lack the heart to mother her child? Cathryn wondered. Or was her sense of Vanya some inner knowledge of the woman's involvement with the craft? Troubled and exhausted, Cathryn desired rest even more than answers.

As she moved closer to the cottage, Zephyrus began to bark. He ran to greet her, then led her to Vanya's door.

"Cathryn, it is the middle of the night." Vanya said, greeting her with a candle.

"Please, let me sleep here tonight. I shall try to explain everything in the morning."

"Of course," Vanya replied. "I'm glad you came. At last I can help you defend against your guardian."

"It's too late," Cathryn cried.

"Too late?"

"He may already be dead—I stabbed him."

Vanya put her arm around Cathryn as her step appeared to falter. "Here, sit down." She assisted Cathryn to cushions before the fire.

"I could not wait for you to help me."

"My dagger—yes?"

Cathryn nodded. "I pray he's dead."

"His death at your hands will mean your death as well."

"At least then I should not have to endure his touch," Cathryn cried, and related her experience to Vanya.

Vanya stared at Cathryn thoughtfully. "I imagine you have only wounded him—which only makes the moment more auspicious. You shall spend the remainder of the night here, of course, but in the morning you must hasten to return and very soon give Gerald some of the decoction I've prepared."

Cathryn's eyes grew bright with fresh hope.

"I am sorry you have had to wait, but there are reasons your wait was necessary—for one, the process of preparing the decoction is long, and until now, the signs of heaven have not been right—nor the blossoms in their bravery."

Vanya rose from the cushions and returned with an uprooted plant bearing a profusion of brown, bell-shaped flowers on a multileafed stalk. "You must give this decoction to Gerald each night, which with his weakness will cause his yearnings to quickly vanish. But be cautious. Too much will accomplish what the dagger did not."

Cathryn touched the soft woolly leaves of the plant. "It shall be a temptation to use it for that end."

Vanya laid the plant near the hearth. "It's been a long while since I've been called to use henbane—more often, as you know, the request is for something to enhance wantonness." She smiled. "I don't suppose tonight you thought to bring me some of his hair?"

"I almost forgot," Cathryn said, and withdrew several strands of Gerald's hair wrapped in a linen handkerchief.

From a nearby basket, Vanya collected several long pieces of straw, which she bent and tied quickly to fashion a figure of straw. In the straw man's head she wove the strands of Gerald's hair.

She kneeled and called for Cathryn to kneel beside her, then sprinkled salt over the figure of straw. "I bring thee to life, Gerald Seymour," she said, and took up another long strand of straw and lit it in the fire. Then slowly she inscribed a circle three times over the straw figure. "Trouble me not at all. Stay thou away from me. From flaming fire to cold ashes with thy lust," she chanted three times, then set the straw figure on fire, igniting first the hair.

Quickly the figure burned until only ashes remained.

When the ashes cooled, Vanya swept them into a linen pouch, which she tied with a silver thread and placed in Cathryn's hand. "With this spell and the decoction, the fire of Gerald Seymour's passion will die."

Cathryn held the pouch of ashes in her hand and prayed Vanya Russo's spells and potions had the power she claimed.

"Now the time has come for sleep," Vanya urged, and made Cathryn a bed of cushions.

In the morning, with some hesitation Cathryn returned to Gerald's house. It was early and as usual she toiled in the garden before venturing in the house. When the children came to her acting as though no disaster had occurred, she joined them for breakfast.

Even Bridget Seymour seemed her usual dour self. "My brother has taken to his bed—a bloody flux," she explained almost casually. "You will need to prepare an agrimony decoction. He seems in much pain."

Cathryn nodded and concealed her disappointment over the news that Gerald Seymour's health was not worse. "I've just the cure for him," she promised, and sat waiting for someone to come forward and accuse her of trying to murder him.

"You shall have more responsibility for the children again now that their father is down in bed," Bridget reminded Cathryn when she finally rose from the table to gather the herbs for Gerald's cure.

"Of course," Cathryn replied as she retreated to the garden, and prayed in his misery Gerald would forget his threat to separate the children from her.

Later she oversaw the preparation of the medicine to ease the ailment he claimed, adding a spoonful of henbane syrup to

Gerald's cup, watching as Bridget carried the steaming brew away to him. Cathryn begged God for success and waited.

Without their father's hawkish observation, the children's daily routine progressed pleasantly. They spent many more hours than usual out of doors. With Cathryn they pruned the orchard and stacked the wood for wattle fences to be made the next spring when the wood had dried. In secret, a long way from the house, Cathryn and the children constructed a tent with linens pilfered from the wash left drying on the grass.

The four children were especially merry, causing Cathryn almost to forget that they were the somber Seymour children. Yet when they trekked back to the house, all laughter ceased and sober faces returned, their songs silenced abruptly in their throats.

"Back to our cells," Cathryn muttered. She and the children lived two lives: one in the house and one in the out-of-doors—and out of view of their stern overseers.

In private, Cathryn waited to be accused of making an attempt on Gerald's life, but none was made. Bridget sputtered her alarm when she discovered Gerald's bloodied clothing and gaping wound, but Gerald refused to give her any information, forcing her to remain ignorant. Mentally she stored away the odd event, adding it to the growing collection of concerns she had about her brother, yet life in the Seymour household went on as if her brother had only taken ill.

Then his fever rose and Gerald sent for Cathryn.

"In my sickbed, I see you floating naked above me riding your goat, and I hear you laughing. Spare me, Witch, I beg you. I vow still to be your slave," he raved in a hoarse whisper, truly frightened.

"You are mad!"

"You have made me so." He reached for Cathryn, but she stepped aside. Gerald became frantic. "I swear, I'll tell no one of your vile nature. No one will ever know of my pact with Satan for you—only spare my life," he begged.

Cathryn's head reeled at his accusations. "If I had power, why would I spare you? You're more evil than anything you fear of me."

Weak from his effort to persuade her, Gerald closed his eyes. "Remember, Witch, you need me as much as I need you," he muttered as he fell deeper into delirium.

Cathryn lay awake in her bed half the night the next few nights, waiting for news that Gerald Seymour was dead, but by morning of the third day his fever had passed.

Again he called Cathryn to his bedside. "I won't forget that you have spared me."

"I did not spare you," she insisted. "I have no power. I am not a Witch."

"The daughter of a witch is always a witch." He smiled in a way that made Cathryn's stomach lurch. "But I won't betray you—as I've not betrayed your mother all these years."

"She's not a Witch. And she's *not* my mother."

"Oh, but she is. Vanya Russo came from Venice with my brother, leaving you behind—perhaps Ashley felt one Devil's Woman under his roof was plentiful."

"If she's a Witch, why has no one spoken against her?"

"Her magic is strong."

"She is only a wise woman using her knowledge of herbs for healing. She harms no one."

"An old woman needs the Devil's power to survive."

"She is quite able, and survives without any help from Satan."

"No woman can survive alone. She has incubi to do her work—that great uncanny dog, for one. She's made a bargain with Satan for the power of bestowing life."

Cathryn looked down at the floor. Part of what he said was true. Vanya often was called to births by desperate women in the district.

Cathryn's instincts continued to tell her Gerald Seymour was mad, though suddenly she felt uncertain.

If what Gerald said was true, why had Vanya not revealed herself to be her mother? Were the faded silk cushions Cathryn sometimes sat upon once vibrant red, the very colors she remembered in her dreams?

If Vanya was her mother, what was in her mind, both now and in the past? Why had Vanya abandoned her? Why had Vanya approached her now?

Vanya Russo made no pretense to be an ordinary peasant woman. What protected her from Witch finders, who profited from the conviction of a Witch and from madmen like Gerald Seymour? Was it a special power derived from hell? If not, what form of dispensation allowed Vanya to live the way she did?

There was nothing in the glen to signify that Vanya was a

Christian, and many pagan symbols were to be found about her place. She had saved many lives with her possets, decoctions, and the like, and had served as a midwife to many a laboring woman— all survivors witness to the fact that Vanya Russo had power over life and death as all Witches had.

Soon Gerald Seymour's ravings diminished into troubled sleep, and Cathryn breathed an enormous sigh. Though frightening in their implication, at least his ravings had not descended to his usual lustful obsession with her. The henbane had worked a cure, and for as long as she continued to administer the drug, Gerald Seymour would be impotent!

Cathryn felt joyful, and though she could have slipped away, she continued to stand at her guardian's bedside. She shivered at the sight of his twitching and trembling in unrestful sleep and wondered over the source of Vanya's gift for healing—and for poison.

Vanya Russo was not merely an herbwoman with gifts any physician would covet. Cathryn thought of the straw man and of Vanya's spell on Gerald. Perhaps there was good reason to fear the woman. At the very least, Cathryn had a few questions she wanted answered.

But there was one question she had no need to ask—if Vanya confessed to being her mother and a Witch—for the daughter of a Witch was always a Witch.

Chapter 45

Cathryn believed in Witches. Who did not? For all her worldly opinions, even Comtesse Dansette admitted to believing in Witches and consulted sorcerers. Protestants and Catholics alike warned against them and campaigned for their extinction. The Bible of both religions ordered a Witch's death.

All at once, curious, sometimes upsetting remarks Cathryn had heard over the years fell into place. She remembered Perdita's hopeless sighs and references regarding her seductive behavior, and Father Vittorio's suggestions that her mother was a Witch from the East.

Had Father Vittorio known her mother to be a Witch, or had he only presumed her to be an Eastern seductress? Had he imagined her the daughter a Witch sent to collect and tether men's souls to assuage his conscience?

Something burned within Cathryn as she felt herself maligned, and in her mind's eye, she saw her accusers—Perdita, Gerald, and Vittorio—standing together. It tortured Cathryn to visualize the three against her. How could the two who claimed to love her stand with Gerald Seymour?

Cathryn struggled with tears of utter despair and tried to regain her composure. When she succeeded, Cathryn called the children to her side. Their uninterrupted days together were at an end. The children's father was well enough, he claimed, to at least sit with them during their Scripture lessons, and it was time to come before him.

"Today the Scripture lesson to ponder is Exodus, chapter twenty-two, verse eighteen. Please read it aloud for us, Jacob," Gerald instructed his son when they were all seated in the study.

"Thou shalt not suffer a Witch to live."

"What do we know of Witches?" Gerald asked the children, his eyes on Cathryn.

"They are ugly and old."

"They suck the breath of babies. Then they eat them."

"They use others to do their evil work."

"They anoint their ugly naked bodies with ointments blessed by their god Satan so they can fly through the air to do their evil."

"They cause crops to die."

"And storms."

"And men's souls to turn away from God."

"They are mostly women."

"Father," Comfort asked in the midst of the litany, "God commands us to kill a Witch. Why, then, do you consent to the Witch's presence in our wood?"

"Who accuses her?" Gerald demanded.

Comfort was silent.

"You have warned us," answered Jacob.

"She *perhaps* is a Witch."

"How might we tell?"

Gerald looked Cathryn up and down. "She gives potions and casts spells. She uses magic for evil. She hunts men's souls and turns them to do Satan's work. She lures her victims with beauty and seeds their souls and minds with lust. She punishes with pain and death."

For several moments Cathryn stopped breathing.

"But the woman in the wood is not beautiful."

Gerald still stared at Cathryn. "The men she seduces believe her beautiful. To them she is more desirable than the promise of heaven."

"No wonder God would have us kill a Witch!" Jacob cried, the Lord's reasoning quite obvious to him.

"It is our duty to see that *all* Witches die," Gerald said.

Cathryn knew he meant his words to be a prophecy, and she hid her terror even from herself, for the moment, imagining her guardian still too unsteady from fever and his wound, and the debilitating effects of Vanya's decoction to be dangerous.

Cathryn recognized how foolish she had been to think her troubles would be over if only Gerald Seymour's lust were cooled and, worried, stayed away from Vanya's glen, arguing the children needed more of her attention, a sufficient argument only as long as the henbane decoction was plentiful.

"I've missed you," Vanya said to Cathryn when she finally was forced to appear at Vanya's door again. There was a question in Vanya's voice.

"I couldn't come until now. . . ."

"But now you need more of the decoction. . . ."

"It has worked magic on Master Seymour."

"Indeed,"Vanya affirmed, letting Cathryn inside the cottage. "I've missed your company, but I've missed your music, also." Vanya smiled. "Come, play for me while I replenish your supply of henbane."

Cathryn unwrapped the Amati and caressed the gleaming maple of the violin's gently arched back. She admired the beautiful grain that gleamed through transparent varnish. A lifetime ago she had been completely absorbed in the act of making heart-wrenching music spill from this miraculous instrument—living a life in which a whole day might be dedicated to the perfection of a few pages of a single composition.

Cathryn rested her eyes on Vanya again and stared at the woman Gerald Seymour insisted was her mother. What would my life be now if I had not been left behind in Venice by a mother whom others proclaim a Witch? she pondered.

Vanya's gross disfigurement was no longer startling to Cathryn, but she could not yet overlook the scars in the first minutes each time they met. For that reason alone it was no wonder she had not recognized the woman as her mother! What Vanya had been as a young woman Cathryn's age could hardly be discerned. The effects of aging and the brilliant mane of white hair further deceived the eye.

Not taking her eyes from Vanya, Cathryn lifted the violin to her shoulder and laid her chin lightly on its satin surface. She perched the bow over the strings, then closed her eyes and played a song of remembrance—of when she was happy in Venice; of when she felt loved. Through the music, Cathryn mourned her loss of innocence, her knowledge of the world only making her long more deeply for her protected past.

Cathryn feared yet burned with questions that had to be asked of the woman who now sat totally still before her.

From memory, Cathryn continued to play the violin, but her mind churned on the subject of her mother. Vanya had been kind, even affectionate, befriending her as no one else in England had, yet as Cathryn considered challenging the woman with questions about her past, Cathryn acknowledged a forbidding quality about Vanya Russo that went beyond the purely physical.

Robust in spite of the fine-boned frame of her small body, Vanya deported herself like royalty, sure of her every step and motion, with an aura about her that spoke of more than human health. From the moment when Cathryn first saw Vanya, she was warned she was evil and a danger. For the most part, Cathryn had overcome her fears, yet Vanya's mystery made Cathryn approach her with caution.

"I know your guardian's health is not what has kept you from the glen and I sense you've come to me tonight for more than henbane," Vanya said when Cathryn's song ended.

Cathryn laid the violin aside and took a deep breath, inhaling deeply of the incense that always filled the cottage.

"Are you my mother?"

"Who told you this?" Vanya asked in an even tone.

"Gerald Seymour."

"Did you not describe him as mad?"

Cathryn nodded.

"And did he tell you I am a Witch?"

Cathryn's eyes widened in reply.

Vanya continued, "Yes to both accusations, Cathryn. I am your mother—the woman who gave you life, and I am a Witch."

A palpable silence descended between the women as Cathryn's eyes filled with tears. "But why?"

Vanya smiled. "Why am I a witch? Or why did I abandon you?"

"Both."

"I had no choice."

"Why did you not tell me you're my mother? Why did I have to be told by Gerald Seymour?" Cathryn could not hide her outrage or her pain.

"Look at me, Cathryn. Examine your heart. Would you have believed me? Would you not have thought I was an insane old woman wanting something of you?"

Cathryn struggled to control her tears. She stared at the composed woman who had just confessed she was her mother. Vanya reached out to embrace her distraught daughter, but Cathryn pulled away.

Vanya understood Cathryn's rebuff. "I am not a common woman, Cathryn, nor a common mother, which you shall come to know," she said. "Did Master Seymour also reveal who your father was?"

"Lord Ashley Godwyne."

It was Vanya's turn to nod. "It seems so very long ago . . . I never dreamed to see you again," she mused. "And, I fear, like all other women, someday you shall come to realize how children easily die—are lost and forgotten . . . but long ago in Venice, Cathryn, Ashley was my lover, and when he returned to England, he insisted we leave you behind.

"By threatening to desert you, he believed he could force me to marry him, which I refused to do, and he would not bring you to England without marrying me.

"I loved him passionately, more than I ever loved another soul. He was like no other man I have ever known, but he could be brutal in his way, and nothing could change his mind once it was made up."

Vanya paused a moment to observe Cathryn's reaction to hearing her father had forced her to abandon their child.

Cathryn met her mother's gaze with a cool stare.

"I discovered I was to have another baby and expected to die in childbed as I almost did when you were born. Ashley did not know I was *incinta*, I made him swear he would look after you until you came of age, if I would go with him and leave you behind as he wanted. Since I believed I would die in childbed, I thought it best, and Ashley loved me enough to make and then to honor his promise."

Cathryn did not quite understand, but she comprehended well enough that Vanya was subject to the whims of the man she loved but would not marry. "You never married but were his mistress all these years."

"Perhaps you cannot understand—your father never did. And perhaps I cannot explain."

"Please try," Cathryn implored.

"I did not want to die."

Cathryn's look was one of utter bewilderment.

"You look at me just as Ashley did." Vanya smiled yet worried Cathryn would not comprehend, certain what she was about to say was contrary to all Cathryn had ever been taught.

"When a woman marries, she becomes her husband's possession, his property—not unlike a sheep or a cow—a slave—and I have been a slave.

"I came to Venice from the East a slave. From the time I was a young child I was sold to one man, then another. I doubt you know what it means to be free, Cathryn. It is a peculiar word in this world, but once freed, I swore as long as I lived I would never again be another man's possession."

It had been difficult for Cathryn to contemplate having a mother whom she might know, but Vanya Russo overwhelmed her.

"I've created more questions than I've answered, I see."

Cathryn nodded. "You were a slave?"

"I was. And I am a Witch."

Cathryn was not quite prepared for Vanya's forthright answers.

"There is nothing to fear. I said I am a Witch, but *not*, as you think, a disciple of Satan. I worship God, but in a different manner than you do."

"When you said you would take care of Gerald Seymour, I had heard rumors. I hoped . . ."

"I would dispatch him with a wave of the wand."

Cathryn nodded.

"I delayed helping you because I needed to confer with the other Witches of my coven for their opinion and consent. A Witch does not use her power for harm—only in rare exceptions, and Gerald Seymour is."

"But my guardian knows you're a Witch. Aren't you afraid he'll report you to the sheriff? You could be . . ."

"Burned at the stake?"

"Yes. When Father Vittorio accused me, even in jest, I felt afraid."

"Who is Father Vittorio? And why would he accuse you of Witchcraft?"

Cathryn hesitated, sorry she had spoken Vittorio's name. But Vanya had been so direct in answering her questions, she felt compelled to answer. "Father Vittorio was my teacher and my friend."

"A friend who betrays you and calls you Witch? You have neglected to tell me something, Cathryn."

"He was my *amoroso*."

"Ahhh—I see," she said. "And when he could not bear his priest's guilt, he called you Witch and all the name implies."

Cathryn nodded.

"Whatever the reason, if a man fears a woman, he calls her a Witch," her mother said.

"Are all men mad?"

"Sometimes it seems so!" Vanya spat.

"Vittorio's love for me seemed to drive him mad," Cathryn explained, wanting Vanya to understand what she herself did not completely comprehend. "I loved him, and I shall love him forever."

"*Forever*, dearest Cathryn, is a very long time."

"Will you not love my father forever?"

Vanya smiled. "I have loved Ashley through all eternity."

"And I, Vittorio."

Chapter 46

With gratitude Cathryn accepted more henbane syrup from Vanya. "Keep the portion steady. Increase it only if the effect you desire begins to wane."

Cathryn contemplated the precise effect she wanted but settled for Gerald's continued disability. With her guardian's general improvement, Cathryn now worried that an opportunity to give Gerald the decoction might not present itself, but she found that in offering to help serve supper, she would rarely miss an opportunity to slip the sweet concoction into his ale.

Bridget Seymour came to rely on Cathryn greatly in all manner of things and saw her gift for growing herbs as an additional blessing to the family. Without awareness she counted on Cathryn's increasing knowledge of white magic and conferred with her regularly so she might improve her brother's health.

As the days passed, Gerald continued to be indifferent to Cathryn and she assumed he was impotent, but unfortunately, he did not forget his threat to send the children away, almost as soon as he was out of bed, at once dispatching Comfort to a Puritan family a full day's journey from Wollingham.

"Why must I go?" Comfort cried; she found her father's argument that she needed to learn the art of weaving cloth and return to train her sisters unconvincing. "I can acquire the skill much closer by," she pleaded to no avail.

"I will not be challenged by a child," her father said.

"But, Father, I only wish to understand."

"You have only to obey!"

All four children frowned at his reply. There was no use in arguing.

"Perhaps it won't be for long," Cathryn said in an effort to lift Comfort's spirits.

"A day will be too long," Comfort wailed, and sought Cathryn's embrace.

"You must dry your eyes. We shall write to each other every day and share secrets just between the two of us."

"I'll miss only you," Comfort said as Cathryn tied her hat beneath her chin.

"And I shall miss you, too."

Cathryn lost a treasured ally. She missed the gentle girl's quick intelligence and her ready but respectful questioning of her father's point of view.

Jacob and Diligence drew closer to Cathryn as if they feared they would be next. "Your father needs you here," she told Jacob, and, "You're too young," she offered Diligence, knowing that reason had nothing to do with Gerald's decisions.

Cathryn lay awake nights wondering what lay ahead for her in Wollingham. She envisioned spending her days toiling in Gerald Seymour's household, ever fearful of her master. How long would it be before he became accustomed to the henbane, and there would be no useful effect?

Perhaps I'd be wise to put my eye on some young man, she thought, and realized the greatest stumbling block to such a plan was the necessity for her to prove she had converted to the appropriate faith. "Never!" she swore, and slammed her fist into her pillow, in her fury knowing that if it were possible to escape Gerald Seymour, she would make the pretense of conversion on the morrow.

Already, Cathryn knew, she held the eye of every bachelor for miles around. Some were bold and on market days tried to corner Cathryn and lead her from the market center, but until now she had not encouraged prospective suitors. In her heart she was already betrothed—taken long ago—but marriage, she remembered, was rarely for the sake of love, and only a kind of bargain the Church advised to avoid fornication.

Cathryn considered the eligible men of Wollingham. Could she sell herself that way? Could she afford not to?

"Dear God." She sighed.

There were a few men of means, widowers with children by the score, and eager, no doubt, to welcome more. Cathryn shuddered. The only thing the unmarried men had to offer above the widowers was youth!

Surely there must be someone I could stomach! Cathryn sighed, discouraged. She racked her brain and cast out each man she considered. She contemplated her whole life under Gerald's roof and decided it was by far a worse future than setting her sights on Giles Jefferies.

Of average stature, Giles was fair-skinned with brown hair and blue eyes, by trade a farrier. He was young and sturdy and, Cathryn prayed, tractable. He seemed earnest but not overly devout. On further contemplation Cathryn deemed him quite acceptable.

Her mind made up, Cathryn set about to woo him and, more distasteful, to become a Protestant convert. The latter process almost startled Gerald from his torpor. He sat amazed while Cathryn, without a hint of sarcasm, revealed her spiritual awakening to an attentive Puritan meeting.

"It has been revealed to me that there is but one God who speaks through the Scriptures to believers without the interference of other voices or false saints. Each believer in Christ, accepted by God, is a saint himself. A man is saved by the Word of God and by faith; not by sacraments alone, or by confession and penance.

"At first we are all godless, stained by the sins of Adam and Eve. We are cleansed by the mercy of God and by enlightenment through understanding His Word. The days of our lives are symbols of God's salvation and our sanctification.

"We are saved from Satan by knowledge of the Scriptures. A person ignorant of the Scriptures lives in sin, and is a friend of Satan. Grace is available to the soul only through devotion and understanding of God's Word. We are naturally wicked and corrupt in nature, but knowledge that is available through Scripture will restrain us from evil.

"Before the Fall, God promised man salvation for perfect obedience. When Adam disobeyed God, man was damned eternally and is only redeemed by faith in Christ, which God grants only to men whom He chooses to save. A man is not saved finally until he is united with God in heaven, but on earth his life must be filled with acts motivated by God, and his goodness visible.

"I am burdened of many sins, yet strive to do God's will, and God provides me many opportunities to know His Word and obey Him. He has helped me love my neighbor, and kept me from sin. He makes me faithful to his Word. He shows me to renounce my Catholic beliefs; to trust in the Word of God, and not in the promises of priests.''

The attentive saints smiled at Cathryn Godwyne, murmuring their approbation. They glanced at Gerald Seymour in admiration, whose confusion amused Cathryn as she was welcomed into the fold of God's chosen, no greater hypocrite, she reasoned, than Gerald Seymour, who readily took congratulations for his triumph in salvaging a pagan soul by setting so worthy an example.

''I confess I thought your sanctification would never come,'' Bridget congratulated Cathryn, quite put off guard. The girl was righteous enough, Bridget reflected, though her behavior continued at times to be troublesome. Her increasingly frequent absences bothered Bridget the most, yet all things considered, the household ran smoothly, and the remaining children in the household continued to thrive. Why then, Bridget wondered, did she continue to have a premonition of doom when she dwelled on Cathryn?

With her doubts, Bridget unwittingly became Cathryn's ally in her pursuit of Giles Jefferies, and when the Puritan began to pay court to Cathryn, Bridget spoke to Gerald in Giles's behalf.

Cathryn smiled as Giles escorted her to Gerald's door after morning worship. ''Mistress Seymour bids you welcome any time you care to call on me,'' she said, and watched the color rise to his cheeks.

''I hope Master Seymour approves,'' he said.

''I cannot imagine his disapproval,'' Cathryn lied, regretting to have to trap Giles Jefferies as she felt she must.

Gerald's eyes narrowed to slits each time he saw the man, and to Cathryn's terror, he began sometimes to neglect his evening ale, complaining of the taste, though no one else agreed. He stared at Cathryn as if he wondered what part she had in the ruin of his drink—a curse?—a potion?—a spell?

Cathryn lowered her eyes and feigned innocence until he finally looked away; she began to hold her breath, fearing the return of her guardian's unquenchable lust.

Chapter 47

When Cathryn next went to Vanya, she revealed her worries about Gerald to her mother, who consoled her. "As long as he consumes a dose the following day, you shall be saved."

"Bridget has asked me to brew a tea to 'embolden Master Seymour'—as if I cared to do such a thing."

"Then we shall mix something." Vanya gave Cathryn a gallipot containing a fragrant gel. "This shall improve him."

"Not too much, I hope."

"Not to threaten you."

Cathryn tried to breathe easier and confessed her conversion to the Puritan faith.

"I see your Catholic God did not strike you dead."

Cathryn blanched. "He knows I feign this dreary and demanding faith and that I only simulate devotion for convenience. Perhaps He understands."

"Tell me, Cathryn, why you follow so cruel a religion at all—Catholic or Protestant, it is quite the same."

Cathryn was clearly astonished by her mother's question.

"Why do you worship at the foot of a cross—a vile instrument of torture? Why do you revere a God who consents to the murder of His only son? Why not a compassionate and loving God?"

Cathryn was nearly rendered speechless by questions she had never dared consider. "I never thought I might choose to worship God in any way but what I do," she answered with a shiver, all at once fearing Vanya approached the subject of her own religion. At the moment Cathryn was in no mood to be persuaded to consider conversion to yet another religion.

Instead she told Vanya of Giles Jefferies. "Now that I am a Puritan, I can marry in the faith. I pray to be Mistress Jefferies before the new year."

"I know of him. He's kind and won't punish you," Vanya said. "But he is rumored to be shy."

Cathryn rolled her eyes in exasperation. "I've begun to imagine he is not made as other men."

"Not every man's a drooling devil," was Vanya's amused reply.

Giles's patient pursuit was quite infuriating to Cathryn. He strolled with her at market every week when she attended and sometimes even carried her bundles home. He brought her dill seed for meeting refreshment and admired her new though undistinguished Puritan cap. He walked her home, a long way out of his way.

"You surely are one of God's fairest creatures." He smiled.

Cathryn offered him her hand to hold.

He declined, making her feel almost a harlot for the boldness of her gesture.

Gerald condemned him over protests from his sister. "I am not convinced he is truly elected by God. I sense he believes a man might contribute to his own salvation—that God alone does not choose his saints—and I am certain he believes there is more than one way to interpret Scripture."

Bridget Seymour frowned over her brother's reservations. "Perhaps my brother is too harsh in his judgment of Master Jefferies. Gerald is still not fully recovered from his latest disease," she said, more concerned with ridding her brother's house of Cathryn's presence than with the future of the young woman's soul as the bride of a dubious saint.

While Cathryn waited for Giles to proceed at his own slug's pace of courtship, she continued to glean all she could of her mother's knowledge of worts and simples, recording recipes for possets, electuaries, conserves, troches, and teas on paper. "I can't remember all you've told me," Cathryn informed her mother, and produced a stack of papers with Vanya's recipes carefully copied down. "How do you ever keep them all in your head?"

"As easily as you've committed so much music to memory."

The women worked side by side, the mother passing her store of knowledge on to her daughter. "Collect bitter buttons from the wild," Vanya said of tansy, showing her a delicate and lacy plant with a pungent odor. "A tonic made from these robust winter posies purifies the humors of the body after winter. Use it also to stay miscarriage by applying the bruised herb to the navel. Then boil it in cider and have the worried woman drink it to ease the womb.

"It shall also repel flies," she continued. "Lay it on meat in summer, or use it to preserve a body from the summer heat by strewing the herb generously."

Cathryn made note, hoping to have little use for her mother's last suggestion.

"The magic of mugwort is well known to travelers hoping to stay fatigue and wild animals, and it is good for pains of the head. Combine it with sage, gentian, and chamomile and boil in honey, then apply warm to the forehead and back of the neck."

Vanya offered Cathryn some tea made of mugwort flowers, but she declined, wishing instead to take up her violin. Each time she visited, the glen rang with sounds of joy and love and, sometimes, sorrow as Cathryn played Vittorio's music, even though she knew he would have been vexed by her unlimber fingers.

Nonetheless, Cathryn managed to enchant her audience of one, and Vanya's heart slid up and down an emotional scale, depending on her daughter's mood.

Sometimes Cathryn could not hold back her tears. "I must discard my violin if I'm ever to be happy," she threatened, but both women knew it was an idle threat, for if there was a moment when Cathryn revived from the burdens of her life, it was when she cradled the Amati beneath her chin. Then her heart traveled to Venice and through imagination fled straight into Vittorio's loving arms. Cathryn kept alive her conviction the dark priest loved her, fearing if she abandoned that dream, she would begin to wither and to die.

Someday he'll come for me, a voice in Cathryn's heart whispered.

Cathryn laid her violin aside. Only a fool would continue to dream of love, she knew, but, without her dreams, reality was harsher than she could bear.

As the days passed, Gerald kept from her bed, his interest and ability diminished, but he was quite able to punish her in other ways, arranging for Jacob to be sent to America with a childless cousin. "I take in a good sum and punish you in the same bargain," Gerald informed a tearful Cathryn after Jacob was gone.

"What do you mean?" she demanded of her self-satisfied guardian.

Gerald fingered a pouch of coins. "I profit from his going in more ways than one."

"You have sold your child?" All Cathryn's illusions that Gerald might possess a scrap of integrity, at least on matters that did not pertain to her, were dashed.

"Such arrangements are common as every day the means to live grows more scarce," Mistress Seymour later tried to explain, but even Bridget visibly lost heart. She seemed not to love her nieces and nephew with any great depth of feeling, but by her reckoning they were kin and deserved, at all odds, to be held together within the family. Soon after Jacob left, Bridget pressured Gerald for Comfort's return.

Comfort's letters, which only Cathryn received with any regularity, were few and pitiful. She was not abused, only lonely— for Cathryn.

Cathryn wrote Comfort to encourage her but had abandoned her other correspondence. "It is just too painful," she confessed to Vanya, "to pretend all is well, and not to inquire why my lover does not come after me."

When she had last heard, her friend Simone was married to a man more than twice her age and several times a widower, and by now had given birth to her first child. Perhaps, Cathryn worried, Simone, like too many brides, was wed and bred and dispatched to her reward before a year was out, dead in childbed, and she vowed to write Perdita at once for word of her friend. It would be only her second letter to Perdita in a year.

In secret, Cathryn had written many letters to her priest, then destroyed them, shocked by the candor of her passion and the ease with which she wrote of her dreams and her desires. "I'm certain he would curse me, for he has cured his passion, while mine is only banked by necessity," she told her mother. "In every letter, I beg him to come for me."

"But he has denied you."

Cathryn sighed. "I should beg you, Mother and witch, for a potion, charm, or spell to unite us, and should forgive him everything if he were only to come to me," Cathryn admitted, showing Vanya her latest letter to the priest before laying it in the fire.

Vanya could neither read nor write and thought it remarkable that Cathryn could.

"Surely my father could have taught you," Cathryn said.

"What use would reading and writing be to me?"

Few women knew how to read, and if it had not been deemed a necessity among the Puritans to study the Bible for oneself, there would be fewer still. There was a blessing to being Puritan, after all! Cathryn thought, realizing the degree of her own education to be quite exceptional.

Though Vanya did not appear to need to record her knowledge for herself, Cathryn refused to rely on her memory for the scores of receipts Vanya had given her. Some potions had seven or more herbs combined in exact sequence, instructions that Cathryn copied down in careful script. "A Witch's daughter might always be a Witch, but some take to the calling more readily than others," Cathryn lightly observed in a moment of ease.

Indeed, Vanya Russo was a wise woman, as the seekers of her wisdom called her. The distinction would not be made by many, and sometimes to the list of ingredients Cathryn recorded for decoctions, possets, salves, conserves, and troches was added a simple verse to enhance the power of the medicine's effectiveness, an incantation not unlike a prayer, but for the world a charm and not far from a spell.

Vanya invited Cathryn's curiosity. "Is there anything more of me you want to know?" she asked her daughter, who by blood alone would need no initiation into the craft. But Cathryn, the child of a Witch, was free to reject her powers if she desired—to choose her path upon the earth—and to her daughter's questions, Vanya explained the objects on her altar. The pentagram, a five-pointed star drawn inside a circle, symbol of wisdom and of mystic power. Inside the figure, the elements: a censer filled with burning incense to represent air; a dish of salt, symbol of earth and life; a chalice filled with water; a candle to signify fire; all elements necessary for survival. "My purpose is to heal, to celebrate life, joy, and love. I revere two deities, a Goddess and a God."

Cathryn listened with growing fascination but could not deny the prickle of fear that crept along her spine. She trespassed now in territory the Church declared more dangerous to Christ's teachings than any other.

"I do not worship the Christian devil, as I know you fear. I believe in two deities, a Goddess and a God, who together rule the universe. She is fertility, birth and rebirth; spring and summer; her sign the moon. Her consort, whose symbol is the sun, is the lord of life and god of death. He commands the hunt, reigning in fall and winter, ruling the seasons of maturity and death or dormancy. One complements the other. One makes the other whole. I believe and trust in the natural world; in love expressed in life; in love between a man and a woman, which the Christian church so roundly condemns."

Though she felt great apprehension, Cathryn was surprised to feel her heart drawn to her mother's religion. Might the God of Catholics and Protestants also be one of love? Cathryn wondered suddenly. Not angry and in constant need of desperate appeasement? Perhaps the Puritans and the Catholics were wrong about God.

"Do you watch heaven, Cathryn?"

Cathryn nodded, remembering especially the nights in Venice when she and her lover priest had disguised themselves and stolen away to sometimes sit for hours and gaze at the moon and stars.

"The cycle of the moon is the cycle of all life, its birth each month a new beginning. As the days pass, as life continues, the moon becomes full; then begins to wane and die and pass into darkness, just as all life does, to be renewed eternally. Her cycle should give men hope. It is the promise of eternal life."

Cathryn reflected on her mother's explanation. Though a pagan notion, it was a simpler road to eternity than either the Catholic or Protestant religion offered, whose promise of eternal life through faith in Christ often was appended with myriad nearly impossible requirements.

"Have you noticed there's been no moon for the last three nights? Tonight there will be a new moon. Stay and celebrate with me. There shall be a ceremony of thanksgiving and hope and love."

"I cannot."

"You are afraid."

"Yes."

"The God of Gerald Seymour and your Catholic priest is one of fear and eternal punishment, Cathryn. Someday I hope you will open your heart to more," Vanya said. "There is love in God's universe if you can accept it."

Cathryn often thought of Vanya's words and reflected on the deities her mother's religion offered. The Old Religion seemed much less damning—but did man deserve to be loved by God? Cathryn asked herself.

Vanya's religion did not damn the love felt and expressed between a man and a woman, nor did it forbid a woman to love a man who was a priest. Nor could Vanya comprehend God, who was the source of love, being offended by love or naming its expression sin.

All Cathryn had heard appealed to her, yet her fear remained—the wrathful voice of the Christian God rumbled in her ears.

Yet when some weeks later Vanya invited Cathryn to another Sabbat, she was impelled by her attraction and by curiosity to attend.

"This eve we convene to celebrate the full moon. Put aside your Christian fears and join us, or, if you must, rely on your God to protect you from the evil that does not exist in our midst."

Cathryn hesitated.

"Attending is not an irrevocable act, my child."

Cathryn agreed.

"I will send Zephyrus for you," she promised, and stared at her beautiful daughter, whose innocence and purity, in spite of her experiences, still shone to illuminate her soul. "Abandon your fears, Cathryn, for they alone can do you harm."

Waiting for Zephyrus that night, Cathryn tried to remember Vanya's admonition, but it was not a simple thing to do. Attached to the forbidden practice of Witchcraft were far too many superstitions, and though her mother, who admitted being a Witch, showed more tenderness and charity than some of the professed Christians she knew, Cathryn could not prevent her trembling.

While she waited for her summons to the Sabbat, Cathryn watched a glorious full moon slowly rise in the night sky, but before it ascended to its zenith, the white dog appeared and sat in clear view of her window as if he sensed she watched for him.

Dressed in a hooded black robe Vanya had given her for the occasion, Cathryn's heart beat wildly as she left the Seymour house, aware as she followed Zephyrus that the course of her life would be changed forever.

Chapter 48

Zephyrus, the Witch's messenger, led Cathryn well beyond his mistress's glen through the woods a considerable distance to another, more hidden clearing. The air was thick with incense and those already gathered in the appointed place stood together around the outer edge of a nine-foot circle cut in the clearing's grassy floor.

Six inches inside the outer circle another circle was inscribed and transected by a pentagram. Four of the star's five arms aimed north, south, east, and west. The fifth arm lay between south and east. Strange symbols were inscribed into the earth between the cardinal points, and within the inner circle, almost in the center, facing east, stood a large stone altar. At the cardinal points between the circles lay four chalices, and outside, four torches blazed.

With Cathryn's entrance into the clearing, the gathered closed tightly around the outer edge of the circle, leaving one space where she took her place. With her presence, the gathering numbered twenty-one, and except for Vanya, who wore shimmering white, everyone was dressed in long black hooded robes that concealed one's identity completely. Keen to the illicit nature of their assembly, the dark, faceless figures reminded Cathryn of Catholic monks, and in the midst of the pagan worshipers, she clasped her hands together to restrain herself from making the protective sign of the cross.

As moonlight fell down upon the assembly, Vanya anointed the forehead, lips, and inner wrists of each worshiper with a pungent oil. At first the oil produced a burning sensation, which quickly passed, and Cathryn felt her entire body flush with warmth. Then she had the sensation of floating, as though her feet barely touched the ground.

Cathryn stared at her mother, whose silver hair in the moonlight seemed made of precious metal. She held an enormous gold

chalice, which she raised above her, and in the air she inscribed
the sacred circle and a five-pointed star.

Vanya put the chalice to her lips and kissed the rim. She
offered the cup north, where lay another chalice containing sand.
"To earth," she said, and drank from the cup she held in her
hand.

She offered the cup south, where a candle burned. "To fire,"
she said, and drank again; then west to air and its symbol
mistletoe; and east to water. "With this consecrated wine, we
unite as one body to gather power and to worship in peace," she
said, and passed the cup in a clockwise motion around the circle.

Like the others, Cathryn received the cup and drank deeply,
almost at once feeling the effects of the sweet, heavily spiced
wine. She felt the night begin to shimmer, and a glowing warmth
flowed through her veins. A bright mist seemed to descend upon
the gathering and fill her eyes.

Arms outstretched, Cathryn turned to hand on the cup, but the
worshiper beside her hesitated.

Cathryn's hood slipped a little from her head, and in spite of
her dreamlike state, a sudden chill washed over her as she
realized her face was clearly visible to this reluctant worshiper,
whom she knew by stature and build was a man.

Perhaps he was a Witch finder spying on the evening's ritual,
she reasoned, terrified.

Unsteady under the watcher's intense scrutiny, Cathryn felt
stripped naked, as though the watcher's eyes roamed hotly over
every inch of her bare form. Then, without warning, he reached
for the chalice, gripping Cathryn's fingers in his, and caused the
hood of her robe to fall back and completely expose her face.

At contact with the stranger, Cathryn felt jolted as if by
lightning. Shivers of tangled emotions danced within her as he
forced her to raise the chalice to his lips, then with deliberate
slowness lowered the cup.

When he finally released her, Cathryn felt the stranger's eyes
lock onto hers. He reached to raise her hood, slipping his hands
inside to hold her head, turning her soft face into the brilliant
moonlight, and for the briefest instant he moved a hand to caress
her cheek.

Cathryn shivered from head to toe.

In silence, Vanya took the chalice from her daughter's trembling
hands and entered the circle. She went before the altar and in

slow motion invoked the circle three times with the chalice before she set it down. Next to the chalice lay bowls of water and salt; a censer filled with burning incense; a lighted candle; a sword and knife. In the center of the altar lay a softly bleating lamb.

Vanya raised the sword and invoked the pentagram, then dipped her fingers into salt and cast it upon the circle. She did the same with water, then clapped her hands three times.

In silence she turned to face twelve of those gathered and invited them into the consecrated circle, where they kneeled facing east. To those who remained standing outside the ring, Vanya indicated a place to stand, separating each watcher from his neighbor an equal distance.

She returned to the altar then and folded her arms across her breasts, palms open, and closed her eyes. She meditated in silence for a while, then placed one hand upon the bleating lamb. "We are thirteen. Sun, moon, and stars. Praise be to the God and Goddess who are one, the Creator, one with the universe and its vessel, the earth. Bless us, we beseech you, to do honor to this place and to assist those who spend time within this realm." Her quiet voice seemed to echo through the night. "Bless us with your knowledge and power."

She took the knife and swiftly sacrificed the lamb, then raised her arms to heaven. "We purify ourselves with the blood of this innocent lamb and bow down to you, Mother Goddess, grateful for your blessings. We worship you, God the Father, provider of plenty, and pray for charity."

Vanya anointed the foreheads of the select inside the circle with blood of the lamb. "We are grateful for the gifts bestowed on us—especially for healing and foresight. We humbly ask to continue our work and pray for enlightenment in this dark age. Do not desert us, we beg. Speak to us. Send us your power. Bless us to do your bidding, to live in harmony with the elements. Let the rain be plentiful and gentle, the harvest ample. Make our hearts pure and receptive, we beseech you. Amen."

"Amen," came the united reply.

Then began supplications from those who kneeled, with Vanya's arms upraised the while.

"Grant me a more open heart."

"Give me patience with the seasons."

"Give me strength to battle our legion enemies."

The prayers continued until there was silence in the glen.

Vanya raised the altar candle to invoke the circle and the pentagram, then ignited the nest beneath the lamb. As flames rose to consume its body, a mournful wail of a solitary pipe filled the glen. The circle of worshipers rose in a body and, with the watchers outside the consecrated circle, began to sway to the rhythm of the song. Gradually the tempo of the music increased and in clockwise motion a dance began.

Within the circle, the dancers paired to dance a kind of energetic reel, inscribing the figure-eight around the altar. Those outside the consecrated circle moved clockwise, exchanging places until each one had danced in every place around the circle.

Then the dancers clasped hands, forming two separate circles. The pace quickened as the two groups whirled, exhilaration overcoming exhaustion.

Outside the circle, a second chalice of wine began to pass from hand to hand, the sweet contents fueling energy until at last the pipe's song sighed a final note.

For a while, Cathryn's heart beat violently; she was surprised that her energy and emotion had not been completely drained away. She felt at peace, unexpectedly comfortable with the rite she had witnessed, and realized she might pray to her Christian God in much the same way—but to a God more loving than the one revered by either her guardian or her priest.

Cathryn looked around her and saw the other worshipers breathing as heavily as she did, yet their faces did not reveal exhaustion as she imagined they should.

A thrill of fear shot through her when she realized all hoods but one were down about the shoulders of the worshipers, and the man who remained hidden was the one who had hesitated to take the cup. Why did he not let himself be seen? a freshly terrified voice inside Cathryn cried.

She forgot her question as Vanya and those inside the circle joined the others outside. One by one the thirteen from the circle embraced the others, and as if by magic, a feast was laid out in a circle upon the clearing floor.

Sitting down beside her mother, feeling as though she still were dancing, Cathryn's heart would not be still. Before her eyes all shapes were distorted. She rubbed her eyes, hoping to clear her vision, but continued to view everything as though gazing through a glittering silver haze.

To her right, Cathryn discovered the hooded stranger, but before she could respond, Vanya passed the ever-brimming chalice, radiating joy. "Drink, my child. This cup will bring you happiness."

Cathryn drank deeply and with every swallow grew more at ease, ignoring the stranger beside her. She ate little of the feast—spicy, tender lamb, ripe, luscious fruits, and an abundance of almonds, breads, and cheese—but greedily consumed more heady wine, with each swallow seeming to require more.

The stranger seated beside her offered Cathryn a bite of bread, which she accepted without hesitation. He followed the morsel with more wine. She laughed as he continued to feed her, taking cherries and bits of apple and orange from his benevolent hands.

Strong feelings of warmth and tenderness washed over Cathryn, and, suddenly free of all foreboding and care, she smiled at the hooded stranger. She began to feed him, also choosing the most succulent bits from the bountiful feast.

As Cathryn fed the stranger, his appetite seemed to grow rather than diminish, and from time to time, he licked the last morsels from her fingertips, making Cathryn quiver with delight. When others began to dance, moving with gentle, swaying motions to the pensive music of ocarinas and lutes, Cathryn declined. She wished only to concentrate on the dark stranger at her side with no more warnings from within as he induced her to lean into his arms and sip more delicious wine.

Much later when Cathryn looked up, the clearing was empty of all but the stranger and herself. Confused, Cathryn remained in the stranger's arms for a moment, then bolted.

As she got to her feet, she swayed and almost fell, disoriented as she stared into the surrounding darkness to see all evidence of the Sabbat gone. The scars of the circles and pentagram cut in the forest floor were covered, and the altar was simply a pile of stones. The other hooded worshipers, the torches, and the implements from the altar—all had vanished. Even the ashes of the lamb were gone.

Then, in the dim, Cathryn saw Vanya standing to the side of the quiet glen, in part hidden by trees. Cathryn breathed a deep sigh and started toward her mother, but Vanya raised a hand and bade Cathryn halt. "Stay," she commanded, and, when Cathryn blinked her eyes, vanished into darkness.

Chapter 49

In spite of the obvious signal from her mother to remain in the clearing with the hooded stranger, Cathryn felt a rush of apprehension, though she was almost delirious with wine.

Billows of dark clouds scarred the perfect night sky and almost covered the full moon as Cathryn sensed the stranger at her back. He placed gentle hands on her shoulders and turned her to face him, offering again the chalice of wine. Cathryn took several desperate swallows, then drained the cup, hoping for courage.

Her vision veiled and senses stirred, she tossed the chalice to the ground. She closed her eyes and felt her heartbeat and the slow surging of her blood. She inhaled the fragrance of approaching morning, but when she opened her eyes, she was aware of nothing but the enigmatic stranger who still hid from her behind the hooded robe.

With a brazen gesture, Cathryn pushed the hood away, and though she did not know him, her heart began to leap inside her throat.

His hair, which grew almost to his shoulders, was deeper than the night, as was his close-cropped beard. Though she could not clearly see them, she felt the power of the man's dark eyes as he looked down at her and quickly drew her into his spell.

Intoxicated in a way she had never been before, Cathryn was not afraid, but eager. "I was promised there would be no demons here," she whispered.

He laughed softly as he moved his lips near hers.

Cathryn closed her eyes, inhaling his scent of almonds and sweet spiced wine. When he kissed her he tasted inexplicably familiar.

At first his kiss was cool and lingering, and when it warmed, it made the blood rush in Cathryn's head. He sucked at her mouth and at the faint trace of her will. His hands, at the small of her back, bade her fold herself against him.

No matter that the Host and planets looked down, as night music sang in Cathryn's ears, all that existed for her was the sweet, vital stranger in her arms.

Cathryn felt the rush of her heartbeat and the intake of his breath as the pressure of her body thrilled him. She moved her hands inside the opening of his sleeves, stirred deeply by the warmth of him. Her own breath caught as her fingers surveyed the strength of his muscled arms; the firm flesh and fine hairs; the smooth bare skin. As she touched him, her fingertips seemed to call the sensation of this very man from memory and made her issue a small whimper of need, begging for more than his tender embrace.

He answered, beginning to explore, to undo the ties that fastened the hooded black robe to her body. He unwound the cord that cinched her small waist and pushed the drape of the robe aside. With eager hands he searched for the final satin ribbon at her hip and freed her.

He paused to peer down at Cathryn and she trembled; as the moon escaped the clouds, the Witch's cloak slipped from her shoulders. In the starlight her body seemed to glow, and his eyes were seared by her perfection.

A sigh sounding almost of anguish escaped his lips, and for a moment he did not touch her. Then he lifted his hands to Cathryn's abundant hair, which was twisted into a heavy knot and laced with ribbon. She raised her hands to help him, and together they let her ribbons one by one fly away on the gentle wisps of wind.

"I'm cold," she whispered, and drew his fingers down.

As his caress trailed over her inviting body, she untied his robe. She sighed at the sight of him, knowing he could promise her more than she would ever need in the way of warmth.

He radiated heat and Cathryn slipped her arms around him, savoring the wonderful hardness of his manhood against her tender flesh and his increasingly tight embrace. His touch was new yet excitingly familiar. She had tasted of his kind of passion many times before.

He closed the loose robe protectively about them and kissed her with a fierceness that drove Cathryn's passions to fever pitch. He caressed her round buttocks and pulled her hard against him.

She replied with feathery strokes the full length of his hard-muscled back and made him groan with the staggering intensity of his desire.

To Cathryn's ears there was music in the stranger's voice, each sound a remembered chord. "Vittorio, Vittorio," she called as suddenly even the breath of her body seemed not to be her own and she responded to his sighs. In her wine-deluded state, the lover who touched her was Vittorio.

He lifted her, and she embraced him with her legs around his hips, urging him into her with one swift thrust.

"Vittorio!" she cried, and held him fast.

Strong, he allowed her to lean away from him, cradling her in his arms and, with her, sighed for pleasure as she rode him. Her motions alternately forced her luscious breasts close to his hungry mouth, then withdrew, and finally he captured her and forced her to be still.

Slowly he sucked each inviting nipple, sending delicious vibrations to her very core, and he continued until her craving for the caress of his thick shaft overpowered her and he relinquished control.

Cathryn wished to go on riding him forever but soon cried out with ecstasy. "Vittorio," she sang as he plunged himself deeper still, the force of his thrusts increasing until, breathless with satisfaction, he crushed her to him.

Gasping for breath, enveloped in her body's rapture, Cathryn closed her eyes and inhaled their mingled scents. She clung to the lover she dreamed was Vittorio. "*Più! Più!* More! More! Do not leave me," she cried as though she were in Venice begging of her glorious, dark, demanding priest.

His breathing still ragged, barely in possession of his senses, a laugh rumbled in her lover's broad chest. He laughed with obvious amusement, hugging Cathryn closer, eager to provide whatever she desired, and before his body slipped from hers, he raised her mouth to begin again the ritual of enchantment.

He swelled and throbbed within her, her body exquisitely tight as she sheathed his manhood. He moaned with each delicious expansion and soon matched Cathryn's desperate hunger.

When they lay down together on the grass, her discarded robe beneath them, Cathryn savored his warm body over hers, only vaguely aware of how muddled with wine she was. Her eyes and whole being continued to play intriguing drunken tricks on her as she drifted in the fading night, wanting to weep, wishing to indulge in the mystery of the night forever.

Cathryn drew her lover's lips to hers, enchanting him with her passion. She invited him to explore her with his kisses, her whispers and her sighs soon making him as delirious as she was.

As he devoured her with his suckling tongue and advanced on her secret recesses with torturous deliberation, Cathryn felt herself on fire. He opened her legs to caress the satin of her inner thighs and teased her hair with gentle strokes. "You torture me!" she whispered urgently.

He laughed and seized her mouth with his. She grasped his hand to urge him on, but knowing what he wanted for her and for himself, he would not be hurried.

Impatient, Cathryn reached for him, thinking she could force him to make haste, but he seemed almost to ignore her ministrations, pleasuring himself instead in the excitement of her tender woman's flesh. He put his mouth to her and Cathryn abandoned all but the enjoyment of his touch and almost too quickly experienced her soul take flight.

He would have sought her pleasure again, but with determined tugs, Cathryn insisted he come to lie beside her. She embraced and kissed him and, with one graceful leg, drew him very near. "I shall show you heaven's light," she promised, alluding to lights her priest claimed he sometimes saw when he came to rapture in her arms, and compelled, intoxicated with more than new wine, Cathryn held nothing back.

In her deluded sight, she lay in Venice with Vittorio, whom she alone could excite and please.

Transformed by delicious fantasy, the body of the stranger became utterly familiar. She savored the contours of his firm flesh—each long, hard muscle, every glorious inch of skin—and just as she had driven the priest to a state beyond his wildest dreams, besotted, Cathryn dedicated herself to bringing her Sabbat lover blinding ecstasy.

She had shivered at his touch only moments before, and now he trembled at hers as, descending his torso, her kisses nibbled and teased while pliant fingers kneaded him with joy, then stole below, applying gentle but insistent pressure to the bulging sac beneath.

She paused to watch him as he lay at her mercy, eyes closed, mouth curved in a half smile, the long length of him taut and eager, every muscle gleaming in the starlight. For a time, Cathryn indulged her eyes with the beautiful sight of him, almost drowning her own senses, but then she returned to attend him, to apply delicate, cool kisses at the base of his hard shaft.

His blood surged at her touch and he struggled desperately for some measure of control. He thought he had forgotten true ecstasy but as Cathryn's mouth closed over him and brought him glorious release, all memory came back.

Afterward he pulled her into his embrace and with contentment sighed and kissed her, tasting of himself.

Cathryn closed her eyes and nestled with the stranger. His arms were strong, a warm cocoon, tender and familiar.

Before long, the dream began to fade. "I must go. It's almost light," she whispered, wanting suddenly to escape, yet she could not move, and for one last moment Cathryn lay still and pleasured in the magic of her dream.

Chapter 50

Cathryn put on her robe again and fled, not thinking of how she would find her way until Zephyrus rushed from behind her and took the lead through the overgrown woods. She arrived home long after daybreak, numb from head to toe, and finding no one about to question her, slipped exhausted into her bedchamber and into bed.

She slept the day away, slumbering as though she were dead, waking the next night with an excruciating headache. She finally sat upright, only to reach for her aching head, imagining it to be swollen twice its normal size.

Cathryn massaged her temples, puzzled for a moment by the unfamiliar robe lying on the floor beside the bed and by the fact that she was naked, since lately it was her habit to wear at least a nightdress. Then she realized the lamp on the table beside the bed was lit, burning far too brightly for her pain-tormented eyes.

Cathryn considered the candle. It was too fresh to have been lighted by her, for she was certain she had been asleep for hours, if not days. As she slumped back upon her pillows, she remembered Vanya's invitation to the Witches' Sabbat. Her mother had given her a peculiar black robe—the one that now lay discarded on the floor.

Did she remember a strange ceremony conducted in the silver light of a full moon, she wondered, or had she been ill and only dreamed the eventful Sabbat?

Cathryn noted the furred feeling of her tongue and seemed also to recall heavy, sweet red wine. She closed her eyes. The wine could easily explain her throbbing head—and, perhaps, her vivid and erotic dreams.

Cathryn shivered at her memories. If dreams could be so real . . .

But dreams did not produce tender, swollen nipples, nor the scent of a man between her legs, she acknowledged as she pushed back the covers from the bed and with an abrupt motion sat upright.

At once Cathryn regretted her sudden movement, feeling as though her head had been snapped from her slender neck, and taking more care, she slowly got out of bed.

Had her mother's Witchcraft transported the priest from Venice, as Cathryn's senses insisted?

Could it be only that Gerald had recovered fully and visited her bed, and while she was in a stupor made use of her without her knowing?

Cathryn shook her head in willful denial, but, head throbbing, she thought better of the motion. No. It was not Gerald Seymour who filled these dreams and made her body quiver with the memory of her pleasure. All Gerald Seymour left behind him were nightmares and desecrated flesh.

It was not possible to think through the last hours or come to a clear recollection of events unless she had a little something to fill her stomach, Cathryn reasoned. After bathing from her basin, she dressed, intending to head for the buttery, but when she opened her door, she found Bridget standing in the hallway.

"When you failed to appear this morning, my brother sent me

to your room. I couldn't wake you. And so soundly did you sleep, I began to think you dead.''

Cathryn grimaced at the woman's loud voice. ''If I were dead, my head would not be hurting,'' she replied.

''You've no fever that I can tell, but I'm sure you have a brew that shall set you straight.''

Cathryn did not trust Bridget's concern for her health but followed her to the buttery and giving the directions, allowed her to brew feverfew tea from last season's dried stamped flowers and leaves.

''I am truly strengthened,'' Cathryn said after several almost scalding cups of tea.

''My brother is most insistent that I cure you.''

Cathryn's blood turned to ice. She turned an almost clear eye on Mistress Seymour.

''He seems to feel you are indispensable in this household.''

''I'm certain you misunderstood.'' The color rose to Cathryn's cheeks.

''He is weak and I believe it wise we mollify him at all cost. We must bend over backward to please him—his condition is that precarious, I fear.''

Cathryn stared at Bridget and assumed the woman did not know what it was she asked. ''I, too, have noticed that he seems to waste. I shall have to find a different remedy from the one I've lately used.'' Vanya would have to prepare something more potent, if not lethal!

''He refuses all suggestions. He even refuses his ale.''

The fresh color drained away from Cathryn's face and Bridget could not help but notice. ''I see that you too are not yet truly well. Come, you must go back to bed,'' she said, and ushered Cathryn from the room. ''One and all, you have given the Seymours quite a scare.''

Chapter 51

Cathryn recovered, and though she slept fitfully that night, by dawn the next day she was up and working. As the days passed, she watched Gerald neglect his evening ale altogether and make a slow recovery. With horror she saw his eyes begin to glint with a special interest in her, and with his sister's encouragement, Cathryn contrived to prepare something to improve his spirits. She was forced to add the henbane to his porridge, meat, or cheese in doses small enough to be concealed. When he reeled back to bed, Cathryn feared she had overdone the applications.

Cathryn returned to the children's bed again, using the first opportunity of illness to abandon her own.

Gerald disapproved, but to Cathryn's surprise, Bridget defended her. "She is only doing what is wise," Bridget answered her brother. "No point in having her rushing up and down stairs all night, disturbing those who'd rest. As you'll recall, from the very first, I thought it foolish to build a room for her. She has used it little enough."

One illness led to another as colder weather settled on England, and several weeks passed before Cathryn managed to return to her mother's. In the interim, she worried over the degree of her entanglement with Witches, knowing the medicines she made from herbs and the prayers uttered in conjunction with their administration were enough to see her burn. But the most damning evidence of all, Cathryn confessed, was her behavior at the Sabbat, where, not at a Witch's bidding but by an act of her own will, she had committed the sin of fornication with either a stranger, or a spirit conjured from Venice—or, perhaps, from Hell.

Cathryn shuddered with her memories, then continued to argue with herself, defending that everyone used magic. Herbs were gathered from the wild or grown in gardens for cooking and medicine and magic by nearly every housewife. Angelica and mistletoe were commonly used to frighten off Witches, and mugwort was used to protect travelers against outlaws and wolves. A woman collected morning dew to preserve her youth and beauty, and no one thought twice about the practice.

Without shame or fear, a young woman conjured her future husband's face in a dream using herbs, or a mother countered the evil air of sickness with a fire in the bedchamber of a threatened child. A bride carried a rosemary bouquet to bind her husband to her in loving friendship.

Even pious Bridget Seymour used magic. She kept vervain, dill, and rowan, and other herbs as amulets against Witches. One of her favorite plants in the garden, vervain, good for staunching bloody wounds, was also known to be widely used in Witchcraft and sorcery, and had to be crossed and blessed when gathered to be truly effective. She wore bay leaves sewn to her shoulder in threatening weather to protect against thunderstorms and reminded her brother that Prudence, who had been born with the caul over her head, would have a life of good fortune.

What, then, distinguished the common person or a magician from the Witch?

Witchcraft was evil magic and Satan's doing. To Gerald Seymour and countless others, blood alone made one a witch. Vanya confirmed there were hereditary witches in the craft, yet she also claimed Cathryn had perfect choice. "You shall be what you wish, my child. There is no devil lurking in my cottage fire to lure you from your heaven."

Did using her mother's potions to disable Gerald and praying in earnest for his destruction convict her of Witchcraft? Cathryn wondered. Might it be evil and a sin to defend herself against rape instead of trusting in God and accepting His judgment in what befell her?

Had she not participated in a ritual of Witchcraft and indulged in evil behavior for which sabbats were infamous? She, as well as everyone else, knew Witches brought demons from Hell to perform degrading acts that were disgusting to all decent, God-fearing men.

Cathryn bristled now. No wonder Father Vittorio had been convinced she was a Witch. Perhaps she was!

Is there any doubt that I would drink my mother's image-distorting wine again? she asked herself. Is my admission not proof that I am infected with her nature?

Though my mother denies it, as Gerald accuses, have I already become the handmaiden of Satan? Will I one day strangle and burn at the stake as my lover and priest envisioned?

Restless and cramped as she lay squeezed between Diligence and Prudence, troubled by disturbing thoughts, Cathryn could not sleep and, in the bitter morning cold, slipped out of the children's bedchamber and at last hastened to her mother's.

She found Vanya seated before the fire. "Child, I feared you were angry," she said, startled to see Cathryn emerge from shadow.

"My head hurt for days," she said. "I thought you offered cures." Cathryn tried to smile.

"Potions work differently on some than others," Vanya said.

For the moment, Cathryn concealed the troubles of her conscience, but she lost no time explaining her problem with Gerald. "His appetite is so uncertain, I administer the herb in unknown doses, never knowing how much or how little he'll consume. Sometimes I fear the effects have completely worn off and at others that he'll die before the meal is finished. Haven't you more destructive magic?"

"Like everyone else, you believe that a Witch consorts with devils." Vanya sighed.

Cathryn lowered her eyes. "I seem to remember a demon from the Sabbat."

"My religion, Cathryn, is aligned with the natural world, and yes, I believe in evil, daughter, and spirits, but the demons you fear are in ourselves and not in evil angels at war with God for souls. Gerald Seymour does not wrestle with demons, but himself.

"What I say is truth, Cathryn, and I am willing to die for it rather than bow to men whose lies corrupt the universe and condemn us all to a living hell of their invention.

"As for your demon at the Sabbat . . ."

"A demon in a man's form, Mother," Cathryn interrupted, "smelling of sweet almonds and spiced new wine, who lured me with visions put before my eyes by Witchcraft. You all but laid me in his arms."

"Perhaps the only demon was the wine, and you saw only what you wanted to see."

"That may be," Cathryn acknowledged as she sat before the fire. "But the wine you provided wasn't ordinary—why did you numb me?"

"My powers are not all you would have them be."

Cathryn looked hard at her mother, dissatisfied.

"You have drawn down power, daughter. What you experienced with your lover is not the sin your church would have it be. The acts the fathers of your church so despise are ones which bring us very close to God," Vanya counseled. "Answer me this, Cathryn: If with more wine you would see your demon a second time, would you take the cup from me?"

Cathryn's heart leapt to answer yes, as she felt herself all but able to feel the arms of the demon bind her to him and taste his feverish kisses. Her body warmed to the imagined sensations of his touch. "I saw a stranger, but Vittorio held me. I swear his touch was as real as the breath I take now. . . . Yes, if you promise to bring Vittorio to me again, I would drink your wine."

"You are afraid but would consent to Witchcraft to hold your priest in your arms?"

Cathryn nodded.

"Trust me, Cathryn, I promise what I offer is not a pact with your dreaded Christian devil. I do not believe in him."

Cathryn looked at her mother in disbelief.

"But I know you believe, child, and it will take more than a promise from a woman with a hideous twisted face to change your mind," Vanya said, and stared at her daughter in silence for a long while.

Then she sighed. "Though I am not the mother you would have me be, I am sorry for my decision to leave you behind in Venice. I should have kept you by my side and raised you in the true, the Old Religion."

While in many ways Cathryn leaned toward her mother's concepts, she was quite horrified at the prospect of being raised the daughter of a Witch. Then without a doubt she would have been a Witch herself. She then would be, just as Vanya was, outside the Church and if not in truth in league with Satan, then certainly a pagan who bowed to unlawful gods. Despite Vanya's explanations of her faith in beliefs tuned to the rhythms of nature, to Cathryn paganism meant mysterious, fobidden rites of barbaric sacrifice and sex-laden magic. Her experience of the Sabbat did little to diminish that impression.

"If your God, Cathryn, is one of love and mercy, then hateful men have made him cruel. His word is corrupted by men obsessed with wealth and power above charity for the faithful. Your Christ is kind, but your church is not.''

Vanya watched her daughter's pensive face. ''Does it not seem, Cathryn, that your devil is more powerful than your God?'' she wondered aloud.

''You fear magic and you fear demons when you should fear the men who covet the power of the very magic they condemn. They would steal the mysteries of the Old Religion for themselves, and sanctify its knowledge, giving it another name, and use it for their purposes. Their doctors steal our worts and simples, calling it medicine; then they call for Witch hunts. Your churchmen substitute Latin prayers for ancient ones and, when the patient is cured, call it a miracle. What is belief in miracles, Cathryn, but belief in magic?

''Each year the lawful sovereign of England blesses the sick with the royal touch. Is that not magic, daughter?

''Your Christian magistrates even use magic of their own to send a witch to burning.''

Cathryn looked puzzled.

''Are you unfamiliar with the practice of swimming Witches, daughter?''

Cathryn admitted she was.

''A suspected Witch is bound and thrown into a large body of water. If she sinks, and most likely drowns, she is deemed innocent by her judges, but if she floats, she is deemed held up by devils and therefore a Witch to burn. Yes, Cathryn, there are devils in the world,'' Vanya swore, ''but they are only men!''

Chapter 52

Not long after confronting Vanya, Zephyrus appeared at the window of Cathryn's bedchamber and fiercely scratched on the panes of glass, his enormous head bobbing with eagerness. She was dressed for bed, intending to sleep in her own room once again, certain Gerald would not trouble her for at least a fortnight, for he had taken to his bed again with fever.

Startled at first, Cathryn looked to the window fearfully, but when she saw the giant dog, she gave a jubilant cry. In an instant she removed the black Witch's robe from the trunk at the foot of her bed and not bothering to change from her sleeping gown, covered herself with Vanya's robe. Then, extinguishing her lamp, she ran to meet Zephyrus at the outside door.

Cathryn's excitement was contagious and Zephyrus yelped and danced about her. "Hush," she commanded, capturing his muzzle in her hands. "You'll give us away." She hugged him with affection. "Are you the Witch's familiar come for me?" she wondered of the eager dog who licked her face.

She freed him then and they were off, running to the glen. The dog bounded on toward the cottage, but Cathryn paused to catch her breath, or so she told herself.

In truth, she needed a moment to think. Vanya had sent for her, and by appearing, Cathryn gave her consent to delve again into the mysteries and the forbidden world of spirits.

Cathryn pressed a hand against her breast, her heartbeat not yet restored to normal; in fact, it was thudding even faster than before.

Was what she was about to do in truth so wicked? Was it unforgivable, by mysterious and unknown means, to conjure her lover from the mist, to steal him from his slumber in Venice and bring him here to be with her? Cathryn knew the Church would condemn such magic and cite a long list of grounds. But did the men who ruled the Church know all there was to know? Or did they only bow down without thinking to the dictates of other, more powerful men, as Vanya had said?

Cathryn knew for certain only two things about the situation she faced. First, she knew that in her lifetime on earth, she might never know the truth about which argument was right; and second, she admitted again that if it was necessary to consort with spirits and participate in magic to bring Vittorio to her side, she would do it gladly. It took courage to confess these things, and before stepping into Vanya's magic glen, Cathryn could not help but cross herself.

"By my Church, I openly defy You," she prayed directly to God, "for I am confused. To whom are Your true secrets given? To the Puritans, or to the Catholics, or to my mother, who proclaims herself a Witch? She seems less evil than others I could name, who profess to know You best. Forgive me if I am wrong. Protect me, please, from evil."

Her prayer said, Cathryn entered the clearing and hurried to the cottage door, which was ajar. She pushed the door fully open and found her mother seated, waiting for her.

"You have come for the cup," she said, and Cathryn nodded. "It waits." She indicated a silver chalice resting by the hearth. "Drink, then be seated."

Cathryn hesitated.

"There is no other way," Vanya reminded her.

Cathryn removed the heavy robe, then did as she was told and took the cup and downed the familiar spice-sweetened wine. Feeling the effects before she drained the cup, she was forced almost at once to sit down.

The room began to whirl around her. "Tonight your magic is stronger than it was before," she whispered.

"The potion is weakened by feasting."

"Yes, of course." Cathryn nodded and watched the room sway before her eyes.

In the grate, a fire burned brightly, attracting her gaze, and as she sat hypnotized, the colors of the flames became more vivid than she had ever seen. Mesmerized, she soon lost all sense of reality. As she sat, she wondered what she waited for, growing conscious of her every heartbeat, of a pounding in her ears, of the flow of blood within her brain.

"It is time, Cathryn," said her mother.

Cathryn looked at her, dismayed.

"Time for you to seek your demon spirits." She pointed to the cockloft.

Cathryn looked at the ladder leading to the loft, convinced she could fly under the Witch's potion, but certainly not climb.

"You're still quite able," her mother said, aware of Cathryn's turn of mind. She stretched out her hand to help her daughter from the floor. "Sleep, Cathryn, and sweet dreams," she said, and ushered her in the direction of the ladder. "Remember, Cathryn, nothing is possible without dreams."

Cathryn imagined she climbed a mountain, the hem of her nightdress in one hand, casually clinging to the ladder with the other. At the top she paused, parting heavy silk curtains, and surveyed the open loft. Cathryn had often wondered what lay

hidden behind these silky drapes but had never inquired, since
Vanya had never invited her above.

With her mother waiting below, Cathryn passed behind the
drapes. Her nostrils were assailed with the scent of heady incense burning in a large brass censer to one side, before which
lay a pile of satin comforters atop a sweet straw bed. Strewn
over all were myrrh, aloes, and cinnamon—like the harlot's bed
of Proverbs, Cathryn was still alert enough to notice.

The brass censer illuminated the space with a gentle light,
and, eyelids heavy, Cathryn lay down. She raised a few petals
from the floor and crushed and spread their juicy fragrance on
her hands, but when she put her head down, she fell at once into
dreamy but restless sleep.

In her dreams, Cathryn wandered on a hill, collecting flowers,
discarding those whose fragrance was only cloying and not
sweet. She wore her nightdress, her body warming in the sun.
Then off it came, and she was naked.

A man she did not seem to know approached her, and except
for a close-fitting black hood tied at his neck, he, too, was
naked. She gave him peonies and sprigs of lemon balm.

Gentle but demanding, he bent to kiss her lips, then moved his
hands upon her body, his large member swelling hard against her
soft flesh.

There was no need for Cathryn to open her eyes, to wake from
dreaming, for she knew him and his kiss that tasted of heaven.
Her skin tingled with delight as he found all the tender places to
fix his kisses. She became delirious with joy.

He kneeled and brought her with him, turning her to face
away. At his bidding, she leaned against him, and he pressed his
mouth against her ear. He cradled heavy breasts in hands with
practiced fingers and tantalized their tips. She swayed her hips
against him, eager and ready.

His fingers stroked her hair, then gently delved inside her
woman's lips, where with ease he found her throbbing center and
made sweet honey flow. She ached for him to fill her and began
to beg.

He declined and coaxed her to even greater passion, insisting
she still her hips that with impatience battered him. Then he
withdrew his fingers and returned them to her breasts. He
nipped and teased and fondled while she writhed.

She reached for him, but he evaded her, and when she caught

him, he laughed, knowing he would have to pay for his delightful though unmerciful teasing play.

Demanding and deliciously ungentle, Cathryn soon made him ache with more than pressing need, forcing him to seize her.

She welcomed his fierce touch, crooning eager consent as, bending her before him, he drove himself deep. "*Vittorio. Mio Vittorio,*" Cathryn cried, and with vigor pushed against his thrusts.

Panting with exertion, he drew her up and back against him, tightening his arms about her. He settled his fingers once more into her eager lips, and together their bodies and their spirits soared, transcending into ecstasy.

For a long while afterward, as he lay with her on the petal-strewn bed, Cathryn listened to his heartbeat and still labored breathing. Idly she stroked his beautiful body. "Why, my love, do you hide your face from me?" she asked, suddenly conscious of his woolen hood. "Or have you come this time disguised as an executioner to kill me, the daughter of a Witch?"

He did not answer aloud but lifted his hands and lightly encircled her throat.

"I, like the witches, believe in life eternal—in life after life," she whispered. "Would you not, my life, my love, join me on the other side?"

In solemn agreement he kissed her and Cathryn closed her eyes and fell to dreaming that he gently took her life.

Chapter 53

When his health permitted, Gerald spied on Cathryn, especially watchful as the phases of the moon changed and he imagined she would be called to pay special homage to the Evil One. Gerald felt certain he had seen Cathryn slip away from the house at least twice and, determined to have proof of her vile collusion with the Devil, vowed to follow Cathryn at the next opportunity.

Once again he lingered late by his window, and at sighting the white dog that approached his house in the bright moonlight, he began to sweat, excitedly anticipating the appearance of his late brother's mistress.

Disappointed when Vanya did not come from the shadows, Gerald continued to wait when the dog disappeared from his view. "Of course!" he muttered to himself a moment later. The Witch had sent her so that she might be in more than one place at a time.

Gerald rushed to descend the stairs in time to see Cathryn slip out the entry door. Before she closed the door behind her, he saw the animal rear up against her in a joyful greeting, his tail whipping back and forth. Gerald's heart began to race as he recalled how often he had spied on Cathryn without success! And now, he raged in silence, still unwell after yet another fever and reluctant to follow Cathryn even as he hastened to the door, the triumph of catching Cathryn was diminshed by the bitter cold night air.

Swift yet silent, surprised to see her use the door instead of departing through the keyhole, as he knew all Witches bound for assignations should, with nothing but his dressing gown over his clothes to protect him from the cold, Gerald ran to keep Cathryn in sight. It was his duty to go after her, he reasoned, breathing hard from the exertion. As her guardian he was obliged to see for himself that she worshiped with Witches.

There now was no doubt in Gerald's mind that he had fallen under Cathryn's evil spell. How else could he explain his behavior? When well, he groveled at the young woman's feet, performing at her command, and when he had given her all that she craved—his soul—with the perversity of her kind, she poisoned him. Satan had acknowledged to him that Cathryn was his disciple, but Gerald would see with his own eyes.

Indeed, if he had not been poisoned or cursed, what explained his grand lethargy and his shriveled interest? Where else did a man's impotence originate but from the spells and potions of a woman versed in Witchcraft?

Suddenly Gerald ceased his pursuit of Cathryn, stopping in response to her lack of movement. He gripped his painful side with a trembling hand and gasped for breath, but he kept his eyes on Cathryn.

Intent on her goal, Cathryn did not once look behind her, though Gerald feared she might and therefore, to better conceal himself, stepped back into the shadows, giving himself a better view of what lay in Cathryn's path.

In the moon-drenched night, he saw the great white dog lie down at Cathryn's feet and behind him, on a crudely fashioned table of rock, a large lighted candle next to a shimmering silver chalice.

Gerald watched, fascinated, as Cathryn stood before the pagan altar. She held her hand over the candle, then withdrew, to his shock reacting as though she felt the flame.

Gerald shrank further into shadow as Cathryn turned and looked at her surroundings.

In slow motion, her gaze swept the grove, searching the darkened shapes: the trees and fallen logs; random bushes and scattered rocks; the almost human shapes. How deep these woods were, she marveled, surprised again to find yet another secret sanctuary, the thought comforting her as she knelt and raised to her lips the cup of dizzying, dream-laden wine.

Grateful for the seclusion of the private bower, Cathryn felt her blood begin to race. Soon, for the third time, she would slip again into a world apart, into the realm of ghosts and visions of which the waking world seemed to live in terror. But to Cathryn, who knew the waking world could be far more horrible, those fears were quite unfounded.

Eyes closed, and trembling with anticipation, Cathryn drained the cup, then let it fall to the forest floor and, kneeling, waited until she felt her lover's radiant presence beside her.

He knelt before her and pulled away her Puritan cap, forcing her hair to tumble from its knot, then held her head in gentle hands.

Cathryn raised her eyes, her drug-widened pupils reflecting the nearby candle flame, and glowing with radiant desire, she pouted, imploring her lover for a kiss.

At first he did not comply, but tilted her face to better his perusal. For several moments he stared at her from behind the deeply hooded black robe he wore again, then bent and kissed her, savoring the sweetness of her touch, sighing as if he had come upon a bit of heaven in the moonlit wood.

As Cathryn wrapped her arms around him, opening her lips to receive his full kiss and the gentle explorations of his tongue, he thrilled to taste her, to the tender warmth of having her against him. He kissed her again and again, as if sampling succulent morsels from a splendid feast, and soon his passion surged, driving him to want more than tenderness from her. He wanted her next to his skin, to be inside her. He seized her, trying not to crush her in his fierce embrace.

In body and soul Cathryn echoed her lover's need, and in a thrilling instant, she soared to another level of rapture that made her crave to be united fully with him. Her passion gave her daring and she pulled down the hood from his head and stripped away the robe that bound and concealed his body. With his eager assent, she assumed the lead, and while he plundered her eager mouth, she stroked him, reducing him to trembling, on the verge of bliss.

Though he had no desire to wrest control, he pulled her down with him to the forest floor, moaning with his pleasure. She lay on top of him and as soon as she untied her cloak, his hands slid with delight over Cathryn's satin skin.

She let her cloak fall over them and stretched as far as possible along his length, wishing to touch every inch of him, made warm by his body heat and the flame of passion. She caressed and kissed him everywhere, then curled her legs around his hips and, with delicious and deliberate ease, forced him into her.

He groaned as if he suffered and she smiled and resisted what her body urged for her to do. She bore down but did not ride him, holding herself quite still. She waited and she watched.

Her lover's passion ebbed a scant degree, his eyes luminous as, buried deep within her, he willed himself not to end what was a most exquisite torture. He forced himself to follow her lead, but tantalized her excitement-swollen breasts, his fierce mouth suckling her tender nipples, and enjoyed her deliciously tight woman's body as it sheathed his manhood until Cathryn writhed, sighing with the rhythm of her ecstasy. Helpless then, he soared with her, their spirits seeming free of all familiar bonds of earth. They seemed to fly above the normal world and spiral into a world of incandescent peace.

With great reluctance, their vivid sensations not quite memory, the lovers descended to a plateau of ordinary sight and sound. Within moments each lay beside the other hungry still, as if he had not yet filled her; her lover knew her wish and pulled Cathryn beneath him, eager to explore again the enchanting realm of bliss.

Chapter 54

Chilled as much by fear as by the cold, Gerald Seymour watched
Cathryn fall to her knees and worship, then imbibe the pagan
wine. Then, with his own eyes, he swore he saw a beast emerge
from the bowels of the boiling earth and, in an incandescent
glow, take on the human form.

Horrified but aroused, he stood enthralled, rooted to the ground,
and observed their rite. He envied the beast his ability to overpower Cathryn and would have traded all he possessed for that
power alone. Gerald coveted her lover's capacity and dreamed
himself the object of her impassioned mating in the Devil's stead.

As they lay entangled, sated, upon the forest floor, Gerald
also panted for breath, exhausted by viewing their primitive
ritual of unnatural love. But if they were in rapture, so was he.
He had proof, even if by his own hand, that he had overcome
Cathryn's evil spell. He was still a man and not forever damned
to be a witch's quivering eunuch.

The warm semen now smeared upon his hand proved to
Gerald that he was holy—a man blessed by God to triumph over
the power of the Devil's chosen woman—for to Gerald's eye,
Cathryn possessed the Devil's heart, indeed, his soul—if that
fallen angel still had one.

Gerald watched Cathryn make the Prince of Darkness a slave
of her needs and saw the Devil transfigure himself from a
snarling, horned, hairy, cloven-footed beast to a most perfect
man, except for his organs of lust, which were not of normal
human size but of unusually large proportion. Else he could not
satisfy her, Gerald reasoned, and if not pleased, Cathryn would
not do his work upon the earth.

All that Gerald saw confirmed for him that he had been
seduced by Satan's ablest vixen. But he stood aghast while he
observed the lovers for a second time, making love as if they had
not yet embraced each other. Again he was aroused, staggered by

their passion, which electrified the night. He would never forget their animalistic enjoyment, forgetting himself, as if he, too, participated.

Close enough to hear their sighs, he could almost distinguish their whispers of endearment. Her lover worshiped Cathryn's body with his tongue, feasting on her supremely tender flesh, raining kisses that left her delirious. It was obvious she found him equally delicious, and, staggered, Gerald watched her use her mouth to perform the act the Devil always required and reduce the Prince of Demons to mewling.

His eyes full, Gerald shivered with satanic envy and would have preyed on her himself when at last she wandered home, but, to Gerald's fury, reluctant to be separated from his woman, the Devil escorted Cathryn to Gerald's own door.

Gerald's mouth burned with the final kisses Cathryn and her lover exchanged, one with them, his body flaming with their heat. But as Cathryn disappeared into the house, Gerald caught the beast's red raging eye and he reared up high on his massive hind legs, his large copulative organs still exposed to taunt the merely mortal man. Then the beast charged toward him, snorting when he stopped nearby to paw the earth. He reared again and pawed the air and, with a maniacal laugh, cursed Gerald with a clammy cold sweat, turning Gerald's lust into the fire of a fevered brow, and shriveled Gerald's already shrinking member. Satisfied, the horned beast then vanished into a sulphurous mist.

Grateful still to be alive, Gerald trembled and limped the final steps home to safety. His strength sapped, he had great trouble even pushing the door open, and the stairs were quite beyond him. The next morning, Bridget found him incoherent and slumped upon the floor.

Chapter 55

Gerald folded the unsigned document and concealed it beneath his nightshirt. Ten readings of the letter did not improve its contents or give him any better insight into what his course should be.

Discouraged, he pulled the bedcovers under his chin, and though he felt better than he had in weeks, he decided he was not yet up to taking any action on the correspondent's unasked-for information. He had planned to rise today but reasoned another day of contemplation would be to his benefit.

Again, God had spared him, but in Gerald's view, this time it was not a particular sign of favor, and he would be wise to consider his few existing choices with special care. His last foray with Satan had resulted in something less than triumph.

He had not lost his wits in total, as some men do when they come face to face with the Devil, for he was not yet fool enough to believe he could bring Cathryn to the attention of the authorities with impunity. Nor could he in safety accuse Vanya of Witchcraft. The risks to his own welfare were much too great. Mother and daughter would turn on him and accuse him, and with their power drive him to the stake with them.

At the very least, Cathryn would implicate him for his crimes with her, though he were innocent and only an instrument of her kind's overwhelming lust. And although it was well known that a Witch could transform a man, willing or not, and use him at her mercy to satisfy her carnal nature, this common knowledge would not protect him. Nor did Gerald imagine that Cathryn would hesitate to call on her subterranean lover for assistance. Reviewing his most recent personal encounter, he was not eager to engage in any sort of battle with the Prince of Darkness.

Gerald touched his diminished genitals. He had no urgent wish to confront the prince of darkness directly a second time. On the very night he had witnessed Cathryn with her demon, Gerald's organs of copulation had swelled painfully to more than twice their normal size, as punishment, he reasoned, for his envy of the Devil's prodigious ability and size. When Gerald's brow had cooled, so had all his ardor—and all capacity as well.

Yet now, at least, for the first time since he had laid eyes on her, Gerald could look on Cathryn Godwyne and not be reduced to groveling. But he still was ill at ease, for he feared that in conjunction with the pact she had made with her master, she could at her whim restore him and put him to licentious use.

The anonymous letter now concealed against Gerald's breast announced to him that others besides himself knew of Cathryn's wickedness, which would make it easier for him to accuse her. However, the fact did not console Gerald entirely, for his correspondent also spoke of Vanya Russo and questioned why Gerald harbored her.

The missive stated Vanya Russo was a well-known Witch, known to many persons for her curses and her cures. If a need for magic arose in the neighborhood, everyone knew the disfigured herbwoman would have a useful potion. She was the wise woman on whom they called when the time came for a woman with a babe-swollen belly to face her hour of death, and this included his own wife, Phoebe, at the birth that had cost her life.

Were not midwives Witches with the power of life, sometimes taking lives of babies for their satanic rituals? Was his own last child a victim of the Witch?

Why, Gerald's correspondent asked, did Vanya Russo continue to live free of harassment on the Godwyne estate? Why had Gerald not driven her away? Had he made a pact with the Witch in exchange for her protection?

Gerald winced. He had made no such pact with the Devil. On his hope to enter heaven, he had given his solemn oath to Ashley to honor his last wish, but now it seemed to Gerald the vow might lead him straight into the fires of everlasting Hell.

As for his other sins, Gerald denied complicity. He had committed no willful sin. All blame rested with Cathryn, the evil one, true daughter of Eve and practitioner of the Craft.

As all men did, Gerald knew sin originated with the first woman and passed down the generations solely through her blood from mother to daughter to the present day. All her daughters were Satan's handmaidens, unless a dispensation was granted through grace. Even so, a woman could be corrupted with ease, as worldwide convictions of the female sex for Witch-craft were ample proof. Far more women than men were tried and punished. Ten women for every man.

The wise men of the world knew whom to blame.

Still, Gerald reasoned, he could not afford to take a chance on the wisdom of a few.

Perhaps even in his own household there were persons who presumed his guilt. He regarded his sister with worry as he watched Bridget enter the room with another vile infusion, harboring suspicions about the hot mulled drink she brought him, the contents of the cup smelling little better than the slop jar hidden beneath the bed boards.

Without argument, Gerald drank the vile contents of the cup to fortify his strength. Bridget had nursed him through many a crisis, he noted, rubbing his distended belly, and now was hardly the time to question her loyalty.

Bridget seemed exceptionally weary. "I would have some relief today," she said. "Cathryn will bring whatever else you need. I must go to bed."

"No. I cannot have her wait on me."

His sister frowned. "She's well able and I must get off my feet."

Gerald felt a wave of sudden weakness. "I insist."

It was rare for Bridget to defy him. "In this instance you cannot."

For the first time Gerald noticed the blue color of his sister's lips and fingernails. At last he agreed. "I can see that you're not well."

"And you, brother, should be up and about your house, but in the meanwhile, Cathryn is more than able to take care of you."

Gerald stared at Bridget. Did she make a statement of fact, or did she mean more than she said? Her opinion of Cathryn had changed these four years since Cathryn came to them from Venice. How had this usually unbending woman come to rely on Cathryn's help and judgment?

Bridget no longer nagged him about Cathryn's absences and wayward, independent ways. Was it because Cathryn never failed to do her work and, on the Lord's day, the first day of the week, bowed her head on bended knee at meeting? Was it because Cathryn dutifully wore the austere Puritan dress and somber stare with such perfection and no more questioned her place? Did it please Bridget that Cathryn bore with saintly patience the attentions of her pathetically slow suitor, thereby appearing innocent and pure?

Why did Cathryn not use her Witch's lure upon Giles Jefferies? Gerald wondered. Did she have some reason for preferring to remain under his own roof?

Gerald began to sweat. What evil design did Cathryn have? What plot had she contrived with her master? Was he to be her only victim after all? Even Bridget, his devoted sister, trusted Cathryn now, leaving her quite free to commit whatever vile acts she pleased.

In the next days, as Cathryn performed her duties, Gerald watched her every movement, standing at the window even when exhausted, watching her weed and plant and prune.

Cathryn was oblivious to her guardian, absorbed by the tasks at hand and, secretly, by the needs her encounters with her silent lover had reawakened.

"Why do you withhold the cup?" Cathryn had demanded of her mother when her woman's longings had driven her wild.

"The drug is too potent to use often," Vanya had replied, "and I fear you've already used it overmuch."

"Let me judge," Cathryn had pleaded like a child, pouting when she did not prevail, and much like her mysterious, spirit-laden dreams, Vanya's power had faded before Cathryn's eyes.

"Some things cannot be," Vanya had tried to comfort her.

"No! Please, no!" Cathryn had insisted.

"Do not despair," her mother had said at last. "You and your lover shall be joined again someday."

Cathryn had tried not to be depressed, but despite the Witch's promise, she'd felt abandoned again to an eternity of empty nights.

In the garden, Cathryn rose from her knees and pushed several stray strands of rebellious hair beneath her cap. She raised her eyes to Gerald's upper-story windows. She knew he watched her. She could feel his stare.

She prayed her guardian's disabilities this time were permanent, for she began to feel she no longer had the strength or the will to fight him. She'd lost faith in Vanya's magic. She'd abandoned hope that Giles would ever marry her. Cathryn's courage seemed to fade like her hopeless dreams.

She bent to scoop a handful of black earth from her garden

plot, then raised her hand and released the dirt to fly into the bitter whipping wind. For comfort she had only to turn to the new religion she feigned. "Indeed," she whispered as the particles of rich soil disappeared, "the Lord God giveth, and He taketh away."

Chapter 56

Gerald Seymour knew almost everyone in the district and had never seen this man before. Beneath his rain-sodden cloak he was well dressed, and Gerald marveled that he had ventured to travel on such a miserable day.

"My business canna wait," the man said as Gerald ushered him into the study. "I come to speak of the letter ye recently received."

Gerald's heart seemed to stop beating, but he forced himself to remain calm. He sized up his visitor, whose rich clothing was insufficient to conceal his coarse and feral nature. With hollow cheeks and sunken eyes, he looked like the specter of death, a man returned from the grave.

Yet he was very much alive, quick and nervous, and in a hoarse whisper related details to which no one, save a ghost, should have been privy. As he talked, Gerald grew paler than his guest, fearing not only what he said, but what he did *not* say.

"I will not ask how you came by this information, only why you bring it to me. If you accuse me, surely I am not the one to tell."

"I bring ye also a solution." The man laid a packet on his desk. "I've three documents for ye to sign. For Yer Honor's endorsement, all debts to yer departed brother's estate will be considered settled. No one'll be the wiser. And because me and me master can keep our mouths shut, ye shall escape the disgrace, not to mention pain, of dangling from the sheriff's scaffold like a thief. Yer children will be spared from prison, and maybe not grow to be beggars."

Gerald reviewed the papers. In exchange for an amount well in excess of the funds Gerald had siphoned from Cathryn Godwyne's rightful estate, he was to sign a contract giving custody of

Cathryn Godwyne, said Puritan woman, an unmarried female of good health and, likewise, reputation to the proprietors of the Dunstan Holding Company, a society chartered by our Sovereign Lord, King James, and do charitably agree forthwith to provide for her reasonable welfare, until such time as an honest and sufficient husband can be found, or a position of servitude in a home of the same Christian piety and charity as she was sent from hence.

In setting her hand to this document, Cathryn Godwyne doth confirm she hath not made a vow of perpetual chastity in the world, and shall submit to her husband, and to God's command to be fruitful.

Gerald stared in silence at his guest. In all his thrashing about for a solution to the problem of his responsibility for Cathryn Godwyne, Gerald had not considered sending Cathryn to the Colonies as a prospective bride of some worthy Puritan colonist.

He doubted Cathryn would have to accept servitude, for he imagined there would be a long line of panting unmarried men for her selection. And while it seemed a perfect means of disposing of her, Gerald balked, for no matter what other vows he broke, signing this agreement seemed to violate his solemn pledge to Ashley.

"I must have time to consider your offer," he told his guest as he rose from his chair. He opened the study door to show the visitor out.

Unnerved, Gerald had trouble walking to the outer door, agonizing while the man donned his cloak and gloves. At last, however, he let his guest out into the driving rain and turned, intending to return to his study to reflect and pray on the perhaps providential offer. Instead, he was forced to face his frowning sister.

"I could not help but overhear," Bridget said.

"What you mean is, you spied on me again."

"The man seemed dangerous."

That Gerald could not deny.

"You have not agreed?" she asked.

Gerald shook his head.

"You must."

"I did not expect you to be the man's ally," Gerald answered, stunned. "Am I mistaken, or have you not become Cathryn's friend? Of late you defend her at almost every turn. Now you would turn her over to that grotesque creature?"

Bridget shifted her weight. "I have come to tolerate her presence."

"She is one of us, but you would send her away at the first opportunity."

"She is quite miserable here."

"Our faith tells us not to expect happiness in this life," he argued. "We only await the kingdom of heaven. But I think you exaggerate Cathryn's misery. She loves the children. Did you not notice how joyful she was at Comfort's return? It was as if a lost child of her own had been restored to her. And though I forbid it, I hear her singing all the time."

"She cries herself to sleep."

Gerald turned quite pale. "How would you know that? Do you spy on her, also?"

"By chance I heard her one night when she retired. It has been the same for weeks."

His color began to return, but he was greatly agitated, not wanting to discuss any aspect of Cathryn's possible departure. "You are imagining it. Do you make a habit of leaning against bedchamber doors?"

"Not as a rule!" Bridget glared at her brother.

He became angry. "She will never consent."

"You are her guardian and have the right to sign for her marriage. Please, Gerald, God has sent you the means to cleanse your conscience."

"What do you know of my conscience?" he all but snarled.

"I am aware that it could not be possible for you to have paid your debts these recent years unless you had access to assets other than your own."

"You know nothing of the kind."

"Tell me, then, brother, out of respect for truth, where did these assets come from? How is it that this foreign orphan, who came under our roof through some peculiar deathbed agreement you made with our half brother, came by property and money for you to steal?"

"What makes you conclude I've stolen anything from her?"

"My ears. By God's mercy only, the man who was just here neglected to bring the sheriff to our door."

Gerald did not reply at once. "If we are blessed, heaven will swallow our recent visitor. Or would you inform on me, dear sister?"

"To save your soul."

"To save my soul?" He began to laugh and could not seem to stop. Bridget's eyes widened in alarm.

Suddenly his demeanor changed and he turned on her, his voice boastful, low and vicious. "You cannot save my soul, woman, for my crimes are almost too numerous to count."

Agitated, he began to pace. "If I were to send Cathryn away, her mother would work some terrible curse on me." He thought he could see Bridget's hair rise on her scalp.

"Her mother?" She hoped she had misheard him.

"Her mother, fool, is Vanya Russo. And her father, our dear departed brother." It gave Gerald perverse pleasure to inform Bridget of these facts. "Where do you think she runs to, but to her mother's knee, to learn the Craft?"

It was Bridget Seymour's turn to pale.

"And I assure you, my virgin sister, Cathryn Godwyne, the Devil's daughter, has worked many a spell on me. And quite probably on you." He laughed.

Bridget looked around to determine if any of the children or the servants could overhear. To her vast relief, there was no one in sight.

"She has often spirited me to her bed and forced me to perform unspeakable acts to satisfy her unquenchable Witch's lust, just as, I'm sure, her mother bewitched our brother."

Bridget had to sit down.

"Is this overwhelming, dear sister, or are you only making yourself more comfortable so that I might give you the details of our assignations?"

Bridget covered her ears and began to cry. "How dare you? And how dare you not consider your visitor's offer? Cathryn is our brother's child, your near kin. Would you bring the wrath of God on us all?" she demanded when she could stifle her outburst of tears.

Gerald resumed his nervous pacing. "I do not send the whore away because I do not *wish* to send her away!" he growled.

In despair, Bridget put her face in her hands. " 'Get thee behind me, Satan,' " she prayed.

Gerald sat down. "Too late, sister, unless I rid myself of her," he said. "But the solution is not God-sent, I promise. It is rather a plot hatched by the Devil himself. Our visitor this day is another of His agents."

Bridget looked about as if searching for ashes to sweep away. "We must prepare a witch bottle to break her spell—your finger-nail parings; a clip of your hair; a few drops of your blood or water in a bottle and buried under the doorstep. I must hang fresh vervain, dill, and rowan in the house."

Gerald nodded in agreement with Bridget's plan to overcome Cathryn's influence, then rose from the bench and hastened to his study. "At last I rid my house of evil," he said, and with Bridget as witness, endorsed the documents, sealing Cathryn's fate.

PART THREE

The New World
1691–

The
Harvest

I wished for you
to be born a daughter
though we know
that daughters
cannot but be

born for burning
like the fatal
tree.

> *from* "Baby-Witch"
> *by Erica Jong*

Chapter 57

If no one traveled on English roads at night, Cathryn's companion had not been so informed. But very likely, Cathryn felt certain, he was just the sort one avoided by not traveling at night. Except for his expensive cloak and superior mount, he had every appearance of an outlaw, his chronic glare vicious.

Cathryn had first met her companion many long hours ago, when after being awakened from a sound sleep by Bridget and told to dress for a long journey. She then was brought before Meldon Archer. "You shall be going to London with him this very night," Bridget advised her. Incredulous, Cathryn stood before Gerald alone, bemused and sleepy, while he explained that he had arranged a marriage contract for her benefit. In a few months' time, she would be living in New England somewhere in the Massachusetts Bay Colony. He showed her the official documents, demanding she put her signature to the contract.

For some minutes, Cathryn tried to convince herself she was only captured in a vivid and disturbing dream, but little by little, she realized she was experiencing no simple nightmare.

"So, you would sell me to the highest bidder. Do you suppose it is a Christian thing to do and I should be grateful?"

"It is in fact an act of charity," he replied. "If you stay, you soon would be accused of Witchcraft." He showed her the anonymous letter he had received.

Cathryn grew faint at the details of her movements recorded in accusatory language. Her first thought was of the stranger at the feast who had been reluctant at first, but then . . . But why would he betray her? Cathryn stared at her guardian in utter confusion.

"Vanya Russo shall also be accused if you do not go away. As you see, there is at least one witness to your collusion," Gerald announced. "I imagine it should not be difficult to find other witnesses to testify against my brother's whore. Though she is reduced to a crone by her evil, few would doubt, if informed, that she is your mother. You, Cathryn, are too beautiful to be good.

"I have been witness with my own eyes to your evil, but I should be reluctant to testify against you. More, I should hate to hear your screams while your interrogators persuade you to confess your liaison with your master, the Devil."

He smiled at Cathryn's silent fury and offered her a quill to add her signature to the marriage contract. "You have no choice but to sign, showing your eagerness to participate and submit to the contract."

As Cathryn put her name to the agreement, Bridget entered with a valise and portmanteau.

"I shall say good-bye to the children," Cathryn said when it was obvious there was nothing left but to go, and she started for the stairs, almost unable to control a flood of threatened tears.

Bridget moved to stand in Cathryn's way.

At first, Cathryn met the woman's hard gaze, then let her glance fall to the stairs; the floor of the stairwell was littered with flowers and leaves.

"Angelica?" she whispered, surprised.

Bridget nodded. "To rid us of your evil influence and to ward off any future invasion of Witches."

Cathryn cast her a bitter smile and attempted to push past her. Bridget grabbed her by the arm and Cathryn struggled, then stopped when she heard her name called down from the top of the stairs.

"Please, what is happening?" Diligence demanded in alarm from the second floor. Prudence stood clinging to her sister. "Are there Witches in the house?" She began to tremble, but Prudence hurried down the stairs and tugged at Cathryn's free arm.

Bridget tugged on one arm, Prudence on the other.

Cathryn managed to hoist Prudence to her hip and Bridget began to struggle to seize the child. As she fought to stay in Cathryn's arms, Prudence began to scream.

"Let go of her! She's a Witch!" the child's aunt screamed.

"No!" Prudence cried, and held to Cathryn more fiercely, her screams reduced to sobs.

Bridget ceased her struggle for Prudence, letting Cathryn comfort the distraught child.

Diligence descended the stairs until she stood eye level with Cathryn. "Is it true, are you a Witch?" she asked with perfect calm when her sister's crying suddenly ceased.

"What do you think?" Cathryn asked the child.

There was silence as the evidence of Diligence's doubts crossed her face. She looked at her father and her aunt, and at the frightening visage of the unnamed visitor, who stood glowering to the side. Then she looked at Cathryn again. "I had begun to love and trust you," Diligence said.

"Don't believe their lies about me when I'm gone," Cathryn pleaded as Gerald stepped forward to take Prudence from her arms and the ugly stranger came forward and dragged Cathryn to the door.

Cathryn could no longer suppress her tears. "A lasting curse upon your head and house," she swore at Gerald as she was pulled from his house. "Damn you to Hell, Gerald Seymour!"

It was a wild struggle, but Meldon Archer succeeded in getting himself and Cathryn in the saddle. He forced her across his lap. "Ye can gallop to London in this fashion, or ride like a lady on yer own horse, mistress. Have yer choice."

Cathryn quickly decided to ride alone, but her violent tears would have caused her to tumble to the ground had her ugly companion not had the foresight to tie her to the saddle.

Archer took her horse's reins and seemed deaf to her raging tears, neither trying to comfort her nor demanding her silence as Cathryn indulged her fury and madly screamed her outrage over the predicament in which she found herself. She stopped shrieking only when she was too weak to cry more.

After daybreak the travelers rested and ate by the roadside, and on the second night they slept at a bustling inn. Stone silent by now, Cathryn waited for her companion to speak to her again, but he never did.

She feared the worst as he locked the inn room door behind them and pocketed the key. But sullen, he sat before her on a stool and, leaning against the door, fell asleep. No fool, Cathryn took the hard, narrow bed.

After the first night's ride she was no longer tied in the saddle, but her horse's reins were still held by her companion, and in the confusion of London, where they arrived just before dark, she was glad to have a guide. Staggered by the sights and smells of England's largest city, Cathryn stared at all she saw, barely missing the damage and the trauma of being struck full face by flying stinking refuse that rained from an overhanging window above her on one narrow twisting street.

"In London, never look up," her companion said at last, and Cathryn arrived at her final destination exhausted but unscathed, quite glad of his advice.

When they arrived at their destination, the door that opened from the street to them revealed a dimly lit interior, and from their dress and manners Cathryn knew at once those who gathered were Puritans. Her welcome was quiet, but not unkind. "Meet your sisters," her host said, introducing her to five somber young women dressed much like herself. "Like you, they travel with the Lord to a new beginning on a distant shore."

If there was also rage and fear within their hearts, Cathryn did not see it in their nods of greeting. "Welcome, sister," each said to her. Feeling numb, Cathryn adopted her new companion's silence after her escort vanished, leaving her clutching her packet of papers without a farthing in her pocket.

"Your papers, please, mistress," demanded the stern master of the house, directing Cathryn to a bench, where she was offered food and drink and watched with interest while the other women continued the task of making bread.

In whispers, the other women revealed their stories to Cathryn. Unlike her, they wanted to leave England. They were poor, widowed or never married, and in desperate need of husbands to keep them from starving in the streets.

Almost twenty-two years, Mary was almost too old to be considered a likely bride at home in England. The sale of her marriage contract would see that her mother and her brother and sisters survived the coming year. The terms and prospects agreed with her. She was thin and already missing a few teeth, and Cathryn wondered if Mary would live out the year herself.

Anne and Elizabeth had tales similar to Mary's, and Ida, a widow with one babe, who lay sleeping in a basket by the hearth, was just as grateful for a chance at a fresh start in the New World. She sought an earnest husband who had settled in the Puritan colony "according to the laws of God."

Beatrice, fifteen, was both sad and eager. She was not a child, she insisted, but leaving her family was hard, she admitted, tears welling in her eyes. "But I shall obey God's will," she promised to a chorus of amens.

The five young women turned to Cathryn, who, after the emotionally wrenching journey from Wollingham to London, had no more tears to shed. "I'm an orphan and my guardian sends me to the Colonies to hunt a husband," she said.

Ida stepped back. "I'm surprised there were no suitors here in England," she said, a question in her voice. She gauged Cathryn's lustrous black hair as it peeked from beneath her Puritan cap, her perfect teeth and flawless skin, her erect and voluptuous figure.

Cathryn blushed.

"Perhaps the Lord God has a husband waiting for her in the New Jerusalem," Beatrice suggested kindly.

"Virtue is to be more prized than beauty," Ida speculated, appraising her competitor.

"I'm sure, Mistress Barrett, that you did not intend to be unkind with your remark," Anne interrupted Ida. "We've a long journey ahead. It shall be that much easier to bear as friends. Our faith instructs each of us has been selected by God. Do we dare to doubt His choices?"

At Anne's challenge, Ida shook her head, but she continued to bear in silence her reservations about her sister, Cathryn Godwyne, the final woman to enter their midst.

Chapter 58

As she approached the imposing bark Cynthia Ames *that would* take her to the New World, Cathryn felt as if she were bound with a rope tied around her neck, the noose her only inducement to board the ship. Bitter, she remembered once swearing she would never again board a sailing vessel unless it was bound for Venice!

At about one hundred twenty-five feet long, with a deeper draft, the *Cynthia Ames* was much larger than *Il Vento,* and she bore an English flag. A ship heading for the English colonies would bear no other, and Cathryn tried to reassure herself that her pending journey would have little resemblance to her last sea voyage with Capitano Salvadori.

But once below decks, where even on this raw day the air seemed close, Cathryn remained ill at ease. After two weeks in London she still felt uncomfortable with the other five Puritan women and knew that for the most part they were no less ill-at-ease with her.

Ida's baby began to squall, and Cathryn sympathized with the child. Your mother must have told you we'll be sharing these miserable quarters with some thirty men for at least two months, she thought while Ida did her best to silence the unhappy child.

How can it be? Cathryn wondered as she glanced around the cramped passenger hold, her stomach growing queasy at the prospect.

Within the passenger steerage, two decks below the main deck, as elsewhere aboard ship, not a square inch of space was wasted. Each passenger was assigned a narrow bunk and issued a thin wool-filled mattress and blanket for warmth and comfort. It was impossible to sit upright in one's bunk, for underneath the bunks, which were stacked two high, was storage for personal belongings. Ida would share her bunk with her baby, of course, and though not private in any sense, the women were allotted one corner of the cabin as theirs.

Cooking for the passengers would be done by the women on the main deck in the cook's cabin, but the passengers would spend most of the next months below decks confined to quarters, a horrid prospect from Cathryn's point of view.

But unlike Cathryn, who in private railed against the notion of traveling to the New World, all of the others relished the coming voyage. Most had left nothing behind worth having. Visions of riches or at least modest success in the new land replaced the reality of lives of poverty and bleak futures. Stories of others who had gone before them were repeated like a litany.

The first night, when all but one lamp was extinguished in passenger steerage aboard the *Cynthia Ames*, Cathryn admitted she, too, had little to mourn in leaving England. Yet she cried herself to sleep for the twelfth night in a row. The blessing of escaping Gerald Seymour was not sufficient to make up for her other losses.

She missed Vanya; she ached for the Seymour children as though she had been torn from her very own offspring. The distress on Diligence's face and Prudence's wails at her departure echoed in Cathryn's heart. The visions of her priest, she realized, were lost to her forever now, except in ordinary dreams.

At times Cathryn feared she had gone insane; she was certain her companions thought so, too. She withdrew, becoming a sullen prospective bride, lacking obvious gratitude, her Puritan devotion in doubt. The only solace her overseers had was that, though she was not happy, she at least was not defiant; the sound of her tears was an odd comfort to new guardians.

Beatrice tried to cheer her, an effort Cathryn appreciated but which she suspected was intended more to improve Beatrice's own lagging spirits than to comfort Cathryn. "You shall see, mistress," Beatrice told Cathryn. "The Lord shall give you a brave husband and you shall make a home in the wilderness, and, together, grow fine sons."

Cathryn knew the young woman dreamed this for herself, so she acknowledged Beatrice's words with a smile. She even indulged in Beatrice's fantasy, but instead of the charming suitor of Beatrice's dreams, Cathryn envisioned a man more like Gerald and swore she would not marry anyone who did not please her. She would die in servitude before she would allow that to be her fate!

With extreme caution, Cathryn looked upon the male passengers aboard the *Cynthia Ames* and felt her skin crawl. At first glance, not one appeared to her to be a reasonable prospect, though they were not at all unlike the lot from which she could expect to draw. "God help me," Cathryn muttered.

"He shall, if you are faithful," Elizabeth answered.

Cathryn cast the Puritan woman a doubtful look but said nothing. Oh, to have faith! she thought.

Her faith in everything almost gone, Cathryn resorted to more tears and then to dreams. She dreamed of violins, hearing music that would have made her weep even under ordinary circumstances, and mourned her Amati, which remained in Wollingham with Vanya. Without her violin she felt an utter pauper, reduced to penury, no better than a beggar in London's teeming streets.

Cathryn decided that perhaps she should be grateful for the opportunities awaiting her in the New World. Her life in Wollingham had been cursed, and after hearing Gerald's prophecies, she had elected life over death by signing the contract; but as she looked around passenger steerage, she admitted this life was not quite of her choosing, either.

Cathryn sighed, admitting she dreamed even when there was never any hope. An utter fool is what I am, she damned herself. But dreams are all I have. Nothing is possible without them.

Her mother had urged her to believe in the magic of dreams and had offered her a cup brimming with a froth of magical visions; all Cathryn's doubts about Vanya's power had vanished with those dreams. However, it was also obvious that her mother's magic was not supreme; otherwise she would not be sailing now from England's shore.

In fact, the cup containing the most magical of dreams had been denied her of late, and her mother's motives in that denial were unclear to Cathryn. What had been Vanya's purpose to encourage her to dream, to give her the means to fulfill them, and then to deny her?

Perhaps, Cathryn reasoned now, the dream-inducing cup had been only a deceitful ploy to delude her and woo her to the Craft. Cathryn remembered Vanya said she regretted leaving Cathryn behind in Venice, because Cathryn had been raised a Catholic and not in the Old Religion. Perhaps it was her mother's only regret.

In Wollingham, Vanya had trained Cathryn to be an herbwoman and exposed her to the Craft. Though she'd promised otherwise, perhaps she had intended to groom her daughter to replace her in the coven. Would a witch not use ploys, from spells to poison, to have her way?

Cathryn's heart sank deeper into the gloom. She'd been abandoned by her mother; then for convenience wooed back. Was there perhaps a familiar pattern in her life of being claimed and discarded for the purposes of others? Had not her priest and lover also used her and then cast her away?

Even Gerald, the pious Puritan, her guardian and kin, had ignored his obligations and because it had suited him, had abused and then sold her. Mother, lover, guardian, all three had failed her.

Cathryn looked into the faces of the other passengers in steerage. She knew that the invisible dreams which floated almost tangibly in the air and fueled the colonists' will to struggle against the very odds of survival were nothing but cruel visions that others were free to use against them. Perhaps, Cathryn reasoned, she was only more worldly than her fellow travelers— this odd collection of believers in dreams. She stood apart however, and without hope forevermore abandoned dreams.

Chapter 59

Aboard the Cynthia Ames, *the women's status was not much* more elevated than cargo, commodities for sale to the highest bidder, but how the other passengers treated the women depended on the character and individual means of the man. A third of the men traveled under similar conditions, but only their labor was for sale. The rest were free men, some of whom looked on the women almost as equals.

In addition to the women, the passenger bill listed thirty men: three yeomen, three carpenters, two clerks, a sailmaker, an ironmonger, soap-boiler, farrier, merchant, cooper, sowter, ropemaker, draper, miller, and an innkeeper. Eleven others were listed as servants. Thrown together as they were in close quarters night and day, each passenger had an opportunity to know perhaps more than he wished about his fellow travelers.

Life aboard the *Cynthia Ames* was harsh, and time was passed in various ways. Except for the women, who toiled in the cook's cabin, everyone was forbidden to leave steerage, the order given to prevent passengers from interfering with the work of the ship's crew.

The women kept busy with the task of feeding the men, one or two at a time going to the cook's cabin to help prepare the meals. They also stitched new dresses from bolts of fabric provided them as part of the bargain struck on signing their marriage contracts. They prayed and studied the Scripture so important to their faith, but time passed slowly for Cathryn, who found more hours than she wished to speculate on her future and brood about the past.

All the women dressed in somber Puritan style, alike from

their plain shoes to their hair-concealing caps. No lace adorned their collars, and no jewelry of any kind detracted from the utility of their clothes or the implication of their humility and purity of spirit. Cathryn blended well with the other women who were born to serve.

Each woman received the scrutiny of the men, even those who were in no position to give the idea of a wife a second thought. Reasoning it could do no harm to look, a silent consensus allowed that Mistress Ida Barrett was the most desirable of the women. She was pleasant and had experience. She knew what to expect of married life.

Perhaps even she would have been surprised to know the amount of sheer will it would require to exist in the Colonies so far from England's shores. It was a life for the most part deprived of even the slightest luxury, but at least she knew firsthand the elementary requirements of marriage. She was fertile, both a blessing and a curse. Children meant more mouths to feed, but without children a man had little help with his endless work.

Next to the virtue of experience, there was something appealing about the hearty but innocent Beatrice, garnering her second place among the women. Then Anne, Elizabeth, and Mary vied with an equal number of votes. The three had the look of adequate and willing wives.

Considered least desirable was Mistress Cathryn Godwyne. Without a doubt, she had been the first to catch the men's eyes, but under practical consideration for a wife, she would be chosen last. Despite her unattractive Puritan dress and sober manner, even the dullest man had intuition enough to sense her exotic spirit. She was too much like a thoroughbred to be reserved for the stables of kings, not to be wasted and ill used on civilization's harsh frontier. She at once was deemed out of place.

But even the humblest man was not restrained from his idle dreams. If he were a better man, or at least more elevated in station, he might be one to reach an agreement with the overseers regarding Cathryn's contract. Nor were those with tangible resources beyond their brawn prevented from assessing their exact abilities to afford this extravagance of kings.

Not one of the men could fault Cathryn's behavior, for she was as dutiful as any of her Puritan sisters, serving beside them without stinting her labor, and she kneeled with apparent devotion for prayers. However, her total indifference to the men, unlike the other shy but available brides; her mysterious air, which made her delectable; and her dark eyes and soft pouting mouth registered something deep within almost every man. They were attracted to her as moths to flame.

Of the men, only one, Will Clement, caught Cathryn's eye, and it was not the man so much as it was his flute.

The first night she heard its voice, Cathryn banged her head as she sat upright in her bunk and strained to listen to simple tunes seeming to come through the steerage bulkheads. When she identified the man who owned the flute, she lost no time and with boldness struck a friendship, almost dying with her envy of his possession of the instrument.

The other men took jealous notice of her move toward young Will; boyish and underfed, he seemed an odd sort to gain Mistress Godwyne's attention. They stared, having no inkling of what attracted her to him.

Before she smiled on him, Will Clement never fancied Mistress Cathryn Godwyne might turn to him, the disparity of his station and her luminescence being very clear to him. Cathryn never intended to seduce him, but from the moment she turned her eyes on him, he harbored the hope that something more than an acquaintance would develop.

She did the forbidden, following him outside steerage into the passageways to pretend to learn to play his flute. "How is it you possess a flute?" she asked, not daring to reveal she was more proficient on the instrument than he could ever dream of being.

"It belonged to my father's brother, who was a musician at court. When he died, my father, who had no use for either flutes or Charles the Second, gave the whistle to me. My uncle died a pauper and my father considered the flute a toy fit only for children."

"You taught yourself to play?"

Will nodded. "I'll teach you, if you like," he offered, the thought warming his heart.

Cathryn's progress on the instrument astounded him; she accomplished more in weeks than he had in years. "I should give my flute to you," he marveled.

Cathryn smiled at him. "It is enough that you have shared your music and yourself with me," she whispered in the ship's passageway, then lifted the flute and began to play melodies Will had never heard before.

The music came from the depths of Cathryn's soul. She closed her eyes, transporting herself on waves of thrilling sound from the *Cynthia Ames* to her mentor's knee.

She saw her former teacher nod at her rendition, then grimace at a tiny mistake; but "Splendid," he would have confessed when she was finished.

Perhaps he might have kissed her and whispered other things, but when she opened her eyes, Cathryn was no longer in Venice but at sea, she remembered, with another man and headed for another world, a greater distance from the salons of Venice than she could ever imagine.

Will Clement was speechless at first, and not knowing what to say, he changed the subject. "I go to Marysland," he said, explaining to Cathryn's surprise that the *Cynthia Ames* would land there before heading north to Massachusetts Bay.

He told her how a friend of his father had gone to Marysland as an indentured servant. "After seven years, he was a freeman, acquiring, at first, fifty acres of rich tobacco land. Now he has servants of his own—but mostly slaves. The days a man with no craft, like me, can go to the Colonies and make a new life are ending. Slaves, black souls from Africa, soon shall take the place of men like me."

Cathryn looked at Will with envy. He had the chance of being free when his indentureship was up, while her marriage contract promised nothing of the kind. Oh, to be a man, she thought. To have some choices. To be free!

Cathryn realized her only chance for any kind of freedom was to refuse to marry the men who offered to buy her contract and force the Dunstan Holding Company to indenture her for a specified time in order to salvage their lost revenue. The period of her indenture would depend on the price that Gerald had struck. Knowing Gerald always drove a hard bargain, Cathryn imagined she no doubt would be committed to labor for the rest of her natural life!

In any event, at the end of a specified amount of time, perhaps seven years, Cathryn would be free to do as she wished, and she began to dream of independence, a new but appealing idea. She would live alone like Vanya in the woods. She would not starve. She would . . .

"Cathryn, what do you say?" Will asked, waiting for a reply to some question that for dreaming she had not even heard.

"I beg your pardon?"

"I said, I wish you could wait and marry me."

Cathryn blushed, grateful that in the dim passageway Will could not see the deep color of her face. "I would be grateful to be your bride, Will, but never has my fate been in my hands." She sighed, then leaned to kiss him on the cheek and, without her knowledge, left behind a burning brand.

Chapter 60

In the instance of Will Clement, Cathryn thought it fortunate she did not control her fate. Without question, Will had been kind to her and she was grateful for his friendship, but Will wanted more from Cathryn than she could give him. He wanted Cathryn to love him, and while she was fond of him and grateful for his kindness, just as her consent to marry was not hers to grant, her heart was no longer hers to bestow on any man.

Cathryn knew that she was comely enough to attract more than one bid for marriage. Proposals of marriage would come from more serious sources than a dreamer like Will. There would be offers that she and the Dunstan Holding Company proprietors would have to consider carefully.

As soon as word could be passed that the *Cynthia Ames* carried Puritan women who were available for marriage, the wharves would be crowded with clamoring men. In truth, Cathryn knew her brave words to refuse to marry were empty threats. Whether or not she believed she could love a particular man, or whether he would ever love her, would be of no consequence. Her beauty would be a prize, but a prospective husband would be more interested in her strength and capacity for work. Her health and the number of her teeth would take precedence over beauty. Her flawless skin, shining eyes, and cascading raven hair would count only as evidence of good health. In the end she would be forced to make a bargain with the highest bidder, and the prospect of love would have no bearing on that bargain at all.

With this knowledge fixed firmly in her head, Cathryn cried herself to sleep and dreamed of a spray of orange blossoms and rosemary leaves that Father Vittorio had once left for her in the salon she always used. The fragrance of the leaves and blossoms clung to her fingers, perfuming the very music she played. She dreamed of violins and hearts and bodies in concert, waking in the dim of the steering cabin believing she still heard strains of that music.

Cathryn raised her head. She felt feverish and dizzy; desperate for a breath of fresh air. She threw her legs over the side of the bunk and lowered herself to the deck. As she put her feet down, the deck seemed to roll and with it Cathryn's stomach.

She took a deep breath and listened. She swore she still heard faint strains of music but, listening again, heard only the creaking of the ship and the now familiar whines and wails. It could only have been her vivid imagination.

Cathryn crept to the main deck, wrapped in a heavy gray shawl, and made herself invisible in shadow. It was cold, but at least the air was not fetid with tainted breath or stale hopes and wild dreams.

She often prayed her own ceaseless dreams would end. To be plagued much longer with visions and whispers would drive her truly mad, she feared. She had earlier vowed against them, but to no avail. One more night with the feel of Vittorio's kiss on her lips and she would be consumed by the fire her memory engendered.

Hidden in the shadows near the cook's cabin, Cathryn tried to lose herself in the rhythm of the workings of the ship; suddenly a dark figure emerged from the captain's quarters across the deck, at once drawing Cathryn's attention, and she involved herself in watching him prowl about.

He seemed at ease, stopping without urgency to speak to the sailors at their various watches, and for a while, he took the helm to sail the ship before the wind. From his bearing, Cathryn knew this dark figure to be the captain; there was no mistaking that he held command—his lady, the *Cynthia Ames,* would do her master's bidding in spite of all her wayward inclinations.

Cathryn and most of the other passengers had never met the captain face to face. As far as he was concerned passengers were cargo, and for all his interest, they might have been hogsheads of tobacco. He never came below, and whenever Cathryn went above to cook he was nowhere to be seen.

From a distance, with a careful eye, Cathryn now surveyed him. He wore a short, close-fitting dark coat that accentuated his broad shoulders and tight canvas pants that covered his lean hips and flat stomach. The prominent codpiece invited speculation. He moved as if he were an intricate part of the ship itself and, inexplicably, Cathryn felt drawn to him. She sensed a restlessness, a yearning that stirred her emotions uncomfortably.

But within a short period of time, the captain retreated from the deck, and Cathryn allowed herself to relax. Soon she leaned farther into shadow and, for the first time since she had left England, realized she felt oddly at peace.

Later Cathryn fell asleep and, when she woke, lay in her bunk convinced she had dreamed the whole excursion topside. She had also dreamed of music and of Vittorio, who came and sat beside her to whisper her name and tell her that he loved her. It seemed so real—at least as real as the dreams induced by Vanya's potions! She sighed, becoming aware of her parched throat and the cloth that was cooling her brow.

"You were raving when they found you. One of the seamen brought you below," Beatrice whispered as she applied another dampened cloth to Cathryn's forehead. "You've lain delirious in your bed for three full days! We thought you'd be the first to die."

"Your words hardly bring me comfort, mistress," Cathryn whispered.

"I'm sorry, but I was afraid." Beatrice handed Cathryn a cup of hot tea. "This shall fortify you."

"Except for my parched mouth, I don't feel ill."

"Thank God, for you are sorely needed."

Cathryn arched a brow.

"Except for Mary, the other women are not well," Beatrice confided, then lowered her voice. "Mistress Barrett's baby died last night."

Cathryn gasped in horror. She covered her mouth reflexively, unable to stifle a sob of surprise as tears sprang.

Helpless, Beatrice nodded her head. "The miller is also very ill. Like yours was, all fevers are frightfully high."

Cathryn wiped her tears with her sleeve and tried to take a deep breath. A stab of pain beneath her ribs caused her to flinch.

"It leaves one with sharp pains below the heart," Beatrice said as Cathryn eased herself to the deck, steadying herself on the young woman's arm. "Perhaps you ought to stay in your bunk."

"No. I need to move about," she insisted, not wanting to lie in bed and become a victim of an epidemic.

She stayed on her feet most of the next two days to aid the sick, as one by one the passengers fell ill with fever, some rapidly developing a barking cough. The stagnant air of the passenger hold filled with the stench of sickness and death.

Day and night Cathryn helped nurse the sick and tried to ignore the signs that she grew weaker by the hour. The most visible and vocal of saints, when all was right and steady, withdrew, ignoring their Christian duty to aid their fellow men. Cathryn understood their fear of the evil influence of disease, yet she was surprised that they did not have the confidence of their loudly proclaimed convictions that the Lord God would spare the righteous. How many times she had been forced to listen to sermons that declared God would protect His select, His chosen. Disease was proclaimed to be a sign that the soul was in jeopardy. But the righteous would be protected. If they were as holy as they insisted, would they not be safe?

Knowing she was not similarly protected did not make Cathryn flee her fellows. She saw the fear in the eyes of those who fell ill and could not turn away, regretting only that she had had no opportunity to collect a cache of herbs before she left the English countryside. She longed in particular for a decent supply of coltsfoot, feverfew, horseheal, and horehound. She also wanted a few dozen bags of rosemary to overwhelm the bad air and prevent contagion.

The ship's store of medicine was woefully incomplete, and while others prayed for the return of health, Cathryn and Ida comforted the sick with simple ministrations, showing, if not their faith, at least their concern. They brewed hot teas and ale steeped with dried gillyflower and violet blossoms to soothe the chills of fever, and made plasters of thyme. It was the best they could offer.

At the end of the first week, three people died: Mary, then the cooper, then Beatrice.

"For a time," Ida said, wiping away her tears, "I thought God only punished me." She believed, as did the others, that the death of a child was retribution. But God was not displeased with Ida alone, for in all eight lives were taken.

For Cathryn, the hardest death to bear was Will's. He died in the morning of the fourth day of his illness, while Cathryn sat beside him, tortured, listening to his labored breathing. She tried to soothe his raging fever with cool cloths soaked in lavender water.

Weak and bone-weary herself, Cathryn wept in anger and despair. She mourned his death and regretted the pride that had kept her from telling him a very simple lie. How wrong could it have been, she wondered, to let him imagine that she loved him? It might not have made any difference in the course of his illness, but she knew it would have brought him ease. "I'm sorry, Will," she whispered. "Forgive me."

Chapter 61

Will's death was a turning point for Cathryn. For days she stumbled on, caring for others, then collapsed from exhaustion and for two days slept as though she were one of the dead.

"I'm sorry for my unfair judgment when I first met you," Ida apologized when Cathryn was on her feet again. "You have been the most faithful of all."

Cathryn acknowledged Ida but withdrew into herself, seeking solitude, and often disobeyed the rules clearly laid down for passengers by stealing away at night to hide in isolated passageways and play the flute bequeathed to her by Will.

Only in those moments did she find solace, though at first Cathryn spent most of her stolen time trying to stifle a racking cough, which she induced by her efforts to play the instrument.

And, sometimes, she cried. She missed Will, not realizing until it was too late how fond of him she had grown.

She wondered if somehow Vanya knew she had been sent away and prayed that her mother would invoke a more potent curse than her own upon Gerald Seymour's head.

Cathryn knew a curse was surely on her own head. God had surely disowned her long ago. He had given her a mother who had quickly abandoned her, then had cursed her to love a priest—and, perhaps, doomed her to love him only. But she deserved His ire, for she had dared to love a man coveted by God. She had been cruelly tossed out into the world, and those she should have been able to trust had hated and abused her. What further proof did she need that God despised her?

Seated on a wine barrel in a dark alcove a deck below steerage, Cathryn searched her soul. Though she loved a priest, she did not feel especially evil. Until she had been raped by her guardian, the strongest emotion she had felt was love, although, she admitted, it was quite obvious her love had been misplaced. Father Vittorio deserved her respect and honor, but perhaps not the passion that had erupted unexpectedly from her childish admiration and loving regard.

But this minor prince of the Church was not altogether blameless, a demon in Cathryn insisted. After all, the priest had stirred, then fanned, the first flames of her affection until a searing, uncontrollable fire had roared within her. Even when he had felt remorse, it did not seem to her that he had tried very hard to douse her passion. He had rebuked her for her evil, wanton ways, and then had seduced her, disavowing his crimes by crying out, "*Strega. Strega bella!*" at the peak of passion.

How convenient it was for men to damn her for their sins!

Gerald Seymour did not spew lyrical Italian phrases in climax, preferring to administer physical punishment rather than poetic curses.

If Cathryn needed further proof that God despised her, she had only to wait a few nights until, returning to steerage through passageways she knew by heart, His disfavor took yet another form.

Some nights before, a sailor discovered Cathryn prowling and reasoned a maid as willfully disobedient of the captain's rules deserved harsh punishment; with this twisted logic, night after night, he lay in wait for her. She eluded him until one night coming up the ladder from the deck below, she saw him and, in terror, tried to flee.

For a moment Cathryn forgot to scream, but when he touched her, she raised her voice in shrill alarm, fighting with strength she did not know she had until an enormous fist, aimed at her face, stunned and knocked her down. She struck her head and, mercifully, lost consciousness.

When she woke, Cathryn at once closed her eyes again and

tried to sleep, but though she felt weary beyond belief, bright shafts of light forced her to open her eyes. Cathryn sat up with deliberate slowness, trying not to dislodge a throbbing head from her slender neck.

At first, her surroundings did not seem real. She seemed to be encased in a silky blue cocoon, and from the heady fragrance exuding from the mattress, she would have sworn she lay on a bed of rose petals. Only when she felt the ship roll and heard the familiar groan and creak of sails did Cathryn realize where she was.

Memory returned and she remembered a man's enormous fist flying in the direction of her face. She touched a swollen cheek and reckoned the sailor's blow was responsible for her aching head, the most excruciating pain emanating from deep inside her skull.

A sound outside the canopy made Cathryn hold her breath. Instinctively she shrank away as the cocoon that surrounded her split open.

"No need to be afraid," the man said. "I've only come to look in on your progress."

Cathryn recognized Master Joshua Bledsoe of the Dunstan Holding Company, owner of her contract.

"The captain has graciously granted you permission to recover here in his quarters, where the air is less rank than that below."

"A very kind gesture," Cathryn murmured.

"Indeed it was, Mistress Godwyne, considering you've already displaced him from his bunk for a full two days."

Cathryn felt both surprise and guilt.

"Now let me look at you," Master Bledsoe insisted, sitting down beside her. He lifted a small lamp beneath the canopy and tilted her face to the light. "Much improved," he decided. "Perhaps your woman's vanity allowed you to wake only when your face healed sufficiently to bear examination." He raised one eyelid to examine the eye. "Often, for a time after the head is injured, the center of the eye expands," he explained. "But you, mistress, look fine."

"Then I shall not inconvenience the captain any longer," Cathryn said. "Please thank him for his unusual concern."

Master Bledsoe did not move from the edge of the bed. "Your assailant was keelhauled," he informed her.

"I don't understand."

"It's a not uncommon practice, but it's a particularly brutal form of execution."

Cathryn paled.

"But perhaps only what the man deserved," Master Bledsoe added.

"I don't remember much of what happened."

"Oh, you were rescued before he'd done you much harm." He gestured to her ripped clothing. "But the captain's rage was not assuaged until the villain was bound and thrown overboard. But I sensed our captain might have preferred to kill the miscreant with his own hands."

Remembering her own disobedience of the captain's orders, Cathryn's mouth went dry.

"Only when they pulled the body up after it had traveled the length of the ship's keel did the captain seem content."

As Master Bledsoe rose from the bunk, Cathryn felt she could have easily managed without the details of her assailant's execution.

"Before you go below, Captain Ruggero has ordered you a bath. He said you'd most likely enjoy it." Master Bledsoe's expression showed the idea did not appeal much to him. "I think it unnecessary, but I don't believe a bath will do you irrevocable harm. Nor do I believe it prudent to defy him." He smiled. "I judge you almost fit, Mistress Godwyne. By the time we reach Marysland, you shall be recovered in total," he said as he went to the door.

When he opened the door, a seaman carrying a wooden tub entered the cabin, followed by a silent stream of sailors bearing water-filled buckets until the tub was full of steaming water. "The captain says, also, to choose a dress from one of these chests," Master Bledsoe instructed, and pointed to three trunks standing against the bulkhead opposite the canopied bunk.

Left alone, Cathryn watched the steam rise from her bath only for an instant before she disrobed, unpinned her hair, and gingerly stepped into the tub. She did not understand the common reluctance to bathe, taking to the soothing liquid warmth as if it were the most natural of elements. Witches, she remembered hearing, had an affinity for water.

Cathryn sighed and leaned back a moment, savoring the delicious warmth, but she did not lounge for long. Choosing one of several fragrant soaps stacked in a large marble dish beside the tub, she began to scrub. Yet despite the luxury offered her, she was not completely at ease. She forced herself to hurry, lest the water become frigid or the captain grow impatient for his quarters.

Most of all Cathryn did not wish to offend the captain. In spite of his kindness in offering her the use of his cabin, a bath, and a new dress, she worried she might be due some sort of punishment. She had disobeyed him in wandering the ship and had been the cause of the death of one of the crew, the definition of keelhauling all too fresh in her mind.

Lastly, Cathryn washed her hair and then rinsed all with a bucket of warm water that stood beside the tub. She dried herself, then wrapped a towel around her for warmth and used a comb, also provided, to untangle her hair.

In a hurry, eager to rummage through the trunks, she towel-dried her hair. She wanted a new dress very much, she admitted, and hoped the trunks contained something other than drab Puritan attire. How she longed for garments made of silk and satin, or even cotton! Something stylish with an ornamental collar, a puff of fur, or perhaps a fringe of lace.

Why torment myself? she thought, struggling for a moment with the first chest's latch; then, opening it, she gasped in surprise.

Within lay gowns made of astonishing fabrics, dresses she would love to own and wear, but after inspecting and admiring each garment, she laid them all aside. "Not a one is suitable," she grumbled and assessed her discarded dress for mending.

How stupid of me, she thought, to think that the captain of the *Cynthia Ames* would store three chests of dresses suitable for a Puritan in his quarters! Such commercial items would be carried in the hold. These were dresses he stored for someone very special.

Cathryn inspected the second chest, but it did not offer any better selection. She sighed over each and every garment, then repacked the second trunk and looked with doubt at the third. She did not think it very probable that the last trunk would contain anything to meet her needs.

Still, she could not resist and opened the lid, her hands shaking as she lifted the first item from the chest.

Tears stung her eyes.

Of course! This was a bride's trousseau. The bridal gown was packed beneath a veil studded with minute seed pearls, and nestled in the décolletage of the bodice was a pearl-encrusted headdress to top the veil.

Gently Cathryn clutched the veil, undoing the length of shimmering silky gauze, unwinding yards and yards of train. Who in the Colonies would need such an extravagant trousseau? Even in Venice a gown and veil like this would be spectacular, and the Venetians loved extravagance. Perhaps the queen of France would do this ensemble justice.

Cathryn sighed and pictured herself dressed in the gown, imagining a thousand candles illuminating a midnight Mass; the angelic voices of a hundred little girls singing as she moved down a cathedral aisle; scented petals of roses, lavender, and rosemary strewn beneath her feet.

Tossing the towel from her body, Cathryn lifted the airy veil over her head with utmost care and let it shower down the full length of her graceful body, savoring the soft mist of fabric as it enveloped her.

Standing tall, Cathryn crowned the veil with the pearl headdress and closed her eyes and dreamed she moved down the long cathedral aisle.

At the altar, her lover raised the silky veil and, together, they knelt down to make their vows. He held her fingers to his lips while she promised to love and honor the man who would forever fill her dreams.

Adrift in the frothy web of fantasy, Cathryn was startled by the sound of the opening of the cabin door. A rush of air extinguished the cabin's only lantern, and in the dark, Cathryn stood frozen, helpless, naked, trapped in a cloud of precious lace, alert as the emotions of both fear and anger washed over her. She feared the captain's rage at finding her dressed as his bride, yet she was angry that he would dare invade her privacy.

She fixed her gaze on the shadowed figure standing by the door, her eyes adjusting slowly to the cabin's faint light. Sensations of terror from her recent violent encounter flashed through Cathryn as she realized the intruder might not be the captain. She tried to back away but in her haste only trapped herself more securely in the diaphanous train and veil.

Utter panic swept over her. She feared for herself and dreaded she might destroy the precious bridal veil. "Please, if you have a shred of honor, you shall leave me to finish dressing," she demanded, hoping to appeal to the intruder's sense of chivalry.

He answered her with silence.

Cathryn imagined she felt his gaze drift over her and turned her back, covering her breasts with one arm and the triangle of hair between her legs with her other hand. "Please," she begged, on the verge of tears, infuriated at her own helpless response. "Please, go away!"

"You speak of honor, *cara*. I've no honor where you are concerned," he said. "Not one shred is left to me."

Confused and dizzy, Cathryn whirled to face the intruder again, her petulant mouth open in surprise. Time seemed to stand still as the intruder reached to pull a curtain from a porthole at his shoulder to allow more light.

Beneath the airy veil, Cathryn stared wide-eyed and touched the still tender side of her face. Was it possible? Had the blow to her head produced hallucinations? Or had she all at once assumed her mother's powers to conjure dreams?

Dazed, mistrusting her vision, Cathryn forgot her nakedness and boldly stared at the intruder. A moment before she had heard Vittorio's voice, yet when she turned to face him, Cathryn did not see her priest. If her eyes did not deceive her as her ears had the moment before, the man dressed in sturdy clothes befitting a ship's captain was the lover she had met at Vanya's Sabbat feast.

Cathryn felt faint but steadied herself as the captain doffed his loose-brimmed hat and stood motionless, inviting her scrutiny.

He was Vittorio's height, but his body was hard, leaner than the priest's, and unlike the priest he wore a short beard and his very black hair came to the collar of his coarse wool shirt.

While her priest had an arrogant side to his nature, the whole posture of the captain bespoke absolute authority. Even from the distance that separated them, Cathryn could feel his power and in an instant understood how other men would without question obey him. She had understood this quality about the captain the one other time she'd caught a glimpse of him. Now she also sensed a hostility in his demeanor, the kind of emotion that at a decisive moment allowed him to keelhaul a disobedient member of his crew.

His mouth was tight, his jaw tense under his close-cropped beard, and though in the dim she could not see the color of his eyes, she felt the heat of his intense gaze.

Cathryn drew a ragged breath and shook her head to try to clear her vision. She had not recognized him as her lover that night in the shadows but now recalled her first sensations at seeing the hooded stranger at the Sabbat and the sense of menace he had projected. She had been wary then, until quantities of dream-inducing wine had allayed her fears.

Once more Cathryn became conscious of her nakedness and crossed her arms over bare breasts. From forehead to toes she felt herself turn crimson, and she shivered with a renewed sense of fear. She shuddered also with a sudden misery, faith in her mother's magical powers all but destroyed.

Vanya had not conjured her errant priest from Venice at all, as Cathryn had wanted to believe! Instead, this stranger, the captain, had come forth from God knew where, and under the influence of drug-laden wine, she had been convinced that her mother had spirited her priest from Venice. She now also reluctantly remembered that Vanya had suggested the illusion.

Cathryn's eyes brimmed with tears that began to trickle down her face.

"*Cara*, why do you cry?"

At the sound of his voice, Cathryn covered her ears. Truly, I am insane! she thought.

"Do you hear me?" he said.

She shook her head violently in denial.

He laughed as he breached the distance that separated them until he stood a breath away from Cathryn. "Do I not speak clearly?" He pulled her hands away from her ears.

"I am used only to your silence," she murmured, trembling with uncertainty and at the thrill of his touch. His radiant smile unnerved her.

"Ah, *angelica*, if you only knew how much I wanted to cry out your name." He raised the bridal veil and smiled down at her, cradling her face, he stroked away her tears. He marveled at her astonishing beauty and observed that her countenance was only slightly marred by the swelling of the attacker's recent blow. He hoped her heart was as unmarked by the sorrows that he knew had touched her.

Her skin was soft, unblemished, her face still as pure as the innocent Madonna's. "Truly, *cara*, you were the bride I had in mind when I chose this veil," he whispered, smoothing the misty fabric over the headdress. "You, above all others, should be my bride." Cathryn stared at him, her eyes wide and luminous.

"Indeed, you already are my bride," he swore, folding her

into his arms. "Surely no man ever was more wedded to a woman than I am to you. My very soul is yours," he murmured, lifting her lips to his.

His kiss was deep and long, stirring the fires of eternal passion, and still trembling, completely bemused, Cathryn gave herself up to glorious sensation. At first she matched the driving hunger of his kiss, then suddenly she pulled away, her breathing ragged, her heart beating out of control.

He sought to capture her again, but summoning strength, Cathryn grew fierce. "No!" she commanded in a throaty yet determined voice. She gripped his arms above the elbows and held him away. "Am I hopelessly deranged? Is this yet another dream? Or would you only have me believe myself a deluded fool?" she demanded, pushing him away.

He smiled at her challenge. "You are no fool, *cara*, nor are you insane. Only a beautiful, too desirable woman."

"A designation fraught with sin on my part," Cathryn retorted, and turned her back to him.

"God knows you are not alone in sin, *angelica*. My sins are beyond counting."

A melancholy note in his voice caused Cathryn to turn back to face him. "Captain. Demon. Lover. Priest," she whispered, confused.

He stared into her question-filled eyes but saw those questions begin to fade away as she gazed at him. Slowly Cathryn and the captain were drawn into a silent and welcoming pool of abiding love. "Forgive me, but I love you," he whispered as she came against him again.

With his kiss, she melted in desire, remembering only that she loved him, and when he knelt before her as if he worshiped her, and put his mouth to her tender breasts, she could not resist.

He used his tongue to tease her satiny nipples erect and soon, with soft sighs and a slow undulating motion of her hips, she urged him to suckle her more fiercely.

For a while he answered her desire, then freed his mouth to rain feathery kisses below. His lips drifted as though without aim from delicious breasts to the wild pulsing of her heart; along her waist and hips, onto her belly, and down to the very center of her flame. With his gentle kiss, he opened her woman's lips, touching, exploring, probing the limits of her passion; the sound of his voice, his moans of pleasure, echoed in her ears.

Then he rose to remove the veil and headdress from Cathryn's head and led her to his bunk; climbing under the canopy, he closed the silk drape, sealing the scent of roses around them. With his hands on hers, he invited Cathryn to undress him.

She unbuttoned his shirt, letting soft kisses fall wherever she exposed his skin; then, unbuckling his belt, she pulled his shirttail from his pants. Before the breeches passed his hips, she let her hands idle and caress him.

Fully engorged, he moaned his pleasure, eager to have her practiced hands excite him more. She knew him so well. But did she remember all, as he did? he wondered, certain he could recall every touch, every sigh and whisper, every thrill of delight they had ever shared. Would it be as mystical, as magical, as before? Now that he possessed her, now that she belonged to him, if he but chose?

But he did not ponder long, for Cathryn's touch soon drove him to the brink of rapture, and he rolled onto her, and seized her mouth, kissing her with a fierce and hungry passion born of tremendous need. But Cathryn was not ready and struggled, drawing her lips away. She planted kisses like feathered silk upon his face and, taking his hands from her eager body, began to kiss them: the fingers that were kind to her; the open palm that craved her round breasts.

With her kisses, she made a feast of him, every cell and fiber of her body alive and pulsing, her mind unclouded by drugged wine. Once she had feared she would never again know that splendid desire for a man to fill her body without the assistance of wine or Witchcraft. Now, trembling with desire, Cathryn indulged her whims with joy.

His body was fully responsive as she drove him ever closer to explosive release. "*Cara, cara,*" he cried, the sound of his passion thrilling her.

With a deliberate slow pace she rediscovered every contour of his body, every sensitive inch of hard male flesh, and he let her explore, bringing him almost to frenzy until he forced himself to overpower her and brought her beneath him once more.

His voice was strained. "I love the selfish pleasure of your mouth," he whispered, "but this first time, I want to come inside you, to have you pressed against my heart."

He raised her hips and she opened to him as his heart beat

with a deafening thud inside his chest. He slipped inside her and was enfolded into her intoxicating warmth.

Fevered, evolving a perfect rhythm, he moved within her until Cathryn writhed beneath him, emitting soft, stirring cries. Soaring, he clutched her to him fiercely, in memory and desire, blending with her, ascending swiftly into brilliant ecstasy.

They held each other fast, their descent coming about slowly. "Thank God I have found you," he cried, and drew Cathryn nearer against him.

"Yes, thank God—whoever that might be," she answered in a whisper, her heart racing and her mind beginning to whirl. He cuddled closer, wrapping powerful legs around her. Unable and unwilling to protest, her arms and body still deliciously full of him, Cathryn nestled and relaxed. She lay at peace at last and listened to him croon of his contentment until, blissful, she fell asleep.

Chapter 62

When she awakened, Cathryn found herself alone. She touched the empty side of the bed and found it warm and, smiling, closed her eyes again, preferring to sleep. Awake, she had too many troubling questions. Asleep, she was consoled by dreams.

A moment later, Cathryn felt a draft, and opening her eyes again, she saw her lover standing over her.

Still naked, a soft smile curved his mouth.

"Are you enjoying the view?" she murmured, sleepy, and retrieved the silk sheet that had slipped below her breasts. Then Cathryn's lazy gaze became a stare.

He laughed at her unsettled gaze; the music of his pleasure sent chills through Cathryn. "While you slept, I shaved my beard and cut my hair."

"I see." How could she *not* have known? she wondered. Why the masquerade? Why had it been necessary to distort her vision and blur her consciousness with drugged wine? Why had he always been so silent?

Vittorio bent to kiss Cathryn, but she pushed him away. "Why? How?" she demanded.

He made a slight frown. "Do you not still love me, *cara*?"

"I do not like to be deceived."

"Everything I've done, I've done because I love you."

"That may be, but I believe I'm due a full accounting."

"You want my confession, *cara*?" He smiled.

"Every last word," she insisted, unable to return his smile.

"Then we'd best make ourselves comfortable," he suggested, plumping pillows and seating himself in the bunk. He patted the bed, inviting Cathryn to lie close to him.

She gave him a wary look and settled at arm's length. With a prim tug at the comforter, she covered the lower half of his body. "Lest you be distracted," she said. "Now, tell me every last detail, Vittorio."

"To start, I am no longer called Vittorio, I left the Church . . . because of family misfortune . . . and because, truly, I was unfit."

"That's not true," Cathryn argued.

"Oh, but it is, *cara*," he replied. "Once I tasted you, I forgot all my vows. I put my love for you above my obedience to God. When you left me, I imagined I would forget and, some way, learn to live with my guilt. But I found there was no absolution— and no ceasing of my love for you. Then, on the verge of admitting defeat, I was called home.

"Perhaps you remember my brothers, Luciano and Piero?"

Cathryn nodded and pulled the sheet more tightly about her. She would never forget his brothers or their treatment of her.

"They abused you, and I'm sorry, but they are dead now and I have forgiven them."

Cathryn felt no grief, nor any inclination to forgive them.

"You remember how superstitious they were of you, calling you a witch, fearing your curse on them and me? Well, it appears they had reason to fear, for, in fact, their ship did sink and their lives were lost."

"Not because of me!" Cathryn insisted.

"It doesn't matter now."

Wanting to hear his story, Cathryn bit her tongue and for the moment at least let the matter go.

"With their deaths, I had yet another reason to leave the priesthood, for somewhere between Venice and Dalmatia their bodies lie at the bottom of the sea and, with them, my family's fortune.

"Not long after you left for England, I went home to aid my mother settle my brothers' affairs and try to repair the family fortune. I had my mother to comfort, though my leaving the priesthood hardly brought her ease. In fact," he reflected, "I think, perhaps, that desertion was the final blow. Or, perhaps, it was because I abandoned my music."

Cathryn could not believe her ears. "Perhaps you are too vital a man for the cassock, Vittorio, but surely you did not have to give up your music, also."

Vittorio gave Cathryn a rueful smile. "You left me with a thousand songs to rend the soul, *cara* . . . but for whom could I play such sensuous music, and not reveal my secrets? For my mother?"

Cathryn lowered her eyes from his intense gaze.

"If I'd played my music for my mother, she'd have known in an instant that I had not left the Church solely for the sake of family." He spoke lightly, but there was a touch of sadness in his voice.

"When she died, I said I would take up the violin again, but then I felt I had broken her heart. Of everything, my leaving the Church was her greatest sorrow."

Cathryn frowned and tossed her head. "You cannot have given your music up completely. I swear I've heard a violin aboard this ship. Or do you intend to tell me I've only been drinking from *my* mother's cup?"

Vittorio could not resist reaching for a handful of Cathryn's hair, which fell over one of her shoulders when she shook her head. He lifted a handful of satin curls as black as the raven's breast to his cheek. "Cathryn, promise me you shall always remember that I love you."

Startled, Cathryn paused to stare, to take in the beauty of the man she felt sure she would love forever; at the moment, however, she held herself stiffly away from him. In silence, she rejoiced to recognize him, to see him looking at her with adoration. "Why do you need my promise? Will it give you absolution?" she asked.

"Probably not." He sighed, then shrugged and from beneath the bunk produced her violin.

Cathryn leapt at him. "My Amati! How can you have my Amati?" she cried, overjoyed to have the precious violin in her hands. "I was not dreaming. I did hear you play!"

He nodded as Cathryn lifted the instrument and began to play a breathtaking passage.

"Oh, thank you, Vittorio!" she cried as she put the violin down. For joy, she kissed his hands, his face, his mouth. "I thought I'd never see my violin again. I thought . . . But tell me, Captain, how did you come by this instrument?" She pulled away from Vittorio's embrace and settled back into the bunk, cradling her precious Amati in her arms. "I told you I shall not be satisfied until you tell me *everything*."

Vittorio took a deep breath while they both pretended to ignore the pronounced effect her kisses had had on his body. "For a while, I insisted to myself I would forget you. I took back my family's name—from birth I am called Matteo Francesco Ruggero—and I occupied myself totally in my family's affairs.

"But I found that I could sooner forget how to breathe than forget you. You haunted me. On every breeze, I heard your sigh; in every ray of sun, I felt your smile. Soon I knew I would not find any peace until I found you. I would have searched to the ends of the earth for you, Cathryn Godwyne, till the last of my days," he swore, reaching for her.

Cathryn slipped into his arms, no longer able to ignore her instinct to embrace him. "Vittorio, Vittorio," she whispered, and hugged him fiercely. "Thank God you found me."

He enjoyed the delicious pressure of her body and pulled her down with him into the bed, intending to take full advantage of the moment.

But she resisted, meaning only to give him a brief reward. "No, you must continue," she insisted, pushing his eager hands away.

He sighed in resignation. "At last I acknowledged my obsession and returned to degli Innocenti to inquire of you. Signorina Perdita was still furious with me and refused to give me even a scrap of information."

"But why was she angry with you?"

"I had ruined her reputation."

"I don't understand."

"When I left degli Innocenti the reputation of the school declined. Perdita Fabiani took it personally."

Cathryn smiled and shook her head. "She did not understand your loyalty to family?"

"She is too proud to understand anything but the prosperity of her school."

Cathryn sighed as much for Perdita as for her priest and herself.

"But Bianca reminded her how fond you were of me and I of you and tried to play upon Perdita's sympathy. However, that turned out to be a grave mistake, for the wise old owl read more than friendship in my face, and began to howl of her suspicions. I received no help from her. Indeed, I barely escaped with my life!"

Cathryn put her head on her lover's shoulder and laughed. She thought of his difficulty in finding her and the many letters she had written but destroyed because they too clearly revealed her passion for him. But her mirth did not last long.

For Perdita to have guessed her affair with the priest disgraced Cathryn. "Perdita never once accused me in her letters," she consoled herself aloud.

"She loves you, *cara*. It is easier for her to make me the villain."

"Because you are." She pursed her lips in a firm but pretty pout.

"If you want me to finish my story, you best not tempt me," he suggested. "A sailor is always a very needful man."

Cathryn adjusted her face to a frown. "Pray continue."

"I began a search for the ship that carried you from Venice, and when I found Capitano Salvadori, I told him only that I was in love with you. At first he was hostile, but later he was of immeasurable help to me. He succeeded in obtaining a license for me to trade in England within the year, an almost impossible feat—it is fortunate that the English lust for malmsey overrides that country's concern for protecting trade. Salvadori said he owed a debt to you that helping me would settle." Matteo Francesco Ruggero looked to Cathryn for an explanation.

Cathryn smiled. "Is every ship's captain a seducer of women?"

His face hardened. "He harmed you?"

"No, but he intended to."

His color darkened. "If I had known, I would have—"

"Never found me," Cathryn interrupted. "Please go on, Vittorio."

"Matteo," he corrected, looking hard at Cathryn, for a moment feeling uncertain; then he went on. "I traded with England, sailing back and forth from Venice at such a speed I wore out several crews. And each time I arrived in England I would inquire after you. Though I usually landed at Bristol, I knew from Salvadori that you'd arrived at Ipswich. I could not comb every hamlet myself, so I hired a man to search for you in my place."

Matteo pulled Cathryn to him and this time found no resistance. He kissed her forehead, then an eyelid, a silky cheek, and, at last, he captured her mouth. For a short while he indulged himself extravagantly, then was forced by Cathryn's demand to pull himself away. "For almost three years," he continued, "with the devotion of a knight after the Holy Grail, my man searched for you.

"Eventually he led me to Vanya Russo. She looked at me as though she could see right through me. We talked for days, and just when I despaired of her helping me, she demanded that I play your violin. When I did, I think she began to trust me, though she cursed my Church, my God, my selfish soul. She only promised to help me because she said she knew you loved me."

Cathryn leaned into Matteo. She needed comfort to think about her mother, whom she did not quite fear yet did not trust completely, either. At the least, Cathryn admired her. Vanya certainly had courage.

Part of Cathryn loved Vanya fiercely, but only part, for most of Cathryn's heart belonged to the man who now held her fast in his arms. Ever since she could remember, Vittorio—now Matteo— had turned lonely darkness into glorious day, and at least for as long as he embraced her, there was no space in her heart except for him.

But Cathryn was not as easily distracted as Matteo. He wanted to make love; she only wanted to be held and hear the rest of his story. "There are more pressing matters to attend to," he insisted, lightly teasing the flesh between her thighs.

"Not until you tell me everything," she said, and pushed his hand away. "Why did you not come to me directly? Why the masquerade?"

Matteo sighed and continued. "Do you not believe in Vanya's power, Cathryn, even now?"

"At the moment I don't know what to believe, or whom to trust. Even what god to worship."

Matteo tried not to let his shock at her remark show.

"Vanya is gifted beyond most and, I thought, unusually tender and kind. Even among the Puritans there are those who preach a gentler religion than that which Gerald Seymour supports. They believe God is love and preach hope to men and women. Of course, many followers of such philosophies have been burned for Witches." Cathryn flinched. "Perhaps Vanya only has His power, though she calls Him by a different name," she mused. "But you distract me, Captain. Tell me why you did not come to me in person."

Matteo looked at Cathryn and regretted having to explain. "I did not come to you because I feared what I already had found, and because your mother insisted that we meet the way we did.

"The first time I saw Vanya Russo, it was growing dark. A cold mist had gathered in the glen, and from the devious and winding route that monster of a dog took, it could have been Hell he dragged me to. It took all my courage to stand my ground before your mother, for she looked like she'd come straight from Hell—with the Devil's hideous brand seared upon her face.

"A wind blew, whipping her wild hair about her as though she were surrounded by a pack of invisible demons. Yet as hideous as she was, in an instant, I knew she was related to you.

"All the things I knew of your mysterious history fell into place. Many times, I'd heard Perdita say under her breath that you were too foreign-looking, or—when you'd misbehaved—you were too like your heathen mother. In fact, at our last interview, Perdita warned me that your mother was a Witch.

"I learned Vanya's reputation in the district. She's known to be a Witch, known for her cures and potions, for her good and for her evil—I'm astounded she has survived so long."

Cathryn sucked in her breath as Matteo said aloud what she truly feared. Someday someone would point at Vanya and scream "Witch."

"I am a fairly brave man, Cathryn, and, in most things, prudent. But I did not care to risk conflict with a woman who looked to have flown straight from Hell, and when Vanya insisted we could meet only at the Sabbat as participants in the rite, I agreed.

"She tried to convince me she did not indulge in Devil worship, but my skepticism was plain, and I imagine she believed the only way to convince me she was not as dangerous as she looked was to force me to attend the Sabbat. I would have walked into the mouth of Hell to find you, and she knew it." Cathryn nodded, appreciating Matteo's determination to find her as well as her mother's wisdom to have Matteo see for himself that she was not a disciple of Satan.

"Before I had word of you," Matteo continued, purposefully changing the subject slightly, "I had reason to believe you might have gone to the English colonies. I made arrangements to trade there. It is also a very restricted trade, but with connections I had through my family and by various other means, I've established myself firmly in the New World.

"And new it is, Cathryn, with opportunity. I am a rich man, making my fortune in tobacco I both grow and trade to England, and by carrying all manner of goods to the Colonies. I engage in trade between Marysland and the northern colonies, and sometimes the Indies.

"I have a plantation in Marysland—three hundred acres. Imagine, Cathryn, three hundred acres! In Venice I never dreamed of that amount of land.

"If you listen, Cathryn, you can hear music in the forest that surrounds my estate. The vegetation is so thick there is hardly room to travel through the woods. You have to notch yourself a trail if you wander from the house."

Matteo paused. "I have not spent as much time in my home as I would like, for in addition to searching for you, the sea, it seems, runs in my blood. But now that I have found you," he said, relief plain in his voice, "perhaps I shall settle down and take up my violin again. Perhaps I shall at last write all the music that crowds my heart. Now that I am allowed to be an ordinary man, I am free to reveal my heart."

"That, of course, depends on what you have to say."

"Only that I adore you and I always have."

"I'm not sure the world is as interested in your confession as I am," Cathryn teased, pushing him on his back to lie on top of him.

Matteo's body responded instantly and would no longer be ignored. "I'll not let you turn away this time," he said as he attempted to thrust into her.

"I've no wish to, Captain." she said, making him gasp as with one swift movement she took him into her. He closed his eyes to savor how she mastered him.

Cathryn ruled with grace and tenderness until she found a tempo that more suited her, administering delicious torture that time and again almost brought Matteo swift release. But she denied him repeatedly, until he ached with need. "Cathryn, have mercy!" he begged, enjoying every minute.

"You don't want mercy, miserable priest, you want absolution."

He laughed and she settled, waiting for his momentary ease. "If you came after me seeking absolution, Captain, you have troubled yourself in vain," she said, brushing his lips with hers. "I bring you only love."

Matteo smiled up at Cathryn. "No absolution?"

"Not a drop," she insisted, and he pulled her mouth to his and kissed her hungrily.

"If you shall but love me, Cathryn, I have troubled myself not at all," he vowed, and swiftly brought her beneath him to take glorious pleasure in her fierce and passionate embrace.

Chapter 63

After making love, they dressed. Matteo wore high boots, canvas breeches, and a woolen shirt. Cathryn donned a red silk bedgown and a sable-edged white satin robe he selected for her from the three large trunks of clothes.

Although she was curious about the trunks, Cathryn remained silent, wanting more than anything else to believe his whispered promise of the night before. She wanted to imagine that the clothes had all been designed with her in mind and, for a little while longer, was content to recline in his bed like a pampered pet.

Matteo ordered food brought to his quarters, where they feasted, growing at least as intoxicated with each other as with wine.

Ravenous, Cathryn ate her fill. "I suppose I shouldn't be surprised that the captain's fare is better than his passengers'," Cathryn commented lightly, pushing her empty plate away at last.

"Someone who spent her youth learning to play the fiddle shouldn't tell her hapless shipmates she can cook. Perhaps the sailor who attacked you was hired by the passengers so they could have another cook."

Cathryn made a face. "Everything I know I learned from you."

"Then you're not a cook."

"What am I, then?" she asked, quite serious. "For what have you prepared me?"

Matteo laughed and when she gave him a look that might have reduced a boulder to grains of sand, Matteo reflected, trying to be as serious as she. "You are suited for . . . well, not for serving men like Gerald Seymour. When I heard that you were treated as nothing better than a laundress and a scullery maid, I went into a rage." He drew her hands before him for examination. "You should have been protected from abuse."

"My hands were not all that he misused. But what of you, Matteo?" she said, turning his hands over into hers. "You were not meant to be the master of a ship, but the master of musicians." With her finger she traced a fresh scar, then bent to kiss his open palm.

He pulled his hand away. "I have more salt water in my blood than you imagine. I sailed with my father and brothers almost from the moment I first walked until I entered the priesthood under protest. If I had not been my father's third son, I would never have been forced to be a priest. If I had had my way, my gift for music would have been ignored; only acknowledged, perhaps, when I was at my ease. It was the mistake of a foolish mother, protecting her last born, to dedicate me to the Church."

"You dismiss your brilliance too simply. Surely God intended you to be a musician. Sailors and their captains are conceived every day. A talent like yours is very precious."

He smiled. He had used similar arguments on her only a few years ago. "You won't argue that it was an error to cloister me with a brood of tempting young women?" he teased, pulling her onto his lap, opening her robe front to nuzzle playfully at her throat and breasts.

"Perhaps," Cathryn conceded. "Perdita must surely wonder just how many of her children you led astray. Every last girl adored you."

"*You* seduced me, remember?"

"I did nothing of the kind!"

He smiled, enjoying her pique. "Cathryn, lying is a sin. I recall your beautiful eyes often resting on mine in chapel. How chaste and pure you seemed, all the while plotting the corruption of a holy priest."

Cathryn's face was red. "Until you corrupted me, I hardly gave you a moment's thought."

"I see your face, Cathryn." He laughed, seeming to take the subject lightly. "Did you not, at confession, admit your impure thoughts, and I, of course, never dreaming that one as innocent as you had wicked intentions, issued easy penance."

She jabbed him in the chest. "You really believe that I seduced you, don't you?"

Matteo squirmed.

"Vittorio!"

"Matteo."

With a nod, Cathryn acknowledged her lapse and reflected with sadness about how the priest in Venice had needed to believe she was guilty of seducing him. "I remember your accusations well, priest. *Strega, strega bella!*" she gasped, duplicating the inflection of his voice at the moment of release.

Her chant excited him. "*Sí, cara. Strega, strega bella,*" he whispered. "Use your Witch's wiles now. I ache for you. Wield your power over me." He drew her mouth down and kissed her, groaning as she aroused him further, her tongue darting into his mouth.

Seated together on a stool, Cathryn swiveled her hips and wrapped her legs around him, shrugging the robe off her shoulders, her motions inviting his hands to explore the straining breasts beneath the bodice of the red silk gown.

"Dear God, how I've missed you," he cried, aware of the sudden intensity of his need, lifting her breasts from the folds of the silky gown. Insistent at her tingling nipples, his mouth sent waves of pleasure rushing through her loins to the center of her brain.

The sweet musky scent of her desire made Matteo's senses reel, and he slipped a hand beneath the skirt of Cathryn's gown. He sought her woman's warmth, letting his fingers play in the fringe of her love-moist curls, the pressure of his knowing fingers bringing her inexorably to release.

Her voice, musical and alluring, begged him to continue, then, in sublime ignorance of how she made him crave her, her fingers seized and petted him until, loving the wet warmth of her, he slipped his fingers into her.

She was soft satin to his touch, crying out with every stroke as he caressed and coaxed her. "Matteo, I need you. I want you inside me," she breathed.

"No more than I want you," he answered, lifting her with him to the bed. "Attending to you excites me almost as much as your attention to me," he confessed. "Witch or no, I worship you."

All at once there was no respite from his passion; his kisses were demanding, his pleasure in her taste measured in his voice. "I am so hungry for you," he murmured, feasting the length of her, from mouth to succulent mouth, until she begged for him again.

Cathryn brought him to face her. "You give me everything and yet deny me," she accused him, breathless from need.

They moved together then in a timeless rhythmic motion, her jubilant cries bringing him with her, freeing their spirits to merge and dissolve into the molten core of ecstasy.

Afterward they stroked each other with gentle hands; Cathryn sighed against him, blissful. Vittorio! Vittorio! He would always be the passionate priest who risked his soul to love her. Perhaps he would always see himself a priest—seduced away from the priesthood, and if not from the priesthood, then from his more vital calling, music.

Cathryn sighed, and to Matteo's ears, the sound was one of fulfillment and peace. He watched her, loved her, and desired her again, though his body still trembled from the last encounter.

Cathryn smiled up at her lover, not wanting to delve too deeply now into whether he did or did not believe that she had seduced him, for fear that she would hear again that the daughter of a witch is also and always a witch. For another few moments at least—for the night, if not for eternity—Cathryn wanted to lie at peace, in the glorious shelter of Captain Ruggero's arms.

In the silence, eyes brimming with love for him, she watched Matteo, until with the faintest tremor of her lashes, Cathryn closed her eyes to dream.

Chapter 64

Matteo basked in the joy of Cathryn's unceasing love, awed by the trust she bestowed on him. Yet he had only the faintest understanding of what it meant to love another without conditions. Captain Ruggerio had not told Cathryn all there was to tell, and he felt compelled to conceal many things, including his involvement in her departure from England, declining to reveal that he had masterminded her escape from her predatory guardian. He had also failed to inform Cathryn that he now owned her marriage contract, but he sent word to the other passengers that Cathryn would convalesce from her injuries in his cabin. He let it be known that as master of the ship he felt responsible for her ill use by his crewman, that he had obtained her contract from the Dunstan Holding Company and intended to release her from its obligations. When Mistress Godwyne was well he would offer her employment as a freewoman in his household in Marysland. The legal documents rested safely in a locked box on a flat upper corner of Matteo's high, slant-lidded desk.

Legalities aside, God must have intervened in these events, Matteo reflected, because if it had not been for Cathryn's misfortune to nearly fall prey to the lust of an errant seaman, Matteo might never have revealed himself to Cathryn, given the complexity of the obligations which bound him, and the unresolved doubts which continued to gnaw at the edges of his bliss in their reunion.

Several times a day, perched on a high stool, Matteo made entries into the ship's log at the desk, from time to time lifting his gaze to a view of the endless ocean trailing behind his ship from the aft porthole. Often, without being aware, he rested a hand on the locked box, as if reassuring himself its precious contents remained tucked away, comforting himself with the knowledge that Cathryn was safe. But just as often he sighed, his heart truly not at ease. Cathryn's ultimate course, and his, was much less sure than a ship's upon the uncertain sea.

With vague attention, Matteo listened while Cathryn limbered her fingers on her violin, to cringe when the Amati's gut strings squeaked and sometimes broke. Cathryn cursed in a fashion that made him smile. She had picked up some quite colorful phrases in her many early morning walks in Venice.

Matteo realized, however, that Cathryn's vocal irritation was only a symptom; she also was not as at ease as she pretended. In truth her head did not rest as comfortably on his shoulder as one might guess from the eager way she nestled in his arms. He noticed sometimes her soft face was drawn, seeming angular in its tight rage as helpless fury smoldered in her dark eyes. If Matteo pried, heated words would spill, releasing her anger at Gerald Seymour and her bitterness that circumstances had rendered her powerless, making her his slave and victim.

"At least now I understand why my mother did not marry my father," she said. "To have been a slave is to forever respect freedom, and not surrender it lightly, for the sake of mere respectability." With those two sentences she made it all but impossible for Matteo to confess he was the legal owner of her marriage contract. He had more power over her than she dreamed—or that he wished for her to know.

Certain that in private Cathryn would admit he possessed her body and soul, Matteo could not admit to her his literal possession of her person, knowing that, like her mother, she despised the notion of anyone owning her. Upon reflection, Matteo decided Cathryn's attitude defied reality, for throughout her life, a woman belonged to one man or another. First, she belonged to her father, and then, as a rule, to her husband or some close male kin. A widow might wield some power over her own destiny, but as a rule, she quickly relinquished that authority to another man. Born to be subservient, most women knew their place in God's design, but, Matteo sighed, not Cathryn Godwyne, the woman he loved. The most desirable woman on the face of the earth.

She fit him to perfection, enticing him and molding herself to his form and his command. Yet as willingly as she committed herself to him, as exactly as she did his bidding, Matteo admitted that part of his fascination with Cathryn derived from his sense that he would never control her completely. In so many ways, Cathryn remained a mystery even to the man who loved her.

When he felt generous, Matteo admitted that on those occasions when he sensed he did not entirely command her spirit, his ultimate conquest was sweeter. But when he reflected on the truth of his own existence, he felt wary of Cathryn's demanding desire to belong to no one but herself, as if she were not mere chattel. Her rebellious notion made Matteo ponder Cathryn's heritage.

Since Venice, she had changed; obedient acceptance of God's will in her life had been replaced by rage at her fate. Was this the influence of the Old Religion and Vanya's efforts to convert her daughter? When Cathryn spoke of understanding her mother's choice to remain free of Lord Godwyne, Matteo felt his blood run cold. After all, the woman was a Witch.

Vanya Russo professed not to worship Satan, nor conspire with his host, but Matteo could not dismiss her aura or his sense of her magic. Nor could he dismiss his memory of her majesty, despite her small stature and disfiguring scar. The shape of Vanya's scar might even be a signature, God's way of marking her, the inverted cross a sign that she was in fact in league with Satan, though she vehemently denied it.

Warned by his own agent that Vanya Russo was disfigured by burns, Matteo had been prepared for her to be grotesque. He had resolved to reserve judgment on the rumors of her allegiance to the old religion, but it had been difficult after he'd laid eyes on her.

He was used to the deference of women, and Vanya was proud, not the least cowed by humility. Protective of Cathryn, she had challenged him, demanding to know what Matteo wanted of the woman he sought, not settling for simple answers. She had pressed him with questions that probed for more than he'd wanted to reveal to her, a stranger. Only when he'd learned Vanya was Cathryn's mother had Matteo begun to understand her inquisitive, almost combative stance.

Matteo was certain he would never be able to forget the Sabbat conducted by the high priestess, Vanya Russo. The nature of the rite he had witnessed was primitive, yet to his surprise, it had all the qualities of holy worship. The former priest could not recall any clergy he had ever known commune more directly with God than Vanya did when she invoked Him, and in all honesty, he had to agree there seemed some logic in her respect for the universe created by God and for His order, some blessing or sense of correctness in her belief that man created evil in the world. It seemed true enough to Matteo that mankind did not need any help from fallen angels to commit vile acts.

Yet by her own admission Vanya was a pagan, and though Matteo had renounced his orders, though he had made a mockery of his vows and even now did not presume to claim he led an exemplary life, he had not fully renounced his faith. He could not quite align himself with the natural world that Vanya proclaimed.

At the Sabbat Matteo had felt her power and, at the time, imagined a divine presence at the rite. He had enjoyed the surge of primitive energy, had felt charged and uplifted, but regardless of Vanya's assurances, regardless of what he had felt and seen with his own eyes, in his still Catholic mind a pagan was presumed evil and anti-Christ. He still believed in Witches—and in the Christian Devil whom the Church declared they worshiped.

In the wee hours of the morning, physically exhausted and sexually sated, but consumed by doubts, Matteo often could not sleep. He lay awake and reviewed his life, searching his heart, worrying most about Cathryn's proclaimed acceptance of Vanya's approach to God. In the dawn he argued with himself against his love.

In his heart Matteo inclined to Cathryn, uplifted in spirit by his love for her, in rapture because of Cathryn's love for him. His instinct was to cast all reason aside, to respond to the soundings of his soul, but intellect demanded his full-hearted feelings be weighed against more objective evidence, and for the former Roman Catholic priest there was ample proof of the corrupting influence of Cathryn's love.

Matteo confessed to himself that in his physical responses to Cathryn, he was reduced to the level of an animal in search of the most elementary form of gratification. In the throes of passion, he grimaced and panted and groaned like a frenzied beast, a victim of his lust. Yet this act, which was vile according to the teachings of his Church, brought him as close as he had ever been to God. If that sense was an illusion, he feared then that nothing would ever elevate him above a rutting animal or give him distance from God's lower creatures.

But was this grace, when with a look, with a kiss, with a touch, Cathryn destroyed the creative man he was before he drowned himself in her seductive whispers and sighs? She made a mockery of his vows to God, and though his stated reasons for abandoning the Church did not involve Cathryn, the truth remained to burden him with guilt and shame.

A man less burdened than he by the depth of his emotions for Cathryn could argue that her abuse by Gerald Seymour had defiled her for eternity, but Matteo's love forbade this not uncommon reasoning. For he could not avoid the truth: He cherished Cathryn Godwyne more than life itself.

But no man could allow the heart to rule above the head for long. Matteo might listen to Cathryn as she played the violin and be convinced no two people created by God were ever more in tune. He might listen to her sighs as she lay entwined in rapture with him and feel they breathed from the same source of air, or stare at her and know he would never love another soul as he loved Cathryn; but the captain also accepted that the voice of the heart must be subject to the voice of reason. It was an unalterable though regrettable fact that when the *Cynthia Ames* docked in Marysland, his adoring heart would certainly submit to his impassioned head.

Chapter 65

The dawn of every new day brought Cathryn and Matteo closer to the Marysland shore, and Matteo began to live two lives. He was reminded of his life in Venice, where he had pretended to be a priest when, in fact, he was only a man.

Aboard the *Cynthia Ames*, Matteo began to wake from dreams in which he held Cathryn in his arms forever, and he was haunted by the truth; when he looked at Cathryn, he began to feel enormous sadness for his deceit. She trusted him, while he knew he again would soon betray her. The pain of his remorse was physical.

Matteo vowed never again to use Cathryn greedily and damned his man's body until he could lie beside the woman he loved without responding naturally. He reminded himself of the abuse Gerald Seymour had inflicted on Cathryn and held her gently in his arms, swearing to replace her pain with memories of his tenderness.

He focused his attentions on soothing any of her discomforts. Without demand, he stroked her temples and rubbed her back and limbs until she fell into soporific sleep. He consented to play the violin for her, sharing none of the erotic compositions she had inspired. He read to her from his log and entertained her with his dreams for his plantation.

The more sensitive he was to her, the more intense his guilt, and even while he ministered to her, he withdrew.

Cathryn loved Matteo more for his undemanding devotion and read in his eyes his love for her. Under his gaze she thrived, blooming as though she were an exotic flower whose roots all at once had found a source of nourishing rich soil. From force of habit, she thanked God for the blessing of His returning her to her true love, and while they sailed the forgiving sea, Cathryn all but forgot the bitter years of separation.

Cathryn was so at ease and so enamored of Matteo, she neglected to pursue the questions he quite deftly had skirted. She looked no farther ahead than the day or night that lay before her; every question she had about the future was answered when she opened her eyes and touched him and realized he was no phantom of drug-distorted vision.

For a while Cathryn enjoyed Matteo's undemanding attention, but eventually desire flared and she pursued its clarion call.

"I cannot perform my duties as captain of this ship if I'm flagged from bed. I must have control over my passions if I am to fulfill my responsibilities," he explained when Cathryn wondered over his abstinence. "Your loving arms, I fear, debilitate me."

Cathryn stared at Matteo, perplexed. She drew energy from love and had come to subscribe to Vanya's notion that the act of love drew down power from the heavens.

As Matteo continued to maintain absolute control over his passions, Cathryn's confidence began to ebb. She was forced finally to confront the mysteries which until now she had avoided. But whenever she brought up the questions that nagged her conscious mind, Cathryn realized she felt drowsy, though in fact she had recently enjoyed an excessive amount of sleep. Eventually she realized her sleepiness only masked her dread of uncovering the truth.

When she had first come to the captain's cabin, Father Vittorio's appetite for her had seemed to pale next to that of Captain

Ruggero's. In fact, at times Cathryn had wondered when Matteo slept. He worked most of the long day, almost always dressed and on deck shortly after dawn, and at night he had seemed inexhaustible. He had never needed encouragement, his body always ready for hers. She had been driven to wonder how he had survived four years without her eager presence.

Uncomfortable now with the answer to that question, Cathryn rose from the captain's bunk and retrieved a yellow satin dressing gown from the cabin floor. She tied the sash of the robe around her waist and poured herself some tea.

Did she need to ask Matteo how he had satisfied his usually hungry male instincts while she lay nowhere near?

Cathryn smoothed the fabric of the robe against her thighs. Originally the notion that the fabulous wardrobe that filled the trunks in the captain's quarters had been ordered for her had delighted her. And though Matteo had whispered he had been thinking of her when he'd bought the bride's veil and headdress, Cathryn knew better than to believe he had taken total stock in dreams.

She believed it coincidence that she sailed aboard the *Cynthia Ames*—some peculiar twist of fate that brought her to the captain's bed—and now was free to fear the magnificent trousseau packed in the captain's trunks was destined for another woman.

Who could it be? she puzzled. A colonist in America? If not, why would Matteo carry the chests to that shore? So little did Cathryn know about the Colonies that she could not imagine a colonial woman needing fine garments such as those the chests contained. She knew only what she had heard—of opportunity and the wild, abundant land—and never dreamed of wealth and luxury.

Cathryn wanted to believe that the trousseau was hers, just as she had prayed and dreamed that one day Vittorio would come to England to take her from Gerald Seymour, by force if necessary; but the fantasy could not last, and in its place sprang the vision of another woman who had lain in her lover's arms these years—a woman who had inspired him to buy the most alluring of diaphanous gowns, gowns with sleeves showered with pearls, bright flounces of fashionable new petticoats to peek with boldness from beneath a draped overskirt, and plunging bodices that revealed almost all of Cathryn's ample breasts.

Cathryn dwelled on Matteo's waning passion. He was too

attentive of her every comfort and whim but one, foiling almost too easily her efforts to seduce him, and she knew without a doubt that if he were unattached, she would have succeeded in wooing him away from his ridiculous excuse that loving her depleted him of necessary energy.

Cathryn thought of the fetching wedding gown that curiosity had forced her to try on for Matteo. The hem of the skirt had been a trifle short and, on Cathryn, the bodice too revealing for a bride. But Matteo had said nothing when she'd made a comment about the too tight fit, unnatural behavior for a man as lusty as she knew him to be. The priest would have pulled at the lace that barely concealed her breasts and made them spill forth into his eager hands.

Cathryn tried but could not conjure the face of her rival. She tried and tried again, but only succeeded in reducing herself to tears. Did Matteo love this colonial more than he loved her? she wondered. How could it be? How could there be any room in Matteo's heart to love another woman when there was no room in her heart for another man?

But Cathryn lacked the courage to bring herself to challenge Matteo about the woman she knew existed. Would there ever come a day when she would be brave enough to probe his true loyalties? She wondered, yet knew there was nothing on earth that could make her shatter the fragile cocoon she had spun around herself and the man who filled her dearest dreams.

Chapter 66

Cathryn was aware of the scent of land before she saw it and was not taken by surprise when Matteo announced landfall.

"I'm anxious for you to see my plantation, Cathryn," he said, his excitement showing in his eyes, "but it needs your touch."

"What of my contract?" she pressed, hoping for some exact statement of Matteo's plans.

"Leave that to me," he stated simply, and proceeded to

apprise her of some of the details of his Marysland home. "From my bedchamber, you can see the woods and beyond to my fields of rich tobacco and corn and sections of livestock. I am a rich man, Cathryn, but richer by far in having found you," he said, and cradled her against him with love.

On their last morning at sea, Matteo returned to his quarters and surprised her bathing in a steaming tub. He seemed especially cheerful as he seated himself on the high edge of the wooden tub. In his hand he held a small squirming sack.

"A parting gift," he said, untying the bundle, and from inside the sack popped the small head of a golden-eyed black kitten, who began a surprisingly loud protest.

"How precious he is!" Cathryn cried as she touched the kitten's shiny black nose with a wet finger.

"She," Matteo corrected her, petting the furry kitten. "There are five of them. I thought we might spare you one."

"I'm glad to have a friend. I surely need one—is she supposed to keep me warm nights now that we reach land?"

Matteo lifted the now purring kitten and placed it on the deck beside the tub. "In a few hours," he said, ignoring Cathryn's last question, "I shall send for you to come on deck prepared to land. Then one of my men shall row you ashore and accompany you to my home while I continue with the ship to join you . . . later."

"Later?" Cathryn's eyes widened. "When?"

"In, perhaps, a week."

Cathryn frowned. "Why must I go without you?"

Matteo smiled a distant smile. "You must is all, *cara*. You must."

Cathryn stared at Captain Ruggero. There was nothing to argue, she could tell, but a stray tear of fearful anticipation escaped her eye. Not wanting him to see her doubts, she casually tried to brush the tear aside.

"You must not cry."

"Aye, Captain." Cathryn forced a smile but had to turn her face away.

"Always remember that I love you, Cathryn, no matter what I do or say."

She turned to face him again. "What is it you're trying to tell me, Matteo?"

"Only that I love you, *cara*."

"Then hold me!" she begged, and he drew her dripping from the bath and pressed her fiercely against him.

"I shall be bereft without you." He nuzzled her.

"You only say that to placate me!" she challenged. "I know someone waits ashore to take my place."

"No one shall ever replace you, Cathryn, I swear."

Cathryn began to weep. "I don't believe you!"

Desperate, he tried to soothe her. "You fear for nothing, *cara*. I love only you."

"No," Cathryn sobbed, "you do not love me anymore, I know it!"

Matteo pulled her more tightly to him. "You are wrong. You are wrong."

"Then why do you never *show* me that you love me!"

"How have I been unkind?" he asked as if he did not know exactly what she meant.

Cathryn dissolved into angry tears, and the longer he held her with gentle arms the more she cried, continuing until she was exhausted. "You know very well how to comfort me, Matteo," she murmured finally.

Staring down at Cathryn, Matteo smiled. "I know, *cara*, I know." He sighed as he bent to give her a kiss of shattering bliss. "But there is no time left this morning for what you want," he said as he released her and moved directly for the cabin door.

Left speechless, Cathryn had no recourse but to prepare for Matteo's call. Only shock over his abrupt announcement prevented her from shedding more tears as she dressed and packed her few possessions.

Eventually she grew angry with how Matteo had so deftly sidestepped her questions of the past and future during their brief reunion. Much of the time he also had flatly ignored her desires, Cathryn remembered, recalling in particular one of the last times she and Matteo had made love. On that night he had left the drapes around the bunk half-open to allow a candle-soft illumination of them while he'd seduced her with his voice and gentle hands. She had curled herself against him as he'd rubbed her back in measured slow strokes until she'd been quite unable to move, on the verge of falling into dreamless sleep. Then he had gradually revived her to a very narrow consciousness, making her only just aware of every delicious sensation he aroused.

"If ever I doubted the existence of Witches, Cathryn, you've made me a believer," Matteo had whispered, "for no simple woman has ever had such power over me. Your touch alone reduces me to abject slavery."

At the time, quite besotted, his words had washed over her as adoration, but later the name "Witch" had ripped at her very soul. It was as if she had lain in Venice with her priest, his guilty conscience driving him to accuse her of witchcraft, and all the torment of her memory of betrayal had surfaced once again.

With painful difficulty, Cathryn had begun to single out Matteo's accusations.

"*Ti voglio bene, strega minore,*" he had murmured.

Cathryn had only wanted to hear the words "I love you," but his endearing "little Witch" no longer fell on deaf or adoring ears.

When he had panted, "*Strega bella!*" Cathryn had risen up in anger. "Never call me that again," she'd cried, and had torn herself from his embrace. She'd wanted to run away, to hide, but there was no place she could run from the misery she felt. She had despaired that the end of love again was near. "Why do you desire me to be and call me the evil thing you name a Witch? Yet you say you love me. You drive me mad!" Cathryn had fairly bounced from the bunk, pulling the comforter with her and wrapping it about her.

While Matteo had struggled to recover some composure, she'd demanded, "Tell me, just what do you intend when you call me Witch?"

Matteo had run his fingers through his hair in a gesture of perplexity and, for a moment before he'd answered, had stared darkly at Cathryn as she stood and fumed at him. "Surely, *cara,* a man cannot always be held to what he might cry when he is mindless with ecstasy." Matteo had risen from the bunk and approached Cathryn cautiously. "Do you say that you have never tried to bewitch me? And do you not also believe that there is something almost magical about our love?"

Cathryn had felt confused. "Please," she'd said, "do not ever call me 'Witch' again. Or I shall not forgive you."

As she remembered now, Matteo had not answered her precisely but led her back to bed and, with skillful and deliberate effort, made his peace with her. However, from then on, Cathryn had felt very like a note of music sliding up and down the scale, first high, then low, then swiftly high again. Not long after that exchange, Matteo had claimed lovemaking drained away too much of his energy. He had remained tender and attentive, but he had declined to respond to her desire and, remarkably, had neither exhibited nor expressed any of his own. Yet, Cathryn told herself, only a fool would imagine Matteo did not love her.

When called to disembark, Cathryn was ready and emerged from the captain's cabin, calm and sober, a Puritan once again. Cloaked in gray, she looked demure and, as always, beautiful. At the poignant moment of their parting, Matteo wondered how he had ever been able to resist her abundant charms in the last weeks. With seeming indifference, however, he escorted her to the side of the ship and handed her to a waiting man.

In parting, he managed to whisper a few words of promise to her, but because he feared they might be overheard, he forced himself to sound cool and impersonal.

How he hated sending her away! But he knew there was no avoiding what lay ahead.

After watching the departure of his very heart, Matteo once more reflected on events that now forced him to chart the course he did. Waiting for him on the eastern shore of the great Chesapeake Bay was a fate from which he saw little hope of extrication, and he damned himself for his position. When he had counseled Cathryn that his sins were too numerous to count, he judged now that he had been quite accurate, and that the crop was about to come to harvest.

Matteo smiled bitterly at the wide horizon. His brother Piero had cursed him for his association with Cathryn, and Piero's legacy to him would fulfill that curse. Who was he, Matteo Ruggero wondered, to dare not to believe in sorcery!

In addition to the duty of restoring the Ruggero fortune at his brother's death, Piero, the eldest brother, had left him with a peculiar legacy, an obligation to marry a woman not of his choosing.

Matteo had not known of this duty at the beginning of his quest for Cathryn. Perhaps the knowledge would have made a difference and, from a complex sense of guilt and family duty, he would have given up his search for Cathryn, the woman who held his heart in bondage.

Perhaps, Matteo sighed, perhaps.

But Matteo had not known of this obligation to marry Avis Ames and, obeying the dictates of his soul, had gone in search of Cathryn Godwyne. Then, in the process of taking over the family business, Matteo had come into contact with Milton Ames, with whom Piero Ruggero had had complicated commercial dealings and, unbeknownst to Matteo, other agreements that Matteo would eventually feel bound to honor.

Milton Ames became his partner, the source of his entrée to trade in the English colonies. Ames had made his fortune in both lawful and unlawful enterprises. His legal wealth was tied to the tobacco trade; the illegal to traffic in pirated East India goods. His greatest fortune, though yet to be acquired, was in the traffic of slaves.

A shrewd, sometimes cruel man, Ames had only one weakness of which Matteo was aware, and that weakness was his only child. Not long after her mother, Cynthia Ames, had died, Avis took her mother's place in her father's affections. There was nothing she wanted that her father did not provide.

Consequently, in a moment of supreme despair after months of fruitless searching for his beloved Cathryn, Matteo had been prevailed upon to honor an agreement Piero had made long years before with Milton Ames, which promised that a surviving brother would marry Milton's daughter in the event of Piero's untimely death. The obligation should have fallen to Luciano Ruggero, not Matteo, but God had obviously decreed it otherwise, and Matteo had fallen prey to Milton Ames's manipulation in his daughter's behalf. At the time, Matteo had told himself his reluctance to wed Avis was due only to his unwillingness to accept that it was time for him to give up his dream of finding Cathryn. In accepting Avis's hand, he had also realized that at the very least he would lose his head should he ever think of disappointing her. Now Matteo feared for Cathryn far more than for himself. Milton Ames would have to take only one look at Cathryn to know Matteo Ruggero had been unfaithful to his daughter. Ames was known to be ruthless and barbaric, often employing any means to obtain a goal, and Matteo felt certain he would not hesitate for an instant to inflict his revenge on Cathryn if he saw her as the cause of Avis's disappointment or unhappiness.

While a willful, tempestuous child, at seventeen Avis Ames was a beauty, as different from his Cathryn as night from day. Rather soon after meeting his future bride, Matteo discovered that beneath the angel's face surrounded by pale blond angel's hair, and looking out from sky-blue eyes, was a flirtatious imp. She was bold in her eagerness to part with her virginity and without his coaxing gave Matteo a husband's full rights. At first he had been reluctant to indulge in her charms, but she had persuaded him, begging for the memory of his love to help her endure the time he would be at sea and separated from her.

However, Matteo soon learned Avis was in no rush at all to marry, and in spite of her readiness to fulfill the obligations of a wife, at heart, Avis was selfish and cold. She wanted to be fondled and held, like a pampered pet, taking far more than she was willing to give and giving herself only for the purpose of gain.

At first Matteo hoped for more from Avis than the simple use of her body, dreaming of affection and love. With patience he showed her what gave him pleasure and expected to give pleasure in return, with skill awakening in her a true woman's desire, though he could not help but compare Cathryn to his betrothed.

It had been Cathryn's nature to seek her lover's pleasure almost before her own, enjoying variation, while Avis did not seem to consider anyone except herself. Though soon proficient, her responses seemed too routine. With Avis, Matteo could afford to be a complacent, even careless lover, a behavior he had never considered with Cathryn. She had been a partner in the fullest sense, and never had Matteo imagined Cathryn's cries to be rehearsed.

When he took his pleasure with Avis, Matteo often closed his eyes and, at the moment of exaltation, troubled himself not to cry out Cathryn's name for Avis to hear. When he found Cathryn again and could afford to end his silence, he felt free.

"Cathryn, oh, my beloved, Cathryn," Matteo now cried, and knew, regardless of their fate, he would love Cathryn Godwyne alone, throughout eternity.

Chapter 67

As Cathryn looked out the windows of her bedchamber, she decided she might possibly be viewing heaven. Everywhere she looked she saw green—woods, orchards, pastures, cultivated fields—against a blue sky sprinkled with occasional puffs of clouds. Not far from the house the Patuxent River flowed into the waters of Chesapeake Bay, a gateway to the world if one should choose to roam from heaven.

In the early morning especially, everything seemed harmonious and serene, but beneath the surface the order and tranquillity was an illusion, Cathryn feared. The sun might filter through the clouds above the western shore of Matteo's Marysland, caressing her and lulling her into believing she was home to stay, but in her heart Cathryn knew better. There were too many things pointing to the fact that her welcome would soon fade.

For one, Cathryn had been forced to deal with the certainty of another woman in Matteo's life when, with the exception of the items she had worn, the trunks in the captain's cabin had been repacked and secured with leather straps for unloading, but not with Cathryn at Matteo's private dock. The wedding gown and veil were bound, Cathryn imagined, for Captain Ruggero's intended bride.

Perhaps, she gauged, Matteo intended to keep her in addition to a wife, but, though his house was large, no house she could imagine was big enough to shelter both a man's wife and his *amante*.

When his bride had been the Church, Cathryn would have agreed to be Matteo's mistress, she reflected. But the circumstances she envisioned now were not the same. She could have tolerated Vittorio's devotion to the priesthood, but she could never accept Matteo's loyalty to a flesh-and-blood wife.

But troubling Cathryn almost as much as her thoughts about Matteo having a wife was the man who had escorted her from the ship to shore. He had turned out to be none other than the man who had carried her from Gerald Seymour's.

When Cathryn saw him waiting for her in the boat lowered to the side, she almost fainted, but at the moment, her emotions running high, there was scarcely time to exchange farewells, and no time at all for questions.

It was all she could do to remain composed as Matteo whispered, "*Addio, angelica*. I shall come to you sooner than you imagine," and handed her down to the man waiting in the boat below.

Seating herself, Cathryn settled a hostile stare on her escort, wondering if he intended to tie and drag her ashore. But of course on this occasion he would have no reason to truss her.

This time Cathryn was very subdued, with no uncontrollable tears for him to deal with, no horse from which to fall, and, she observed, absolutely no danger in the world of her throwing herself overboard.

Cathryn held on to the sides of the shallop for dear life, worried about the pathetic mewing kitten, while the man exerted himself and oared steadily toward the shore. She took one last look behind her to see the *Cynthia Ames* headed to the distant eastern shore, for a long time staring at the aft cabin where, it was hard for her to believe, she had spent almost a month.

To Cathryn's surprise, when she at last turned her gaze from the ship, the man at the oars smiled. "I know ye must be thinking the worst, mistress," he said with polite deference.

In spite of her anxious gaze, he continued. "I be Meldon Archer, in service to yer . . . Captain Ruggero. I spent near all of three years combing east and north of London, England, hunting ye.

"The captain, he'd've hunted ye himself, but chose me instead. He weren't English enough to get nowhere with the likes of your guardian."

That was true, Cathryn had to agree.

"And my face gave me advantage, scaring people to answer when they'd rather shut up. Ye've no reason to fear me. I'd give me life for ye."

Speechless, Cathryn continued to stare.

"The captain loves you, mistress. That's enough for me."

While Cathryn struggled with a reply, Meldon eased the shallop to a weathered but sturdy dock and, climbing out, secured a line, then stretched out his hand to assist her.

Leaving a number of small crates behind for another trip, he shouldered Cathryn's one trunk, and she clutched her violin and the mewing cat. He led her up a wide, heavily wooded trail to Matteo's much cherished house, and she followed obediently, curious and anxious to see the home about which Matteo had spoken with a light shining in his eyes.

Matteo had warned Cathryn that though his house was impressive for the Colonies, it would not approach the grand houses of Venice; and while it was not a palace, the full two-story redbrick house was welcoming and quite beautiful to Cathryn's eye. A stair tower at the front of the house, and dramatic chimney stacks positioned at each end, balanced the large rectangular form. On the inside, all the rooms were finished with a brilliant white plaster made of oyster-shell lime, Meldon Archer said.

Downstairs, in addition to a kitchen, a dairy, and a buttery, there were a large hall and a smaller withdrawing room; upstairs, there were three bedchambers, a salon, and a sitting room. Every room had leaded windows that overlooked the plantation and gave abundant light. All the furnishings were massive but sparse, giving the large rooms an open yet occupied feeling.

Matteo's bedchamber, which adjoined the one Cathryn occupied, was austere and so like his room at degli Innocenti that Cathryn had gasped aloud upon seeing it for the first time. The oak floor was covered with a luxurious carpet, rich with dark colors; his bed was covered with white silk; the windows were draped with wine-colored velvet. A massive gold candle holder decorated a highly polished rosewood table by the bed, and across the room stood an enormous rosewood armoire. The only exceptions to the image that this room had been transported whole from Venice were the absence of a large gold crucifix adorning the wall opposite the bed and the presence of two carved marble birds that seemed to perch on the fireplace mantel, staring in fixed concentration into a tall mirror framed in gold. Cathryn felt as if the birds watched her from the mirror as she stood in the doorway.

She was also amazed, and a bit disturbed, by the fact that what had been assigned as her bedchamber was identical to her bedchamber in the *palazzo* in Venice. The room held the same deep blue and rose carpet; the same dark rose-colored satin quilts and velvet drapes; the same pale rose brocaded wall covering. Even the walnut bed had clawed feet and a headboard of carved flower faces, the same as her bed in Venice. Cathryn wondered what had possessed Matteo to duplicate their rooms, touched by his having joined his to hers.

Another door from Matteo's room led Cathryn to a music salon. The walls of this room were covered with stamped leather, and four large chairs had seats and backs of the same material. Two finely carved violins—a Guarneri and a Ruggieri—a viola, a cello, an oboe, and a flute lay on a polished ebony table, and several sheets of staff paper with scores she did not recognize were scattered about. It was obvious someone dusted the room every day and arranged each instrument and paper with care, leaving the impression that the person whose work it was might return at any moment.

A few minutes after entering the room, Cathryn took up the music that lay about and began to hum the difficult score. She tuned one of the violins and began to play, grimacing over her efforts to achieve the degree of dexterity the passages required. It was not a composition for an inexperienced musician, and Cathryn concluded the passage could not be the composition's start. She rummaged through the papers and tried again.

Yes, this was a much better beginning, she reasoned as she played, repeating the major melody and slowly building a theme until, breathless, the violent passages she had first tried fit with perfection. Then came the decline, the eventual ebbing, but with the repetition of familiar melody. The whole was brilliant, the score full of stimulating dissonance, perhaps exemplary of both the composer's passion and his frustration.

So beautiful, she thought, then read the dedication beneath the final bar: *A Caterina, la mi' adorata*.

Elated by the master's dedication, all at once she felt embarrassed, as if she pried. "Abandon your music, my eye," she said aloud to cover discomfort. "You dare to tell such lies?" she huffed as if Matteo stood before her to be chastised.

There were several volumes of bound scores on a shelf behind the table, and intrigued, Cathryn leafed through some of them. She recognized many of the themes Matteo had written over the years, and she continued to browse until she heard her name called from two rooms away.

"Mistress?" came a young woman's voice again, and Cathryn closed the volume to answer her summons. Before she started for Matteo's door, however, she picked up a folio of loose music from the table. She would read the music before she went to bed. Before Matteo returned to his home, she vowed to learn a new score to surprise him.

Then she might hear her teacher's comments and, perhaps, his praise, and for a time it would seem that nothing had changed. Perhaps, Cathryn thought as she passed from Matteo's room into hers, this had been Matteo's dream as he had prepared their rooms to imitate the ones in Venice, then searched the earth to find and bring her here.

Chapter 68

Every night after a late supper and a hot bath she at first had difficulty arranging, Cathryn crawled exhausted into bed and slept soundly with no memory of dreams. She fell asleep as soon as her head touched the pillow and when she opened her eyes again, it was morning and Meldon Archer was at her door.

On the first morning Meldon invited Cathryn into the garden, where he surprised her with crates of cuttings, roots, and seeds that called for her immediate attention. "How did you come by these?" Cathryn asked as she touched plants and seeds she knew must be from her mother's garden.

"They come w' ye from England."

"Not with me," she answered, "and you know it. Who gave them to you?"

"All I did was to hover o'er 'em aboard ship in order to keep 'em hardy."

"Did you know my mother?" Cathryn tried to narrow the distance between herself and Meldon Archer, but he stepped away. "Did my mother give these plants to you?"

"I admit none such, mistress."

"Then how did Captain Ruggero come by them?"

"Ye must ask the captain yerself."

Cathryn gave up in dismay, but if Meldon could not give satisfactory replies to her questions, he did point her in the direction of a fresh plot of cleared land, and soon Cathryn was up to her elbows in newly turned soil, worrying whether the cuttings would survive. "The one thing I don't have to fret over is comfrey." She smiled at the hardy root.

The day after she arrived, Meldon Archer also produced a woman to measure Cathryn for a new wardrobe. She would replace Cathryn's Puritan garments with outfits of finer cloth and would also design several other dresses of very acceptable style. With two girls to help her, the woman was kept busy night and

day for a week, completing a ducape hooded cloak; five silk
petticoats, one blue, one red, one black, and two white; a black
silk gown; a white taffeta waistcoat edged with lace; six colored
bodices; seven Holland aprons; a red waistcoat; nightgowns for
all seasons; a morning coat; and two printed calico dresses.
Cathryn was overjoyed. Why, if there was another woman in his
life, would Matteo go to this extravagance? she wondered, and
tried to convince herself it was an auspicious sign.

Still, many questions remained for Matteo to answer. Meldon
Archer's presence alone proved to Cathryn that Matteo had
played some essential part in her departure from Gerald, but
when she recalled her marriage contract, which made her little
better than property for sale to the highest bidder, she was filled
with anger.

The ugly truth of her status as a commodity to trade made
Cathryn think of Vanya, who had been many a man's slave, and
she wondered what part her mother had played in the arrangements that had brought her to the Colonies. Vanya must have
had some knowledge, Cathryn reasoned, or else she would not
now have seeds and cuttings from her mother's garden—nor
possession of her Amati.

Cathryn shivered; the idea of Vanya being her mother still
produced chills sometimes. Vanya could haunt a person with her
aura alone, Cathryn mused. Her mother admitted being a Witch
but was not evil, unless one believed Vanya's devotion to a God
different from Gerald's or Father Vittorio's made her inherently
corrupt. Yet Gerald and Father Vittorio would each accuse the
other man of worshiping a false God, and they were each, by the
acclaim of many, godly men.

Cathryn frowned, at once more at ease with her mother's
Goddess than desirous of the favor of a God revered by either
Gerald Seymour or the priest. Surely, Cathryn prayed, God was
something more than these men made Him.

Cathryn now sat in the middle of her bed and swore that when
Matteo returned, she would make him answer her once and for
all about his and Vanya's involvement in her departure from
England. For tonight, Cathryn resolved, she would not worry
over questions she could not answer by herself. Tonight, with a
week already passed in Marysland, Cathryn resolved to find the
energy to study the folio of music she had taken from Matteo's
salon.

Before her eyelids became too heavy, Cathryn began to leaf through Matteo's folio of loose music, hoping to learn at least one score to dazzle him. As she sifted through the scores, Cathryn felt certain that despite his protests, Matteo could never give up his music, though he tried hard to convince her that their affair had destroyed his inspiration. *Why does he want me to feel guilty?* As busy as he was aboard the *Cynthia Ames*, Cathryn had often caught him scribbling notes of music, sometimes even jotting notes in the ship's log.

"Now that we are together again, sometimes I dream whole scores," he confessed, startled.

"You see, I am your inspiration. You thought I destroyed you, but I made you, instead."

He laughed. "You praise yourself too highly. You are first a distraction. When you are near me, I think mainly of making love," he said, lifting himself above her.

"And when I am absent?"

He smiled. "I think of having you near," he said, and began to kiss her.

She kissed him lightly in return. "It is my fault you come panting after me?"

"But I know you want me—need me." He stroked her, letting his fingers slide between her thighs.

"Mmmmmmm, yes," she admitted, caressing him in return. "And you, whom do you need?"

"We need each other," he replied, hungrily succumbing to her influence.

Before her now Cathryn had proof enough that Matteo had not been entirely distracted. She held a folio thick with hand-drawn staff paper and page after page of composition.

She studied the music, humming as she read. "You are mad, Vittorio," she whispered. Even if the priest had contemplated abandoning his music, inspiration had not abandoned him.

"Brilliant," she cried as one theme in particular leapt out at her. She went for her Amati and tried the notes, repeating phrases until they flowed triumphantly; but she realized she would have to practice many long hours before she had the courage to play for the composer.

Cathryn leafed through the folio, thoroughly awed by Matteo's productivity, then all at once stopped to stare at several ink drawings positioned in back of the compositions.

The first was of a woman of extraordinary beauty whom the artist apparently knew well.

Cathryn had not had an inkling Matteo could render a drawing. Perhaps, she thought, taken aback, it was a talent she did not inspire. The strokes of the artist's pen were bold, just as his music was, and on two facing pages there were several small sketches of the woman, as if when the artist began he was merely distracted; then the larger, more complete drawing emerged. The woman was young, not much more than a girl. She wore a thoughtful, seductive pout.

Cathryn stared at the sketches a long while. In the larger drawing the woman sat stiffly, in profile, her long hair pulled back to the nape of her neck, falling in ringlets to the middle of her back. From the strokes of the artist's pen, Cathryn assumed the girl's hair to be blond and her eyes light. The subject's nose was straight, her brow perfection. By the artist's rendering she seemed arrogant, and Cathryn instinctively disliked her.

For a moment, she did not have the courage to turn over the drawing. She did not want to see any more likenesses of the woman she instantly knew had taken her place in Matteo's heart.

How dare he?

How could he?

Of course he has not been faithful to me, Cathryn admitted to herself. This sketch was of the woman for whom the trousseau had been made—the queen to wear the bridal crown and veil. With reluctance Cathryn confessed the beautiful woman would do it justice.

Summoning her courage and overwhelmed by curiosity, Cathryn turned the page.

Her mouth dropped open in shock.

"Matteo!" she gasped as she saw on the page before her a woman and a man unclothed, locked in love's embrace. Memory and desire stirred as Cathryn recognized the couple. The man lay on his back, the woman astride him with dark hair flowing, head thrown back. Her eyes were closed, her mouth slightly open, as his hands grasped her round breasts, his body thrust into hers, soft sound seeming to escape her lips as she found ecstasy.

One by one, Cathryn turned the pages, as music notation gave way to astonishing and skillful drawings; she feasted her eyes, happy to discover the explicit sketches were always of the same impassioned lovers.

Quite overwhelmed by what she saw, Cathryn closed the folio at last. If Matteo intended to send her away to marry someone else, if he did not still love her, at least he would not soon forget her.

But it was not enough for Cathryn, and in the dim of the very late night, she frowned and feared Matteo might persuade himself he could live without her in the flesh, believing his memory and sketches would be an adequate replacement.

Cathryn's stomach tightened in a fierce knot, and her lower lip began to tremble, her eyes shimmering with hot, crystal tears. Her dream had ended.

She knew Matteo would arrive soon and she must be ready for his announcement that she would have to go. She resigned herself to the unpleasant but obvious truth, and, she vowed, he must never know that his betrayal had wounded her mortally.

In anticipation, Cathryn imagined herself standing before her lover, and though she felt his dismissal as if it were a series of violent blows, she did not flinch, or beg. Though at his command to forget him her heart broke into a thousand fragments, Cathryn saw herself standing erect and knew when the time came she would quite simply walk away.

Chapter 69

A flutter of Cathryn's eyelashes revealed his entrance into the room disturbed her dreams. Yet she did not wake, and for a while Matteo stood watching over her, wishing the moment could last forever.

But despite his fondest dreams, Matteo knew he would soon have to find the courage to inform Cathryn of his plans to marry Avis Ames.

As he stood beside Cathryn, Matteo reasoned with himself that by all logic it should be easy for him to use Cathryn, then be done with her. For in the scheme of things he knew women were created solely for men's use, and those whose charms a man could not resist, a man enjoyed without regret.

Once again he argued with himself about her heritage. "She is a pagan," he breathed unsteadily. "And exceptionally head-strong." She had the worst of female tendencies: the effrontery to think for herself and the daring to disagree vociferously.

Matteo sighed with resignation. The man who invited into his home a woman who considered speaking out against his stated opinions allowed hornets to nest in his chimney. Yet for Matteo there could be nothing casual in the act of sending Cathryn away.

Who else but a woman like Cathryn Godwyne could be more to him than the standard comfort in the night, the mistress of his estate, and breed mare to supply him with heirs? Who else but Cathryn had ever touched him beneath the skin? She alone understood him, knew what drove him, felt the unwritten music of his soul. He had found no one else to inspire him, and without her there was no music; nothing to record.

Matteo took his gaze off Cathryn for a moment and spied his unbound folio on the floor beside the bed, wondering at once if Cathryn had thumbed far enough into the folder to discover his graphic sketches. Had she realized the drawings portrayed more than his lust? Or had she been too shocked to see and be flattered that his thoughts strayed only to her?

Matteo remembered he'd begun to sketch Avis in an effort to forget Cathryn, but no matter how he had tried to focus on the alluring Mistress Ames, his vision had blurred with images of Cathryn. He wanted her, he admitted, regardless of all logical prohibitions. Even now his body betrayed him and, stripping away his clothes, he pulled the covers from Cathryn's sleeping form.

She stirred at once, opening her eyes, and without hesitation, moved for the comfort of his arms. "Matteo," she murmured, "at last you've come to me," as if their separation had been an eternity.

Matteo wanted to promise that he would never stray from her again but instead pulled Cathryn tightly to him. His body was atuned to hers, the days of forced abstinence keening him to her. They kissed, the heat of passion surging between them, and all arguments against his love for Cathryn evaporated into air.

Long and tempting, Matteo's kiss filled Cathryn with languid desire. She parted her lips, and he slid his tongue into her mouth, exploring the warmth within.

He unfastened her gown and raised it, lowering his mouth to her breasts before the garment passed above her head. Completely absorbed by the ripe bounty of her form, Matteo suckled at length, his delight hers. She trembled under his mouth, every caress compelling Cathryn toward ecstasy.

Then he began a search for every gloriously tender place abiding in Cathryn's flesh, his kisses sending thrills of sensation throughout her body and into her limbs. She moaned with excitement as his kiss descended down her back and settled just below her waist, making her crave his most intimate touch. She drew one of his hands over her firm satin buttocks, inviting him to explore between her legs, gasping with delight as he fulfilled her unspoken wishes to perfection.

Cathryn could not imagine more knowing fingers than Matteo's as he coaxed incredible sensations, his touch making white bursts of fire explode inside her head, until, moved by his own mounting desire, he entered her, his increasingly vigorous motions triggering responses that made Cathryn tremble from their intensity. Joined fast to him, Cathryn felt as if her soul escaped her body and merged with his.

As Matteo crushed her to him, he felt their merging, also. "Only with you," Matteo panted. "There is music only with you!"

Yet as soon as his delirious cries abated, Cathryn felt Matteo recede from her, both in body and in soul, and even as he held her in his fierce embrace, Cathryn began to mourn.

To Cathryn's surprise, Matteo did not send her away the following morning, or the next, and for a fortnight he held her in his arms. He worshiped her with his body and with words, exclaiming again and again that he would love her for eternity. Matteo showed Cathryn his plantation every day from horseback, proud of the order and the bounty, wanting her to be acquainted with every acre of land. They rode together on a spirited rust-colored gelding. Cathryn rode behind him in the saddle, her arms wrapped around him in a joyful embrace, the pressure of her body making Matteo acutely aware of Cathryn's tender loveliness and how he craved her.

He tried to convince himself that soon he would have his fill, and with conscious effort he tried to wean himself of the tremendous effect she had on him. When she leaned against him in the saddle, he commanded his body not to respond.

But at other times he delighted just in her presence and caught her hands possessively while they walked on the narrow trails that wound over his property.

Once, long before he was betrothed to Mistress Ames, Matteo had dreamed of finding Cathryn and bringing her to Marysland. He had imagined carrying her up the staircase to her room and then to his, and on into the music salon. He had dreamed they would live forever in those rooms, making love and music, their passion for each other never ceasing, the music of their love inspiring the music of their violins.

But there were other plans that could not be changed for the sake of love alone, and with every passing hour, Matteo watched his dreams of bliss with Cathryn draw to an end.

With a mixture of purest delight and devastating pain, Matteo watched Cathryn settle into his home, saw her grow fond of everything that was dear to him; at the same time, he watched the calendar: the date of his marriage to Avis Ames was drawing near.

In the drawer of a cupboard downstairs lay Cathryn's contract of marriage, the groom's consent already obtained. All that remained for the document to be legal was the signature of the bride.

In a few days, Matteo would carry Cathryn to Ameston on the Ames River on Marysland's eastern shore and stand beside Avis and her father to watch Cathryn Godwyne promise herself to another man. Again and again, Matteo tried to envision Weylin Rodman taking Cathryn away.

He succeeded in imagining taking Cathryn to the Ames plantation. He saw himself witness the formality of the wedding vows, as, rigid and erect, Cathryn stood next to Weylin and, unsmiling, promised faithful devotion to the man who would be her husband. But in his mind's eye, when she turned to be embraced, Cathryn did not turn to Weylin but to him, folding herself into his aching arms. For no matter how he tried, Matteo could not imagine Cathryn cleaving to another man.

Yet Matteo knew the event surely would come to pass, for along with the whispers of love for Cathryn that echoed within Matteo's brain, there reverberated Milton Ames's blood-chilling threat.

A spy, a sailor aboard the *Cynthia Ames*, had reported to Matteo's partner an account of the captain's suspected affair with

Cathryn. This provoked the indignant father to defend his daughter's interests and honor.

At first, Milton Ames used what little charm he possessed, urging Matteo to abandon his mistress for reasons of innate greed. "My daughter's dowry is fairer than any slut," he urged his prospective son-in-law.

"She was a diversion for the voyage," Matteo insisted, sensing the father's rage, attempting a light denial of the fact that Cathryn meant anything to him.

Milton Ames stared at Matteo. "You lie," he finally replied, and suggested the younger man pause to consider how fate could be manipulated. "I don't especially yearn to have my only child see your rotting corpse dangling from the king's scaffold, but since you trade under papers which I know to be forged, you might want to avoid offending me. The Crown don't like to see a foreigner taking profits in the Colonies."

That tack also failed to bring Matteo to his knees, which forced Milton Ames to throw down a final card. "If you care nothing for your own life, dearest Matteo," Milton finally growled, "be certain you hear this, for unless you send the whore away, I promise one day you'll wake and find her throat was slit while you slept soundly beside her in her filthy bed."

Only to that threat did Matteo bend, not the least uncertain that the man who sometimes beat errant slaves to death just to prove a point would have a second thought about carrying out his threat to murder Cathryn.

As Matteo looked over the green rolling land of his plantation, he sighed and accepted that his wish to have Cathryn beside him would have a very different end than in his dreams. Fate and a vengeful partner had decreed that Cathryn Godwyne soon would turn away from him forever, and for the first time in his fantasy, he was clearly able to see Cathryn give her husband a prim kiss. Then in the dream Cathryn raised her eyes and in silence declared to Matteo that he would never again know the sweetness of love's thrilling embrace.

Chapter 70

Matteo's announcement of his approaching marriage to another woman had been inevitable, Cathryn knew, yet hearing him say he intended to marry brought her excruciating pain. She felt his words as a knife into her middle, when one morning she woke to find him dressed and sitting on the edge of her bed.

She saw his mournful look and waited for his words, unable to smile, almost unable to breathe.

"I am betrothed and shall marry soon," he said, for the moment erasing for Cathryn all memory of recent long, glorious nights of making love.

"Tell me, then, that you do not love me anymore," she demanded in an unexpectedly calm voice.

"I cannot love you anymore."

"And your promise to love me for eternity?" She sat erect.

Matteo was silent.

Anger overrode despair. "I swear, Matteo, I wish only to be the Witch you would have me be! I'd damn you to burn with love for me 'for all eternity'!" she swore, and turned her face away, barely able to control the raging flood of tears that swelled behind her eyes, almost unable to hear Matteo's explanation of the arrangements he had made.

"A marriage has been arranged for you to a decent and quite prosperous man, not disagreeable to the eye; a widower with no family, but youthful and fit. The wedding shall take place two days hence."

Cathryn stared dumbfounded as Matteo thrust her contract of marriage under her nose. A quill and inkwell waited nearby. "How can I refuse your splendid offer?" she asked sarcastically, daggers of impotent rage seeming to spring from her eyes.

She scribbled her name beneath Weylin's precise signature and from that moment put on airs, seeming to accept her fate without remorse.

Though she cared not at all, Cathryn demanded the details of her future husband's assets—his ships, his foreign plantations, his personal property.

"In addition, I'd wager his immediate assets to be in excess of two thousand pounds sterling," Matteo advised, a little startled by her demands for an accounting.

"I do not intend to be pawned off on a pauper," she snapped at his surprise.

After his announcement, Cathryn was icy with Matteo, but when at last she met her husband-to-be at the Ameston plantation, a shy and modest warmth befitting a bride came over her. In the difficult day and a half before she and Weylin Rodman exchanged their vows, Cathryn tried to know her husband, privately conceding that her lover had done decently by her.

All the while Matteo watched Cathryn from the corner of his eye, saw her shy smiles, and strained his ears at the gentle murmurs of the bride.

"You are strangely interested in this contracted bride," Avis noted of his preoccupation with Cathryn. "Did she not journey with you, Captain? Perhaps I should be jealous. She is an extraordinary beauty."

"I am concerned only that the match agree with Master Rodman."

Avis made a coy and pointed reply. "I did not know you and Master Rodman to be fast friends," she said, still a little annoyed by the short notice of house guest Master Rodman's marriage, though it had given her yet another perfect excuse to delay her own wedding. She had patted her French-styled powdered wig and begged her father to consider the need to entertain and celebrate the marriage of one of his partners free of any preoccupation with the demands of preparing her own wedding.

In fact, Avis had pointed out, the importance of her father's business with Weylin Rodman exceeded that of his involvement with Matteo, and his marriage in Milton's home merited special attention. Hailing from the Massachusetts Bay Colony, Weylin Rodman was an investor and merchant who bought large consignments of cargo from her father's ships and stood to prosper even more as his and her father's slave-trading enterprise grew.

There would be almost no ceremony, only witnesses to the signing of the legal documents and a verbal exchange of agreement between husband and wife, in keeping with the Puritan tradition, which did not view marriage as a religious rite but strictly a civil matter, though the lives of the couple were subject to the teachings of the Church. Avis thought it prudent to follow the formality with a celebration, and her father, who seemed almost more anxious for this wedding to take place than for the marriage of his own daughter, had agreed.

Pleased by how smoothly she had once again arranged to put off her plans to wed Matteo, Avis nevertheless could not avoid her future husband's obvious but shackled anger at the prospect of waiting longer to claim his bride. His impatience both annoyed and amused her, but she allowed herself to be distracted by the arrangements for Master Rodman's wedding feast.

Matteo's special eagerness to see Weylin's marriage take place continued to nettle Avis, and it dawned on her that her fiancé might have grown jealous of the attention she was paying to her father's house guest.

After consideration, Avis could only laugh at the notion, for though a handsome, even charming man, Weylin Rodman could never hold her interest for long. In addition to her distaste for his religion, Avis was only interested in men who, unlike Master Rodman, a devout colonial, had strong ties to home—to England— not to the wretched Colonies. At one time, Matteo's ties to Venice had sparked her interest.

In secret, Avis dreamed of escaping the colonial shore, wishing to return to England, perhaps to enter an extravagant life connected with the royal court, perceiving herself as equal to royalty and worthy of the rumored splendor of the court of Charles II and Catherine of Braganza, of which she had heard in some detail and on which she based her dreams. Used to having her way, it did not faze Avis's ambitions that the Restoration court had been replaced twice. All that mattered to her was the dream itself, and at the moment she was closer to achieving her aim than she had ever been.

One of her father's constant house guests was a Monsieur André Chapin, her present lover, a flamboyant and extravagant French nobleman and the epitome of the class of man with whom Avis most desired to associate. In spite of the fact that the French were devoutly hated by the English, Avis's father never lost an opportunity to make money and engaged in lucrative arrangements with Monsieur Chapin, ignoring politics and legalities. Her father's only loyalty was to profit and at the moment the French needed allies like Milton Ames in the English colonies.

Milton Ames noticed his daughter had not restrained her charm on the French visitor, but he also knew Avis would keep her place. She had been raised to marry Piero Ruggero and Matteo in his place. Avis's waning interest in her husband-to-be did not concern her father in the least, especially now that he had made his point about the captain's mistress. The captain would bend to him in this matter, and it would not suit him to have his daughter suddenly rebel.

Not a word had been exchanged between Avis and her father on the subject, but since his mind was set, Avis knew it was of no consequence that she preferred another. At first, Matteo had seemed to her a quite acceptable husband. He was handsome beyond the ordinary and a man of vast means and experience. He surrounded himself with the very best of material possessions, which by contrast made her father's estate and holdings seem at least colonial, and in dreadful lack of style.

Avis had seen Matteo's plantation only a few times, and then, because she was forbidden to venture beyond the first floor, she was forced to steal up the stairs to view the upper story. Once there, she was taken aback by its purity and elegance, stunned by the unusual arrangement of rooms, and as a result Matteo's allure increased several degrees in Avis's clear blue eyes.

At first, Avis had even enjoyed the attention of Matteo, an accomplished and splendid specimen of a man; too late she realized she had gone too far with the virile captain. Her wish had been only to secure Captain Ruggero on a tether of guilt by allowing him to steal her virginity; instead it seemed her wiles had unleashed a wild animal.

Avis hated the demands all men seemed to make on her but liked even less Captain Ruggero's attempts to bring her pleasure. His efforts required she participate to a degree she found repellent, but she pretended to enjoy his efforts and forced herself to learn what gave Matteo satisfaction.

From a very early age Avis had realized her delicate face, pale blue eyes, and lavish blond curls would be the key to her good fortune. Her own father doted on his fair child and spoiled her extravagantly. But with other men—Matteo as well as other lovers that soon followed him—she knew she would have her way only if she acquired a few accomplishments.

Though sex repulsed her, Avis knew men craved a willing woman, and if she wanted more in life than to waste her time in the colonial swamps, she believed she would have to have more than her beauty to recommend her. She pretended to agree to the Ruggero marriage but plotted to escape somehow with a man of her own choosing.

Avis smiled. Her vision of sailing away from the Colonies forever might soon be realized with Monsieur Chapin, though she had altered the setting from England to France to accommodate her current lover.

Since his return to Marysland, Avis had been careful to keep Matteo and André separate, a fairly easy task in the bustling Ames household. The unusual, large, one-and-one-half-story house was a series of open bedchambers hosting a variety of guests with as many as five large beds in a single room. Even the kitchen had its bed. No one considered it improper to roam from room to room or to entertain all manner of guests while still comfortably ensconced in bed.

Privacy was easier to come by out of doors, where Avis tried to console Matteo over the latest postponement of their marriage. "Now, Captain, it shall be only a brief delay. And you can't expect me to share my ceremony with another bride, especially one brought to bed on contract. It's unthinkable."

"What do we have but a contract between us?" Matteo answered, annoyed and miserable at the idea of Cathryn marrying another man.

Avis tried to console Matteo with persuasive caresses but managed to arouse him only after a surprising amount of effort. This time he sought relief with little regard for Avis's pleasure, not in the mood to accept her logic about yet another postponement of their marriage.

"You are so anxious, *chéri*, though already you have the privileges of a husband," she whispered, lowering her skirt modestly after their lovemaking on the grass.

She tried to conceal her own anger at him for being so disagreeable. "You must not be angry with me. I shall give you your freedom only a little longer," she purred, and nuzzled him, seeking his mouth with hers.

She felt the detachment of his kiss and it chilled her. "I test my father's patience, also. So do not worry, Captain Ruggero, soon I shall be your lawful wife."

"The delay shall be longer than you planned, *chérie,*" he said, mimicking Avis's French. "I must be at sea again—for six months."

"Oh." Avis sighed with pretended disappointment, careful to arrange a pout at her pretty mouth. Then she smiled, realizing she soon would be free again to spend all of her time with André. "I shall make you anxious to return to me," she said, and began to kiss Matteo with a warmth she did not have to feign. "You shall wish you never left my side," she promised.

She undid his collar and uncovered his chest, letting her kisses fall as her hands aroused him. Then, summoning her courage, Avis bent her mouth to the largeness of him, but to her surprise he pushed her away. "No," he commanded in a harsh whisper. "We must go back."

Perplexed, Avis hurried to repair her dishabille, staring at Matteo as he dressed, humiliated yet relieved to be spared an act she loathed to think about, much less perform.

Standing upright, Avis stared at her handsome but glowering future husband. The longer she knew him the less she knew of his nature, she conceded. André often demanded she use her mouth to give him ultimate satisfaction, and she had reasoned Matteo also would enjoy the favor.

Matteo saw Avis's expression and read her confusion, but he had no intention of explaining why he had pushed her away. He stared at the woman he would marry and realized she would put her mouth on him only as another means of barter. Poor selfish Avis, he thought, you have no way of knowing how much I crave the gesture, but I long only for Cathryn Godwyne's touch.

In her embrace, the gesture was an act of love.

Chapter 71

Matteo saw his vision of Cathryn realized as, a little pale and sometimes trembling with apparent shyness, she stood before those gathered at the Ames plantation and promised herself to Master Weylin Rodman. Her voice soft, a whisper, she vowed to be a faithful wife and accepted her husband's light kiss with eyes lowered, but when she raised her eyes, they rested on Matteo. "Never again shall I be yours," they said to him as clearly as any spoken words.

Then a celebration ensued, more lively than any that groom Weylin Rodman had seen fete a marriage. He was accustomed more to the civil formalities of the Puritan tradition, which consisted of committing a wife into the custody of her lawful husband and was rarely followed by festivities of any sort. However, Master Rodman did not consider declining his partner's hospitality.

Avis Ames fulfilled her role as hostess to the party with great skill, liking nothing better than to have a house full of guests. She watched the bride and groom—and in particular the bride. If Avis had reason to suspect her Captain Ruggero had an interest in the beautiful bride, she had no reason to doubt the new Mistress Rodman. So shy before her marriage, Mistress Godwyne had barely raised her eyes to any of the house guests but her intended, and never, that Avis could tell, to Matteo. Only when the bride danced a reel at her own wedding feast had she even come near him.

Even then Mistress Godwyne seemed afraid of him, if not of the other men attending. Stiff, she danced in Matteo's arms and looked away, though he seemed almost to stare at her, leaving Avis to think the current of electricity she imagined she felt in the air between them was only the early warning of an approaching thunderstorm.

For a moment, Avis tore her eyes away from Matteo and the

trembling bride, spying her father, who throughout the day had glowered as if he had lost a ship and its valuable cargo; when she scanned the room, she found few of the other guests as caught up with the dancers as she. The other guests drank and ate ravenously from an ample spread of food, a display for which the Ames plantation was noted. An enormous harvest table fairly sagged with filled dishes and kegs of wine and cider.

When Avis turned her gaze back to the dancers, the partners had changed; the young bride and Matteo were nowhere to be seen. But before she could inquire of the missing couple, she was interrupted.

"Mademoiselle Ames," Monsieur Chapin said as he captured Avis's eye. "You must teach me this peasant's dance."

Avis's cheeks burned. Peasant dance is what it surely was! "Of course, monsieur," Avis replied, eager to be in the arms of her lover, soon forgetting all about the disappearance of the bride and her own betrothed.

But Matteo and the bride had not wandered far, only past the lanterns on the terrace so that Matteo could claim a private kiss from Mistress Rodman. "It is an ancient custom for the bride to bestow a kiss upon the witnesses. In fact, I hear in some places it is the custom for all to watch the husband deflower the bride."

Cathryn tried to push away from Matteo's embrace. "Fortunately we are in a civilized land."

"You think so? Have you not seen the wild painted savages who abound on the frontier?"

"I do not fear savages."

"Nor do you have reason to fear me. I only want a moment to say good-bye—to wish you well."

"I do not feel the same need."

"You are cruel not to grant me one kiss. A show that you forgive me."

"Forgive you, Matteo? In truth, there is nothing to forgive. You have saved me from peril; brought me to a new continent, a place of hope and dreams. You have even been kind enough to provide me with a prosperous husband who claims he shall honor and cherish me. I humbly thank you, and I ask *you* to forgive me. Pardon me, for the grief I have caused you. And pardon me, please, for my recent angry words."

Matteo caught his breath. Cathryn's voice was soft, with only the faintest trace of sarcasm; her look innocent, the very look that haunted Matteo's deepest dreams. "Then one kiss shall not undo my charity," he said, and seized her, feeling the thrill of having her pressed against him again as she responded with the passion that always caused a hard swelling of his loins.

His hand swept down her back to clutch her curving buttocks. He pressed her fiercely against him. "Cathryn!" he choked with his emotion.

"Good-bye, Matteo. Forever, good-bye!" she whispered, and fled from Matteo's aching arms.

Chapter 72

Under the prevailing conditions in the Ames household, the union of Cathryn Godwyne and Weylin Rodman would not be consummated until the couple departed the Ames plantation, perhaps not until they reached their ultimate destination of Massachusetts Bay. The possibility quite agreed with Cathryn, who found her husband attractive and cordial but felt not the slightest physical attraction to him.

She kept her emotions in hand, though sometimes she felt she might at any moment break into uncontrollable tears. She excused her nerves on the grounds that a bride who knew next to nothing about her husband had reason to be anxious.

However, the truth lay in a different direction. Her unshed tears were for Matteo and for herself, and every day that Cathryn remained in Marysland made her more eager to leave, if not begin her duties as Weylin Rodman's wife.

Weylin treated his wife with deference, pleased with his good fortune in securing an apparent jewel for a bride. Her beauty was uncommon, yet she seemed genuinely humble and modest. He looked forward to their departure with even more eagerness than the bride, anticipating the assumption of his role of husband to his wife.

While Weylin doted on his good fortune and stared frankly at his bride, Cathryn did not waste the opportunity to observe all that went on about her. She did not miss, as Matteo and Milton Ames did, the clandestine affair of Avis and Monsieur Chapin, and she grew even more enraged with Matteo for choosing such a shallow woman over her. As far as Cathryn could see, Avis was slight and empty-headed, fond of none but herself. The idea that Matteo could not see the truth beneath Avis's fragile, perfect face made Cathryn eager to please her husband, and she began to believe that God might have granted her good fortune at last.

"Before we leave this shore, I want to gather some wild growing herbs. Perhaps you'd care to come with me?" Cathryn asked her husband.

Weylin gladly accompanied Cathryn into the wilds, carrying a second deep basket, but at the first opportunity, he took Cathryn into a determined embrace.

"We're as private in this forest bed as we would be in my house with the door bolted behind us," he responded to Cathryn's protests.

His arms began to bind her and she stiffened, but Weylin was not offended. A virgin would be unsure.

Weylin kissed Cathryn with passion, leaving her numb. She did not respond, but he seemed not to notice, his focus already narrowed by the wild stirring of his blood. He felt the delay in consummating the marriage had already been overlong. He had felt forced to stand by idly as if he were not aware Cathryn was wonderfully, essentially female; endowed by her Maker with a perfect body; as if he had not taken in her luminous dark eyes and glorious bounty of shining black hair. Well he could see that Cathryn's eyes shone whenever she saw that he regarded her.

Weylin pressed Cathryn against him, his kiss hot and unyielding upon her lips.

All senses alert, Cathryn forced herself not to pull away from the unnatural feel of Weylin's demanding body. She told herself she should be glad for his attention, grateful for his passion, which would serve to keep him loyal to her, but she had a fierce struggle with herself, revolted by his obvious arousal and her knowledge of what he wanted of her.

She saw his light brown eyes rimmed with dark lashes, his trim brown mustache above his firm lips, and imagined the texture of his light brown hair. At a distance he had pleased her, but close, Cathryn was of another mind, and when Weylin forced her to lie down with him, she focused her senses on the sweet smell of the grass beneath them. She tried to ignore the feel of him and the sudden urgency of his touch.

He raised her skirts and separated her legs with bold, possessive fingers, having no soothing word for her as he shoved his fingers inside.

Cathryn gasped at the suddenness of his approach and without having to make the effort, her body tried to repel his invasion, which only served to substantiate his knowledge of her purity. And though his body yearned for him to proceed with swiftness, he delayed, stroking her with deliberate gentleness. "Mistress, you must give way to me," he advised her as she lay desperate and tense beneath his touch, "or I shall hurt you."

Then he straddled her and tried to penetrate her tight body with his. "This first time shall be painful," he warned her.

Cathryn tried to make herself relax, to force her body to respond to her husband's acknowledgment of her discomfort, but she could not. Not even her husband belonged where her heart insisted Matteo had the only rights.

An intense struggle developed as Weylin grew ever more excited. He began to sweat, panting with his effort, and Cathryn closed her eyes, fighting her rising panic and the sudden memory of her struggles with Gerald Seymour, until Weylin prevailed against her flesh, with violence thrusting into her, making Cathryn cry out in protest. She gripped his arms as if she would push him away, trying not to shed the tears that stung her eyes.

Oblivious, Weylin did not slow his motions, and it seemed to Cathryn that he would never finish. He bore down on her dry, unwilling body with a frantic pounding rhythm until she began to ache. At last he gasped and fell against her, heaving for his breath.

Cathryn felt raped rather than loved, and it was all she could do to keep from retching as she tried to contain the sobs that threatened to burst her lungs.

As Weylin rolled off her, Cathryn pushed her skirts below her waist, too weak with emotion to get to her feet.

"It shall seem easier as time goes on," Weylin tried to reassure her as he reclined in the tall grass, making no effort to repair his clothing.

Cathryn nodded solemnly.

"I hope you shall come to accept this part of your wifely duty,

Mistress Rodman. I've no particular wish to hurt you,'' he said, and Cathryn began to cry.

Weylin felt sympathy for Cathryn and tried to comfort her. "I am truly sorry." He sighed.

Again Cathryn acknowledged his effort to be kind with a nod and prayed in time she could accept her husband as her lover.

Chapter 73

When they returned to the main house from their outing, Matteo knew that Weylin Rodman had claimed his bride from the look of wild distress in Cathryn's eyes.

Even Avis noted her expression, smiling at Cathryn's reaction to her first duty as a wife. She knew Cathryn's body would soon be less sore but admitted there was little pleasure in the chore God punished women to perform. "Try to remember it is the one means we have to manipulate a man,'' she counseled Cathryn in private. "I advise you learn to pretend gratitude. Of course, I only know this from women's gossip,'' she hastened to add.

Cathryn's face flushed in horror that the events of her outing seemed to be known to all and that her unhappiness was so apparent. She especially abhorred the thought that Matteo might know her misery, though she did not mourn the fact that he should be aware that her husband had consummated a union in which now only he had rights.

Weylin had forced himself on Cathryn a second time and Cathryn suspected he would have done so again, but it had begun to shower, requiring them to return early to the shelter of the house; the herb baskets were almost empty.

"For a while he shall be at you night and day. Men like to make sure a woman is at least well broken in,'' Avis offered.

Cathryn grit her teeth to stifle a reply and prayed for a downpour. She cursed the idea to collect herbs and feared Avis was right about Weylin's intentions. Already he insisted they must collect more herbs as soon as it stopped raining. "I don't want you to be disappointed," he said.

Cathryn watched the rain continue to pour for three more days with gratitude, and when it ceased, Cathryn and her husband boarded ship for the voyage from Marysland to Massachusetts Bay, sharing a main deck cabin with twenty other people. At night they bundled together in a narrow, cradlelike bunk.

Aroused each night as they lay close, Weylin raised Cathryn's gown and in the darkened cabin made use of her, relying on Cathryn's modesty to prevent her from making any serious protest. At first he barely penetrated her body before he finished, his excitement intensified by the boldness of his open act. But soon his confidence increased and he slowed his pace, prolonging Cathryn's misery and magnifying her fear of discovery.

Weylin's hands became familiar with Cathryn's every contour, and he took pleasure in the details of each curve and hollow, the different textures he found. His breathing ragged, he urged her to acquaint herself with him, but she declined, which Weylin accepted for the time being. He convinced himself it was proper that their public quarters should cause her to recoil. It would be different, he imagined, when they were safe in the privacy of his bed.

Throughout the voyage, which lasted more than a week, Cathryn felt nauseated and dizzy, thinking that the choppy sea, as well as the behavior of her husband and her continuing distaste for him, caused her to feel unwell. She also kept up the pretense to herself that she had chosen her course, and whenever she wavered even slightly from that approach, she forced herself to remember the pain of realizing Matteo preferred Avis over her.

Avis, she suspected, was a woman Matteo could not use with lies and pledges of eternal love. With a father to protect her honor, she was a woman Matteo would have to marry and give his name. Well, Cathryn comforted herself, Matteo quite deserved Avis Ames.

Over and over again Cathryn tried to tell herself that in losing Matteo, she did not lose much in the way of a man. Avis, she believed, would find Matteo was a man destined to break all vows.

Yet even these hateful thoughts of Matteo served to make Cathryn sad.

"I shall feel better when we are home," she promised the black kitten she had named Regina as she stroked the faithful animal's silky back. She was certain that when she at last had a home to call her own, she would forget Matteo. She believed she would grow at least fond of her husband. Then she would be happy; she would have reason to smile again. As it was, Cathryn feared she now looked more sour than even Bridget Seymour.

But Cathryn worried she would never learn not to cringe at Weylin's touch. Would she ever come to feel delirious in his arms? Or were those delicious sensations reserved only for the moments she lay with her forbidden priest?

She knew the answer, though she would deny it.

Arriving in her husband's home did nothing to allay Cathryn's revulsion for Weylin's demanding touch, and by then she knew her nausea was more than *mal di mare*; yet she continued to ignore all the signs, until her pregnancy was obvious.

There was no doubt in Cathryn's heart who the baby's father was. It was perverse, she knew, but she was grateful to be bearing Matteo's child, doubly so because he did not know. The baby would be Cathryn's, the precious treasure of her love for Matteo and his love for her, a love gone awry.

Cathryn vowed she would see Weylin own the babe as his. No child of hers would be an orphan to go through life without a mother or a father to claim, and she redoubled her efforts to love her husband.

Like most men in the Puritan community of Norman in Massachusetts Bay, Weylin Rodman had strict notions of his role as husband and of Cathryn's duties as his wife. He followed the Puritan faith but, to Cathryn's surprise, was not a selectman, one of the chosen, an actual member of the Puritan church. Reluctant to know the reason, Cathryn did not question why.

Weylin's steep-roofed, two-story wood house was situated close to the wharf a fair distance east of the other houses in the village of Norman, Massachusetts. At first glance, Cathryn thought the house, located on a rise of land, with its small, gabled windows that looked out toward the bay and its adjacent store and warehouse, had a lonely look. It was as if the three buildings huddled together at the edge of the bay, waiting to be invited into the community.

If lonely, the location of the wharf was convenient for receiving goods shipped for trade. Weylin explained proudly that he owned the Norman wharf and that this bit of enterprise had done much to insure his prosperity. "Almost daily I have an offer to purchase this site. But no one person has the capital or anything else of value to make me sell.''

As for the house, Cathryn was a little disappointed with its modest size but admitted it was more than adequate, and quite large enough considering her lack of skill and experience as a wife. The house, well built and well cared for, retained a woman's touch, though Weylin had been without a wife for almost five years before he married her.

There was only one bedchamber upstairs with a hidden storeroom attached to it, filled now with crates whose contents were unknown to Cathryn, but the moment she saw it, Cathryn envisioned a nursery.

At first Cathryn assumed Weylin Rodman to be respected among his peers in Norman, for his business flourished and she was welcomed with cordiality on the Lord's day at meeting. But she soon realized that Weylin's association with his neighbors was limited almost exclusively to commercial transactions, leaving Cathryn to develop friendships on her own.

As soon as possible, Cathryn planted a garden, using cuttings and seeds Meldon Archer sent with her from the plot in Marysland. She worried that the plants would not survive after so short a start in Matteo's ground, but as Meldon said as he swaddled and packed the dirt-covered roots in straw, "Some things a man can't kill, no matter how he tries.''

Cathryn found truth in this observation. It seemed not only to apply to her garden but to her heart, and the reverse was just as true, she found. Some things cannot be nurtured, no matter how sincere one's effort.

Try as she might, love for Weylin did not bloom in Cathryn's heart. Except for the physical demands he made on her in bed, he was indifferent to Cathryn, rarely speaking to and never confiding in her. She feared they would never share the passion and close companionship she had known and expected with Matteo. Night after night Weylin sat on the settle before the fire and stared at her, drinking mug after mug of rum. At first Cathryn played her violin, but Weylin did not encourage her and sometimes complained he did not care to hear her play the instrument.

Cathryn tried to dwell on the bright aspects of her condition as Weylin Rodman's wife. She admitted she had more than most, wanting for nothing: she had food to eat; a comfortable house; a reasonable wardrobe suited to a well-to-do Puritan merchant's wife. Naomi Sheldon, Weylin's servant before Cathryn arrived, remained to aid Cathryn in the house and garden. In fact, Naomi became Cathryn's friend—the only real friend, it seemed to Cathryn, whom she could claim in Norman.

Concealing her pregnancy until the sixth month was not especially difficult, but by then a pronounced and ever-rounding belly gave her away.

"Why have you not said something to me before?" Weylin asked when Cathryn at last informed him, telling him the baby was due in five months, not three, to conform with the date of their marriage.

"I—I can't explain," she stammered, unable to put into words her wish to keep the baby to herself for as long as possible, over and above the truth of the baby's paternity.

"I am the father, am I not?"

Cathryn looked back at Weylin in horrified surprise.

"Forgive me, mistress. Of course I am," he said before Cathryn could form even a simple reply. "I shall send for a seamstress tomorrow," Weylin added with haste, hoping to make amends for his insulting question.

"That isn't necessary," Cathryn answered in a chilled voice, still flushed from Weylin's unexpectedly perceptive query. "Naomi and I can alter what is needed."

"I insist," Weylin said with finality, preferring to clothe his expectant wife in something he provided than have her make do with garments given to her by Captain Ruggero.

Weylin had been surprised by the generous provision of clothing to a contracted bride on whom the captain should otherwise have made a handsome profit. The quality of the cloth provided her was exceptional, Cathryn's merchant husband knew.

Perhaps the captain had made a decent profit after all, for Weylin had paid dearly for Cathryn, expecting from Milton Ames's enthusiastic description that he was buying much more than a willing bride.

Weylin Rodman had purposely rejected taking a Norman woman for a wife, deciding that he did not require in his second marriage as much piety in a woman as the Norman community produced.

Forced often over the years to the public pillory and to pay large sums in fines for "states of gross drunken impiety and general Devilish behavior," Weylin reasoned he did not need a local woman for a wife, for she might be prejudiced against him; and he vowed his intention to reform this time was in earnest.

Weylin Rodman admitted he was not disappointed with Cathryn and was in fact quite delighted by her pregnancy; although devoted, his first wife—plain of face and unremarkable in form—had been accomplished in almost all her duties save the most important: all the years of their marriage, she had been barren.

God's ways were often mysterious, Weylin knew, but it seemed unjust that a woman as devoted to her husband and to the Lord as his first wife had been should fail in her most essential duty. Cathryn, on the other hand, easily the most beautiful woman Weylin Rodman had ever seen, but quite lacking in skill in almost all her duties as a wife, even needing instructions from her servant in most matters concerning the domestic arts, was fruitful at once.

To her additional credit, Weylin allowed that Cathryn had a gift for healing, but in that instance, Weylin doubted he would ever benefit from her ability; except for the regrettable but ever-increasing number of episodes of the ill effects of too much rum, Weylin was never indisposed.

Already the current Mistress Rodman had proven her worth to Weylin's Norman neighbors. An able nurse, Cathryn could cure all manner of ailments, from her arrival making herself busy in his long neglected garden growing edible and medicinal plants, soon having a thriving garden bed. While waiting for the fruits of her labor in his yard, Cathryn lost no time in scouring the surrounding terrain. She collected native herbs, gleaning what knowledge about local vegetation she could from her neighbors, sometimes approaching them with surprising boldness when she came upon them in the field; soon Weylin's house became filled with the aroma of various brews, crowded with drying foliage and blossoms of native plants.

Later Cathryn began to disappear for hours, traveling along the shoreline gathering plants from the sea and shore, often arriving home with a large basketful of sea weeds and berries; later, she would serve her husband a variety of tasty dishes. Boiled potatoes were dressed with glasswort pickles and toasted bread was enhanced with a tart beach plum preserve. Weylin regularly ate many varieties of sea greens and drank a great deal of tea made from the hips of salt spray roses.

Cathryn heard from others of some of the healing properties of the plants she collected, but she lost no time in discovering new ones. Silverweed she found was an excellent drawing plant; sweetened with honey it made a good cure for sores around the lips and mouth. A burn on Weylin's hand was quickly soothed with the milk of a commonly found thistle.

A man working to arrange hogsheads in Weylin's storehouse received a nasty cut, which Cathryn eased with the macerated leaves of another common weed, then covered and bound with a bandage of the whole leaves. Cathryn pronounced the weed "clotburr," for its use and for its prickly appendages.

Quickly, then, Cathryn's reputation spread and soon thereafter she began to be visited on occasion by neighbors asking for cures. Reminded of her mother as she willingly shared her insights and remedies, she wondered if she could be heir to her mother's talent, then shivered with the knowledge that she might be more than "gifted" with the art of healing; it angered her to realize that the appellation "Witch" was a curse, when experience with her mother had proven it worthy of praise.

Cathryn also developed a reputation for healing ailments that afflicted the Lord God's lesser beasts, an ability that became the first uttered contention between husband and wife. Often the wild beasts that Cathryn treated lingered behind when they were cured and soon she possessed a small menagerie of blackbirds, owls, squirrels, and a wolf pup, in addition to Regina, the cat Weylin had no difficulty admitting he despised. The feeling was mutual, Weylin knew, as each night he stared into the eyes of the small black beast where she lay curled on the hearth, giving her host a malevolent stare.

The wolf pup, called Rex by Cathryn, now half-grown, ate from her hand and was growing larger every day. To Weylin's amazement the animal was as docile as a pet dog, better than a sentinel in his vigilance toward his mistress. The beast intimidated Weylin, giving the husband a warning glare if his voice became the least harsh with his wife.

"I heal all creatures our Father sends my way," Cathryn responded to Weylin's objections.

"You overlook that God inflicted the creatures with their pain. By curing them, you interfere with His design that they be diseased or maimed."

"You would rather have me see them suffer?"

"It is God's will."

"How can you be certain?"

"We are told that truth by our faith." He seemed shocked by the doubt reflected in Cathryn's words.

"I sometimes believe there is error in the words men attribute to God."

"A devout woman does not dare entertain such thoughts! You shall forsake that opinion at once!" her husband commanded, outraged.

Cathryn struggled not to reply and turned away to bind the wing of a disabled bird.

It was difficult for Weylin to consider that God had not delivered the creatures to her doorstep when everywhere he turned, the eyes of her loyal patients followed him. Above the door of his house there perched an ancient owl, who Weylin swore slept night and day, perhaps opening one eye only to mark his comings and goings from the house, another evil sentry.

Weylin stared at Cathryn as she ministered to the latest fallen animal. Her silence and lack of even faint passion unnerved him. Would his wife, this beautiful, increasingly enigmatic woman, who would provide him with the child he had wanted for as long as he had been a man, ever be as devoted to him?

She was loyal, and perhaps in most things obedient, Weylin decided, and with a sigh, he reaffirmed his devout belief that a man was a simple fool to demand love where loyalty and obedience were all that was required.

Chapter 74

Weylin Rodman decided he had little patience left for Cathryn, knowing she submitted to him only out of a sense of duty. Willingness out of duty was a tolerable response from his first wife, for her extremes of piety had precluded any other attitude. But from Cathryn, whose Puritan devotion appeared to Weylin to be superficial, he felt he deserved more.

The more he observed her the firmer he grew in his conviction that she had the look of a woman meant for pleasure. Her mouth had a permanent sensuality that no change of expression erased, and her body, even with the deformity of pregnancy, continued to beckon his thoughts from all industry.

Weylin knew his rights and demanded Cathryn perform her wifely duties. She begged his indulgence while she carried his child, but the argument fell on deaf ears. He wanted his child born whole, but he wanted the use of Cathryn's body more. The fate of women in childbed being what it commonly was, Weylin conjectured he might never have another opportunity to indulge in a woman so fair, though it nettled him that when he lay with her she never gave him the pleasure of fawning over him, nor did she ever seem to crave his touch. If his touch did not excite her, Weylin at least expected Cathryn to give better than the half-penny whore in the way of feigning enjoyment. A woman kept in Cathryn's circumstance could at least act pleased, Weylin reasoned nights over many a cupful of mulled cider and rum.

Accepted and common in England, wife-beating was expressly forbidden in the Colonies; nevertheless, on certain occasions Weylin broke the law and made use of his elder whip to try to spur Cathryn's passion. His abuse of Cathryn only marred her beauty, and it failed to excite the passion he desired.

Weylin did not realize that Cathryn was ignorant of colonial law and fully expected her to renounce him at meeting. Her silence made him certain he would yet be man enough to bring Cathryn eager to his bed.

Weylin Rodman sat drinking before the fire, almost immobilized by his thoughts of Cathryn as she prepared her ritual bath. At grave risk to her health, he thought, each night before she went upstairs she would sit in the wooden tub filled to overflowing with hot water and bathe with bayberry-scented soaps she and Naomi had made.

Cathryn massaged her swollen belly with gentle rhythmic strokes, breathing deeply, eyes closed, sometimes murmuring or humming enigmatic melodies in what to Weylin seemed a foreign tongue. Deeply aroused, Weylin would allow himself to be hypnotized by Cathryn's beauty.

A primitive intuition told Weylin Cathryn had not been truthful about herself, and as her pregnancy advanced, she slipped ever further from Weylin into another world. He knew a woman could act strangely as her time drew near, but he feared Cathryn soon would abandon him entirely.

During her nightly baths, especially, she seemed to commune only with the babe. And this baby, he felt sure, did not belong to him.

Though the babe was not expected until two months hence, all was ready. A cradle sat beside the bed and piles of new infant sacks and napkins lay in wait. Weylin grew nervous over the accumulation of the infant's ensemble, fearing he and Cathryn would be challenged by an early birth to stand before the Puritan congregation to answer to the Seven Months Rule, which required a couple who bore a child prior to a seven months' anniversary to confess they had fornicated before they were lawfully wed.

Weylin scowled at the prospect. These days the selectmen of Norman seemed to watch his every move, and if the low position of the babe in Cathryn's belly were any sign, some meeting day soon he and Cathryn would be called to stand before the congregation. Weylin regretted that Norman's chosen of God had not been present to witness her bleed when he took Cathryn for the first time that day in the Marysland meadow.

He poured himself more rum, another bottle finished. If a man's wife did not willingly provide him with a little warmth, then perhaps the lady rum, on whom Weylin often called, would comply. He had even considered calling on Naomi Sheldon for comfort; he knew she, at least, would enjoy his attention. Though the unfortunate girl was an ugly wench, and Cathryn's devoted friend, it now was not beneath Weylin Rodman to seek comfort with her. Long before traveling to Marysland, Weylin had known Naomi wanted to be his bride, but only when drunk and craving a woman's body did Weylin ever consider stealing affection from the girl. Now, however, until he could alter Cathryn's mind, Weylin decided to make use of Naomi to satisfy his own substantial carnal needs.

Still, Weylin confessed, he far preferred to gaze on Cathryn Rodman. Even when she was fully dressed and heavy with child, he could hardly force himself not to stare at her. She kept him in a constant state of arousal, and when she was naked in her bath, Weylin raked her with his eyes, no moment too private for his view.

Now, his eyes traveling over Cathryn's form as she disrobed before the firelight, he sat entranced, aching with excitement as she stood in the tub and stroked her body with soap. He wished to do the same and watched as the nipples of her swollen breasts grew taut with cold before she lowered herself with care into the steaming tub.

She was bewitching; even the stupefying quantities of rum Weylin drank each night did not dull his senses enough to make him oblivious to Cathryn's allure. Time and again, the figure of her ripe body before his eyes drew him from his alcoholic daze, making him desire her. Even by force, he should enjoy her, he thought, placing his empty mug on the varnished oak floor.

She stood reaching for her towel when he approached and yanked it from her grasp. She saw the feral gleam in his rheumy eyes and tried not to shiver with her fear. "Husband," she addressed him in a calm voice, "I am cold and need the linen."

"My rights first, mistress. My rights."

"Have you forgotten your child?"

"I've been dwelling on that, mistress, and it seems to me that you are larger than you ought to be, for seven months."

"You have waited a long time to be a father. Perhaps there is more than one babe growing inside," she suggested, hoping to touch his vanity if not his sodden conscience.

Weylin appeared at first to take her words to heart, then growled, "I have rights, mistress, before the babe, or babes, whatever the case be."

Cathryn shivered. "I deny not your rights, my husband, I plead only for your unborn child, or, as you say, your children."

Weylin wavered, looking about for another bottle of rum to help him decide. Finding none in sight, he stumbled toward her. "I need you, Cathryn," he insisted, clasping her hand and pulling it to surround his straining member.

"You must be patient, as I am."

"I shall not wait!" he shouted, dragging her from the tub; pushing her to the floor.

Weighed down by her own clumsy form, Cathryn struggled uselessly as Weylin's mouth sought her tender breasts. Rough, and clumsy with drink, he savaged them, drawing blood.

Cathryn cried in pain, growing weak as her husband forced her onto her back. He pinioned her arms and shoved himself between her legs. Helpless to prevent her husband from raping her, Cathryn found it an effort to breathe. "No!" she screamed as he plunged at and pounded her, unable to bear the pressure of his weight. She feared not only for herself, but for the baby that might be crushed beneath him.

It seemed an eternity to Cathryn before Weylin rolled over and collapsed beside her; she felt his semen ooze from her as he pulled away, and then a sudden and excessive flow of warm fluid from between her legs.

Cathryn struggled, turning on her side, to be seized by a lightning shaft of pain. Terrified, she lay in a watery pool of blood and realized her hour at the well of death had come. Tears stung her eyes. She had expected pain, but not this excruciating agony.

Weylin lay in a drunken stupor beside her, unable to help her up the stairs to bed nor go for Mistress Sheldon; but Cathryn reasoned that in his frame of mind, he might even refuse to aid her, so she headed for the stairs without disturbing him.

Forced to stop every few steps to gain her balance and to deal with long moments of searing pain, Cathryn grew light-headed. She focused her thoughts on the bed that remained only a few paces away, crouching as she reached the top of the stairs, taking another searing stab of pain in a bent position. She felt drained of all energy, wondering how she would endure what lay ahead, suddenly certain she would die.

Lashes heavy with unshed tears, heavy with sorrow for her baby, Cathryn threw her head back and panted through a long wave of pain. Then, able only to crawl forward on hands and knees, she reached the bed, leaving a trail of blood behind her, and too weak to stand, depleted of energy, she sank exhausted to the floor.

Chapter 75

Between contractions, Cathryn slept through the night, at one point finding the ability to climb into her bed. Little by little, she soaked the mattress and covers with her blood, incoherent with pain when Weylin found her at dawn.

"Forgive me, mistress," he begged, but she did not hear, only barely aware that someone stood beside her. "I swear as long as I live, I shall never lay a hand on you."

"Father, Father, at last you've come," she whispered, her throat dry. "Do you have my rosary, Matteo? Where is my rosary?" she demanded. "Your baby dies within me; I feel it!" she cried, submitting to yet another searing pain. "You must forgive me, now, before I die."

Weylin was silent beside her.

"You've the power to absolve me, holy priest," Cathryn insisted, staring wildly at Weylin, growing frantic. She only halted her pleading to bear another of the now fast-paced contractions. Her face still contorted with pain, Cathryn hissed at the man beside her. "You loved me enough to fill my belly with your child, priest, but not enough to marry me, and by God, Matteo, you owe me absolution!"

She panted through the next contraction, ending with a scream. "God damn you, Matteo! Damn you for all eternity."

Weylin fled before she finished, slamming the door behind him, covering his ears to block her piercing screams as he rushed down the stairs and ran, not stopping until he reached the Sheldon house.

"My wife!" he sputtered in great alarm, completely sober but breathless as Naomi answered his pounding at her mother's door. Mistress Sheldon joined her daughter in the doorway, and quickly covering her head with a woolen shawl, she and her daughter hurried to follow the terrified husband through a shallow crust of snow.

When the three arrived, they found silence in the Rodman house, and as Weylin hesitated below, the women hurried up the stairs, fearing the worst as they followed Cathryn's track of blood.

"Thanks be to the Lord God," Mistress Sheldon muttered as she found Cathryn nuzzling her baby at her breast.

"She is perfect," Cathryn announced to the women who had rushed to her side. "A gift." She smiled.

"One paid for with your blood, if not your life," Mistress Sheldon muttered as, exhausted but sublimely happy with Matteo's precious baby, Cathryn drifted into dreamless sleep.

Chapter 76

Naomi was at Cathryn's side throughout her long recovery from Celestine's difficult birth. For a time, a fever threatened the young mother's life, but Naomi nursed her friend to health with Cathryn's own recipes for possets and infusions, using herbs and simples from the garden and the wild.

Disturbed by Cathryn's ravings the morning of the baby's birth, and overwhelmed with remorse for his brutality, Weylin tried to drown himself with ever-increasing amounts of rum. He dwelled on Cathryn's admission that the child she bore was Captain Ruggero's and only in rare moments paused to consider his wife might have been deranged by pain or driven mad by his cruel use.

Weylin heard an evil voice. "You should never have allowed her to bring the child of her detestable sin to life," it said.

Who was this woman he called his wife? he wondered. She called to a priest and for her rosary. Was she a Catholic and a Devil, or a Witch, hiding her pagan nature under a Puritan collar, deceiving and tormenting innocent men with her beguiling form, forcing godly men to succumb to her lasciviousness?

How many men had she seduced?

The country surrounding Norman must abound with Witches, Weylin reasoned, for Norman lay not far from Salem, where a score of the Devil's servants had been arrested and examined.

Weylin trembled as he realized that he might be harboring a Witch under his roof and wondered why God had not protected him.

A devil in the bottle of rum beside his hand snickered out loud, causing Weylin to shiver with abject fright.

Why had he turned to drink again? he asked himself.

Because of Cathryn Godwyne.

Because he, a mortal man, was defenseless against her lure. Because he was afraid. And because he had always suspected

Cathryn was too beautiful to be the simple woman she pretended to be.

Weylin contemplated beating Cathryn again; while beating her did nothing to stimulate her woman's passions, the act stirred him greatly, and at the same time, it would lessen her power. Beating a Witch always diminished her effect.

"We are under a Witch's influence," Weylin confided to Naomi as she served his dinner.

Naomi's eyes widened.

"You thought my wife your friend?"

"I adore her and the babe," Naomi confessed, thinking how at first she'd hated Cathryn for marrying the man she worshiped and slaved for as cook and housekeeper. "And does her babe not look just like her?" Celestine had the same raven-black hair, the same deep expressive brown eyes.

"Beware, Naomi, a Witch's child is always a Witch."

"Do you know what you say about your wife?"

"Naomi, Naomi." Weylin sighed. "You are still too much a child. Though," he confessed to her startled gaze, "in truth, I admit, I should have married you. But because of my multitude of sins I was subject to the Devil's use. He had but to flaunt her beauty before me and I was duped."

"Master Rodman, you indulge overmuch in rum," Naomi accused in a stern voice.

"Perhaps, but what I say is true. But it is also true that a man must cure his sorrows."

Naomi ladled Weylin another bowl of stew.

"These herbs have magical properties, have you not noticed?" Weylin demanded, lifting a leaf of some stewing herb with his knife.

" 'Tis only common basil," Naomi corrected.

"Nay. Your sight is affected by the Witch, too."

"My poor sight is not your wife's doing, Master Rodman."

"It pains me that you take her side against me. I have been your friend for longer than she has. How can you abuse me so?" Weylin reached for the girl's hand and stroked it, then pressed it to his cheek.

"Tell me, Naomi, if my eyes had not been blinded by the Witch, could you have looked on me with favor?"

Naomi felt weak; her yearning for Weylin Rodman had lessened only gradually as her affection for Cathryn had grown. Weylin's touch sent chills up and down Naomi's spine.

"I need you, Naomi, and I need you now. You must help me break Cathryn's evil spell."

"But how?" Naomi whispered.

Weylin stood and drew her to him. "You can love me. Counteract her evil with your pure and tender love," he answered, and kissed her, feeling her press herself against him as he without relenting pursued her long suppressed desire.

"Yes, I shall love you," she answered, her whole body burning from the heat of Weylin's kiss. Yes, Weylin, Naomi thought, I shall lie with you again, but this time I'll not allow the drink to let you forget.

Chapter 77

"I feel I'd now be in my grave without your help, Naomi," Cathryn told her young friend. "And I'm sure I don't know anyone else who would be as devoted to me as you have been," she said, handing Naomi a cup of flavorful spiced tea. "This is something special to ease your bones and improve your mind, I promise."

Grateful for Cathryn's kind words, Naomi took the cup. She had been working hard of late, toiling the long day in both the house and yard, since Cathryn was not yet fully on her feet, while Weylin was demanding many of her hours at night.

"Of all that has befallen me, I count you as one of the few blessings to come my way—and Celestine, too, of course." Cathryn turned her glance to the baby sleeping soundly at last. "I think you can begin to sleep in your own bed at home again. I'm strong enough at last. Think what a pleasure it shall be to sleep the whole night through!" Cathryn laughed. "While I've a life of interrupted sleep to look forward to."

"With six brothers and sisters, there's no sleeping through the night," Naomi reminded Cathryn, feeling quite uneasy in light of her frequent betrayal of Cathryn's trust. She did not know she was welcome to Weylin as far as Cathryn was concerned, though

Cathryn would not have tolerated her husband using the girl in the fashion he did.

"I've wondered how your mother could spare you all these weeks." Cathryn sighed.

Not willingly, Naomi knew, but she had been unable to turn away from Weylin Rodman's attention, knowing he would spurn her the moment his wife was well enough to permit him to resume his rights.

Weylin might rave about Cathryn being a Witch, but Naomi felt certain he longed to be her lover again. She saw his lustful eyes wander over Cathryn's voluptuous breasts as she nursed her child and saw how his male body responded to his wife.

Weylin might deny the babe was his and claim she was the Devil's issue, but he could not conceal his hunger for the baby's mother. "My lust is only proof that she's a Witch," Weylin pleaded when her guilt and jealousy emboldened Naomi to challenge him. "Her Witch's power overwhelms my reason. If you do not continue to help me, I shall soon become her unwilling victim again. You know she sends you away to prey on me."

But Naomi was forced to resume her normal course, coming to the Rodman house at break of day and leaving at dusk. The nights she shared with Weylin were over for good, she feared. She adored him but was torn by her deceit. Sometimes she stole to Weylin's storehouse, where they furtively made love, bearing the indignity of lying on the cold floor for a few moments in each other's arms.

Weylin pretended passion to make use of her, soaking his conscience with rum, but his mind and his performance deteriorated with every passing day.

As his consumption of alcohol increased, the number of his customers declined; his ability to reason diminished, also, and he blamed his reduced profits and his Norman neighbors' informal proscription on his Witch wife. When Mistress Sheldon forbade her daughter to serve Cathryn, Weylin began to spend even more of his time in contemplation with expensive rum.

On the occasions when her husband did not saturate his lust beyond all desire and performance, Cathryn became his target, but he feared her almost as much as he wanted her, believing his own wild inventions about her nature. Weylin saw Cathryn as the pagan goddess of forbidden carnal pleasure and himself as a wounded husband deprived of his wife's rightful devotion, converting jealousy and anger into hatred and rage. No longer trusting his own judgment, he felt the fool.

In his mind he repeated his experiences with Cathryn a hundred times and his pride suffered, knowing she had been no virgin bride, only reluctant, eager for the touch of her lover, Captain Ruggero—or perhaps Satan. Never once had Cathryn shown her lawful husband passion, but he knew the Witch was capable of returning the passion he yearned to know from her. He imagined that if he had been Matteo Ruggero, the lover she raved for even in childbed, her passion would have illuminated his nights.

But Weylin knew his rights; Cathryn was *his* wife, and no man save he was entitled to know her better than he did. He owned her body, if not her soul, and she cheated him by withholding her passion from him. Weylin swore Cathryn would give him his due.

Cathryn worried as she watched Weylin desert his trade and begin to drink more rum than he had a tolerance for, until one day, with a low warning growl, Rex sauntered to her side to stay, the wolf dog knowing his mistress was in danger.

"A man should not have to rape his wife," Weylin complained at bedtime as Cathryn suckled Celestine, turned as far from her husband's view as possible. He reeked of rum and Cathryn was overwhelmed with nausea.

"Please," she whispered. "Do not raise your voice. The baby must sleep."

"She is the only one in this house who does!"

Cathryn knew what he said was true. Weylin often lay awake in bed for hours, aroused; the rhythm of his breathing alerted her to his desire. And while he lay beside her, she lay rigid and on guard, Rex restless on the floor beside her.

"You scrub and clean until your hands are red and raw. Then you let the filthy beast inside, almost into your bed. No wonder our neighbors reject us." Then Weylin had an insight he had not had before. "Of course—a Witch would prefer a wild beast to a man."

Cathryn was outraged. "You are mad!"

"And you, wife, are a Witch!" he shouted, fleeing from their bed, startling Rex with his sudden movement.

The animal crouched and bared his teeth, and, growling, prepared to spring.

"Call him off!" Weylin begged, suddenly meek.

"No, Rex!" Cathryn commanded to Weylin's violent trembling, and, still snarling, the wolf dog lay down.

Sweating profusely, Weylin edged past Cathryn's sentry and rushed from her door into the night. He preferred, he decided, to make his bed in his storehouse to sleeping with the Witch and her incubus, and thereafter he began to live among his casks and crates. When he was visited by Naomi, he raved about his wife and her vile associates, and even Naomi thought him mad.

Chapter 78

Cathryn continued as if nothing were different. She cared for her child, the house, and the kitchen garden, and Weylin, after a fortnight of sleeping in his warehouse, returned to his bed and resumed his trade. However, as he had feared, Celestine's early arrival caused the Puritan elders to invoke the Seven Months Rule. Cathryn and Weylin were ordered on the first Lord's day that Cathryn returned to meeting after paturition to confess their sins of fornication.

Before the congregated village, Pastor Curtis reminded the baby's parents that their failure to confess would jeopardize Celestine's soul. "Your pride threatens the babe with eternal damnation," he threatened.

"We have nothing to confess," answered Weylin from his position at the back of the church.

Sitting apart from her husband among the other women, Cathryn, whose experience left her with little faith in the rightness of Puritan opinion, likewise had nothing to confess before the congregation.

Therefore, along with several dozen others condemned from the pulpit for a variety of crimes, Weylin Rodman and his wife were renounced as sinners.

"You may remain silent before the congregation, but you shall confess to me," Weylin swore as they returned home, giving Cathryn a hurried shove through the doorway before Rex could enter, leaving the large mottled-gray-and-black animal behind to rear on his hind legs and paw frantically at the door.

"It's no use, you devil, I shall have my way this time," Weylin shouted in jubilation at the dog as he threw the bolt.

Cathryn fled upstairs, only managing to put the baby into the cradle before Weylin reached her.

"I have waited a long while for this moment, Cathryn," he said, and seized her roughly, shaking her hard.

"You say I am a Witch; then you must know my power is greater than yours! You cannot harm me!"

Weylin pulled Cathryn tight against him, pinioning her arms at her sides, her face only an inch away from his. "Yes, mistress, your power is great and you have been successful. You've seduced me to your needs and I have given the Devil's daughter a name, but your power is not so great that I cannot inflict great harm to you."

Seeing in his eyes the light of madness, Cathryn pleaded, "Please, husband, I spoke in fear of your anger."

"Husband? I am not your husband."

Cathryn felt her heart pound in her throat; Weylin's grip was a crippling vise.

"A wife submits herself to her husband. Whenever do you submit yourself to me?" he demanded, tearing at her clothes, and through a violent struggle reduced her to a petticoat.

Both Cathryn and Weylin panted from exertion. Several times she had managed to escape his grip, only to be caught again, receiving angry blows each time he recaptured her.

For good measure, Weylin struck Cathryn again, making her fall dizzy to the floor, blood trickling from her nose and lip to blend with tears of pain she was unaware she shed.

Then Weylin dragged her from the floor and threw her on the bed, but she struggled to her feet only to feel a fist as he knocked her unconscious.

When she woke, she felt his hands clutching her milk-swollen breasts as he tore his way inside her, pressing her down into the bed, his motions furious.

Cathryn summoned the last of her strength to try to force Weylin from her. " 'Tis good, mistress," he panted, taking pleasure from her struggle. "Fight me, so that I might enjoy this more."

Cathryn began to scream, causing him to finish. He then fell with his full weight upon her as she sobbed for breath.

"Do not sigh for relief, Mistress Rodman. I am not finished with you yet. There are words I want to hear from you, confessions you must make before you die."

He raised himself a little, making her conscious of his rum-heavy breath. When, she wondered, had he had something to drink? Turning her head, she caught sight of a bottle and a wooden mug lying on the table by the bed.

"You lay stunned a long while. I had to ease my thirst. And by the way, your baby cried, and being a generous man, I shared a little with her. 'Tis better than mother's milk, as you can see."

The idea that Weylin had touched Celestine and had given her God only knew how much poisonous rum gave Cathryn sudden strength. She fought with Weylin for a look at her child. "Let me see my baby!" she screamed, and he yanked her with him to the cradle, holding a furious grip on her wildly disarrayed hair.

Celestine lay quite still, several rum stains soaking the blankets.

"Take a final look, Witch, and name her father to me." Weylin dragged Cathryn away from the deep-sleeping infant. When Cathryn stared at Weylin, remaining silent, he struck her. "Tell me the father's name."

"Master Weylin Rodman," she all but hissed.

"Do not lie to me. You were not chaste when I first had you. Tell me, did you spawn with Satan, Witch?"

"The child bears your name in the village book," Cathryn answered.

Weylin appeared to calm down. "You deny that you have mated with Satan?"

"Of course I deny it," Cathryn replied, desperate to control the hysteria she felt. She heard the wolf dog's bark outside below the window and reached for her discarded clothing.

"It is nightfall. Why do you not dress for bed?"

"I wish to eat," Cathryn lied, hunger from fasting on the first day of the week being the least of her concerns.

Naked, Weylin followed Cathryn to the keeping room. "I shall eat, also," he said as Cathryn stirred the fire and whipped eggs, adding Johnny-jump-up blossoms to the mixture. Weylin sat near the fire on the settle watching Cathryn, taking swallow after swallow of rum as they both listened to Rex bark and rake at the door.

Hiding her fear, Cathryn arranged thick slices of bread on a long-handled toasting ladle, placing it strategically above the fire, then stirred the pan of eggs. As if nothing untoward were taking place, she set the table and poured warm cider into two mugs.

When Weylin came to the table, Cathryn served him a hearty portion, laying a round of cheese on the table between them. He ate as if starved, the day of fasting obviously more difficult for him to bear than it was for Cathryn, who under the circumstances consumed little.

She watched as Weylin ate and drank, distressed to see him drain his mug of cider and refill it with rum. She prayed he soon would fall into a drunken stupor and forget his rage.

Cathryn saw no way to escape from her husband's mad temper. She could complain to the congregation and to the court, but where would that leave her? Weylin's own accusations would leave her no better off—and might even cause her to be hanged.

How had she ever arrived at this dreadful state? Cathryn pondered to Weylin's increasingly vacant stare. On a path littered by sin, she judged, the greatest of which was loving a man perhaps more than she loved God. And now, as punishment, she sat with a madman for a husband, a lunatic who hated, beat, and raped her, and threatened her life.

Surely Hell was an invention of man's imagination, Cathryn mused. Nothing could be worse than this existence.

Weylin finished his supper and returned to the settle, seeming not the least affected by his total nakedness. With studied patience, Cathryn sat at the table in silence, hoping her husband would fall into a heavy, rum-induced sleep. Then Celestine began to cry and, nervous, Cathryn rose slowly to go upstairs.

"Don't move, mistress," Weylin warned.

"But I must."

Weylin ignored her. "Remove your clothes," he ordered.

Terrified, Cathryn pretended not to have heard and started for the stairs.

Instantly she was seized and thrown back into the room. "Did you not hear me?" Weylin raved. "Undress! Or shall I do it for you?" he asked, ripping at the apron that covered her dress. A small knife fell from the pocket to the floor.

"What is this?" he cried, stooping to retrieve it, with fury stabbing the blade into the table, the force of his thrust causing the plates to clatter. "Did you secret a knife to plant into my heart?"

"Of course not," she lied. "I used it to slice bread and cheese."

"Another lie. But no Witch has respect for truth. You lied from the start, pretending to be a virgin, pretending to bleed."

She tried to control her voice. "I told you no lies."

"Your pardon, mistress. You are right. You did not speak of your virginity, but lay silent, pretending the part. And I, a foolish man, awed by beauty that stuns the senses, believed you innocent and pure. When you bled, I thought 'twas only right. But you invented that smear of red to fool me."

Cathryn bit her tongue to keep from saying that it was his clumsy use that had caused her to bleed. "You are mistaken," she said as evenly as possible, choking back her rage, hoping her tone of voice would calm him.

Celestine's cries grew louder.

"Please, I must attend the baby," Cathryn said, trying to pull from Weylin's grasp, milk from her full breasts staining the bodice of her dress.

Weylin eyed Cathryn's breasts beneath her bodice, immediate excitement causing his flaccid member to grow large and stiff. "No, mistress, you need attend to me," he said, reaching for her.

Cathryn fled across the small room, where Weylin caught her and twisted one of her arms behind her back. He dragged her to the kitchen hearth, grabbing several strips of leather hanging near the hearth.

"I tire of chasing after you," he said as he forced her onto the rug before the hearth. Then he stripped her of her clothes and separately bound her wrists, lashing each to the leg of the table so that her hands were forced above her head.

Terrified and exhausted, Cathryn still tried to struggle. "What do you intend to do?" she screamed.

"I am only subduing a Witch. Giving you another chance to confess your sins before you die. I've not found the rosary you clamored for, nor am I a filthy priest, but I shall hear your confession nonetheless."

Cathryn managed to plant a furious kick at Weylin's chest before he bound her feet together at the ankles.

Rubbing his ribs, Weylin stood over her to appraise his work. "It should suffice," he judged, grasping the knife that a moment earlier had fallen from Cathryn's apron and examining the blade in the fire's light. "Torture, they say, serves to loosen a witch's tongue."

"At the worst, Weylin Rodman, you have made a bad bargain

by agreeing to marry me. But I am no Witch. Would I lie here helpless like this if I had the power you say? Your accusation is madness."

"I was not mad before you came. You have made me so, hoping to render me useless so that you can wreak your evil on the world. Since you came into my life, I am on the verge of losing everything. My trade declines; my reputation. You've brought the Devil to my door."

With the soapstone from the mantel, Weylin honed the knife blade. "I shall prove your pact with Satan with this knife. I shall search your body as you have made me long to do. I shall find the Devil's Mark." He drew the warm blade against Cathryn's cold skin, making all the tiny hairs of her body stand on end.

"At last you shiver at my touch," he said, pressing the point into her flesh but not breaking the skin. "You are so perfectly made," he praised. "God would not send such a woman among men," he mused, caressing her with the knife's point. Using the flat side of the blade with care, he tilted a heavy breast and bent his mouth to taste her flesh.

"Usually you lie as though you were dead, but now you tremble, mistress. I have long suspected that you knew how. I should have known that fear would raise your passion."

He stopped to take pleasure at her breasts, moaning with intensified desire. "Mistress you have been made for passionate use. So tell me why Captain Ruggero discarded you? Did he tire of you? Or did he discover your nature? Did you try to destroy his manhood as you have tried to destroy mine?"

Cathryn almost laughed through her tears, straining at her bindings. "How can you accuse me of destroying your abilities? Did you not rape me only an hour ago? And are you not able again?" What was the use of trying to reason with a madman? Cathryn wondered, sinking back against the rug.

Cathryn heard Celestine crying in furious protest for being ignored. "Please, Weylin, what do you intend? What do you intend to do with my baby?"

"The offspring of a witch is dangerous. She should be destroyed."

Cathryn began to cry, giving up reasoning as useless, slipping very close to madness herself.

"Lie still so that I may find the Devil's Mark," he commanded, raising a candle above her, here and there tormenting her gingerly, sometimes drawing a trickle of blood. "Do you know how I shall know if I have found the Devil's kiss? I shall plunge my knife and draw no blood, and you shall feel no pain."

Cathryn began to writhe and scream, unable to stop, her piercing shrieks impelling Weylin to slap her viciously.

Outside, Rex was frantic. With blind devotion he retreated several yards from the house, then broke into a lightning-fast run and leapt through the front window, the framed panes of leaded glass breaking free. The crash was heard too late by Weylin; as he stabbed blindly at Cathryn his wrist was seized in the dog's great jaws and torn open, the wound spurting bright shafts of blood.

The ensuing tumble caused Weylin to drop the knife and forced Rex to loose his grip; with his remaining good hand, Weylin grabbed the iron poker from the hearth, but even armed he was no match for the furious animal, whose ferocious growl and facial grimace made Weylin fear for his life.

Man and dog circled each other with Cathryn lying immobilized and helpless in between. "Your master sends a devil to your defense," Weylin panted as, snarling, the dog leapt on him again, this time going for his throat, the viselike jaw propelling his teeth deep into Weylin's soft, unguarded flesh.

There was a loud crash as Weylin and Rex upset the settle and an unheard snap as Weylin collapsed backward, limp and lifeless.

From her position Cathryn could not see beyond the overturned settle, but she presumed, when Rex came to her side to comfort her, that Weylin lay dead. Cathryn sobbed in both horror and relief, her tears licked from her face by the adoring half wolf, half dog.

Cathryn's tears at last subsided and Rex stared at his mistress, waiting for her to rise. He gnawed at Cathryn's bindings, trying to set her free, but she was bound and tethered so tightly it was impossible.

Then Celestine, who had been silent for a time, began to squall again, making Cathryn cry. "Oh, God, this is far worse torture than Weylin meted out," she sobbed to Rex, who turned his head and cocked his ears and tried to understand.

Whimpering, Rex rushed up the stairs and for a time, in agitation, traveled back and forth from cradle to mother in obvious distress. He licked at Celestine, whose resulting fury forced him to back off. Throughout the night, Cathryn listened to her child's despair, her baby's cries growing weaker and less frequent as the night wore on.

The fire died to embers, the candle burned down, and in the stillness and the eerie light, Cathryn's hold on sanity began to ebb away.

Chapter 79

Cathryn's vision filled with dreams of pleasure and of pain; she did not know the real from the imaginary. One moment she was lying in a grassy glen enfolded in the arms of a man who loved her and made the world seem glorious; the next she was lying with a husband who threatened her life. She felt fevered and she felt cold. Masked, she danced in the whirling Piazza San Marco. The Devil had her on his arm. She felt his heated breath, but it was sweet, not fetid: inviting.

Tearing off the mask, the Devil revealed himself to be Matteo, a loving, mortal man. He filled her with his love and, with his kisses, healed wide gaping wounds not even her mother could heal.

Vanya watched and granted her approval as he carried her away to sail a cloudless sky, fire trailing in a golden ship's wake. Then, in a storm of frightening violence, the vessel began to sink. To save her, he said, Matteo threw her overboard, but she fell down and down to an atmosphere in which she could not breathe. She continued to fall until she felt arms holding her at last, and she was dragged to shore.

But her rescuers were angry. They scourged her and they whipped her. They pulled her hair and tore her flesh. They drowned her baby.

Cathryn's screams brought her from her nightmare. She panted and she cried, twisting at her tethers, until her tears subsided and she waited in silence for her child's protests. "Celestine, Celestine," she wailed, terrified of the baby's silence.

Rex no longer lay beside her. Even he had deserted her. She

had been saved from her husband for the torment of a prolonged and tortured death.

At least with Weylin . . . But Cathryn did not care to finish her thoughts, her last memory of his murderous, frenzied eyes making her tremble more.

The hour seemed right, and Cathryn searched her soul. Had Weylin Rodman been a good man once? Had she only used him to escape her misery and shame, and caused him to go mad at her indifference? Had she destroyed him? Or had Weylin used her, also, knowing no one save a woman ignorant of him would agree to marry him? Weylin had damned Cathryn, saying she brought him nothing but bad luck. But from all that Cathryn could see, Weylin had been a hopeless sinner long before she arrived in Norman.

Against the tenets of his religion, Weylin prospered among his neighbors because he had foresight. He saw to it that he had the means and the goods that his neighbors needed to survive in this godforsaken New England. While Puritans applauded success, claiming success showed God's favor on a man, it seemed to Cathryn that Weylin went about obtaining his success in a way that quite abused the doctrine. From the way his fellows held him in contempt, Cathryn felt his Norman neighbors agreed.

Weylin owned the only wharf in the village of Norman, monopolizing the only safe channel entry where ships could dock. Through Milton Ames he had the most desired goods to trade and bought or bartered from his neighbors whatever they had to trade at rates that were not quite the market, making large profits on their beautifully wrought furniture in particular. He profited at their expense; they in turn courted him only to use him, censuring him at every turn.

For a moment, Cathryn lay absorbed by her aching cold and pain, but her sorrow was not strictly physical as she contemplated what awaited her. She could, she knew, lie for days until someone discovered her—perhaps even a week, when her and Weylin's absence from meeting would require investigation. By then, surely, she and Celestine would be dead, Cathryn realized, too exhausted for tears.

Cathryn thought how far she had traveled from sunny Venice. Her music had glorified God and made her feel sublime, but Venice now seemed a distant dream, a lifetime away. There she had been innocent, believing that God's love and hers for Him protected her. Yet the moment she was forced to live the life He set before her, Cathryn had seemed to lose His favor, beset at every turn with misery and by obstacles she had to face alone.

Vanya told her that her Catholic view of God made the world seem crueler than it was, amending her appraisal by saying the Puritans had no better opinions. God was love, her mother said. God gave man the world. The pain and horror on earth was not His punishment, nor necessarily man's due, but often was only the result of his ignorance and his folly, man's mistaken belief that he is better than the universe in which he lives.

Cathryn knew only that most of what she had learned from Catholics and Protestants alike sounded more of hatred and vengeance, than of the divine. Their God was wrathful and cruel, punishing man for His mistake of making man so stupid as to choose evil over good, something Cathryn failed to understand. If God was love, why did reverence for Him seem to foster so much hate?

If God intended to remain a mystery, then He was, and the men Cathryn had met who claimed to have the answers did not.

Cathryn closed her eyes and drifted again, prepared to die.

No world ahead could be worse than the one she was about to leave behind, she reasoned. True Hell was to believe that Matteo felt the same kind of love for her she felt for him, then learn she was mistaken.

She should despise Matteo, Cathryn reasoned, at the very least for delivering her into the hands of her assassin, her husband, a man who would murder Matteo's child. Of course Matteo did not know she carried his child, yet Cathryn knew it would not have made a difference. A man like Captain Ruggero would not weep over his bastard children. Such offspring were the worries of the women who seduced and corrupted saintly men.

Reason aside, Cathryn searched her heart and found that beneath the layers of pain lay abiding love. "I fear I love you still, Matteo," she confessed, and fell into a troubled sleep.

Her head filled with soft sounds and sensations: of mewing kittens and purring cats; barking dogs; soft fur and cold, inquiring wet noses against her skin. She woke with a start to discover Regina curled next to her skin and Rex nudging her cheek. Then she heard a frantic human voice.

"I cannot get in the door."

Cathryn recognized Naomi's voice. "Naomi!"

"Mistress, is that you?"

"Yes!" she answered, louder this time.

"How do I get in?"

"Through the window."

It seemed to Cathryn she waited a long while before Naomi stood above her.

"Mistress Cathryn, what has happened?" she demanded as her eyes tried to take in the scene. She did not want to believe what she saw: Cathryn lying naked and bound, a knife beside her. At first she did not see Weylin Rodman's body behind the settle. She raised the knife that had been Weylin's weapon and stared at it.

"Weylin has tried to kill me."

Naomi gasped. "No. I don't believe you!"

"Why would I lie, Naomi?"

The girl then noticed a dark pool of blood that had oozed from beneath the overturned settle.

"No, don't," Cathryn warned as Naomi moved toward Weylin.

"You have killed him!" Naomi screamed, and began to weep, forced to turn away from the body of her lover. She sobbed out of control for several minutes as Cathryn tried to gather strength.

"Please, Naomi, you must understand . . ."

"I do." She gulped for air. "Master Rodman told me all about you. How you were—you are a Witch!" she said, and shrank from her friend. "You're a Witch! And you've killed the man I love."

Cathryn forced herself to remain calm. "What are you saying, Naomi?"

"If it hadn't been for you, your husband would have married me."

"My husband has lied and deceived you, Naomi. He could have married you before he married me."

Naomi did not care to be reminded of the truth. "No!" she screamed. "I shall not listen. He told me you are a Witch. You forced him to marry you."

Cathryn could not bear to listen. "I must go to Celestine. Please untie me," she begged. "If it weren't for Rex, I should have died from my husband's knife. If he hadn't fetched you and you had not arrived, I should have soon been dead, also."

"He told me the wolf was a demon to do your bidding."

"I fear my husband was completely mad." Cathryn sighed. "Now, please, I beg you, untie me."

"No!"

"Why not?"

"You are a witch. You can free yourself."

"Dear God, Naomi!" Cathryn gasped. "Please be reasonable. I shall lie here until you free me, and my baby . . . For the sake of Celestine—she's gone all night without being fed. Please!"

Naomi was torn, but finally, remembering Cathryn's many gestures of friendship and prompted by her affection for Cathryn's baby, cut Cathryn's bonds.

Cathryn choked back tears of relief and tried to rub some life into her hands and arms, struggling to her feet. She first moved to Weylin's body, retching violently at the sight of Weylin's head twisted on his neck, his throat torn open.

"Everything comes clear," Naomi said behind her back, trembling as she backed away toward the door.

Slowly Cathryn went to the stairs, turning in time to see her friend Naomi flee.

"No, Naomi!" Cathryn shouted after her. "You do not even begin to know the truth!"

Chapter 80

"Celestine, my precious baby," Cathryn cried, lifting her infant anxiously to her breast. She swaddled the wet baby in clean flannel and wrapped her in a fleecy blanket. At first Celestine was listless, uninterested in the nipple that dripped milk, but Cathryn rocked and crooned, caressing the infant's cheek until, reflexively, Celestine began to nurse. She suckled with vigor for several minutes then, and only protested when Cathryn stopped her and offered the other breast.

Physically exhausted and emotionally spent, Cathryn had summoned the strength to climb the stairs from some unknown source of energy. Terrified, she realized Naomi might this very moment be headed to the constable to accuse her of Weylin's murder by means of Witchcraft. She considered fleeing but wondered where she would go should she even be able to find energy to stumble downstairs. A hangman's noose loomed in Cathryn's imagination.

Surely Naomi would recover her senses, Cathryn reasoned, trying to ease her panic. She could understand the girl's hysteria at finding the man she loved dead but tried to reassure herself Naomi would quickly come to trust her friend's statement that Weylin had tried to kill his wife.

Desperately cold, Cathryn moved beneath the covers of the bed and nestled with her child. Not many moments before this, Cathryn had given up all hope of ever again enjoying the comfort and pleasure of her precious baby at her breast, and soon, despite her real fears, mother and baby fell to sleep in a nest of warmth and love, resting at peace until Cathryn wakened to a pounding at the bedchamber door.

"Mistress Rodman, are you there?"

Disoriented, Cathryn at first did not reply.

When she heard her name called again, she demanded, "Who is it?" wondering who would dare to enter her house uninvited and climb the stairs.

"Constable Yarrow," the man replied.

The name registered with Cathryn. Constable Yarrow would have come to investigate Weylin's death. Cathryn hesitated. "You must allow me to dress."

"I shall wait downstairs."

With haste Cathryn bathed and dressed, then left the baby sleeping in the cradle and went downstairs to find Constable Yarrow and Pastor Curtis waiting for her.

Constable Yarrow seemed unusually nervous. "Are you all right, mistress?" he asked.

Cathryn nodded.

"Naomi Sheldon has come to us and made a serious charge against you. She claims you are responsible for your husband's death."

Cathryn shook her head in dismay. "Did she not tell you that she found me bound, unable to move? Did she tell you that the only reason she found me is that my faithful dog summoned her? If he had not, I should still be lying bound."

Constable Yarrow looked to Pastor Curtis. "The younger Mistress Sheldon accuses you of Witchcraft, mistress, and claims the dog you mention is your incubus." The minister pointed to Regina, who stared and swished her tail. "Is the cat not another of your familiars?"

Cathryn felt weak. "The facts are that my husband, whom

you know to drink often to the point of drunkenness, has for weeks been drinking more heavily than usual. I've been afraid of him and have kept my dog at my side for protection, but yesterday, after meeting, my husband locked the animal out and in a mad drunken rage bound and tried to kill me.''

The constable and the pastor looked at each other.

"But by a miracle of strength and cunning, Rex broke into the house and rescued me. He sprang at my husband even as Weylin wielded the knife. Only the dog's intervention saved my life and in the struggle, Weylin died.''

"Do you give your oath that what you declare is the truth?'' inquired the pastor.

"Of course!''

"Naomi Sheldon's report varies in considerable degree.''

"Our servant at one time, Naomi blames me because she foolishly believes my husband loved her.''

"Your husband told her you are a Witch.''

Cathryn did not reply.

"He accused you of seducing him into marriage to acquire his property, thereby to gain control over the citizens of Norman, to make them join you in your craft.''

"My marriage was arranged by contract.''

"That proves nothing in your favor. Furthermore, your husband did have a great deal of influence over the citizens of the village. We were quite subject to him in matters of trade.''

"Of that I'm not to blame.''

"Tell me, mistress, why does the blood of your husband not congeal?'' Pastor Curtis inquired. "Why is his body still supple when, with a natural death, a body should be stiffened by now?''

"I've not touched my husband's body.''

"You may accept my word for his condition, but you must answer my question as to why he remains supple.''

"I can't answer your question.''

Pastor Curtis and the constable looked at one another in silence. A Witch would have the power to keep the victim's blood in a state that her demons could drink and thereby take sustenance. "Is the animal you call Rex not a wolf?''

"Part.''

"You admit it?''

"Yes.''

"Mistress Rodman, the pastor and I have come to investigate a complaint of Witchcraft which has been made against you by

Naomi Sheldon, and being in agreement with that charge, as magistrates of the court, we do hereby arrest you on the charge of being a Witch. You shall come with us now for further examination.''

Thunderstruck, Cathryn only stared.

"Did you not hear the charge?"

Cathryn nodded. "I heard, but I do not care to believe." Cathryn sat down. "I must have something to eat. I have not eaten all day."

"You shall be fed in jail."

Exhausted, Cathryn forced herself to stand. "I must fetch my child.''

Cathryn wearily climbed the stairs and prepared herself and Celestine for a journey from which she had grave doubts she would ever return. She knew several women accused of Witchcraft had already been hanged in Salem, and now she wondered what actual crimes had sent them to the gallows. The condemned of Salem had been accused also by young neighbor girls. What had the motives been for those sentenced to death? Jealousy? Greed? Lust?

Cathryn knew a charge of Witchcraft had seen thousands of men and, in particular, women tortured to death or burned or hanged. Now she had a very personal reason to question the practice and, in light of all that had happened to her, to question the widely held belief, to which she also once subscribed, that God would protect the innocent.

Cathryn could understand the origin of Naomi's accusation. A girl in love could be driven to do many foolish things, and trusting a lover easily could be one of her mistakes. However, Naomi's accusation of Witchcraft hit Cathryn especially hard.

She had not suspected her friend had betrayed her with her husband, yet found it more difficult to believe that Naomi could believe her a Witch.

Cathryn knew everyone believed in Witches. Witches alone were responsible for all unexplained deaths involving babies; they caused destruction, pestilence, and famine. In short, all the evil happenings of the world could be laid to Witches, who did the Devil's work. They sought converts to Satan among men, the soul a constant battleground. Cathryn wondered just what evil Naomi had witnessed her commit.

When Cathryn went downstairs, the body of her husband lay

before the hearth, a blanket covering his nakedness. Cathryn turned her head away.

"You turn away, mistress. Are you sorry for your deed?"

"I have committed no crime."

"We think otherwise," Constable Yarrow said, and began to read the warrant for Cathryn's arrest. "There being complaint this day made before the Magistrates of Norman Village by Naomi Sheldon against Cathryn Rodman, the wife of Weylin Rodman, recently murdered, for high suspicion of sundry acts of Witchcraft done or committed in the village of Norman or in the Colony of Massachusetts, whereby great hurt and damage hath been done or intended, therefore craved justice. You are therefore in Their Majesties' names hereby required to apprehend and bring before us Cathryn Rodman, wife of Weylin Rodman, tomorrow about ten of the clock in the forenoon at the house of Harley Johnson in Norman Village in order to perform examination relating to the premise above said and hereof you are not to fail.

"Signed, Phillip Yarrow, William Curtis, assistants to George Merritt, marshal, and any or all ye constables in Norman or any other town."

Cathryn appeared calm. "You read my death warrant."

"No, mistress, there shall yet be an examination and trial."

"You can be sure it shall be a waste of time."

Constable Yarrow ignored Cathryn. "You are further advised that all property that you might claim as your husband's widow is hereby confiscated by the authorities."

At once Cathryn better understood her circumstances. Naomi only proved a convenient instrument for the citizens of the village of Norman to seize Weylin's long coveted property. "With my conviction for Witchcraft, the village shall possess what it has wanted all along—the wharf and the warehouse, along with all my husband's other assets. Eventually I should have been accused of Witchcraft with or without Naomi Sheldon's accusation."

"You rave, mistress."

"I rave, but you needn't fear. Alone, my voice is hardly loud enough to stop you," Cathryn replied, all at once very weary of the world. "Goodmen, I divine your sin is greater than mine could ever be and say I am totally innocent of any wrong. I confess to you I am many things, but with God as my judge, I am not a witch."

Chapter 81

Cathryn stared at the shackles that secured her feet. Her hands
were not bound so that she might care for the infant, and a small
fire was kept burning to keep her and the baby from freezing.

Cathryn shivered beneath a wool shawl wrapped tightly about
her shoulders, the ends wound about Celestine, who lay snugly
at her breast. Because of Celestine, Cathryn was not detained in
the village jail but housed in an outbuilding belonging to Constable Yarrow. No human jailer was deemed necessary, for the
constable posted a large, ill-tempered dog as sentry, but Cathryn
was not spared any of the other discomforts of jail. The food was
meager and often cold, and the accommodations were just short
of filthy, though she was allowed sufficient water to cleanse
herself and the baby.

She bore her solitude as best she could, waiting for her trial,
certain the magistrates and grand jurors had their minds already
made up.

The day following her arrest, her case was reexamined and
Cathryn told her story of Weylin's death, this time sparing none
of the details. Then Pastor Curtis repeated Naomi's statement,
adding that the young woman had been taken ill immediately
upon reciting her tale. "She is clearly possessed," he claimed,
describing "torment by a Witch taking Mistress Rodman's form."

In the presence of the magistrate's wives, Cathryn was stripped
and her body searched for the Devil's Mark; their examination
was an exceptional ordeal with Weylin's terrifying search of her
body all too fresh in her mind. The examiners found no Witch's
teats from which she could suckle demons, but the Devil's kiss,
his brand, in the shape of a small butterfly, was found beneath
one of Cathryn's breasts. The women and the men looked from
one to another, convinced of Cathryn's guilt, and quickly returned her to her private prison.

Each day that passed allowed more evidence against Cathryn

to collect; reports of her evil deeds were shocking and numerous. Despite the royal command in such matters, spectral evidence would be used against her.

Her husband was buried and the whole village turned out to mourn him as if he had been a righteous and admired man. Only his wife, who sat chained in her cell, did not attend.

Rex had disappeared, and on the order that he be destroyed, rumor flew that Cathryn had sent him back to Hell because his services were no longer required in Norman. Everyone knew only witches could command wolves. His dog blood was completely forgotten.

Cathryn was joyful that some sense had directed Rex to flee, knowing the fact that he had saved her life would never be heard. The animal would forever be a man-killer in the villagers' eyes. "Keep running," Cathryn prayed.

But Regina stayed near, often sitting on the ledge outside the window of Cathryn's jail, meowing to get in.

"Get rid of your familiar," ordered Constable Yarrow.

"She is not my familiar, sir, but my pet. And she is making herself fat on your rats," Cathryn snapped.

The constable made no reply, his mind firmly set that his prisoner was indeed a Witch.

How distorted vision could be, Cathryn mused. Her neighbors' dislike of Weylin had passed on to her. In addition, the villagers stood quite ready to profit from a lie told by a young woman struggling with jealousy and guilt for her own sins.

How easy to place blame for one's stupidity on demons, to rely on men's fears and guilt to produce a chorus of believers in witchcraft. Blame for evil actions and unhappy circumstances then could be placed upon the Devil. No need to look further for an explanation of wrong or evil doings or unknown events.

No one seemed to be immune to searching for someone or something to blame for the tragedies and sins of life. Profane and holy men alike search the darkness of their souls for Witches to share the burden of their sins and sorrows.

But when one conjures up the Devil, the Devil must have his due. When it comes time to pay for sins, the punishment is easier to bear with company at the bar. One need only renounce a witch and thereby not face the gallows alone.

Cathryn saw no way to save herself. If the most learned and lucid men of Norman convinced themselves of her guilt on little more than Naomi's word, then she had little reason to assume the grand jurors would be more enlightened.

Cathryn inhaled deeply and prayed for courage for the coming ordeal. In her mind she traveled back to England and her mother, seeking the peace of the shaded glen. The images refreshed her, then changed. She thought of the Sabbat; of the many hours she had worked beside her mother, the decoctions they had brewed. Was this association, as well as her kinship, sufficient proof that she was indeed a witch?

Had her use of henbane to disable Gerald and her acceptance of the Witch's cup to enjoy her lover been Witchcraft? Cathryn feared the world would judge her a witch. Perhaps God agreed. Had she called down His wrath upon her for associating with a Witch, though that Witch was her own mother? God had not seen fit to save her from Gerald. Perhaps He did not wish to save her now. He had never approved of the seduction of priests by any means and certainly not by the use of potions brewed by a confessed Witch.

Part of Cathryn felt resigned to a conviction for witchcraft, for without love, life was little more than misery, and for Cathryn, a life without Matteo was devoid of love. She confessed this to herself in spite of lingering anger and pain, but she also recognized that her sentiment for Celestine came first.

As she sat waiting for trial, Cathryn worried night and day about her baby. Someone would surely take the orphaned baby in, but in the climate of Norman, how would she fare? Cathryn remembered the Seymour home and the grim spirits of the children raised under cold Puritan stares. What future was there for the daughter of a convicted Witch?

Cathryn strained at her shackles.

Perhaps if Matteo knew of his child, he would provide for her. He would take her to his home in Marysland and raise her in the room he had so carefully prepared for her mother.

Cathryn smiled as she imagined Matteo beside his daughter. Has God given Matteo's child an ear for music? Cathryn could see him patiently showing Celestine how to hold a violin. He would teach her the music that made his very blood flow, and as her mother had, she would look up at him with deep, adoring eyes, convinced his every word came from God Himself.

Cathryn shook her head, hoping to dispel her dreams. Her hair was loose; stray curls fell against her shoulders. How Celestine's father had loved the long raven-colored hair, she remembered; she could see his smile and his deep eyes that told her he adored her.

With a start, Cathryn came back to the present, where a nightmare had come to life for her. She remembered that when she was tormented by Gerald Seymour, she had dreamed of insane accusations being made against her. Now that very fate had come to pass, she realized as she stared at the frayed wrists of a once beautiful heather-colored gown.

Suddenly the door opened and Constable Yarrow walked in. "Mistress Rodman, the grand jury awaits you," he said, and because of her shackles, he gave her his arm to assist her the several yards from his property to the meeting house.

As it turned out, the whole of Norman had come to see Mistress Cathryn Rodman's trial. In the meeting house, she stood behind a chair used in place of the defendant's dock and placed her baby in its seat, which faced away from her; she would be required to stand throughout the proceedings.

Behind a broad table before her sat Magistrates Robert Cory and Charles Tyler, and to the left eight jurors watched her. A more sober set of men could not be found; all were known to be stern judges of other people's conduct.

Cathryn turned her head to see who had turned out to watch the proceedings and found numerous strangers among the familiar faces. "They come from far and wide," she muttered to Constable Yarrow, who because she was deemed a danger to onlookers would continue to stand beside her throughout the trial. But Cathryn's sweeping gaze of the courtroom halted midway around the room and her voice died within her throat; near Naomi Sheldon and others who would testify against her, she spied Captain Matteo Ruggero. Cathryn gripped the back of the chair before her to keep her balance.

"What bothers you, mistress?" demanded the constable, growing alarmed by Cathryn's suddenly ashen face.

She could make no audible reply. And as the proceedings against Mistress Cathryn Rodman, accused of Witchcraft, began, Cathryn stared and heard nothing but the roaring of her blood, the crashing of her heartbeat.

Chapter 82

Captain Matteo Francesco Ruggero's heart began to pound when Cathryn entered the court. He watched her every move, scrutinizing her every gesture and expression. His heart sank to see the exhaustion that placed shadows beneath her eyes and made the soft lips of her sweet full mouth tight with determination to weather the coming ordeal.

Cathryn seemed gaunt to him, though he judged from the size of the infant she cradled so possessively that she had recently given birth. Her body lacked the fullness it was usual for a new mother to display and his heart began to ache.

Matteo tried to listen to the start of the proceedings, to the pastor's lengthy prayer begging the Lord God's guidance to bestow His merciless wisdom on the appointed jurors, but he did not bow his head in reverence. Instead he felt compelled to fix his gaze on Cathryn, who, seeing him, stared as though she could not trust her eyes.

Shield and protect her, he begged God directly in silence while Cathryn continued to stare.

If she was terrified, Matteo did not see the emotion in her expression, and he wondered if she could identify his terror from the careful set of his own features. He had promised himself he would sit impartial and placid throughout the hearing. He would trust heaven to protect the innocent, but he did not smile, for he feared the worst.

In moments of extreme distress, even he had labeled her a Witch, and his own passionate cries of "*strega bella*" rang in his ears. He knew her beauty alone served to condemn her; the modest dress she wore did little to lessen her extraordinary appeal. Even her weariness exaggerated her beauty, making her seem more ethereal than real. The abundance of raven curls cascading well below her waist did nothing to dispel the illusion that with a sweep of her lashes she could put any mortal man into a trance.

Cathryn was forced to turn her gaze away from him to answer the magistrates' questions, but Matteo still stared. She stood erect and still, her posture alert, the lift of her chin defiant to his knowing eyes. In answering the introductory queries of her judges, her voice was firm, and hearing her tone, Matteo could not prevent a small smile from spreading across his face. How often he had heard a proud young girl answer his challenges in that very tone! Now that time they had spent together in Venice as student and mentor seemed very long ago.

Magistrate Robert Cory cleared his throat, then began the formal inquisition. "You have given your sacred oath to tell the truth. How do you answer the charge before this court that you are a Witch, and have on many occasions practiced Witchcraft, in particular, in the death of your husband, Master Weylin Rodman?"

"I deny all charges with God as my witness. I neither murdered my husband, nor am I a Witch."

"You are advised that it is your burden to prove your innocence to the court."

Cathryn nodded but wondered how it would be possible to do so when it was so obvious the court already sat convinced of her guilt.

Fearing for her life, Matteo bowed his head.

The second judge, Magistrate Charles Tyler, eyed Cathryn sternly. "How long have you been a Witch?" he demanded.

"I am not a Witch."

"Why did you become a Witch?"

"I am not a Witch."

"What oath were you forced to give to your master?"

"I have made no oaths."

"What Witch name did your master give you?"

"I have no name but Cathryn Rodman, nor do I have a master."

"Who are the persons on whom you have cast spells, including children?"

Cathryn's face grew red with irritation. "I have never cast a spell on anyone."

"Who are your accomplices?"

"I have no accomplices."

The magistrate produced Cathryn's much used herb book with notes made at Vanya's knee. "What is this, Mistress Rodman?"

"It is a receipt and garden book."

"Does it not contain receipts for Witchcraft?"

"No."

"Then what of this notation: 'receipts of magic'?"

"Magic is not Witchcraft. Do you not use mistletoe to keep Witches away?"

Magistrate Tyler made no reply but yielded the floor to Magistrate Cory. "Naomi Sheldon of Norman Village, the principal claimant in this case, please stand."

Naomi stood slowly and faced the judges and grand jury.

"Please come before the court," Judge Cory instructed, signaling for Naomi to stand beside the jurors and face Cathryn.

She swore to tell the truth.

"Do you identify the woman at the dock as Mistress Cathryn Rodman, your former mistress, and wife of Weylin Rodman, now deceased?"

"Yes," Naomi replied, only glancing in Cathryn's direction before she turned and pressed her gaze upon the magistrate.

"Repeat your accusation for the jury."

As she did Cathryn only half listened, distracted by the heat of Matteo's gaze, which recalled for her the many mornings she had spent in the Fabiani chapel enduring his burning observation. She felt her face stain with color and her body begin to warm with familiar sensations.

How can I still be drawn to him? she wondered. I should hate him. If it had not been for his eagerness to be rid of me, I might not be on trial for my life. He as much as sold me to Weylin Rodman.

What could be the purpose of his appearance? she wondered as she tried to focus on Naomi's testimony. Then it struck her, and, horrified, she could not help but turn away from Naomi and stare at the man who was once her lover. His purpose, along with many others in the courtroom, was to testify against her, she realized.

He shall stand to vilify me, she thought. To confess. To expurgate his soul.

Cathryn gasped with her horror that Matteo would betray her, drawing the attention of the crowd from Naomi to herself. Immediately she stifled the sound and forced her attention back to Naomi. The spectators followed suit.

"How long did you know Master Rodman before his death?"

"Since I was born. He was a friend and our closest neighbor."

"Did you ever know him to lie?"

"No, sir. I trusted everything he told me."

"And what did he tell you about his wife?"

"Well, he warned me that she was a Witch," Naomi said, and looked at Cathryn. "He said not to trust her. He said she forced him to marry her. He said otherwise he would have married me."

"Do you believe that is so?"

"Yes, sir," Naomi answered, wiping away tears from her eyes with the corner of her shawl. "He said the baby Celestine was not his, but the Devil's seed."

As a gasp rose from the crowd, Cathryn grew alarmed and again all color drained from her face.

Matteo's gaze fell to the infant, who lay wiggling quietly upon the large seat of the heavy oak chair, and all at once he knew that Weylin Rodman had been right: he was not the baby's father.

When the room quieted, the questioning resumed.

"Go on, mistress. What else did Master Rodman say?"

"He told me that since she came to him, his trade declined and his drinking of rum increased—a sure sign of her Witchery. He told me a witch likes nothing better than to harm a man and interfere with his affairs."

The magistrate nodded his agreement with the deceased's observation.

"He said Mistress Rodman refused to let him confess fornicating with her before their marriage, because she would not have her baby baptized. She did not want Celestine's soul saved for God's fold but dedicated to Satan."

The accusation brought the court to an uproar.

"Besides the dog, Rex, does Mistress Weylin have other familiars?"

"Many. The animals—her familiars—come and go, but the wolf and the cat she brought with her when she married Weylin are the most important."

"Is that the same black cat that daily visits her in Constable Yarrow's custody?"

"My mistress calls the cat Regina and she often sent her on errands. The cat would be gone for days and whenever she returned, my mistress fed her extra."

"As a reward?"

Naomi nodded. "And the other is not a dog but a wolf that only Mistress Rodman can control. Weylin said he was afraid of Rex."

"Naomi, why do you lie?" Cathryn interrupted, furious at the implication of her statements, for only witches had control over wolves. "You were with me when I rescued the pup. Don't you remember we found the dog mother dead in a trap and Rex half-starved, waiting loyally beside her? Rex is but part wolf."

"Do not interrupt the witness," warned Judge Cory. "You shall have your turn to speak."

Magistrate Cory turned back to the witness and urged her to continue, but Naomi began screaming before he could continue his questions.

"Stop her. Help me, please!" Naomi cried, contorting her body as if she were wrenched and pushed about. "She pinches me and strikes me with her pins. Ooow! Oh!"

"Cease tormenting the witness!" demanded Magistrate Cory.

"But as you see, I do nothing," Cathryn protested, her eyes wide.

Naomi only screamed louder, then fell to the floor. "Can no one else see her? Help me! Help me! Make her stop!"

"The witness has been afflicted with these torments since she made her accusation," Magistrate Tyler explained to the jurors.

"She says if I do not say that I am lying, she shall kill me, too," Naomi wailed, banging her head upon the floor. "Oh!! Now she threatens me with a knife!" she screamed.

The crowd stirred and Naomi's mother cried to Cathryn, "Mistress, please, do not torture my child!"

Cathryn bent to lift her own child, who also began to scream as a result of the commotion.

All of a sudden, Naomi was still.

Constable Yarrow went to her side and helped her to her feet.

"Are you able to continue?" Magistrate Tyler queried.

"Yes, sir," Naomi replied in a very soft voice, visibly shaken.

"You were, I believe, informing us about the wolf."

"Weylin, that is, Master Rodman said the wolf was his wife's incubus, and that she called for him often. He said she preferred the animal to him, changing him to be part man so they could better . . . fornicate."

"That is the usual role of incubi," added Robert Cory. "Tell us now of your understanding of how Master Rodman met his death."

Cathryn took a deep breath, trying to prepare herself for Naomi's insane accusation while attempting to soothe Celestine by rocking her own body to and fro. But the baby's cries became more plaintive, and Cathryn was forced to drape her shawl about herself and the baby, undo her bodice, and with as much modesty as possible, nurse her screaming child.

While the baby suckled, Cathryn listened in disbelief as the only friend she had in Norman explained that Cathryn had killed her husband with the help of her incubus, the wolf Rex, and then had covered her deed by feigning incapacity, even sending Rex to Naomi so she could be a witness to her plight.

When Naomi finished, the spectators and jurors squirmed, murmuring their shock that among them lived a heinous, husband-murdering Witch.

But to the defendant's equal horror and amazement, as soon as Naomi concluded her testimony, there began a parade of other witnesses, claiming to be innocent victims of Cathryn Rodman's witchcraft, including not one but several of Cathryn's Norman neighbors. One after another, her Christian neighbors rose to damn her for acts of healing and humanity. She listened but did not want to hear the good men and women of Norman Village twist her tenders of friendship, compassion, and charity into crimes.

Chapter 83

"*What have you to say to the court at this time, Mistress Rodman?*"

"I say I am not guilty of Witchcraft. Nor have I performed the deeds of which I am accused. My husband was known to you to drink to excess, which affected his reason. In one of those moods he became insane, intending to murder me for deeds of his imagination. I am not without sin, but I am blameless in his death."

"There are others who accuse you," Magistrate Cory informed Cathryn, peering over the assembly. "There is at least one witness who comes a great distance to testify." Cathryn felt her heart cease its beating as she assumed the magistrate referred to Matteo. But he did not yet rise to testify.

The next witnesses called were her Norman neighbors, who

unburdened themselves, reporting Cathryn's malicious and wicked acts against them. To hear their tales was to be convinced that Cathryn had nothing to do but terrify the village, while her husband, at her direction, monopolized their trade. By intimidating her neighbors, impressing them with her Devilish power to torture and ruin, she could force them to renounce the Son of God and do the Devil's work to destroy the Christian church.

The next step in her plan to convert the colony to the Devil's fold was to become her husband's widow and thereby come into legal posssssion of his property and wealth. Then, with Satan directing her, Mistress Rodman could lead the villagers to subvert the entire colony. No one had to remind those assembled in the court that from the earliest maps of the New World, the Bay Colony was identified as situated in the heart of the devil's territories.

As each witness came forward, the spectators and the jury shivered with the knowledge of how close they had come to being seduced by Satan. Rebecca Porter told how after Cathryn brought herbs to induce the pangs of childbirth for Mistress Porter's overdue baby, the infant had been born dead, "never taking one life's breath." Everyone present knew Witches killed babies, and the court took the occasion to remember the number of still births since Cathryn arrived.

"Devout Taylor, what do you have to say?"

"Mistress Rodman put a curse on me because my pigs trampled in her Witch garden."

Cathryn remembered chasing the squealing beasts with a stick, having to redo a day's work.

"What was the result?"

"Our sixth child was born with a scaly serpent's tail on his backbone." The congregation seemed to hold its breath. "But with prayers and zeal the stamp of Satan has been removed," the grateful mother said, and all those hearing her report sighed in relief.

"How was it removed?"

"By prayers which one morning caused the serpent's tail to fall off."

"With no sign or mark left behind?"

"None."

"Indeed, for you had proved your worthiness," Magistrate Cory concluded. "You may stand down."

The magistrate looked at Cathryn. "Now how do you plead?"

"Not guilty," Cathryn answered.

"Let me warn you, mistress, if you do not confess, you add perjury to the crime of Witchcraft."

Cathryn wondered if they would hang her a second time for the additional offense. "I plead my innocence."

"Constable Yarrow, I believe you have knowledge for this court," Magistrate Tyler continued.

"Sir?"

"Evidence."

"Oh, yes. It's about the Devil's Mark. We did examine Mistress Rodman."

"And what did you find?"

"We saw no Witch's teats that were not cut off or hidden from our view. And except for evidence of old bruises and new she claims were inflicted by her husband, and several fresh scratches, she had but one other blemish of note. Some would call it the Devil's Brand. She tried, but could not conceal it from our eyes. We pricked it and it neither bled nor pained her."

"You shall remove your clothes for the court's perusal of your person," ordered Magistrate Tyler.

Cathryn pulled her shawl close about her. "Please," she pleaded. "Is there nothing I can say to—"

"Do you now admit your guilt?"

Cathryn straightened to her full height. "Indeed I do not!" she answered in a firm voice, and, humiliated, let her shawl fall away and began to undress. She tore at the buttons of her bodice, her fingers stiff with embarrassment.

"Shall I strip myself completely naked," she demanded in a tart tone, her anger growing by the moment, "or do you wish to see only the mark that damns me?"

Magistrates, jurors, and spectators all stared.

"Have those who accuse me no scars or marks upon them? Perhaps my accusers should also disrobe for examination." Cathryn's voice betrayed her rage as she stood naked to the waist and used her hand to lift a breast from the faintly dark, raised spot resting underneath. "I suppose I must approach you so that you may better see the Devil's Brand," she said, stepping forward. "The bruises my husband inflicted are more prominent than this," she observed of the purple-and-green marks upon her body.

The perfection of her body stunned. Her boldness appalled. "Have you seen enough? Is a common birthmark evidence of my collusion with the Devil? This proceeding is a pathetic farce. My accusers lie and prove nothing.''

"I order you to return to your place!" Magistrate Cory demanded, never taking his eyes from her full breasts. He hardly saw the mark in question.

Cathryn turned for the perusal of the spectators. ''It has been said that this mark is not the Devil's Brand but the kiss of angels,'' she said, turning her hard gaze on Matteo Ruggero.

Matteo began to cough.

Cathryn faced the judges and the jury. ''Why do you continue this hearing when you have decided my fate?'' she demanded as she dressed. ''Perhaps you wish me to strip further.''

''That is not necessary, mistress. But I inform you that the court shall weigh all the evidence that has come to light. It is our duty.''

''I see. You exhaust me to hang me silent and agreeable, if only to have my rest.''

''I order you to be silent as of now!'' Magistrate Tyler shouted.

''As you order, but I shall sit down and feed my child,'' Cathryn replied, and did as she threatened, much less concerned for her modesty this time.

Having grown agitated and restless as Cathryn spit her accusations to the court, the courtroom spectators settled down once more, and Cathryn tried to lose herself in the act of nursing her baby, whose audible gulps and pleasurable gurgles often disrupted the proceedings.

Trying to ignore the mother and child sitting at the center of the courtroom, the magistrates continued their examination, but Matteo Ruggero did not take his eyes from Cathryn. His heart swelled with tenderness and his vision did not pass beyond the aura that surrounded the most beautiful woman he had ever seen as she fed the baby he knew was his. Matteo felt as if his heart would break knowing he was to blame for Cathryn's presence in the court, and that she had borne his child without his knowledge.

He dismissed Cathryn's agreement to marry a man she assured him met with her approval and berated himself for his arrogant and self-righteous stupidity. When he should have protected her, he had discarded her, saying he did so for her benefit.

It made Matteo tremble to consider Cathryn's fate. She was right in her assessment that all evidence confirmed her guilt. It was useless for her to protest the accusations as lies.

Did God allow the innocent to die?

At one time, Matteo, like his fellows, believed God punished only the guilty, but too much had happened since he last saw Cathryn Godwyne to permit him to remain convinced that that was so.

Matteo refused to think of Cathryn as Mistress Rodman and was truly repentant for casting her into Weylin's arms, though he had been unaware of Weylin Rodman's real nature. He knew her husband had a taste for rum but had not realized the extent of the man's disabling weakness. He had thought Weylin Rodman upright, choosing to view the man's greed as a sign of his ability to provide for Cathryn, a wife due the extravagances a wealthy man could afford.

From the moment the bargain for Cathryn to marry another man had been struck, Matteo had regretted the arrangement. But Cathryn had not stood still long enough for him to voice his doubts. After he had lied to her, saying he no longer loved her, Cathryn had stoutly maintained they had nothing further to discuss.

Angered by her unexpected and vigorous disdain, and the wounding of his pride by her easy dismissal, Matteo had soothed himself by admitting that a reasonable arrangement for Cathryn's future had been made. He'd reminded himself that from the moment she had seduced him, his life had been in constant turmoil.

He had betrayed himself and his family to love her, endangering, if not damning, his soul. Then he had spent years searching the ends of the earth for her, only to learn his doubts about her had been correct. Her mother *was* a confessed Witch, and she, therefore, naturally came by the skills she needed to render a man helpless—a condition in which Matteo often found himself in Cathryn's presence.

At last, overlooking his deepest feelings whenever they rose to the surface, Matteo had reminded himself of the danger Milton Ames posed to Cathryn. To rescind the decision to send her away would have been to sign her death warrant.

Now it seemed the safe marriage that Matteo had so carefully arranged for Cathryn would ultimately lead to her destruction. The former priest, familiar with his Church's furious pursuit of witches, was only too aware that an accusation of Witchcraft was in fact a death knell. Bereft, Matteo stared at Cathryn Godwyne, certain that the earth soon would open up and swallow her.

Cathryn seemed unaware of Matteo's fears and gazed back at him with regal calm, in the act of nourishing her child amidst the turmoil of the proceedings against her. She looked deep into Matteo's eyes, then beyond, reflecting on her judges and her jury—and all the men who ever held her fate in their hands. She had always been judged by men's definitions of good and evil, and at the root of their favorable or unfavorable decisions lay each man's definition of God, she realized.

Behind all the customary questions of her examination, beyond the formality of writs to the king establishing the lawfulness of the proceedings against her, how these Puritan men viewed God would decide the outcome of the court's exercise. It had always been so.

When Cathryn was in the province of Father Vittorio's God, she was damned for the sin of her very existence but eligible for redemption by the grace of sacraments offered by God's appointed priests. In the domain of Gerald Seymour, God was more selective and chose but few, and all who aspired to His favor did not necessarily receive His benediction. The sacraments were fewer and there was no guarantee of salvation. In the Puritan colony across the sea in which Cathryn now found herself, God had not altered much that she could see, but she was aware of other denominations of Christ both on the colonial shore and abroad who disagreed with the judgments of both Catholic and Puritan. Yet in whatever province the sinner bowed his head, God demanded obedience.

Experience had shown Cathryn how one man's perception of God could be vastly different from another's. If men of different vision could have different visions of God, Cathryn reasoned, might the men she had encountered be entirely wrong in their perceptions? Might God little resemble the angry tyrant, the punishing father, as her mother had said? Might God be a more forgiving parent? More loving; more gentle; more kind? Might God be a Goddess? Might the Deity prefer to love rather than damn the children of this earth?

Cathryn's reflection ended as the droning voice of another witness filtered into her consciousness. She fixed her gaze once more on Matteo Ruggero, struck by the emotion she saw in his eyes. What did she see? she wondered. Sadness? Pity? Love? Hate? None or all of these?

Matteo stared back at her, for the moment absorbed in silent prayer. Forgive me, he beseeched both God and Cathryn. He begged for courage—and for the miracle of inspiration.

Chapter 84

Matteo Ruggero regretted many things, but now he looked back and reckoned what had been a trial by fire had been essential for him to endure. Otherwise he might not be able to sit through the testimony against Cathryn without being poisoned by the contagious madness that so obviously affected the others in the court.

Rumor from witnesses whose credibility in ordinary circumstances was subject to doubt became truth almost at once when Witchcraft was at issue. Matteo understood how fear and guilt allowed a man or woman to believe lies, for to conceal his own sins from himself he had once imagined Cathryn Godwyne a Witch.

Now Matteo could listen to the testimony before the court and know the talebearers came to their conclusions to cover their own fears and sins and doubts; for while Cathryn had suffered with Weylin, Matteo had gone through a purifying fire with Avis Ames that had left him badly burned, but chastened. Furthermore, he had suffered believing Cathryn was lost to him forever, too late learning how dear she was to him. She was his inspiration; his hope; his only consolation.

When Cathryn was safe and married to Weylin Rodman, Avis begged Matteo to postpone their marriage once more, leaving him to spend the next six months smoldering in the ashes of his unremitting love for Cathryn Rodman. He thrashed through his lonely nights aboard ship; in port, he eased his misery by filling himself with rum. Matteo imagined his future with Avis Ames and contrasted that existence with what his life would have been with Cathryn Godwyne at his side.

At best, Matteo acknowledged, his life with Avis would remain loveless, and while no one ever married for the sake of love alone, when love was available for the taking, it was a sin to throw it away.

Matteo freely admitted he did not love Avis Ames; nor did he like her much. But he had agreed to honor his brother's obligation in a moment of weakness, when he was certain he had lost Cathryn. And Avis was beautiful, seductive, and pure—or so he had thought. He was certain he had taken her virtue, and a man could not go through life deflowering, then abandoning virgins and hold his head very high.

Each time he returned home, she showed more accomplishment than before, and Matteo wondered how and where she had obtained her knowledge. But he kept silent, preferring not to know. After Cathryn's marriage he traveled to the West Indies, carrying lumber and salt fish. That voyage served to open his eyes; he tried to soothe his doubts and disappointments with the region's rum and available women but found neither brought him much relief. One experience left him with a pounding head; the other made his heart ache for the only woman he would ever love. He was also struck by the fact that Avis was almost as experienced and as bored in bed as a sailor's whore.

By the time he reached Marysland, Matteo decided he could not marry Avis Ames, regardless of the consequences. He vowed not to follow the grave mistakes he had made regarding Cathryn with the stupidity of marriage to a woman he could never love. Every caress would be in exchange for favors, nothing granted except in implicit barter.

Milton Ames might try to ruin or kill him, but with Cathryn safe, well out of Milton's reach, Matteo did not much care. For that matter, life without Cathryn was not worth living.

He planned to leave at once for Massachusetts Bay. Perhaps Cathryn, too, had had a change of heart, and allowing his imagination free rein, he imagined the Rodman marriage might be annulled. Or if Cathryn were as unhappy as he, perhaps she would follow him regardless of the consequences.

However, on arriving at the Ames plantation, Matteo discovered Avis had her own urgent news. "I should never have allowed you to leave me, my darling," she purred, "but then I did not know how shocking a trick you played on me." Avis lifted his hand and placed it on her round stomach. "You are quite wicked, you know, forcing me to get my affairs in order at last. But as you can see, I am ready to marry you this very day."

Matteo refused to believe his eyes but could not refuse to believe the rather violent movement of her womb under his hand. He looked at Avis in dismay.

"I am as shocked by my condition as you are, my dear," she said in answer to his look, "but all shall be put right when the justice of the peace arrives."

Despite some serious doubts, Matteo acknowledged he could be the father of the child that bloomed in Avis's belly, and with her father scowling at their side, Matteo made Avis Ames his wife.

"Dearest Matteo, you cannot possibly think of asking me to travel in my condition," she protested when he wanted to go home. "And surely you shall not desert me," she cried, giving Matteo her most delicate look, which was not difficult for her to do, for pregnancy did not in the least agree with Avis.

Matteo balked at staying on the eastern shore, but remained by his wife until the bitter end. She spared him nothing, including the truth, alternating between anger and depression as her confinement neared sooner than Matteo had reason to expect.

"What could I do? I had to give the brat a name," she raved. "I never intended to marry you. Surely you suspected," she added when his look reflected surprise. "Ahhh. Men are such fools."

"I think you owe me an explanation," Matteo said, but without rancor.

"You do?" Avis snapped.

He nodded.

"What makes you think I should want to marry you and rot in this wretched colony when André promised to take me to France and to Versailles? He promised we would marry, and believe me, he made a laughingstock of all the other men I have ever known, including you, my precious husband. I enjoyed being in *his* arms," she lied.

"I would have been happy to release you from your promise, Avis, which I think you knew."

Avis turned a hateful glare on Matteo. "So you might have that little Puritan? It hardly concerned me whether you intended to give me my freedom or not. I tried without success to kill this child that burdens me, so that I might go with André. He would not have me in this condition," she whined. "Oh, I hate you, Matteo Ruggero!"

When she had calmed down, Matteo could not help but ask, "Why do you insist I'm to blame? It seems to me, from your proportions and my opportunities, that it is unlikely I'm responsible."

Avis stopped sniffling and almost smiled. "You are my husband; therefore, you are the father."

Matteo declined to debate the child's paternity. What was done was done, and in spite of the strength of her spitefulness, Avis was not well. She was bloated, uncomfortable, and terrified of dying in childbed, her own mother's death in childbirth haunting her.

Understanding this, Matteo resolved to be patient while Avis made the last weeks before the birth a hell on earth for everyone who dared to venture near.

The birth, earlier than even Avis's calculations, was long and arduous. Fearing labor and birth, Avis obtained a potion from an unknown source to stay the early pangs of childbirth, but according to Avis's distraught maid, she took three times the recommended portion when its effects were less than she desired. She began to bleed excessively and in her terror fought rather than assisted the birth, only to be subdued and humbled in the end. "Forgive me, Matteo, please. He is not your son," she whispered when Matteo was summoned to her side, her pride and hatred vanished from her eyes.

Matteo pushed stray strands of fine blond hair away from his wife's pale forehead. He took her hand in his. "I forgive you," he answered, and she smiled, the softness that made her beautiful returning to her face. She sighed then, to slumber while Matteo watched, and a little later that evening, Avis Ames Ruggero died at peace.

Chapter 85

Each time a witness sat down and another came forward, Matteo prayed. "I beg You, do not punish me by allowing Cathryn to die." But her fate seemed inevitable. The only known way to cure a Witch was to kill her.

"Master Jared Merit speaks next," Magistrate Cory said.

A thin, nervous man stood and approached the court. "Several nights she visited me," he volunteered.

"But you live many miles away."

"She came on her broom with a cat and an owl on her shoulder."

"She has an owl. Sits on her roof," offered a spectator.

"What was the purpose of Mistress Rodman's visits?"

"To make me sign the Devil's Book."

"And did you?"

"No. I swear."

"Did she leave you in peace, when you refused?"

"No. She bit and scratched me and stabbed me with pins, then forced me to fornicate with her."

"How many times did she visit you?"

"Five. She did abuse me extremely. She did things to me I could never say."

"Was it her person or would you say her spectral image that made these visitations?"

"I think it was her."

"But no one travels at night."

"Witches do," the man answered.

Cathryn shivered and closed her eyes. She was hungry. She was cold. She wished she were dead. "No. No. No. I cannot die. I am innocent. God shall protect me."

"What's that?" Magistrate Cory demanded.

Startled, Cathryn looked up.

"Tell the court what you mutter under your breath."

"I . . . said . . . I am innocent."

"Do not interrupt the testimony, Mistress Rodman," he warned, and turned back to Jared Merit. "Do you have anything else to say?"

The witness shook his head and the magistrate invited him to stand down. Then, in succession, three more men came forward with much the same report as Master Merit. They each reported that the Witch visited them at night and, in the flesh or in spectral form, tried to force them to sign the evil book. Of course, not a man admitted converting his allegiance from God to Satan through her many strenuous efforts. She was a total failure, it seemed, not that her power was weak, but that these good men were strong and devout.

Goodwife Benson revealed that many times when she passed by Cathryn working in her herb garden, she heard Cathryn reciting prayers backward, and that among other suspect herbs, Cathryn bordered one side of her garden with that well-known favorite of Witches, monkshood. She also reminded everyone that the last siege of smallpox to infest the colony commenced the week Cathryn arrived in Norman.

"Methinks the cat Regina, who has sometime visited everyone of us, was only Mistress Rodman in the person of her cat, come by to spy on us," the woman concluded.

Witnesses recalled how their cows stopped giving milk when Cathryn appeared in their vicinity, and remarked upon the unusual number of hailstorms since her arrival in Norman. The only explanation, of course, was Witchcraft.

"You did not explain why Master Rodman's blood had not congealed by the time the constable and Pastor Curtis arrived," Magistrate Tyler pointed out to Cathryn. "Do not Witch's familiars drink the blood of victims for nourishment?"

"I deny all accusations," Cathryn insisted again.

"Your denials do not convince us of your innocence."

"The jury has not heard my explanation of events that led to Weylin's death."

"They shall on another day, but for today the proceedings shall be adjourned."

The spectators one by one rose and filed out while Cathryn and Constable Yarrow remained. When they turned to follow, Cathryn discovered Matteo lingering in his seat.

He stood then and approached them.

Cathryn froze.

"I wish to speak with the prisoner." Matteo addressed the constable.

"Permission can come only from the magistrates."

As his attention was directed to Constable Yarrow, Cathryn stared at Matteo. How little he had changed in the months they were separated, though she noticed he seemed to have a weariness about him.

When Matteo turned his gaze on Cathryn again, she lowered her eyes, not wanting him to see the depth of her misery at such close range. She hated to have him see her in this state, her dress frayed, her face smudged with dirt.

"What business do you have with the prisoner?"

"I did business with her husband."

"All property is confiscated during a trial."

"There are urgent matters that the widow and I must discuss. She is not yet convicted, am I right?"

Constable Yarrow nodded.

"Then she may yet be exonerated and shall live to conduct her business affairs," Matteo suggested.

"Maybe," the constable conceded to the stranger's logic. "But not likely," he added, knowing the probability of Mistress Rodman ever being judged innocent to be slim.

Matteo glowered at the constable. "That may be, which makes my conversation with the widow all the more urgent. Please direct me to the magistrates."

While Constable Yarrow directed him, Cathryn busied herself with her now fussy baby. When she looked up again, Matteo's eyes were fixed on their child.

"How old is she?" he inquired, reaching to ease the blanket away from Celestine's tiny face.

"Four months, but she is small," Cathryn answered.

"A seven months' birth," contributed Constable Yarrow.

Cathryn gave the constable a scathing look, and Matteo gave Cathryn a half smile. "It seems you do not have the support of your neighbors, Mistress Rodman."

"I am growing used to it."

"Is there no one to speak in your favor?"

"You shall have to attend court tomorrow and find out," the constable interrupted. "Come, mistress, it's growing late." He took her arm.

"Let me carry the baby," offered Matteo.

Cathryn paused, then held out her child.

Matteo took the tiny bundle in his arms. He could not help but gaze from the mother to her infant. "Can it be true," he wondered aloud, "that a Witch's child is always a Witch?"

"Give me my baby!" Cathryn demanded, reaching out, stepping closer to Matteo and pulling Constable Yarrow with her.

The constable yanked Cathryn back into place. "He asks a fair question. Let him assist you."

"I spoke without thinking," Matteo apologized to Cathryn.

"Let's go, before we need a lantern to light our way," the impatient constable insisted.

While they journeyed through the village, Cathryn felt her fury mounting against Matteo, and Matteo felt remorse for utter-

ing the thoughtless question, which came to him from somewhere deep inside, an image of Vanya Russo springing too
clearly to his mind.

"Why do you come here?" Cathryn seethed as she hobbled
shackled between the men. "To add your own testimony to the
mad inventions of my neighbors?"

"I came on business," Matteo said, mindful of the constable.

"What business could there be between us?"

"A great deal that is unfinished."

His words echoed in Cathryn's ears later as she tried to rest in
her jail and eat the meager meal she was starving for. She was,
in fact, on the verge of starvation, for the meal portions provided
while she awaited trial had been quite inadequate. From the
village's viewpoint there was no reason to waste food on a
prisoner soon to be hanged, and no reason to encourage a Witch's
strength.

Why had it not occurred to anyone, Cathryn wondered, that if
she were a Witch, she would not sit by lamely for her trial?
Would she not, she reasoned, summon help from the underworld
and set herself free? Cathryn only wished she had but a fraction
of the power with which the residents of Norman imbued her—to
rain destruction, hailstorms, and disease. If any community deserved destruction, it was this one!

Cathryn devoutly believed in the power of evil. She had seen
evidence enough to convince her there was much harm done in
the world by men whose hearts were filled with fear and hatred
of others and events they did not understand. She herself was
about to be both victim and proof of the madness engendered by
fear and superstition. In the prevailing view, there was nothing
observable in nature to explain why a cow went dry, why
hailstones ruined crops, or why disease decimated a family or
village. If one did not accept Providence as the cause, the only
other explanation was the Devil. But for Cathryn, who knew the
truth about herself, the popular explanations were not sufficient.

Her crime had been to love the wrong man, and if that was
evil, then, Cathryn believed, Satan was surely winning the battle
in God's universe. She wished she had been a Witch; then she
would have made Matteo love her with a love that would never
end.

Cathryn began to weep thinking of what lay ahead for their
baby, and she grew quite desperate. Even Matteo, Celestine's

true father, believed the curse upon the mother fell upon the child.

In the semidark room where she and the baby were locked up from the world, Cathryn reasoned that Celestine should die with her, if only to spare her a life of torture as the progeny of the Devil and a Witch. Should she drown the baby? Or should she strangle her? Cathryn felt a raving madness inching over her, but she was not as yet mad enough to kill her child in order that she might save her.

Chapter 86

Very late that night Matteo gained permission to interview Mistress Rodman, and he found her close to complete despair. "Why have you come?" she asked as he sat down beside her on the bench in her private jail.

Instead of answering, Matteo placed a basket he carried with him on the floor and withdrew a bottle of wine and enough food for a small feast. "Your jailer has gone to bed but has allowed me to bring this late night repast, which you must eat. We both know your ordeal is not yet over."

"Have you come to add to my misery?"

"I come with food and drink and my eternal love, and you chide me almost before I can open my mouth," he upbraided her gently.

"I face a sentence of death. I am hardly in the mood for your attempt at humor," she snapped.

"Cathryn, let me begin again. I've come to tell you I've been a fool, and to bring you food to feed your body so that you do not perish before my eyes. I bring wine to comfort your spirit. I come to tell you I regret everything."

"I'm sure you do."

"Either you're twisting my words, or I've stated myself badly."

Cathryn looked away from Matteo's intense eyes and sipped the wine he offered.

He knelt before her. "I love you, Cathryn, and I shall forever."

Cathryn stared at Matteo. "You have told me this before," she said in an icy voice, trying to ignore his loving gaze.

"You have every reason to despise me."

"I do, don't I."

Matteo lifted her hand to his lips, but Cathryn pulled away.

"You did not come to add your testimony?"

Matteo was silent. An expression of dark and powerful emotion covered his face. "I came to learn what happened to you. I came to beg you to forgive me for sending you away. I came to find whether you were content."

"The Lord God's purpose is not to make us happy. We are meant only to learn and bend to His will," she mocked him.

Matteo looked hard at Cathryn. "It is not the will of God for you to be damned and executed a Witch. The accusation is the invention of men with troubled hearts. Well I know the affliction."

"I've no hope, Matteo. Only a miracle shall spare me." Cathryn stared at Celestine. With gentle fingertips she caressed the soft cheek of her sleeping infant. "Part of me no longer cares. I am weary of this life; in particular of men who distort the truth to suit themselves. I long for peace. I long to die."

The possibility of her death loomed so large before him, Matteo felt his heart begin to rend. "I cannot bear to hear you speak of wanting to die," he said as he pulled her fiercely against him. "I love you as no man has ever loved a woman. Your death would be my end as well. I shall not live without you."

Matteo's intensity affected Cathryn deeply. She ached to the bone for his comfort and protection but stiffened at his touch.

"I love you, Cathryn. You must forgive me for the pain I have brought you."

Cathryn began to weep, and little by little, as he continued to hold her in a fierce but tender embrace, her mistrust eased and she felt soothed body and soul.

He kissed away her tears, then touched her lips with his. He was aroused by her but for the moment did not pursue her. Instead he held and caressed her in a gentle and endearing way.

He washed her hands and face with warm water he heated on the fire and combed her long satin hair until it shone even in dim light. He massaged her shoulders and neck, and rubbed her arms and back. He fed her and lifted cup after cup of heady sweet wine to her lips.

"You've not asked me if I murdered Weylin," she said in a voice devoid of challenge.

"I don't need to, though his death is far more than I hoped for."

Too exhausted, too depleted of reason, Cathryn made no effort to decipher his meaning as she bundled her baby and placed her in a basket by the fire. She accepted the mystery of his presence, wanting nothing more than to bask in and believe his promise of love without end.

Matteo spread a fur upon her narrow bed and bade Cathryn to lie down; when she did, he lay next to her, pulling her close.

Now was the time for making love, for wooing and trapping Cathryn in his design. He remembered and used every exciting caress that made her willing to succumb to his emotion. But as he proceeded, he, too, grew dangerously excited, mesmerized by Cathryn's thrilling responses, and was in mortal danger of falling off his course.

"You dare make love to a woman not purified by the Church?" Cathryn asked.

"I do not believe you are defiled by bearing our child," he answered, and in his heart and soul wanted nothing more than to prove to Cathryn that he loved her, to give her comfort, and to bring her trembling, joyous ecstasy. But while he expressed his passion, and filled her with his rapture, he dared not entirely forget his purpose.

With his heart still beating its furious rhythm and his voice barely stilled of its passion, Matteo began his purposeful attack. "Only a fool would imagine such pleasure came to a man from other than its source," he all but panted. "But it does not matter to me. For I am only eager for the joy of knowing you and quite willing to pay your master his due. For such unparalleled reward, I shall gladly sign your Devil's book."

Cathryn's breath stilled in her breast. She felt the sky cave in upon her. "No. Please, no," she whispered.

"I've but one argument with Satan," Matteo continued, ignoring her pleas. "It goes against a man's nature to have his woman used by other men," he said. "Yet I should understand why he would use you as a lure, for surely there could not be another as perfect as you to do his work." He raised himself above her and caressed her face, pained by the weakness of her limbs and how still she lay. He steeled himself and gazed into the black pools at the center of her eyes. "*Strega. Strega bella,*" he whispered.

Her silence was pathetic to him; he knew his words were as a knife plunged into her heart, that each thought he uttered twisted the blade deeper still.

Without a sound, tears began to slide from Cathryn's eyes and blur her vision. They cascaded down her temples into her tousled hair. Naked and helpless, she lay beneath him as, seemingly excited by his confession, he took her again, almost without care.

Afterward, before he left her, he covered her nakedness with the fur blanket. "I must go, and you must sleep, for we have concluded our business this night. Have no worry, Cathryn, I shall not abandon you, nor shall your master."

Cathryn lay rigid and awake all night, distraught, unable to respond to her own baby's cries, hearing only Matteo's last words rebounding in her head. Truly there was nothing left to live for—and not one ounce of false hope left to her.

She knew she soon would die, and though she had spent her life in search of God, she would die damned a servant and ally of His enemy, Satan. She had worshiped as a Catholic and a Puritan; then finding God wanting in these faiths devised by men, she had entertained devotion as a pagan. But she had been abandoned at all turns. No religion, she realized now, could save her from men who invoked the name of God for selfish purposes, who granted power to the Devil by their fears and sinful natures.

When morning came and Constable Yarrow arrived to bring her breakfast, he found Cathryn still lying in bed, naked, curled in a ball, enveloped by the blanket of fur. Her eyes held a vacant stare, and she did not respond to his less than subtle queries.

As he flung her discarded clothes at her, Cathryn responded to her jailer with a hostile glare. "I'll be most joyful, mistress," he said, "when this examination and your trial are done."

"I'll wager not half so glad as I will be," she replied, and vowed in silence to give her Norman neighbors a haunting vision of their Witch that would last them all their days.

Chapter 87

As the court assembled, Cathryn stood straight, her eyes focused ahead, seeming not to be aware of anything or anyone around her.

This morning Celestine was not with her mother, for Cathryn had neglected her throughout the night and her screams of hunger had made her presence in the court impossible. After much searching, Constable Yarrow had found a woman willing to look after her.

Matteo anxiously assessed the success of his desperate plan thus far. At the very least, Cathryn looked the part with her bountiful black hair tumbling down her back in wild disarray, her rumpled clothing, and the look in her eyes declaring her mind bordered on the not quite sensible.

Matteo held his breath as magistrates and jurors seated themselves and the session opened. There was silence in the court as everyone made note of the accused. Then all but Cathryn bowed their heads for prayer.

"Mistress Rodman," Magistrate Cory began. "You have had the long dark night to contemplate the proceedings of yesterday. Perhaps in the night the Lord God has spoken to you and beaten down the barrier of your sins. Perhaps you have reconsidered your plea. In any event, the court this day inquires how you plea."

At first Cathryn seemed not to hear the magistrate, but after a lengthy pause, she raised her voice. "I, Cathryn Rodman, confess before this court that I am innocent in the matter of my husband Weylin Rodman's death. His death was just as I have said—a miraculous accident. As he tried to murder me, I was saved by a loyal and loving animal, who defended me against my husband, turned a drunken madman. I believe his death the hand of Providence." She paused and Matteo held his breath.

"Further, I confess that in all other matters heard yesterday before this court, I have not degraded myself to bother with such trifling concerns, which, it has been reported, have caused this insignificant village to lose so much sleep. You, the citizens of Norman,'' she addressed the room at large, ''far overestimate your worth. You are but petty souls and my master has more significant prey for me to glean. I do not stoop in ordinary circumstances to the likes of you.''

Cathryn whirled about, causing the spectators in a body to jump in their chairs. ''But you dare to meddle in my master's affairs,'' she scolded them with malevolence, ''and therefore are due a little of my attention. Naomi Sheldon. Where are you?'' Cathryn scanned the court. ''Ahh, there you are,'' she answered herself, letting her voice fall with satisfaction. ''You pathetic child, you shall regret your lies to your dying day, I promise, and I curse you by saying that, should you ever marry, your husband shall be as mean and vicious to you as Weylin Rodman was to me.''

Paler than usual, Naomi began to wail.

Cathryn elevated her voice to be heard over the commotion. ''Rebecca Porter?'' Cathryn demanded next. ''For your lies that I murdered the baby in your womb, no child shall be born to you without teeth already in its hungry mouth—enough so that you weep long and loud as you try to keep the babe alive, and to make you wish it, too, had been born dead.''

Mistress Porter fainted.

''Devout Taylor?'' The woman gasped and stiffened, frozen in her chair with fright. ''Henceforth, you shall be barren and so shall your wretched sows.''

Jared Merit and the other men, who dreamed such dreams as could not be repeated, and testified that Cathryn had visited them in her spectral form, she cursed by saying they should spend their nights so occupied by lurid dreams that they would swear they did not sleep and would be forced to spend the day repenting their visions.

''Goodwife Benson shall be tongue-tied for a year,'' Cathryn proclaimed—which might be a curse for Goody Benson, but would hardly punish anyone else, Cathryn realized too late.

She could not single out everyone who had accused her, because as the aisles filled with those trembling and wailing in supposed agony from a Witch's pins and bites, Constable Yarrow was ordered by the magistrates to seize and gag her.

With considerable effort, the constable did as he was ordered, for Cathryn kicked and bit and screamed, making a dramatic spectacle of herself. "And you," she screamed at the constable, just before he gagged her, "you shall have sore teeth for a treble fortnight, and be forced to subsist on the gruel you force your prisoners to eat."

He threw her into the chair and tied her up, yet she sat looking triumphant to all.

Her arms and hands began at once to throb with the ache of inadequate circulation, but she felt certain she would not much longer have to endure the misery, her confession of Witchcraft having accomplished her goal. The village would make haste to hang her now. She would not much longer have to suffer life.

Cathryn longed for the citizens of Norman to be swept away in a frenzy and drag her from the court and hang her. She watched and prayed as the aisles throbbed with the tormented afflicted and the magistrates conferred in a fever of uncertainty.

"Honorable magistrates and jury," Matteo called above the roar. "I have something I must add to these proceedings."

"Bailiff, assist the constable to remove the Witch," Magistrate Tyler ordered.

Cathryn began to struggle and scream beneath her gag as they began to carry her off still tied to the chair.

The magistrates conferred. "No. Wait. She is entitled to hear all proceedings against her. Put her down, men, and assist the afflicted from the court."

While Matteo swore to give true testimony before the court, it was necessary to carry a few of the tormented out. But as the sufferers realized they would miss the conclusion of perhaps the greatest excitement the village had ever known, one by one they recovered their senses.

At last the court was quiet. "Sir, you had something you wished to say?"

"Yes."

"Then identify yourself."

"I am Captain Matteo Francesco Ruggero, owner and captain of the ship which, at present, is anchored at your village wharf."

"What do you have that is pertinent to this case?"

"A good deal. I have known the accused since she was a child."

"Is that so?"

Matteo nodded. "And I have evidence to give."

"Go on."

"When I first met Cathryn Godwyne she was a girl of nine, but even then she was capable of bewitching anyone who saw her. At the time, I was her teacher and a priest under minor orders of the Church of Rome." Matteo paused to allow the facts to settle on his audience. "With every year that passed, Cathryn Godwyne grew more beautiful and inviting, until, at last, I could not resist her charm. She pursued me until I became her lover, seducing me from my calling and my God. I know that you, being of the Puritan persuasion, would say that she had lured me from a pagan faith, yet you cannot overlook that I was committed to God, not only as a simple man but as a man chosen by God to forswear all intimate relations with women, and she knew that Satan considered my soul a special prize."

Matteo glanced over the spectators, magistrates, and jury, secure in the knowledge that he had their full attention. "This Witch drove me from the Church, from my family, from my beloved country. Because of her, several of my family are dead. When my brothers tried to save me from her, she cursed them with death by drowning. Because of her Witch's lure, I have been made to follow her around the world. What I have suffered, you cannot begin to suspect. Surely the pains of Hell could not be worse."

By now Cathryn glowered at him in spite of her knowledge that he only served to put nails into the scaffolding to be erected for her execution. She burned to hear his convincing accusations, and the knowledge that last night she had again believed his loving lies brought her excruciating pain.

"This court does right to try the now Mistress Rodman, for she is descended from a Witch known far and wide in Suffolk, England, to have impressive power and is, in fact, high priestess of her coven.

"But I caution you against the Witch's execution, for her power is unusually strong. To kill her would multiply her power a hundredfold."

The court shuddered in a body.

"As a rule, confessed Witches are not executed, Captain Ruggero," Magistrate Tyler informed him. "That is, if they repent. Only those accused who cannot prove their innocence are sentenced to death.'' Both magistrates looked at Cathryn, who for all the world looked quite mad.

The moment the notion that by confessing she had saved her life sank in, Cathryn's eyes filled with tears and she began to cry, sobbing audibly.

''You see''—Matteo jumped on the opportunity—''she wishes to die to magnify her power.'' He seemed barely able to contain his pleasure at her genuine and tortured performance.

The courtroom buzzed with excitement and horror.

''But I am willing to humbly suggest a solution to Your Honors and the court, and by conferring this form of punishment upon the Witch, you shall, in Christian charity, also grant me a means to begin to expiate the innumerable sins I have committed while under the Witch Cathryn's spell.''

Not certain they wanted to strike an important bargain with a professed Catholic, and a former priest at that, but not especially eager to be saddled with the conversion of a recalcitrant Witch, the magistrates agreed to hear Matteo's offer.

''As I said,'' Matteo addressed the whole assembly, ''my ship is docked at the Norman wharf. I came to transact business with Master Rodman, who before his death was engaged in several partnerships with me. I learned of the tragedy when I arrived, and decided I must stay for a number of reasons, one of which being the unpleasant fact that I am responsible for this Witch coming to live among you.''

The courtroom responded with shock.

''Mistress Rodman came to your village as the bride of Weylin Rodman through arrangements he made with me,'' Matteo continued when the uproar died down. ''Of course, the man had no idea at first what he had bargained for. If you agree, out of the obligation I feel for bestowing the curse of Cathryn Godwyne upon your village, to free my soul from eternal damnation, but at great risk to me, my ship, and my crew, I shall take the Witch aboard my vessel and carry her from your colony. I shall further guarantee that she shall never set foot again within the boundaries of Massachusetts Colony, and that she shall be kept so far away that her magic cannot possibly influence the good people of Norman.''

The magistrates looked at each other. It took them a split second to agree, and another few moments to poll the jury. ''Do you agree to pay the court's costs for the witch . . . and for her child?''

"Of course."

"Then it is the decision of the court of Norman Village to exile the confessed Witch, Cathryn Rodman, in the custody of Captain Matteo Francesco Ruggero. May the Lord God protect you," Magistrate Cory pronounced.

"Bailiff, draw up the order of exile," Magistrate Tyler ordered. "If you wish, we shall leave the Witch gagged."

Matteo suppressed a smile. "That suits me. And her baby?"

"I shall fetch the child," Constable Yarrow offered, eager to be rid of his obligation to look after the Witch.

Matteo nodded and with caution looked Cathryn in the eye, feeling quite unready for the tongue-lashing he knew she longed to give him, since she sat raving incoherently behind her gag. Tendrils of fire seemed to flash from her expressive eyes, until sheer exhaustion caught up with her and she sat still.

The court adjourned, but no one moved until, with the captain holding the bundled, sleeping baby, Cathryn was untied from the chair.

"I recommend restraints," Constable Yarrow said.

"I agree," answered Matteo to Cathryn's furious glare, and with his assent the constable brought Cathryn's bound hands from behind her back and secured them in front, attaching a length of rope by which to lead her.

Constable Yarrow then took a bowl containing a blue dye from his wife. "Stand still," he ordered as he tried to daub Cathryn's forehead.

Uncooperative, Cathryn twisted away.

"Someone hold her still," the constable commanded.

Cathryn was seized and forced to have her forehead painted with an inverted cross. "This woad dye shall stain her skin a long while and shall mark her as a Witch, preparing all who see her to shield themselves against her."

Matteo could not prevent a smile. What poor judges they were of Cathryn's power!

Then with a razor the constable sheared Cathryn's hair to just below her ears, but not without needing further assistance to restrain her. She struggled with a strength Matteo wondered she still had, mourning as the lengths of her beautiful satin hair fell to the floor.

Then a wreath of rue was raised above her and placed as a crown upon her head. "Rue is anathema to Witches," Constable Yarrow informed Matteo. "It causes all venomous things to be harmless."

Cathryn's humiliation was evident in her eyes, but a glimmer of fierce pride caused her to lift her chin in defiance. Despite the intent of the court in condemning her, the addition of the paint and crown and the short curls that sprang about her face only made the witch appear more pagan and savagely beautiful.

Matteo stared and his heart leapt with joy to realize that his beautiful Witch had come to the end of her ordeal. He had taken a desperate chance—after the horror of Weylin's death and the anguish of her examination, his taunting betrayal might have shattered Cathryn's spirit. He might have driven her beyond reach, but from all that Matteo could see, Cathryn had weathered his persecution with a vengeance.

Very soon, Matteo would be alone with her, and as he held her baby and his, he stared at the wild-eyed Witch and wondered if he would dare to cut away her bonds and undo the gag. Looking at her now, he knew without a doubt that for his efforts to save her, for a few of the things he had told the court, he would have the very Devil to pay.

Chapter 88

Celestine in his arms, Matteo led the way. A few paces behind, tethered by rope to Matteo, strode Cathryn. He had removed her gag. "Don't make me regret this charity," he had warned her. She kept silent, though her eyes flung searing sparks upon him.

Church bells tolled as they marched with the magistrates and a parade of at least two hundred villagers in tow. Cathryn seethed and hurried to keep pace with Matteo's long strides, the inverted cross staining her forehead seeming to burn into her flesh. She heard the crowd mutter and felt its passion. Try as she might to ignore her Norman neighbors or, at least, to put herself above them, their hatred singed the edges of her consciousness.

Cathryn focused her eyes ahead on Captain Ruggero, who loomed a hero to those upon her heels. He cradled their small baby in his arms with tenderness, yet looked every inch the part of a conquering soldier: rugged and handsome, moving with a purposeful gait, afraid of nothing, not to be deterred.

Cathryn felt torn and battered, not knowing which of her beleaguered emotions to trust. More than once she had been led by her lover down a meandering lane to be surprised and disappointed, and now, despite his clever rescue, she dared not trust him.

All at once Cathryn remembered Avis and halted her desperate pace, jarring Matteo and interrupting his advance. What was he doing in Norman? How dare he come to her with his promise of eternal love now that he had a wife?

Matteo saw the look of outrage in Cathryn's face and before she could open her mouth to challenge him, he said, "Mistress, perhaps you would like the crowd to hurry your steps with a few stones hurled in our direction?"

Startled, Cathryn resumed the pace and followed Matteo across the village beyond the settlement of houses to the rise of land where Weylin Rodman's house stood and down past the warehouse and store to the village wharf.

Captain Ruggero's trim ship was waiting for them, the crew prepared and assembled on deck. All except those who would assist them aboard stood silent and alert as if waiting for trouble from the mob. It came at once as a few onlookers picked up rocks and hurled them, but they missed their target, and at the command of the magistrates the rowdy element dropped back.

At the dock, with a hand on her shoulder, Matteo forced Cathryn to kneel before the crowd. Silent for a moment, she stared at Matteo as though she despised him; but she had to obey.

The magistrates approached her. "It is your duty to name any others in our midst who have conspired with you, any who have signed the Devil's Book," said Magistrate Cory. "Name your allies among us."

Cathryn gazed over the crowd, sorely tempted to seize such a perfect opportunity for vengeance. She let her gaze roam slowly over those assembled and lingered on those who had vexed her most. By the simple act of accusation, she could see her tormentors punished for their wicked treatment, forcing those she accused to prove their innocence. Finally, however, she declined. "There is no one," she declared.

Magistrate Cory looked doubtful but accepted Cathryn's reply. "You must now remove the spells you have cast upon your neighbors."

"Never!"

Matteo stepped to her side. "Mistress, it is a condition you must meet," he warned in a voice Cathryn cared not to defy, and one by one, those she had cursed came forward for her touch.

"I remove the spell I cast upon you," she said, embracing each victim but in a manner so cold few truly believed they would be spared.

When it was Naomi Sheldon's turn to face Cathryn, the girl trembled with fright. "I loved you and you betrayed me," Cathryn said, tears welling in her eyes, "but I revoke the spell I placed on you this morning. I forgive you."

Naomi swooned, and as she was carried away, Constable Yarrow gave Cathryn a paper for her to read aloud, then sign.

Cathryn's voice traveled clearly over the witnesses. "I, Mistress Cathryn Rodman confess my guilt and acquit this court of any false accusation. I accept my exile from the village of Norman and all of Massachusetts Colony. I certify the justice of the court's sentence."

With haste Cathryn scribbled her name at the bottom of the document, then stood and turned her back forever on the village of Norman.

As she boarded Matteo's ship, she could not escape how close an inspection the crew made of her. To a man, they recognized the symbol of Witchcraft painted on her forehead in blue. She recognized some of the seamen from the *Cynthia Ames*, which did nothing to ease her tension. Yet, she reasoned, if the sailors did not know the accusations against her were false, at least they knew she had Captain Ruggero's protection.

Matteo led Cathryn to his quarters without delay, where Meldon Archer held open the hatch. Cathryn blushed crimson at the gaze of the man who during her few weeks in Marysland had become almost a friend. "Welcome, mistress. The Lord God be praised that ye escaped the mob."

"Indeed. God *and* your captain be praised," Cathryn whispered as she hurried past him, though she was not yet absolutely convinced she preferred the fate of being rescued.

In the cabin, Matteo dropped Cathryn's tether, then carried Celestine to his bunk and put the baby down squarely in the middle of the mattress. When he pulled the side curtains shut, he turned to Cathryn. "I believe I owe you an explanation of my behavior last night," he hastened to explain. "But I fear if you had not confessed as you so brilliantly did in court, I could not have saved you from the executioner. I was forced, therefore, to try to drive you nearly mad."

Cathryn nodded her comprehension of his cruel tactics, but she could not yet trust his tender tone.

Matteo sensed Cathryn's hesitation. "You are safe," he assured her, "but the question now is, am I? Do I dare unbind you? Or will you rend me limb from limb for my unfeeling torture?"

Cathryn was silent.

"Perhaps you do not yet have strength enough, only the desire," he said gently, greatly disturbed by her apathy. Perhaps he had gone too far—perhaps her response was more than exhaustion. Could this be the lethargy of madness? "Have you no joy for being rescued from the hangman? Do you still wish so dearly to die?"

"I am not convinced that life shall be worth living," Cathryn answered in a subdued voice, her eyes conveying only wariness.

"Perhaps this shall change your mind," Matteo said, pointing to a covered wooden tub sitting ready a few feet away. "I ordered it filled with hot water."

Cathryn eyed both the tub and a basket filled with soaps and jars of scented oils. There was also a pile of soft towels sitting on the deck beside the tub. Silently she raised her bound hands to Matteo.

Matteo untied her, suppressing the impulse to draw her arms around him and crush Cathryn against him in his jubilation at having set her free. Instead, he moved aside, giving her freer access to the tub.

But as Cathryn stepped forward, Celestine stirred and began to cry. Cathryn retreated from the inviting bath.

"Duty before pleasure, mistress, I fear." Matteo smiled at Cathryn.

Cathryn sighed with weariness but slipped onto the captain's bunk and settled with her child, filling her eyes with the sight of the precious baby at her breast. "I was certain I should never know this pleasure again," she whispered to Matteo when he sat down before her on the bunk's edge.

Cathryn closed her eyes and breathed in the scent of sandalwood that permeated the cabin. The motion of the ship, which with the tide had gotten under way, lulled her senses. For several minutes she listened to the comforting creaks and groans of the ship and felt the weight of her slide toward total madness and grief begin to lift.

As best she could, Cathryn ignored Matteo's presence as he sat close to her and listened to Celestine's soft sniffles as she nursed. She reached down into the depths of her mind and soul for peace, daydreaming of soft meadows, soft skin, and gentle murmurs; the face and the sensation of the helpless infant in her arms; her memory of the adoring touch of her baby's father; the long-ago, almost forgotten sound of his music melting the icy fear around her heart.

Matteo eased himself from the bunk and kept vigil while Cathryn nursed the baby and dozed. He went to the porthole as his ship got under way and watched as the villagers knelt down to praise their Puritan God for freeing them of their vile witch. He knew the ship would not be followed, though he wondered how far the madness of Norman would reach into the sea. Would rumors of her trial reach as far as Marysland?

In the silence, Matteo blessed his crew of superstitious sailors, who had conducted themselves with bravery under Meldon Archer's firm hand. Although the captain had explained that it was madness to believe Cathryn a Witch, he had worried that the sentiments of a fearful mob might be contagious and, perhaps, even override his sailors' devotion to him.

He was concerned about Cathryn. Was it solely exhaustion that made her look so warily at him from behind dark eyes? Had he been too brutal in his use of her? Would she ever be free to give her trust to him again?

Matteo sat down and closed his eyes. Suddenly, nights without sleep caught up with him, and despite his intentions, exhausted by emotions that had put him on the rack, Matteo nodded off, slipping into a black and dreamless void.

When Celestine stirred from a depleted breast, Cathryn woke. The moment Cathryn moved, Matteo was awake. He looked confused, as if he had awakened from the dead, and Cathryn seemed to almost smile.

Leaping at this faintest encouragement, Matteo smiled at Cathryn. "Welcome aboard my ship, Mistress Godwyne," he said.

"Is she yours?" Cathryn wondered, still sounding somewhat ill at ease.

"My very own. A spirited East Indian."

Cathryn admired the cabin, which was finished in luxurious woods, ornate brocaded fabrics, and stamped leather, reminiscent of Venice; but she did not praise it. She rocked Celestine in her arms a while longer, then put the sleeping baby down and stole purposefully from the bunk.

Closing the curtains again, she went immediately to examine the basket of soaps and oils beside the tub, inhaling the fragrance of each scented cake and flask of oil with eagerness. When Matteo removed the tub's wooden lid, Cathryn poured a generous amount of one flask into the steaming water and, after a moment of consideration, added more.

She ran her fingers through her freshly cropped hair. There were curls, but not enough left to pin. She sighed, then turned her back to Matteo, doffed her clothes, and climbed with haste into the tub.

For a moment, as the almost too hot water engulfed her body, Cathryn forgot Matteo's presence; as she reclined in the large but still confining tub, a groan of pleasure escaped her. Water sloshed over the side, but she hardly noticed as she rested her head contentedly on the tub's hard edge.

Cathryn's emotions and thinking were not yet entirely clear. She felt not unlike a too tightly strung violin, as if the cords that held her body and soul together could snap at any moment and send her parts flying into the air. How an admission of Witchcraft and a defrocked Catholic priest's confession had saved her from the all too eager hangman was quite beyond her grasp.

"Just what do you intend, Captain? What *does* one do with a convicted Witch?" Cathryn asked suddenly.

Matteo hesitated. "One tries to reform the Witch, of course. And the court was of the opinion that you, Mistress Godwyne, shall need constant and diligent effort to be reclaimed. I assured the magistrates that I was just the man to see to your redemption."

"Does your wife encourage that occupation?"

"What occupation is that?"

"The rehabilitation of Witches."

"I have no wife," he answered. "Avis is dead."

"Oh," Cathryn said, and sat up. "Oh," she repeated, and stared in silence at the man who had rescued her from what had been a very certain death. "You must tell me all that has happened since we parted."

Matteo took a deep breath. "Your assumption I married Avis is correct. But she died soon after in childbed. The baby, a boy born perhaps a month early, survived, though it has been a struggle to keep him in this world."

"I'm sorry about Avis. I'm sorrier about your son." Cathryn sighed at Matteo's apparent distress.

"He is not my son," Matteo said matter-of-factly, "yet I cannot help but feel concern for him." He paused to gaze in the direction of the bunk, where Celestine lay. When he turned back to face Cathryn, his voice was stern. "Why didn't you tell me you carried my child?"

Cathryn drew her knees to her chest and clasped her arms around her legs. "Would it have made a difference, if I had?"

"I married Avis."

"One cannot marry more than one woman at a time, Captain." For the first time Cathryn offered Matteo a smile.

Matteo nodded and managed a half smile of his own. "After you wed, I set sail for six months, a tormented man."

"Captain, please," Cathryn interrupted, suddenly coming to life. Her voice was restrained but heated. "Do not attempt to prey more upon my sympathies. You've been a tormented man almost as long as I have memory."

"And who is to blame?" he answered, in a voice as strident as hers.

"I did not force you to love me," Cathryn said defensively.

"No. No, you did not. I loved you because I could not help myself!" he cried passionately. "My weakness for you was as much ordained by God as anything in my life."

Satisfied, Cathryn urged him, "Please, go on with what you were about to say."

Matteo cleared his throat and continued. "When I went to sea, I searched my soul and decided that, regardless of my past mistakes, regardless of Milton Ames's threats, I could not face a loveless life with Avis, or anyone. I planned—"

"What threats from Milton Ames?" Cathryn interrupted.

"He learned about you and me and threatened to have you murdered, but with marriage you were out of his reach, which was all that mattered to me," Matteo said, knowing that eventually he would have to give Cathryn a more exact explanation. "In any event, I returned to Avis to inform her of my decision not to marry her, but when I arrived, I found her hiding from friends—insisting the child she carried was mine."

"Which you had every reason to imagine might be true."

"But the truth is," Matteo hedged, "the child was not mine but the Frenchman's you met at the Ames plantation when you married Weylin. Monsieur Chapin promised foolish Avis things he never intended to provide, and the moment she informed him of her condition, he disappeared. Before she died, Avis admitted she had lied to me."

"And now a motherless child has no father as well." Cathryn sighed.

"I am the lawful father. And, I confess, he seems no more strange to me than the child of my own flesh." He gestured to the bunk, where Celestine still lay. "In fact, now that I've spent many a sleepless night worrying whether the mite would survive another dawn, I've greater feeling for him than I have yet for my own child."

Cathryn blessed Matteo silently, then eyed him with caution as he began to strip off his coat and shirt. He knelt beside the tub and lathered his hands with scented soap, then drew gentle fingers over her face. "Woad dye leaves an impossible stain," he said as he caressed her forehead.

"I suppose it's a small price to pay for my life," Cathryn replied, and shivered.

When she leaned forward, Matteo applied delicious pressure with his fingers up and down her spine. She closed her eyes, sighing with the pleasure of his gentle ministrations. When he caused her to lie back, raising and slowly caressing each length of leg and foot, his touch eased taut muscles and made her feel sublime.

At last he kneeled behind her and pressed his mouth against her fresh-scrubbed cheek, encircling her with his arms. "Thank God you are safe."

"Thank you for saving me." She turned her face and gave Matteo a gentle kiss.

When she stood, Matteo wrapped Cathryn in towels and lifted

her from the tub, but she began to tremble as he carried her to his bunk.

"Tell me, Matteo, do you believe in Witches?"

"I am an enlightened man; of course I do," Matteo replied as he put Cathryn down before the curtained bunk. "But I believe in lunacy as well."

Cathryn was silent.

"Aren't you going to ask if I think you're a Witch?"

"I'm afraid to."

Matteo laughed. "If you're a witch, then I am Satan."

"My exact thought," she replied, "and as proof, if you recall, someone testified the Devil gave me a black cat to be my familiar. Oh, Matteo, Regina!" Cathryn cried.

"Curled blissfully in a basket two decks below."

"Oh, thank you." Cathryn threw her arms around Matteo, then withdrew. "What brings your change of heart, Captain?" she asked suspiciously.

"I needed only to come to reason. I love you, Cathryn, and have come to realize the love of a man and woman is not the curse of Satan but a gift from God. A man can love a woman as I love you and still love God." Matteo paused to gaze steadily at Cathryn. He sensed she yearned to believe his promise, yet remained uneasy. "Forgive me." He kneeled before her. "My guilty passion caused me to taunt you though you were innocent of all but loving me."

Cathryn reached for Matteo and pulled him against her in fierce acceptance of his plea.

"You still love me, don't you, Cathryn?"

Cathryn stiffened in Matteo's embrace, but he clung to her. "After all that has happened, I shouldn't," she said, a very stubborn note ringing in her voice. Then she softened. "Love never fails, Matteo, but abides forever. 'Love beareth all things, believeth all things, hopeth all things, endureth all things,' " Cathryn quoted from English Scripture she once had memorized to save her soul. She stroked his thick black hair with a gentle hand. "Yes. I still love you, Matteo. I have always loved you."

Matteo released Cathryn and rose to face her. He crushed her against him as he longed to do; then, on the verge of breaking down and losing all control over his own tightly wound emotions, he struggled to alter his mood. "What possessed you to finally confess to Witchcraft?'' he inquired lightly, adding, "Though you did exactly as I prayed you would."

Cathryn stared at Matteo, a bit confused by his sudden change of tone. She freed herself of his arms and stepped slightly away from him. "I could bear the condemnation of my dreadful Norman neighbors, but to know that you believed I was the Devil's Woman was more than I could bear,'' she said. "I would rather die,'' she whispered.

"Forgive me!'' Matteo said with the strength of his emotion, and reached for her again.

"I do, my love, I do forgive you!'' she cried, and let him hold her, embracing him in return. "By admitting your own sins, you endangered yourself enormously for me. If God had not been on our side, they might have hanged you alongside me.''

"I love you. I have always loved you,'' Matteo pledged, and sought her mouth to receive her warm and passionate kiss.

They were interrupted by a sudden shrill cry from behind the drape surrounding Matteo's bunk. Startled, Cathryn hastily opened the curtains and lifted her baby into her arms. "I neglected to bring a cradle aboard,'' Matteo realized.

"A small chest would do,'' Cathryn said.

Without a moment's delay, Matteo emptied one and laid a cushion of blankets inside, but Celestine shrieked with displeasure when Cathryn tried to put her down. Finally, Cathryn was forced to settle with Celestine on Matteo's bed and comforted her with a breast, as Matteo lay down next to them.

This was not quite what he had envisioned when he'd imagined rescuing Cathryn, he admitted to himself. And waiting for them in Marysland was yet another child! Yet he found he did not want for more than this mother and her baby at his side.

"Ah, my love, close your darling eyes,'' Cathryn crooned to her still fretful baby. "Our suffering is over.''

"I promise it is,'' Matteo whispered, and moved against Cathryn's back, reaching over the mother to caress the baby's bright cheek. "I regard it a miracle that you still find love in your heart for me—or for anyone—even God. Truly, Cathryn, you are rare among women. The gift of your abiding love ennobles me.''

With Celestine in her arms, Cathryn turned more fully into Matteo's embrace. She kissed him gently and smiled with a radiance that touched his heart. "I expect to be rewarded by the abundance of your love, and I intend to thrive as does our baby." In the course of her life, Cathryn had made many mistakes, and her life had not been without pain, but her love for Matteo had endured all tests. "Surely ours is a love without end, Matteo," she whispered, and stared into his eyes, into the depths of his soul. "Proof that, however one calls him, God's love is eternal."

Matteo nodded in agreement. "Our reunion is yet another miracle; my rescue of you evidence of a more compassionate God than most men have seen or dared imagine," he said, and held her gaze. "I love you both. I shall love you forever," Matteo vowed as he drew Cathryn and the baby nearer to him.

Cathryn leaned her head upon his shoulder in perfect ease and sighed. "Surely we at last are blessed," she murmured.

"Surely," he answered firmly. "And blessed be."

Author's Note

Had I read the courtroom scenes in *The Burning Woman* prior to my research into the history of witchcraft, I would have found the testimony of witnesses and behavior of the court utterly unbelievable. But I assure the reader, although the book is solely a work of imagination, the testimony, the kinds of questions posed to Cathryn in her examination, and the kinds of assumptions on the part of officials, witnesses, and spectators are entirely authentic. Unfortunately, the loathing for womankind institutionalized in the Christian church at that time is also authentic.

About the Author

Best-selling author Jessie Ford began writing part-time nine years ago when her oldest son entered pre-school. Writing is now a full-time occupation for this third-generation Californian who lives in Oceanside, California, with her husband, two sons, and a large white dog, Zephyrus.

Ms. Ford's fascination with social history and psychology inspired her initial research into women's struggle for equality and political power in the seventeenth century. Her total absorption with this era resulted in the creation of THE BURNING WOMAN.

The author is presently at work on a new historical novel and invites her readers to write her care of her publisher.

The
Best Modern Fiction
from
BALLANTINE

TA-20